Praise for *The Life You've Imagined*

"Unpredictable, touching, and true, *The Life You've Imagined* is a stand-out story; I devoured it and wanted more."
        —Therese Fowler, author of *Reunion*

"A richly woven story laced with unforgettable characters. Cami, Maeve, Anna, and Amy will snag your heart as they explore the sometimes-wide chasm between hope and reality. A beautiful book."
        —Therese Walsh, author of *The Last Will of Moira Leahy*

"Backed by Riggle's trademark unflinching honesty and imbued with heart and hope, *The Life You've Imagined* is a terrific novel about love and loss, letting go and holding on. A book to share with family and friends—I loved it."
        —Melissa Senate, author of *The Secret of Joy*

Praise for *Real Life & Liars*

"This book is a must-read for anyone who has ever been both grateful and driven mad by the people they love most: their family."
        —Allison Winn Scotch, author of the *New York Times* bestselling *Time of My Life*

"With ease and grace, Riggle walks the fine line between sentimentality and comedy, and she has a sure hand in creating fun, quirky characters."
        —*Publishers Weekly*

"Funny, sad, and utterly believable. . . . Kristina Riggle is poised to become the Luanne Rice of the Great Lakes."
        —Elizabeth Letts, author of *Family Planning*

THE LIFE YOU'VE IMAGINED

Also by Kristina Riggle

REAL LIFE & LIARS

THE LIFE YOU'VE IMAGINED

Kristina Riggle

AVON

An Imprint of HarperCollins*Publishers*

To my parents, who always helped me "go confidently"

HarperCollins books may be purchased for educational, business, or sales promotional use. For information please write: Special Markets Department, HarperCollins Publishers, 10 East 53rd Street, New York, NY 10022.

FIRST EDITION

Designed by Diahann Sturge

Library of Congress Cataloging-in-Publication Data is available upon request.

ISBN 978-0-06-170629-5

10 11 12 13 14 OV/RRD 10 9 8 7 6 5 4 3 2

Acknowledgments

THE LIFE I IMAGINED AS A STARRY-EYED KID HASN'T COME TO PASS, but what I've got is even better, and I owe that in large part to my husband, Bruce; my amazing kids (you'll appreciate this someday when you can read grown-up books); and my parents.

Much gratitude to my team! At Nelson Literary Agency, thank you to Kristin Nelson for her determination and dogged pursuit of what's best for me, and Lindsay Mergens for helping me understand the author publicity stew. At Avon, I'm blessed with an insightful and warm editor in Lucia Macro, plus the enthusiastic support of Esi Sogah, Christine Maddalena, and more amazing people than I could name here.

To the lawyers (and spouse) who helped me with the Anna character: don't sue me if I got it wrong! In all seriousness, thank you to my brother-in-law, Robert Ringstrom; Bob and Lee Heinrich; and Jill Morrow. If any lawyer types read this and think any part sounds wrong, it's my fault, not theirs. Better yet, call it artistic license, which it probably is.

For more research help from lifeguarding to the best in sewing machines, a hearty thank-you to Maggie Dana, Meredith Cole, Chris Graham, Kate Filoni, Janay and Andrew Brower, and J. E. Taylor. Also, a big thank-you to Maureen Ogle, who helped me find the context and exact wording of the "life you've imagined" quote, which is actually a misquote in the way it's most often repeated.

To my early readers, Elizabeth Graham and Jill Morrow, my utmost gratitude for your kindness and honesty.

To the readers, booksellers, reviewers, journalists, librarians, and bloggers who have gotten behind me, your support moves me more than you know. I'd list you all here, but I'm terrified of leaving someone out. I'll thank you in person, I promise.

Go confidently in the direction of your dreams.
Live the life you've imagined.
(MIS)QUOTED FROM HENRY DAVID THOREAU'S *Walden*

CHAPTER I

Cami

THE TAXICAB EXHAUST CURLS UP AROUND ME LIKE A FIST. I TURN toward the departing cab and raise my hand, my mouth forming around the word *wait*. Then my dad comes out of the house and I know that actually, yes, this is the right place.

He remains on the porch, crossing his arms and leaning in the doorframe. For a blink before that, I could have sworn he looked happy and was leaning forward expectantly. But now he's propped up like he's always standing there and I just happened to catch him.

The house . . . Paint the color of dried blood has begun to peel. One front window shutter is missing and the other is leaning sideways as if trying to escape. The porch sags like a slackened jump rope.

This house was never the Taj Mahal, no.

I stride across the scruffy, weedy lawn and skip a step going up the porch.

"Like what you've done with the place," I tell him, not looking him in the eye as I pass, though I tense up without meaning to.

"You watch your smart mouth." He cracks his knuckles.

The inside smells as if an old folks' home were in a bar: old sweat, piss, and the unmistakable aroma of beer. A regiment of brown bottles lines the kitchen table, a few of them fallen.

"Your room's the same place it's always been."

First door on the right, across from the bathroom, and there it is. A small square with one small window overlooking the neighbors' car, up on blocks in the gravel driveway. It's a different car, at least, from the one I remember seeing.

I can feel him standing behind me. I can almost hear the toothpick he's chewing, something he does in the morning before he starts cracking open beers.

"You get here all right?" he asks, then coughs hard.

"No, I was in a terrible accident and couldn't make it."

He slams my bedroom door so hard the only thing hanging on the wall rattles down to the dirty beige carpet.

I pick up the brown wooden frame and blow the dust off the glass, which has gone foggy with some sticky filth of unknown origin. So I scrub the film off with the hem of my shirt, adjusting my glasses to get a proper look.

There's me, with my hair in pigtails—I always hated to sit still so long to get those dumb braids—looking scrawnier than ever. This, I think, is my last picture without glasses. There's Trent, too, giving the camera a thin smile. As I remember, my dad fought with him over what kind of smile he was going to give, and finally Trent produced this effort to keep the fight from getting worse. For Mom's sake.

My mother, in the center, looks like me. Her face is a little fuller and she wouldn't wear her glasses, so she's got these wrinkles by her eyes from squinting all the time. Her smile is relaxed, and to me she looks relieved that we can finally get the picture and there will be no more arguing.

But maybe I'm just projecting back. Maybe we didn't fight at that moment. It's hard to remember because this picture is twenty years old and my mom is long dead.

I drop my bag on the bed, and the bedsprings squeak. I wish I'd been able to bring my queen-size, but it's not as if I could have stashed it in the luggage area of the Greyhound bus.

I sit yoga-fashion in an old bowl-shaped chair in the corner, with a cushion so thinned by the years that the canes of the chair imprint themselves on my back. I hesitate for a moment before dialing, but I did promise.

"Hey, Steve. It's me."

He's at home. I can tell from the pattern of traffic outside and the way it echoes off the wood floors.

"Hi. So you made it okay."

What is it with men and stating the obvious? I bite down my sarcasm for Steve, though. "Yes. The ride was fine. I had a fascinating conversation with a pothead about the best ways to smoke in public without getting caught. He showed me a pipe that looks just like a cigarette."

He doesn't reply, and the silence is like a slap.

"Look, you told me to call."

"I know. I'm glad you made it okay."

Now it's my turn to be silent, fingering the ends of my hair and pushing my glasses around on the bridge of my nose.

"I'll make it right," I offer.

"You can't."

I stand up suddenly, as if he can see me and it matters. "How do you know what I can't do? I'll be tutoring again in the fall and I'll get a job here this summer."

"And you can gamble some more and win it back? Sure."

I can feel him holding his temper back, like yanking on the reins of a barely tamed horse. I've seen it in his face any number of times. "It was . . . It was a loan you were never supposed to know about. You were giving me very favorable terms. Big of you, actually."

"Ha," is the only thing he says. He lets his retort hang there and I know we're both going back over it, his discovery and my admission and the sordid week that followed.

"So are you going to call me later, or what?" I ask him.

"I don't think I'd better."

Now I sink back down to the edge of the bowl chair. The position feels precarious, and I tense up to keep from falling. "So you don't want me to call you, either?"

"I don't know."

"What kind of answer is that?"

"I've gotta go. I've got another call, Cami. Take care."

He's gone.

I turn the phone over in my hand, again and again, until I look down and realize that's exactly what I do with a hand of cards.

CHAPTER 2

Maeve

AS MY DAUGHTER STEPS ACROSS THE THRESHOLD, DRAGGING HER wheeled suitcase behind her, the word that floats through my mind is *brittle*.

Maybe she senses it, too, and maybe that's why she won't let me hug her tight.

"Hi, honey," I say. "I'm so glad to see you." I bathe her in my smile, loving her from across the waxy countertop of this convenience store that's been my business and home for nearly as long as I've been Anna's mother.

If only I'd known back in her baby days, during all those long nights of feeding and burping and rocking, that my years hugging my daughter would be counted on one hand . . . Well, I wouldn't have looked so forward to her sleeping through the night.

It's disorienting, thinking of her baby days as she stands before me, with her penny-colored hair pulled up tight into a bun on the back of her head and a prim fashionable black suit. Her lawyer gear, she calls it.

Sally bursts in from the alleyway door, where she'd snuck off to have a smoke. The vapor follows her in and she shouts, "Well, isn't this a regular Geneva convention!"

She doesn't wait for permission and wraps her arms right around Anna, who allows it and waits until Sally isn't looking to sigh and send me a look that says, *Geez, that same old joke. Will she ever give it a rest?*

No, of course she won't. Why would Anna expect anything to change at the Nee Nance Store?

"Will you still make that joke if I get married, Aunt Sal?" Anna says when Sally finally releases her. She wheels her suitcase to the stairway behind the beer cooler, which leads to the upstairs apartment. "Because I won't be a Geneva anymore, then."

"Look, doll," Sally retorts, her hand resting on her hip. "You'll always be a Geneva. You can't escape us!"

Sally's black seventies-era-Cher wig is askew, giving her the effect of looking slightly sideways, and with that lopsided huge grin, she could be a maniac. Anna pats her on the shoulder indulgently and begins bumping the suitcase up the narrow stairs.

I could escape being a Geneva, technically. Sally, being my wayward husband's sister, is biologically a Geneva, as is my Anna, of course. But me? I married into the name and with some paperwork could prune myself right off the family tree.

Carla lumbers in to the store and jars me back to reality by asking for some Virginia Slims. It's not until that moment I realize I've been fingering my wedding ring, which is hanging from a chain and normally hangs inside my shirt, unseen.

Anna clomps back down in her heels, hurriedly, as if she has somewhere critical to be. She takes up the mop that I left leaning against the potato chip rack, where I was interrupted by her homecoming.

"Honey, you don't have to do that. You'll get mop water all over those nice shoes."

She shrugs lightly. "I'll be careful," she says, and then of course mop water sloshes all over them. I know better than to say a word, though, and anyway, she's had a rough time of it, I gather.

I wait until Carla leaves to broach the subject. In the old days, we talked about nearly anything in front of the customers. When you live upstairs from your place of business, the line between personal and private gets pretty fuzzy. It was easy to forget they had ears, especially since most of them discreetly pretended there was nothing unusual about a redheaded mother and daughter having a red-faced fight right in front of them.

But since she left town for college and then her Chicago job, she's gotten awfully fussy about that kind of thing. All kinds of things.

"Are you feeling okay?" I ask her. "About everything?"

"About August being dead, you mean?"

That's Anna, cutting through the euphemisms.

"Well, yes, if you want to put it that way."

"I'm okay," she says, leaning on the mop wringer with more force than I could have imagined she had under that fancy suit. She straightens back up and puffs a loose strand of hair that's dropped out of her bun. "It's sad. Kind of hard to be around there now."

She doesn't look at me for any of this. I've tried to catch those avoiding eyes for twenty years now. I miss the childish openness she used to have. I miss the glimpses into those eyes that always reminded me of that line of poetry *Nature's first green is gold . . .*

"Let me know if you need anything, and sweetie, you really don't have to do that."

"I don't mind," she says, and she slaps the mop onto the floor again.

I hope someday she meets just the right man and has babies—a whole passel of babies, more than I could have—so she understands how it kills me now that she won't let me hug her when she's in such obvious distress. Well, maybe not obvious to anyone else. But I'm her mother. I knew the moment she called me.

"Hi, Mom," she said, and that was all I needed to hear.

"What's wrong?" I asked, and then she sighed as if I'd done something wildly irritating.

It was the forced brightness that gave her away, which made her voice just as brittle as she looks here in living color, right now, wielding that mop with the same determination she gave to spelling bees, exams, her finals, and she must now apply to court papers and trials, though I don't see her in action anymore.

Sally has gone silent, thank goodness. It's rare, but even my daffy sister-in-law can be sensitive to atmosphere and know to shut the heck up. She's biting her tongue and working on a sudoku puzzle now, in the office chair behind the counter, that stupid chair her brother bought that is so pointless behind the waist-high countertop.

It was comfortable but useful only if no one was in the store. Like so many of Robert's grand intentions that only sort of worked out.

"Good morning, Maeve!" calls out Mailman Al, his shadow slicing the June sunshine. I wave at him and begin ringing up his Diet Coke and Snickers while he's still plopping the mail on the counter.

The top piece of mail nearly makes me gasp aloud. I slip it off the top as Al turns to get his drink. I slide the letter into the pocket of my pants, where it fits awkwardly, one corner poking out.

Al leaves exact change for his snack and heads back out with a jaunty wave. Anna has disappeared into the utility closet to dump the mop water down the big sink.

"Sal? Keep an eye on the door for a sec, okay?"

"Hmmph." She's chewing on her pen and not looking at me, which is just as well.

I scuttle sideways like a crab to the office, where I yank open a file drawer and drop the letter in the first folder I see, which happens to be *H*, maybe for *husband*, which Robert technically still is. I thank the heavens that Mailman Al started his route only ten years ago, not twenty, when Robert was still here, because then he'd have caught on by now that my husband is writing me letters, and I'm not sure if I could stand his knowing that.

"Oh, Mom, there you are," Anna says as I emerge. "I might run upstairs for a bit, if that's okay."

"Of course. Have a rest, dear. You've had a long train ride."

Sally has closed her sudoku book and she's riffling through the mail now.

"Sally! Do you mind!"

"Just wondering if you have any good catalogs."

"Honestly, Sal. What would I do with a catalog? You think I've got any room for any of that Crate and Barrel crap?"

I snatch the mail away from Sally and steal a glance at the stairs where Anna has just disappeared. Maybe I need to tell her that Robert is writing, not to mention what's coming in September.

But she's had such a shock already, with her friend dying. No. Now is definitely not the time.

CHAPTER 3

Anna

BEFORE MY EYES ARE EVEN OPEN, I'M CONFUSED. WHAT'S UNDER MY arms that's so scratchy?

So I wake up to the sight of brown fake-wood paneling and what's under my arms is a scratchy, nubbly bedspread instead of the smooth comforter that was back home and is now in some storage locker.

Oh, shit, is my first thought. *Back in Haven again.*

Then, *August is dead.*

I told him not to jaywalk and talk. Over and over, I told him. I'd hear air brakes and honking in the background and say, "You're not crossing the street, are you?" and he'd laugh and say "Yes, Mom, I'll be careful," which made me smile because he is thirty years older than I am and has this huge white sweep of hair that makes him look like a lion.

Was thirty years older, I mean. *Had* the hair.

And I *was* supposed to be staying with him since the lease in my apartment had run out and I couldn't close on the condo yet. And for that matter I was supposed to be taking a deposition today and working on that brief, only Mr. Jenison made me take a bereavement leave, though August was not a relative but a mentor, a professional colleague with whom I'd had a pleasant relationship.

I pull off the bedspread and touch my hair. It feels like Velcro that's been ripped too many times. I should have left the bun in and just slept on my side.

Stupid bereavement leave. I should be working, because I'm coming before the partnership review committee soon and now is not the time to be swanning off for a visit home, only Mr. Jenison made it clear that I had no choice.

I open my closet to look at the few clothes I'd unpacked. I brought home primarily my weekend grubby stuff because the rest got all packed up in anticipation of moving in with August for a bit, only then he got hit by a bus. I had to wear my favorite trial suit to his funeral. He would have appreciated that, come to think of it.

I don't want to wear the crummy stuff, so I step back into my skirt and blouse. I skip the pantyhose and heels, though, and slip into my flat sandals. No one will see them behind the counter, anyway.

My phone bleeps. Shelby, sending me a link to an obit about August in the *Tribune. August Canfield, a fixture on the Chicago legal scene for decades, was known for his fierceness in the courtroom and his gentleness outside it, where he served as a volunteer on several . . .*

I know all that stuff, so I toss the phone back on my bed.

Careful footfalls signal Mom's approach. Aunt Sally would stomp, being constitutionally unable to do anything quietly.

Mom pokes her head in. A neglected pencil falls from behind her ear and she picks it up again. "Oh good, honey, you're awake. You have a visitor."

"I do?"

"Cami Drayton."

"Really?"

"She's back in town and stopped to say hello, so I told her you were home and I'd see if you're awake. Should I send her up or tell her to come back?"

Back in town? I wonder if she means for a visit or that she's moved back. That's a girl I never expected would stick around this little speck on the map.

"I guess, send her up. Just stall her a few minutes first."

As I wrestle the frizz back into a ponytail, I try to remember how many years it's been. She was a skinny, sharp-edged girl with huge round glasses who did projects with me in school and worked at the store in the afternoon. We'd be elbow to elbow at the front counter, one of us punching the register, the other doing home-work. People would sometimes ask if we were sisters, which we thought was terribly funny—since we looked nothing alike—until I got older and stopped finding it amusing at all. Rather, it was evidence of how little the customers paid attention to the living, breathing humans handing over the cigarettes. Anyone with eyes could see we weren't related.

We lost touch after graduation, then briefly touched base again during my flirtation with Facebook, before I got tired of having old boyfriends and former clients try to be my pretend-friends on the computer and stopped updating anything on my page. I now try to remember what her page had said about her job, her life. Was she "in a relationship"? I believe she was. Her posts were always cryptic and funny but left few clues as to what her life was really like. Not unlike the flesh-and-blood Cami I remember. Her profile picture was windswept and romantic, black and white. Her glasses were small and rectangular, but she looked much the same as her girlhood self. She was turned slightly away from the camera, as if she hadn't known it was there.

I hardly hear Cami coming up the steps and startle when she comes into the room.

"What are you, a ninja?" I say, smoothing down the last few strands of hair and trying to straighten my blouse.

"It's my night job, yeah? Pays well, but the uniform doesn't exactly catch the eye."

She's wearing a man's shirt tied off at the waist and a pair of narrow black pants. She looks like a modern version of Audrey Hepburn. She's taller than I remember.

"Well, hi," I finally say, having put myself back together as best I can. "What brings you back to town? Vacation?" I smile but don't try to hug her. Neither of us was much for hugging.

Everything on her face seems to pull tighter and close in. "Something like that. I'm home for the summer."

"Home? At your . . . At your dad's?"

"Yeah."

I try not to visibly react to this, which means I've already reacted, in a way.

I clear my throat and say, "I'm home for a couple of weeks." I don't feel like elaborating, and Cami doesn't ask. She was always good like that.

"I thought I'd see if your mom needs help at the store again. Like old times, yeah?"

"Yeah, exactly. Old times."

We seem huge in this room, now that we're grown-ups. If we stood hand in hand we could just about span it with our arms.

There's nowhere else to sit in my room except on my bed. I sit down cross-legged on my pillow such that my back touches the headboard. Without needing to be invited, Cami sits down facing me, also cross-legged, her hands lightly resting on her ankles, posture straight, like a Buddha.

"We used to sit this way all the time, remember?"

Cami nods. "When we weren't stretched out cross-wise on the bed. Not sure that would work these days, though."

Indeed. My narrow twin bed isn't suited for sprawling adults, just daydreaming girls on their stomachs, their legs bent at the knees and their sock-feet waving in the air, their chins propped in their hands. We used to talk about our crushes. Typical in that way, at least.

"Remember that kid, Damon?" I say now, picturing a boy with braces and a popped-up collar. "I used to write *A* loves *D* in my notebook, thinking I wasn't giving anything away by using initials. I wonder what happened to him?"

"Dead."

"What?" My hand flies up to my face, and then drops back to my lap as I wait for Cami to elaborate.

"Yeah, he fell through the ice out on the lake. Weeks before they found him. Left behind a daughter, too."

"How did I not hear this?"

She shrugs lightly. "Why would you? You were in Chicago by then. I only heard because one of the parents where I tutor had been in Haven and saw it on the news. She knew I was from there—here, that is—so she told me. It was about three years ago."

So he was about twenty-seven. Damon had graduated from high school, pumped his fists into the air and danced a little jig on stage in his cap and gown to the delight of the entire assembled crowd of parents and giddy kids. And he had ten years to live.

When I saw August last, he had hours to live, only.

"I don't know why I'm so shocked. I mean, accidents happen. We're not immune." I wonder who else might be dead, the news not having reached my office on Wacker Drive.

Cami adjusts her glasses on her nose, not looking directly at me. "No, we're most certainly not."

A minute or two pass, punctuated by the sounds of cars motoring down the avenue and shrieks of gulls. I'm about to ask Cami about that tutoring job she mentioned when she points to my mirrored vanity.

"Hey, you've still got yours." She indicates a magazine clipping on the mirror above the old brown vanity table. *Go confidently in the direction of your dreams,* it says. *Live the life you've imagined.*

I shrug. "I never took it down when I moved out."

Amy had photocopied it for us out of *Ladies' Home Journal*, too many years ago to count.

"I never put mine up," Cami says, her gaze resting on the tiny octagon-shaped window near the ceiling of my room. "I always thought it was bullshit."

"I don't know. A little confidence never hurt anybody."

Cami smirks, and I give her the respect she gave me and don't ask what she's thinking.

Once Cami left and I went downstairs again—holding my breath against the peculiar stench of the bottle-return bin—Mom apologetically asked me to watch the register for her so she could take Sally to the doctor, nothing serious, she said, just a cough she thought should be checked out.

I happily sent them on their way, grateful for the quiet and the respite from Mom's questioning eyes.

Now I can't wait for them to get back, because the silence isn't silent after all, what with the occasional jingle bells from a customer at the front door and the wheedling of the fan from the corner, blowing its whisper of air now that the June sun is heating up the front windows.

I flick the security monitor on, which shows a view of the alley—no trespassers, just a couple of gulls—and flip through our few broadcast TV channels we can also watch on the tiny screen. But I can't bring myself to sit through the insulting dreck of daytime TV, with its advertisements for paycheck-advance loan rackets and "schools" in cooking and becoming a medical technician.

And that doesn't even take into account the court shows, which make a mockery of my very way of life.

Judge Judy, my ass.

I can't help but look at the clock and remember what I would have been doing now. Yes, that deposition. Rescheduling was a pointless waste of everyone's time.

But when Mr. Jenison shoved that paper across my desk with his forehead plowed by three deep lines, I knew it was hopeless to argue. It was a furious e-mail, half of which was typed in all capital letters, from a wealthy client.

I'd been tired and feeling a little buggy cooped up in the August-less office, weary of the pitying stares ("I know you were so close," people kept saying, which started up the stupid rumors again) and so I decamped to a coffee shop and fielded a phone call about this client's case from my cell phone, during which time I may have been less than discreet.

Chicago is too big a city for his wife to be in the booth behind me; really, how could I be held responsible for such a wild fluke? Mr. Jenison was not persuaded. He rattled off a few other examples of recent mistakes—innocent stuff anybody could have flubbed, whether their mentor got hit by a bus or not—and sent me home.

An hour oozes by before the front windows darken in the shadow of a huge truck. The Pepsi vendor hustles in and plops a clipboard in front of me for my initials. I'm about to sign and go back to my crossword (I almost ask him, what's the French word for *stop*?) when I see that he's brought in an impossibly large order.

We argue for a moment or two about it—I can't accept all this; he says it's what we ordered—and I disappear into the back office to find the paperwork we surely have.

The filing is nonsensical, nearly random, and outside he grows more blustery by the moment. I can't help but picture my assistant, Kayla, clicking over to a file cabinet or tapping keys to come up with just the thing I need.

"Give me another minute!" I call, not wanting my mother stuck with this inventory she'll never unload, and then . . .

A letter. It's oddness calls to me among all the invoices and carbon copies of important business papers.

I drop it as if burned. ROBERT GENEVA, begins the return address, printed in spiky capitals with such pressure that the envelope is visibly dented. Addressed to my mother, postmarked only three days ago.

The vendor appears in the office doorway. "Miss? If you can't show me something different on your end, I'm leaving the order. I have other stops to make."

"A minute, give me . . ." I trail off, gaping at him, until he turns away with a sudden scowling exhale.

My hands go back to riffling the papers, only I can't remember what I was looking for, seeing nothing else for the searing flash of my father's name.

CHAPTER 4

Maeve

I BLINK IN THE WHITE LIGHTS OF THE WALGREENS, STARTLED BY ITS contrast to the Nee Nance. Instead of the rattly fan and Sally's chatter and neighborhood gossip passed over the top of the counter, I can hear only canned music nearly vanishing behind the hiss of industrial-strength central air.

I'm not a Walgreens customer. I've been going to Clawson's Drugs since I was pregnant with Anna. But if I walked into Clawson's today, Chuck Clawson would start readying my blood pressure meds, only I can't really afford them right now. I'd have to tell him a story, either a lie about not needing them anymore, or, heaven forbid, the truth, which would start the tongues wagging of anyone who happened to be right handy, and they'd start up the *poor Maeve* business.

I had quite enough of that twenty years ago, when Robert left.

Of course, this being Haven, even in Walgreens your neighbor or somebody's cousin could be at your elbow before you can say "none of your beeswax."

I don't see anyone I know today, though.

I slide into the blood pressure machine and slip my arm into the cuff. Before I release the quarter into the slot, I take some deep breaths—*cleansing* breaths, Veronica would say—and think: *low numbers, low numbers*. The cuff tightens up like the fist of an angry man.

There should be a way to sneak someone's blood pressure reading, so they can't be anxious about it and have high blood pressure.

I open my eyes and flinch away, then look again, just to be sure. No, that's not good at all.

Well, no wonder, with Anna dropping in all brittle and sad and acting like she's not, and now Robert's letter arriving with her right in front of me. That and the eviction notice, well, of course it's high. That's all, a little stress. In the fall when this is all sorted out, it will be better, I'm sure.

I wonder how Robert has fared, physically. We're in our fifties and no one gets there unscathed, except for those geezers I see in the "Healthy Living" feature in the *Courier* sometimes, running marathons into their eighties.

I picture his liver swimming in beer, and this image makes me grin but also cringe. He was not often fall-down drunk, but he did nearly always have his hand wrapped around a can, unconsciously flicking the pull-tab the way Anna will start to twirl a pencil like a majorette whenever she forgets herself.

I don't imagine he puts it away like he used to. Who could keep up that kind of pace for all those years? The decades are bound to mellow out a person. I don't shout as often as I used to, and if the cash drawer doesn't balance, I don't . . .

"Ma'am? Is everything okay?"

I jump and this crashes my knee into the machine. It smarts

something awful, but I mumble excuses, untangle my arm from
the cuff, and limp as quickly as I can out of the store, ignoring the
pain because what else is there to do?

The first thing I see when I slink back in the store—feeling guilty,
as if I've just snuck out to smoke crack instead of check my blood
pressure—is that Anna has crisscrossed piles of papers spread
out across the countertop. She's stacking them crisply and with
enough force that she's crinkling the edges.

"How's Sally?" she asks, not looking up.

"She's okay, I guess. No pneumonia or anything. She smokes
too much, though she told Dr. Simon she didn't. She also told him
she's fifty-nine when he's looking at her paperwork and he knows
damn well she's sixty-four. So anyway, he starts asking me about
her mental state."

Anna looks up as if she's only just now heard me. "Mental state?"

"Yeah. He actually asked if I've noticed any unusual behavior.
I said, 'Relative to what?' and he looked at me like I was crackers,
too."

"Who's this guy? Simon?"

"Yeah. Setterstrom retired. He just doesn't know her. You
okay?"

Anna seems more pale than when I left, her spray of freckles
standing out against a waxy complexion.

She pulls out an envelope from under one of the stacks and
tosses it into my field of vision.

Oh, no.

"He's writing you?" she says, now folding her arms and aiming
her full attention at me. I've never seen her in court, but I bet she's
got her lawyer face on now.

"So it would seem, and it's none of your business."

"How do you figure that, since he's my father, and for all we
knew he was dead?"

"I knew he wasn't dead."

Anna seems knocked off stride by this. "Have you been writing him all along?"

"No, I just . . ." How to explain to her that I just somehow knew? And that I always believed he'd come back? "Forget it."

"How long has he been writing? Does he want money? Don't you dare send him any money."

" 'Dare'!" I throw my purse down to the floor. In my peripheral vision a customer steps in through the door and right back out again. "Don't you talk to me about 'dare,' young lady. I'm still your mother."

"Well, what does he want, then?"

I try a new tactic, using one of her own favorite lines. "I don't want to talk about it," I say, and whirl on my heel to run upstairs.

I hear the store's front door slam and the lock click into place. I've miscalculated; she's going to follow me after all. I duck into the kitchen as if I can hide in this stupid tiny apartment.

She finds me easily enough.

"What's he been doing all this time?" Her voice betrays her, snapping and cracking like kindling in a fire. "What's so important to keep him away from us?"

It's useless, useless to talk to her about it; I can fast-forward the whole way through the conversation and she'll be angry at any answer I give, because from me it will sound stupid and weak.

"He says he'll explain it all."

"What's stopping him from explaining it so far?"

"He's . . . He wants to tell me in person."

Anna draws back. She's still wearing half of her business suit, and then, for the first time, I see my daughter as a tired grown woman on the precipice of middle age.

"You're not going to see him, are you?"

"Again, I don't see how that's any of your business." I would like to have said that with some conviction, but my words trail off.

"Does he ever ask about me? Or would that be sort of a buzz kill, you know, the abandoned child." She throws that last phrase like a punch and I flinch from it. Anna rubs her hands over her face then, rearranging her features away from anger, and for a moment I see the hurt emerge until she's collected herself. Her breath is at first shaky, then her voice comes out even and precise. "Mom. Please don't write him anymore. I don't know what he wants after all these years, after leaving you the way he did, leaving *us*, but I can tell just from what you've said he's being evasive, which means he's being dishonest. He's not telling you anything now because he knows he has no good reason to have left, and what good reason could there be? No call from him, no visit, never seeing me grow up or anything?"

Words of protest fly to my lips. *He loved me, he was a good man, he made some kind of mistake. Everyone deserves another chance if they're truly sorry.*

Anna holds out the letter to me, and as I take it, I notice her hand is trembling. In her spring green eyes now I can see the tears of twenty years ago as I tried to explain something that is still beyond comprehension.

"You're right," I hear myself say. "I won't. I won't write him. It can only lead to grief, I suppose."

Anna wiggles her nose with the effort of trying not to cry and sniffs hard. "I'm sorry I yelled at you," she says. "It's been a hard couple of days."

I'm crossing the kitchen to her when she turns and trots back down the stairs, saying over her shoulder, "I'd better open up the store."

At the kitchen table, I turn over the letter, which is held closed by the tiniest bit of adhesive. Robert always was in a rush with things like this: sealing letters, putting the right dates on things.

With the barest flick of a fingernail the letter opens.

CHAPTER 5

Cami

MY DAD FIXES ME WITH HIS SLIT-EYED LOOK, THE ONE HE RESERVES
for special occasions, and in response I lean back in my chair at
the kitchen table, propping my knee on the table's edge for balance
and an extra show of nonchalance.

"So, you think you're hot shit, do you?"

This is a classic from the Tim Drayton repertoire, in the vein
of such standards as "Who do you think you are?" and "I brought
you into this world and I can take you out," and my personal favorite, "Get out of my face, you stupid slut," which has a nice al-
literative feel.

I'm not sure this time why I'm hot shit. In school it was for getting all A's in most everything without doing much homework,
and then during family holidays it was for showing up in a car
so fancy that it wasn't missing any windows, hubcaps, or fenders.
Sometimes I brushed my teeth in an uppity fashion.

At the tip of my tongue is this: "Not such hot shit considering my gene pool," but I know better than that. It's too late in the day for that kind of sarcasm. I just want him to get out the door so I can call my brother and then meet Anna at the store, because I'm going to that engagement party for Amy and Paul.

Oh, right, that's probably why I'm hot shit. I wore lipstick today.

I just shrug instead.

"You best leave my room alone, young lady. If you think this place is such a dump, then you can sit your ass in a Motel 6."

Ah. I'm in trouble for cleaning. I tackled my old room first, then experimentally tugged at the carpet and found some pretty nice wood underneath.

I inspect my cuticles and say as casually as possible, "I won't go in your room."

When he breaks off his stare, I stand up and collect my dinner plate. I leave his alone. I rinse mine in the sink, but I'll give it a thorough washing later, as I'd rather not have my back to him that long.

"You best not go in there," he repeats, giving the table a lazy thud. "I'm outta here. I'm meeting the fellas."

He leaves his plate to the flies coming in through a hole in the backdoor screen the size of a softball and stands up as if he's on the rolling deck of a ship at sea.

I close my flimsy bedroom door firmly and drop the hook into the eye near the top of the frame. He hasn't noticed this yet and I hope it's a good while before he does. If he thought I was hot shit for cleaning up, I'd hate to see what he'd think of me locking him out—*of a room in my own damn house!* I can imagine him bellowing.

A keen sense of observation is not one of Tim Drayton's strong suits, however.

When his truck belches away down the road and I'm sure he

hasn't returned for anything, I perch on the twin bed and slowly dial the many digits of Trent's number.

"Hello?"

"Trent. It's Cami."

There's silence for a beat or two and I don't know if this is his reaction or a delay on the international line.

"Is everything all right?"

I can detect a tinge of accent in the cadence of his question. But then I shouldn't be surprised, as he's been in London eleven years now. No, twelve.

"Yes," I say. "Dad's not dead or in the hospital or anything."

"Well, fine. I was worried. It's late here."

"I know, I'm sorry. I just had to wait until he left to call you."

"You're there now? At the house?"

"It's a long story. I'm here for the summer. Look, Trent, I have to ask you about something."

I've got a Bible in front of me as I speak to him. I found it when I was rummaging in the closet, seeking the source of a particularly foul stench. When I flipped through the pages, some photographs fell out.

"Trent, do you know much about Mom's family?"

"As much as you do."

"There's this picture here. It's Mom as a teenager, I'm sure it is, and there's this couple she's with, a generation older than her, not her parents."

"It's probably just Aunt Clara and Uncle Paul."

"No, it's not them; I'd know it. Anyway, on the back it says, *With love to our dearest Pammie.* Who else would have called our mom that?"

"I don't know, and I don't know why it matters."

"It doesn't matter," I respond, mimicking his speech a little, which I know is mean, but it's the first time I've spoken to my brother in three years and he acts like I'm some slightly annoying phone survey. "Except that Mom is dead and maybe she has more relatives than we knew about."

"And why would I know?"

"Because you were a teenager when she died and I was just a kid. You remember more, yeah?"

"If I saw the picture, I might know them, I suppose."

"Give me your address and I'll mail it to you, if you promise to mail it right back."

"Can't you just scan it in?"

"I don't have a computer." Not anymore, since Steve still has the one we bought together. And with online gambling considered, it's just as well.

"You don't have a . . . ? How can a person as smart as you—"

"Can we discuss my technology shortcomings later? I'll mail it to you. So listen, how are you? How's Everett?"

"Exhausted. It's very late and I have a very important meeting tomorrow."

So I get his address and we exchange pleasantries like two vague acquaintances, and that's that.

I suppose to Trent my curiosity must seem mysterious, since he launched himself out of here the minute he could and in fact left the country without looking back, with me coughing in his metaphorical dust.

Though, I don't much care if he forgets about Dad. Can't say as I blame him.

I put Trent's address and the picture back in the Bible and slide it under the bed, against the wall.

I look at my watch and realize it's time to go to the party. I don't feel like a party, but I do feel like getting out of this shack for a few hours. So I slip my wallet into my pants pocket and head for the door, checking the hallway out of habit, though I know he already left.

CHAPTER 6

Amy

WHEN I SEE PAUL'S REFLECTION BEHIND ME IN MY FULL-LENGTH mirror, I snatch my robe off the bed and cover myself.

And he does the most infuriating thing ever. He laughs.

"Oh, baby, are you worried about your virtue?" He strides up behind me, moves my hair aside and grabs a mouthful of my neck. "Let's ruin your virtue again before the party."

I sigh and lean into him for a moment, until he tries to take my arms away from my robe. I tighten up my grip. "Paul! Not now, I'm trying to get ready."

I meet his eyes in the mirror and they look downturned, like he's wearing a tragedy mask. Oh, what a crybaby. Trust men to go all weepy about not getting sex. So I smile at him. "I'm sorry, sweetie. There will be lots of time for that later. I promise you can ruin my virtue all night long."

I turn around in his arms and kiss him for a long time, and

finally he leaves me alone, seeming to be slightly mollified. Goodness, it's so much work, protecting a man's ego.

I slide my dress over my head and turn back to the mirror once it's safely in place. Oh, I love it. It's a silk georgette with a floral pattern in a spring green that perfectly complements my current shade of blonde. I do an experimental twirl. When I'm standing still, the dress falls to the knee, and I'd have to pirouette like a child's top to get it to swirl up high enough to show the stretch marks.

I add my new necklace. Head of the class, Amy Rickart. Amy Rickart-Becker, that is.

Paul is reading the newspaper when I come out. He doesn't move the paper when I stand right in front of him, left hand on my hip so the engagement ring catches the eye.

"Ahem," I say, and he's still reading.

I go for coquettish and cute and bat the newspaper down, kissing him lightly on the lips before I twirl—carefully—in front of him. "You like?"

"It's nice," he says, rising and patting his pockets, then searching the end table for his keys.

"Nice? I spend forty-five minutes getting ready and 'nice' is all you've got?" I try to smile bigger, as if I'm only joking, still flirting.

He kisses me hard and without chivalry on the lips. "You look ravishing, stunning, beautiful beyond measure. Can we go now?"

"Well, gee, I'm overwhelmed." I look away from him to pretend to search for my handbag, though I actually know right where it is.

"I tried to appreciate your beauty in there and you wouldn't have it."

"It's just timing! We can't be late for our own party." I swallow down the next things I want to say, because we really are going to be late if we get into it now.

He's tossing his keys lightly in one hand, his other hand hooked into his pocket. He looks like a Land's End catalog page. "Who cares about the clock, Aims? Or convenience, whatever."

I toss my hair and smirk at him, because I've got him now. "Really? What if I'd climbed into your lap this afternoon during your game, at the bottom of the inning when the bases were loaded?"

"I wouldn't know. You've never tried anything not written in your daily planner." He turns on his heel and calls over his shoulder. "I'll bring the car around so you don't have to trek across the parking lot in those heels."

"Very thoughtful of you," I mumble, but I don't think he's heard me.

As it happens, traffic is backed up on Shoreline Drive and we're late anyway, but maybe that's not so bad. As we walk up the long grassy slope from the circle drive to the garden gate, the party is in full swing and everyone looks so delighted to see us that I feel like a celebrity. I'm waving, grabbing hands, accepting kisses on the cheek. Paul is pulled away almost immediately by some guys, but I don't care; I have him all the rest of the night, since he's staying over.

Nikki has me at arm's length, cooing over my dress. I give her a little curtsy. Sarah and Kristi are right behind her, and Sarah grabs my hand, yanking me half off my feet to look at my ring.

"Ooooooh, it's beautiful," Sarah says, and they all stare at it for a good thirty seconds before letting go.

Kristi hands me a glass of white wine. "No, thanks," I tell her. I'll just grab a Perrier."

"What?" She puts a hand to her chest, mock-scandalized. "At your own engagement party?"

"Do you know how many carbs are in that? Forget it."

Nikki nudges me playfully. "Oh, come on, live a little. You look fantastic! And I know you'll run it all off tomorrow."

I see Paul across the grass, slapping the back of a friend of his, having a big laugh. I wave to get his attention, but he's not looking this way and doesn't notice.

"Well, all right." I take a sip, and it slides down so cool that I take another.

"So, tell us about how he proposed," Sarah prompts, raising her eyebrows.

By the time I finish the story about his proposal—in front of a whole restaurant on our one-year anniversary of dating, down on one knee and everything, the whole place cheered us and I cried like a little girl—the wineglass has emptied and been filled again and is half empty.

I finally catch another glimpse of Paul. I abandon the girls, skip over the grass to him, ooh, gosh, these heels are tricky in the grass, and hang on his arm while he finishes talking about some new development his dad's company is in charge of downtown. When he's done, I tug his arm to get his attention and give him one helluva kiss. With tongue and everything.

"Whoooa!" all the guys say, and there's a whistle and something like a catcall.

Damn right, whoa.

Then I go off to find more wine, and when I find it, I also find Anna Geneva.

She doesn't see me, and she wouldn't recognize me even if she did.

"Anna!" I squeal.

She turns to me and cocks her head, narrowing her eyes like she's trying to focus. I've seen this look so many times.

"It's me, Amy Rickart!"

For just a second her eyebrows shoot up, then she shakes her head slightly and smiles. "How nice to see you!" I'm so grateful that she hasn't mentioned the obvious that I hug her hard, sloshing a little out of my drink. So I lick the rim.

"I'm so glad Mr. Becker saw you in the store and invited you. I didn't even know you were back!"

"I didn't move back or anything. I'm just here for a little visit."

Her eyes dart behind me. "Looking for Will?" I ask her, assuming she's got to be seeking out her old boyfriend. After all, they'd been that high school couple who held hands constantly and sat in each other's laps at lunchtime and basically made everyone else sick onto their greasy cafeteria pizza.

"No, not really," she says, turning her eyes back to me.

"So, what do you do these days?" I ask, though everyone knows she's a hotshot big-city lawyer, which we all think is great, considering her mom had to raise her by herself in that store. So she starts telling me all about it, only I don't really follow her very well. Paul's on the other side of the lawn and I keep trying to catch his eye.

That's when Nikki and Sarah and Kristi catch up to us and I take another gulp of my drink. A big one.

"Anna Geneva! Oh, my God! I never thought I'd see you back here," shouts Sarah.

Anna smiles at her, but only with her lips.

"She's back for a vacation from her Chicago law firm," I rush to say.

"Hey, you know what I remember?" Kristi says. "I remember when the SAT scores came out and you, like, went around telling everybody."

"Yeah," concurs Nikki. "And you had, like, this freaky high score."

I say, "It wasn't exactly—"

"I didn't brag," Anna says, the only changed expression on her face the cocking of one eyebrow, slightly. "It wasn't like I hired a skywriter. I seem to remember everyone asking everyone else for their scores. Anyway, it was just a number, wasn't it?"

"Well, since you're a lawyer now," Sarah says, "I don't suppose it was *just* a number."

I say, "Well, I think—"

"Oops, I'm getting a call. If you'll excuse me," Anna says, rummaging in her purse. I don't remember hearing a ring, or even a vibration. She continues, "This could be a client. Nice to see you all. Congratulations, Amy."

She cuts across the grass toward the house, murmuring into the phone.

I whirl on the girls. "Why did you have to be like that?"

"Like what?" Sarah says. They stare at me blank-faced. "We were just kidding around. It's a compliment that she's so smart and did so well."

"Yeah," Kristi says. "Not our fault she can't take a compliment. She always did have a stick up her ass."

"She was always very nice!" I shout, sloshing my drink again, so I suck it down to keep from spilling it. *Nicer to me than you ever were*, I almost say.

"Geez, Amy, relax. What's gotten into you? We better get you something to eat."

"Not too many carbs," I say, watching my feet wobble in the grass as one of the girls steers me toward the food. "No pasta salad and definitely no bread . . ."

I don't feel so good. Paul is saying something to me, but it's echoing funny, like he's speaking into a metal pipe.

He's talking about getting me home, but I'm having a hard time going down this hill, was it always so steep here, whoops!

He scoops me up like a doll. "I'm glad I'm so thin you can do this," I tell him, but I don't think he hears me. He's saying something like "good grief" and "how many did you have?"

My fingers won't hold still long enough for me to count.

He plops me into the passenger seat of his car and hands me a bottle of water, but I can't get the cap off. As the car starts to turn in the circle drive, it's like a rollercoaster and . . .

Uh-oh. That'll be tough to clean up.

"Dammit!" Paul says, stopping the car and pulling out a hanky from his pocket.

I lean against the cool glass of the window and mumble, "I was only trying to live a little."

CHAPTER 7

Anna

"NICE TO SEE YOU ALL," I LIE, AND THEN, "CONGRATULATIONS, AMY," which is not a lie, because I'm happy for her that she lost all that weight and landed an eligible bachelor.

Bully for her.

When I'm pretty sure the girls can no longer tell I didn't get a real phone call—though it wasn't so plausible, since my phone never rang—I drop the phone back in my bag and turn toward the bluff over the lake, always my favorite spot here at the Beckers'.

The sun is poised like a diver, ready to plunge into the haze over the lake. The sun burns red and casts the clouds around it in blushing pink. There are probably pretty sunsets in Chicago, but frankly I never see them. My office window doesn't face west.

When will Cami get back with the food? I feel like the rest of the party is circling me, wondering why I'm here, and it's only a matter of seconds until someone else approaches to fish for whether I've returned for good. Can't a girl take a vacation? Bereavement leave, whatever.

"Anna? Anna Geneva?"

"Anna-Anna Geneva, at your service."

"As I live and breathe!" Mrs. Becker swoops in on me and touches my shoulders lightly. "I'm so happy that William ran into you at the store!"

Sure, he *ran into* me there. As if the county's most successful property developer stops by the Nee Nance Store to buy Miller Lite. No, he heard from somebody who heard from somebody . . . but anyway, I don't care how. "I'm happy to be invited," I tell her. "It feels like home here."

Mr. Becker comes up behind her, and as he moves to stand next to his wife, I see his son coming up behind him to join us.

I step forward into Beck's embrace, and it's not as tight as it would've been in our huggy-kissy teenage days, but it's comfortable all the same. "Good to see you in something other than digital form," I tell him.

He sets me at arm's length and smiles big enough that I can see his front teeth aren't crooked anymore; he must have fixed them with all that Becker money. His hair is higher up his scalp but still all in sandy curls that never stay combed right. My hand wants to reach up and brush that one curl back in place. His face crinkles up more when he smiles.

I'm sure I look different to him, too.

"Yeah, e-mails aren't quite the same as living color," he says. "You look wonderful."

"Well, thank you, I –"

"Will." A tiny brunette has appeared seemingly from nowhere. "Maddie's tired. We ought to be getting home."

Beck clears his throat. "Sam, this is my old friend Anna Geneva. Anna, this is my wife, Samantha."

"How do you do?" I say. I start to extend my hand, but Samantha has already nodded and turned away from me, so I take my outstretched hand up and fiddle with a curl, as if I'd intended to do that all along.

"Will, we need to go. She's falling asleep on Aunt Tabi."

"I thought I might stay a while, do some catching up."

"She likes to have you read her a story."

"If she's that tired, she won't even notice I'm not there."

"She hates breaks in her routine." Samantha has folded her arms and gone all taut. The elder Beckers and I now pretend to be invisible and deaf, looking at the grass, the lake, anywhere but at the young couple or each other's eyes.

After a long moment, Beck says, "I guess I'd better go. Catch you later, Mom and Dad. Anna?"

I come back to life again, looking at him directly and avoiding Samantha's face.

He says, "It was good to see you. Maybe I'll . . . Anyway. Bye."

Samantha leads the way across the grass and Beck follows with his hands in his pockets.

Mrs. Becker twirls her wedding ring, watching them go.

"So," I say brightly. "How nice about Amy and Paul."

"Yes," William Becker Sr. says. "We're pleased to welcome her into the family. Too bad we couldn't have had you, too." He leans in to take my elbow and peck me on the cheek, and then he's off across the lawn, his own wife in tow.

I glimpse Cami striding toward me across the grass, waving one long arm and balancing a huge plate of food on the other, but I turn my gaze back to the retreating form of Mr. Becker. *Too bad we couldn't have had you, too?* What an odd thing to say to your married son's old high school love.

CHAPTER 8

Maeve

WITHOUT ANNA HERE, THE STORE RINGS WITH SILENCE. EVEN THE customers talk less when there's only me here. Funny, she's only been home a week and already I'm used to her presence again. And now that Cami comes in, too, picking up her old job as if she'd only taken a few days off, the Nee Nance Store is feeling more like home than it has in years.

Just as I'm about to lose it.

When Randy finally finishes scratching off his instant ticket—leaving the discarded cardboard and silver scrapings all over the counter, the dust of his irrational hope—I am truly alone in the store.

I finally get to read Robert's letter. I promised Anna I wouldn't respond; I never said I wouldn't read it.

Oh Maeve, my dearest Maeve Callahan, I've missed you and couldn't wait for you to write again. I just had to tell you something exciting. You know Charley? I mentioned him in the last letter? Turns out he's got some property up north in Michigan! We worked out a deal, and get this, sweetness—at last I'm going to build you that house. Can you believe it? The one I always promised you?

We're going to be coming up in August to check things out up there, and I hope you'll agree to meet me then. I know I have a lot to say, a lot to make up for, and we'll talk about it, I promise.

I'm a new man, finally deserving of you.

Write me back at the Tennessee address, I'll be there a couple more weeks.

With great love from your wayword and repenance Robert.

I smile sadly at his mangled grammar and fold the letter back up, carefully slipping it back into the envelope

He'll build me a house at last, he says. I tip my head back on that old office chair and remember all the times he used to talk about it. He even used to sketch it, back when we lived in the bottom floor of that dodgy rental, when Anna was still drooling and gumming her pacifier.

I can hear him now.

"Baby," he would say, "look at this. Would you like a picket fence?"

I'd just gotten back into the kitchen from placing a drowsy Anna in her crib, having tiptoed down the short hallway for fear of waking her.

I smiled at his drawing. "Why would we need a picket fence in the woods?" I kissed the top of his head, which smelled like tobacco.

"Because picket fences are things husbands are supposed to build for wives."

He started sketching in the little picket points.

I heard a soft knock on the door. "Must be Veronica. She's coming to show off her engagement ring," I told him, squeezing his shoulder. "Why don't you just build me a nice gazebo? Put a hot tub in it and I'm yours forever."

"You better be mine forever, Maeve Callahan."

Veronica plunged into the house, left hand out first, almost like she was punching me. I chuckled and admired her ring and told her to keep her voice down so she didn't wake Anna. We girls had white zinfandel and Robert cracked another beer and we sat in the kitchen, listening to her extol the virtues of her fiancé, Grant. His dad ran a huge boat dealership and repair service that he would take over someday, and his family had not only a cottage in Spring Lake and a house in Haven to be near the business but a loft in Grand Rapids, too . . .

After a while, our smiles froze on our faces. Veronica seemed to forget we were even there, and by the time she left, I was giddy with suffocated giggles because every time she'd turned her head, Robert had pulled a face or kicked me under the table.

When we locked the door behind her, Robert said, "What's up with that broad?"

"Oh, stop. She's happy to be engaged, is all."

"She's happier about that rock, I think. I'm surprised she remembers the guy's name." Robert circled my waist from behind me, squeezing lightly, resting his chin on my shoulder.

"She's not that bad." We'd been friends since middle school, back when we were both new kids in school and neither of us had any money. Why shouldn't she be a little extra giddy because she wouldn't have to scrimp?

I couldn't say that to Robert, though. He'd take it personally and probably pop open another beer or three and be all fuzzy in the morning.

Robert brushed my neck with his lips and murmured, "Would you love me more if you had a big diamond?"

I turned in the circle of his arms to face him. "Oh, honey, you know size doesn't matter."

Robert looked blank for a flash before he got the joke. Then he laughed and silenced his own laugh by kissing me hard on the mouth right there, the porch light splashing onto us through the small windows in the front door. I fumbled for the off switch and we fell into darkness.

"I'll teach you to joke with me when I'm horny," he whispered, and scooped me up caveman style. We fumbled down the hall like that, taking care not to bang into walls or giggle too loudly, lest we wake the baby.

The clanging phone makes me jump half out of my skin.

"Nee Nance Store," I mumble. "Yes, we're open until ten tonight. Yep, bye."

The Nee Nance was supposed to be temporary. Just something to tide us over until we saved up enough to buy some property. What savings, to live and work in the same place! The landlord cut us such a sweet deal on the rent we couldn't refuse. We named it Nee Nance Store after Anna's baby-talk attempt to say "convenience store." She learned to walk cruising the shelves in the candy aisle.

If I'd had any idea that the scrubby grass in the front yard of that old crummy rental house would be the last chance I had at a real lawn, I would have put my foot down about moving here to begin with.

I finger the edges of Robert's letter. Maybe it wasn't my last chance after all.

I slip the letter back in my pocket when the jingle bells on the front door ring. It's Sally. Today she's changed wigs, wearing a bright red eighties-era Reba McEntire number.

"Hey, doll," she croaks. "What's shaking?"

A headache has begun to grind away behind my eyes, but I only now notice it, with Sally's arrival. I fish under the counter for my bottle of Excedrin.

"Nothing, Sal. Need some smokes?"

"Nope, just loaded up at the grocery store. Just feeling like some company."

Business seems slow for a bright Saturday, when people ought to be coming in for their chips and drinks and ice cream treats. So I don't argue when Sally pulls out some cards and starts shuffling.

She deals seven cards each for gin rummy and I keep track of our scores on the tail end of a nearly-used-up receipt tape roll. We break for the occasional customer, and then we get a rush of sorts, five people in the store at once, stocking for a party apparently, as they've got me fetching liquor bottles by the armful.

I hope they're not driving after this party of theirs.

When I turn back to her, Sally is staring so hard at her cards, she might be trying to set them on fire with her eyes.

"Your turn, Sal. Sorry that took so long. Can't stand in the way of a good Saturday drunk."

She doesn't respond and continues staring.

"Sal? You okay?"

"Huh," she replies, still staring. "It's the damnedest thing. I kind of forgot what I'm doing."

"We're playing cards, goofy. Did you forget what cards you were trying to collect? You've been picking up every three, and lots of diamonds, too."

Sally drops the cards right out of her hands, spilling them like drinks off a tray. She pats herself and the counter, frantically. "Where are my keys? I just remembered, I've gotta go, sister dear. Gotta . . . I've gotta go. Catch you on the flip side."

She snatches her keys and is around the counter with surprising quickness.

"Sally? What's wrong?"

"Nothing, doll," she calls out with a wave and a jaunty wink through the hairs of her outrageous wig. "Just heading home, is all. See ya."

I bend down to pick up the cards, and that's when I see that she had plenty of good cards in her hand. In fact, she had enough to lay them all down and crow "Gin!" which normally Sally loves to do, cackling like a maniac as if nothing were ever so fine.

I straighten up to peer out the door and watch her elderly gray Chevette cough and belch its way past the store and up Shoreline Drive.

Her trailer is in the other direction.

CHAPTER 9

Amy

"I'M WALKING ON SUNSHINE!" SINGS KATRINA AND THE WAVES FROM my clock radio. I slap the radio until it stops, and I think I've knocked it to the floor, which is just as well.

"Paul, honey? I need some water."

I've never licked mildewed bathroom tiles, but it's the best description I can think of for the taste in my mouth.

He doesn't respond, and with great reluctance I open my eyes into the stinging sunshine of my bedroom. The warm weight on my bed is Frodo, my chocolate Lab. The dog stirs lightly, then slurps at my nose. I put my hand over my eyes and try to remember the drive home. About the last thing I can clearly recall is Paul setting me in the car, and then . . .

Oh, crap. I should offer to get his car detailed.

I roll back away from the dog and his Alpo breath—normally I crate him at night; he must think this is quite a luxury, sleeping up here—and that's when I see the glass of water with a bendy straw, and a note.

Had to stop into the office this morning. Here's some water and Motrin. Feel better and take it easy.

I sip the water, but it's gotten warm overnight so it's not refreshing and my stomach curdles anyway.

I fumble for my thermometer in my nightstand, but I can't find it. Not that my temperature would be reliable anyway. If you don't get enough sleep—or for that matter, if you drink—it throws off the reading, according to that pamphlet from my OB/GYN.

That means this whole month's worth of charting my basal body temperature to figure out my most fertile time is all a complete waste.

I curl back under the covers and review my decisions of yesterday, starting with letting those silly girls talk me into chardonnay instead of Perrier. Now look at me! And heaven knows what I ate yesterday. The calories, the carbs from the wine. I think I even had cake with buttercream frosting.

It's enough to make me sick, only I already am.

It's a silver lining if I'm too sick to eat all day. That will begin to make up for some of the ground I lost.

Frodo hops off the bed and starts pacing and whining. Paul should be here to let the damn dog out, knowing what a mess I'm in.

Paul whined to me last week, *Why don't we just live together? Then we don't have to debate about which place to spend the night, and you can save money on rent.*

There's no way he could understand my answer, so I just didn't bother explaining that a wedding doesn't count unless it's a couple truly starting out together in life. If a couple is already living together, it's just a big party and a shakedown for presents.

Sometimes I think I'm the last traditional girl on the planet. At least we have sex. It's not like I'm Victorian about it. Oh, sex. Paul didn't get his sex after the party, either. Well, he'll live.

Frodo is pawing at the slider now. If I don't get up, there will be a mess.

In the bathroom, I splash water on my face and yank my hair into a ponytail. My face is mottled and bloated and I have to pause to dry-heave into the sink.

On my mirror I'd taped a piece of paper with the saying, written in glitter pen, EVERY THIN DAY IS A GOOD DAY! And on the other side, like a cheerful bookend, is that old magazine clipping, GO CONFIDENTLY IN THE DIRECTION OF YOUR DREAMS. LIVE THE LIFE YOU'VE IMAGINED.

I need to tape up another one: IGNORE PEOPLE WHO TELL YOU TO "LIVE A LITTLE."

People like me can't afford that luxury.

In retrospect, it was optimistic of me to put on my running shoes.

On a typical morning, I like to imagine stomping down my old self with every stride. *Take THAT and THAT and THAT, thunder-thighs!*

At the moment, though, I'm under a tree with my head between my knees, watching the blades of grass swim in my vision, Frodo's leash around my wrist.

At least he went to the bathroom, so when I manage to crawl back to the apartment it will buy me some hours of recuperation.

Meanwhile, I can feel the fat cells making themselves at home.

I'll get up even earlier tomorrow, before work. Run twice as far, and after work, too.

Frodo lunges, and the movement knocks me off balance, the leash slipping off my wrist. I stand up too fast and my vision fuzzes up for a moment, and when I collect myself, I see him tearing off down the road.

I force myself to plod after him, but he's far too fast; even on a good day I can't catch him. "Frodo!" I shriek, but by now he doesn't even hear me, much less care. "Frodo!"

I speed up the pace, though my head pounds, holding my stomach with one hand. "Frodo . . ." I lose sight of him near the goose pond. We're getting close to the entrance to the apartment complex and the main road where people drive too fast.

I collapse to my knees and dry-heave again, waiting to collect enough energy so I can get up and go find my dog, trying to remember the information on his dog tags, what happens if the animal control people find him before I do, what if . . .

"Miss?"

I jerk my head up. A large, sweaty, egg-shaped man is lumbering toward me with two dogs, and . . .

"Frodo! You found him!"

Frodo jumps on me and slobbers on my already wet face.

"Yeah, he stopped to make friends with my dog, dragging his leash. I figured he belonged to somebody here so I started walking him back through, figuring I'd find his owner soon enough. Soon as he saw you he started pulling for all he's worth."

I finally get Frodo to settle down enough so that I can take the leash.

"My name is Ed," he says. "This here is Lucky."

Some kind of small terrier with a loop-de-loop tail is panting at his side.

"I know I'm lucky you found him," I say, shuddering now with relief.

"Are you all right?" Ed asks. "You don't look so good."

I'm sure I don't, at that. "I'm not feeling so well. I shouldn't have tried to walk him right now."

"Want me to walk him for you? I'll bring him back when I'm done. Just give me your apartment number."

"Well, that's nice, but he's already done his business. I'll just head back now."

"How about I walk with you? You seem a little shaky on your feet, and if he sees another bird or something, he'll knock you right flat."

I just want to get home and back in bed and pretend none of this happened, but the quickest way with least drama will be to let this Ed walk my dog home, so Frodo doesn't yank me into traffic or something.

"Okay, thanks. That's nice of you."

I respond to Ed's questions with the barest of answers. I'm Amy, I tell him, graduated from Haven High, class of '90; yes, I was in National Honor Society and the band. Ed was in the band, too, though he was a freshman when I was a senior. I don't remember him at all, and I can usually remember the other fat kids in school. Not that we were all friends in some kind of obese fraternity. I just recognized the familiar bubble of empty space surrounding them at lunch and in the halls.

If he remembers what I used to be, he doesn't mention it.

"See you around," he says when I finally get back to my apartment.

Inside, I lean against the door and sink straight down, sipping breaths of cool air until I feel like I can move again.

CHAPTER 10

Cami

I TELL THE CUSTOMER, "$19.88, PLEASE."

"Don't you need to ring that up?" she asks, hitching her baby up higher on her hip as she tosses a twenty on the counter.

"Can't. The drawer is stuck."

"Huh." She stares hard at her twelve cents in change before shoving the coins in her pocket and scooping up her shopping bag of baby formula and Kleenex.

"Have a nice day, now," I call after her, whacking the register again with my fist.

Anna comes down the stairs, talking on her cell phone in her lawyer voice. "I can do it Monday," she's saying, "first thing . . . No, it'll be fine. I'll get in Sunday. It's no problem . . . I'm staying with Shelby. Right. See you then."

She clicks off and nods in my direction. She's wearing trousers and a blouse and her hair is blown out straight, and just peeking out through her hair I can see a pen she's left behind her ear. You'd never know she was just getting ready to straighten the canned goods.

"Back to work next week?" I ask her.

"Yes," she says, and crouches down in front of the cling peaches.

"Are you feeling okay, then?"

Anna cuts her eyes over to me. "What do you mean?"

"Your mom mentioned you lost your friend. I was sorry to hear that."

"I'm fine. I was fine before, too. I wish people would give me the courtesy of accepting when I say I'm fine."

"Okay, I believe you. I've never known anyone finer. You are the Duchess of Fine."

She puffs a piece of hair out of her eyes and continues shoving cans around, facing them out, making all the labels even. "Is my mom upstairs?" she asks.

"Yes, she said her head hurts, so I sent her up to rest."

"Thanks."

As the bells chime at the door, Anna pops up, and the effect is prairie-dog-like. She dusts her hands off, touches her hair, and smiles the first real smile I've seen all day, maybe since she's been back.

"Beck!" she says. "What a nice surprise."

Will Becker beams a smile right back at her. As he walks past the counter, he suddenly notices there's someone else in the store. "Oh, hi," he says to me. "Cami Drayton, right? I saw you at the party."

"Hi. Your dad was kind enough to invite me, too, when he stopped in to see Anna."

"We always know we can find her at the Nee Nance," Will says, turning again to Anna. Her smile dies away at this, and Will rushes to finish his thought. "When she graces Haven with her presence. When she's not in her fancy high-rise office building in the Windy City."

He's walked past me now and joined her in the aisle.

She's shifting her weight from foot to foot and has retrieved the pen from behind her ear. She twirls it in her hand, spinning it over and over around her thumb. Used to make our English teacher nuts when she did that, because sometimes she'd lose the pen and it would spin crazily out onto the carpet in the middle of his lecture.

Beck is so tall he looms over her, and the fidgeting and height difference make her look twelve years old.

"Want to come to lunch? Not today, I have a meeting. Tomorrow?"

"Well, let me check my busy calendar . . . um, yeah, I think I'm free between the mopping of the floor and emptying the garbage."

"Great. Portobello at noon?"

He reaches out with one hand, gives her upper shoulder a squeeze. When he walks past me on his way out, he's got this tight little grin, like he's trying to hold in a huge silly smile.

Anna is back to the cans, straightening just like she was, but now she's humming a little tune.

"The cash register drawer is stuck," I tell her.

"Oh, that. I can fix that."

Anna disappears into the back room and comes out with a screwdriver, and damned if she doesn't fix it, lawyer clothes and all.

On the way walking back to my dad's house, I stop in Jack's Hardware and buy some paint with my last good credit card. I've tried to rationalize this purchase twelve different ways since I made up my mind, but there's no legitimate reason to spend money I don't have, money that I should be giving back to Steve, and in fact I shouldn't be working at the Nee Nance but someplace a little more profitable, like temping or even waitressing, which I've done in a pinch. It's not like Maeve can pay me much.

I just need to paint my room, and that seems to be as good a reason as any to do something. Also it keeps me busy, and busy is good because it keeps me from thinking about the closest casino and whether I can take a bus to get there.

I'm rehearsing a conversation with my dad on the way back, as the houses get shabbier and the streets get more rutted, but his truck is gone so there's no need tell him, *You should be happy I want to paint, make this house worth more someday . . .*

Almost makes me wish he were there, since I've gone to the trouble of thinking all that up.

He's forgotten to lock the door behind him. I'd be pissed about that if I owned anything more valuable than a few paperback books.

The door swings into the wall behind it, the doorknob neatly sticking into a hole punched by an earlier, harder bang. It isn't until I yank the door free and close it behind me that I see a body on the couch and shout, "Jesus!"

And the body moves, so at least I know it's not dead.

She's got chlorinated hair with black roots and black around her eyes from makeup applied too heavily, too long ago. She carries the same eau de booze that clings to my father.

"Get out of my house," I tell her.

"Fuck, he's married?" she groans, throwing an arm over her eyes.

"Oh, God, no. Not at all and definitely not to me. I'm his daughter and I'm home now, so get out."

I stomp past the couch and down the hall, slamming my thin bedroom door and dropping the ersatz hook-lock into place. I pick up my deck of cards for some restless shuffling, but no sooner do I spill them out of the box into my hand than the chlorinated chick taps on my door. Least, I assume it's her.

"What," I shout at the door, shuffling the cards rapid-fire so they sound like a tommy gun.

"You gotta light?"

"No."

"You're out of toilet paper and I really gotta wee."

Wee?

I forget the hook is there, and when I yank on the door, it pulls right out of the cheap, thin doorframe.

I stomp past her and rummage in the hall closet for toilet paper. I haven't been to the store in a couple days and I didn't know we were running out. Presumably my dad must have done this kind of thing for himself before I came back.

"Use a Kleenex."

"Why so snippy? If you pardon my expression." She leans on the hallway wall with her unlit cigarette propped between her fingers, ready for action.

"I'm not used to extending Chez Drayton hospitality to random women my dad is nailing. If you pardon my expression."

"I'm not random. I'm Shirelle. Most people just call me Sherry."

She sticks out her hand. I take it and her fingers feel bony and hard. I look at her face directly and I see the makeup seeping into lines around her eyes. She's older than I thought; I'd assumed from the bleach job that she was a youngster, my age or younger. But no, she's probably about dad's age. My mother's age.

"Just go. I've got things to do, yeah? Makes me nervous having a stranger here."

"What stranger? I just told you my name is Sherry. You must be Camille."

I stop in my bedroom doorway, then turn back to her slowly. "He talked about me?"

"Oh, sure. Says you're real smart and everything, can do math in your head like some kinda whiz-kid computer. Too bad about your brother."

"What do you mean?"

"Being a fruit and all."

I take her elbow and start walking toward the front door. She's

wheeling along behind me with her limbs flapping everywhere.
"Hey!"

When I deposit her on the porch, she clutches the railing as if
I'd tossed her like a pro wrestler. "There's a bathroom at the gas
station on the corner. I bet they even have toilet paper." The door
is too light to slam hard, but it's something.

With the curtains off the window, the room looks cleaner already. I would love to jump right to the yellow I bought, but I have
a lesson to learn, I think, about instant gratification. So instead I
pry open the primer can.

Even with primer, the room is better. Disappearing under my
roller are scuffs and scrapes, smears of unknown origin, a sheen
of dirt and neglect. I roll hard though my arms ache, and then I
realize I have to do the ceiling, too, because it's also filthy.

The radio croons behind me, tunes from my days in college,
when I was so dizzy with freedom.

That's when I hear stomping feet down the hall. I left the door
open for ventilation, so I stand and watch the empty space in the
frame until it fills up with my father.

His shoulders are tight and aimed forward. His black hair juts
out from under his hat, and he's got three days of beard going. Now
he smells as much like the shop as he does the booze. It's that pin-
nacle of the day before he really lets loose. Even so, I do not relax.

"What's this I hear about you attacking my girlfriend?"

"I convinced her to leave, yeah? After she didn't respond to my
subtle hinting along the lines of 'Get out of my house.'"

He smiled. "Oh, your house, is it? Yours? Bitch has been back
one week, crawling back because your boyfriend threw you out,
and now this house is yours? And now you think you can paint,
too?"

"Why not? It's in my room, which you never see. Someday
you'll sell this house, and then you'll be glad I fixed it up."

"So my piece-of-shit house isn't good enough for you." His eyes dart down. "You stupid slut, you're getting paint on the carpet. Ain't you heard of a drop cloth?"

"I'm going to tear up the carpet, so it *is* the drop cloth, yeah? There's hardwood underneath."

"And what if I say no? It's my goddamn house and if I want carpet, I want carpet. And what if I tell you you've gotta get down on your knees and scrub off every little paint splotch? Whaddya say to that?"

"I say fuck you to that."

As he swings, I only have time enough to close my eyes, so it isn't until I hear the smack of his hand into the wall that I know he didn't hit me. When I look, he's grinning at a black, greasy hand-print he's left on the wet primer, and smeared straight down a good three feet. He wipes his hand on his overalls.

"I'm going out. With Sherry. And you know what? She'll sleep here if I want her to and she'll stay as late as she feels like. And if you lay a hand on her again, I'll call the cops and have your un-grateful ass thrown in jail for assault. Don't think they won't do it, neither. Betcha your fancy tutoring people wouldn't take kindly to a teacher with a criminal record."

After he storms down the hall, I hear something hit the floor and shatter. And something else, six or eight of them. Beer bottles, is my guess. The beer bottles leftover from last night's partying with Sherry. He's wearing his same heavy boots he always wears to the shop and he'll crunch right over it.

I'm barefoot, though. And my shoes are by the front door.

I lower the roller into the primer again and roll a swath over his handprint, again and again, until it finally fades from view.

CHAPTER 11

Anna

WHEN I WAS TWELVE, WALKING IN HERE MADE ME GASP IN AWE. I stared at the fine woodwork, fingered the linen napkins, and stole furtive peeks at the other diners, making up elaborate stories in my head about what they did when they went home. They went to their mansions and played pool in their downstairs rec rooms, I figured, the grown-ups holding cocktails at the bar and watching their children play. And in my fantasies of other people's lives, even the rich ones never got out of the fancy clothes they wore to dinner. I imagined they kept those clothes on because they knew how beautiful they looked and wanted to stay that way.

Now, standing in the purposefully dim Portobello Ristorante, I'm wearing nice clothes myself. I know that the people in pretty dresses go home and sit in their pajamas and watch TV, same as anyone.

Well, they probably watch a nicer TV.

Beck is a little late. I imagine his wife grilling him about where he's going, and with whom, although it's probably nothing more than a work delay. I know how those things go.

Mom took me here after Dad left, as a treat for getting straight A's. I believe the real reason was to distract me from his absence. I wore my mother's jewelry and some cloying perfume she bought from the Avon lady. I tried very hard to pretend that we were going to keep our pretty dresses on all evening.

I wasn't the only one pretending.

I was holding the giant leather-bound menu, and it was so tall it blocked my mother's face. I insisted on ordering from the adult menu, and Mom was talking about school and how I joined the swim team. Then she said something about how "Your father will be so excited to see you swim. Do you know he's quite a good swimmer himself—"

"He's never going to see me swim. He's never coming back. For all we know he's dead."

I slammed the menu shut, and when I flopped it down on the table, it caught the basket of rolls by the edge. They spilled out across the tablecloth. Mom and I hurriedly shoved them back in the basket, lest it look like we were going to cram the rolls in our purses or something.

Mom's hand was shaking. I folded my hands over my menu so I wouldn't fidget. When the waitress arrived, I ordered the "quee-chee" and blushed hard when the waitress replied, "The quiche, then? Or maybe the young lady would prefer some pasta?" with a sideways glance at my mother.

Now I hear the heavy door squeak open, and the man is framed by a corona of sunshine, coming right at me with arms outstretched.

I return Beck's hug warmly.

"So good to see you," he says, and we follow the hostess to a booth. It might be my imagination, but as he glances over his shoulder, it looks like he's worried about being seen by someone he knows.

banter, he'd never before complained about his wife. "Ever occur to you to put the dish away, Boy Genius?"

"Well, of course, I should . . . Hey, whose side are you on?" He smiles but quickly looks away, back at his sandwich, which he's still not eating.

"We're taking sides now? I'm just saying, it seems pretty simple to me. Put the dish away. Ta-da!"

He shook his head. "Marriages aren't that simple, and then adding a child adds a whole other level . . ."

In other words, I know nothing about having a family. I cross my arms and tune him out.

"Hey, I'm sorry." He reaches across for my elbow, but he can't reach it and I don't give in to the gesture. "I shouldn't have started complaining and all. It's fine, it'll all work out. Let's stop carrying on about me. Are you enjoying your vacation?"

"It's not a vacation. A friend died and I was distracted at work, so they sent me home."

I've caught Beck with a mouthful of sandwich for this, so he can't reply except to wrinkle up his forehead and kind of murmur sympathetically. I wave away his stricken look.

"It's fine. I mean, sad, of course. But everything will be fine. I'm looking forward to going back because I'm up for partner soon and I really need to be working now."

He's finally swallowed. "Congratulations. I always knew you'd make Haven proud."

I shrug. "Actually, I am worried about my mom. She's been . . ."

Now it's my turn to look around the restaurant. It's dim but sparsely populated today. The waitress is leaning on the bar talking to the bartender, but they glance over this way, probably just to see if we need more drinks, but they could also be actively listening. For all I know they're Nee Nance customers. The store is just down the block.

Beck has nearly plowed through his sandwich already. So I say, "Got time to take a walk?"

I'm glad I skipped the pantyhose today, because now I can dig my toes into the warm sand. I tip my face up toward the sun. I'd forgotten how good this feels on a perfect June day when the sun is just warm enough to be pleasant instead of burning. Beck and I are sitting on an old picnic blanket he found in his trunk. He's cross-legged on the blanket next to me, still wearing his shoes and business clothes.

It's crowded at the beach, but no one's paying us any attention. Moms are watching their children; teenagers on summer vacation are watching each other.

Beck rolls up his shirt sleeves and loosens his tie. "So, what's wrong?"

I sit up and turn toward him. He's giving me that steady look of his, the one that seems to say, *Let me have it. I can take it.*

"My dad is writing my mom letters."

He startles and turns to face me more fully. He takes one hand of mine in two of his. "Are you sure? Is he okay? Have you talked to him?"

"No, I haven't talked to him, and he's at least okay enough to be writing. Yes, I'm sure. I found the letter and she confessed immediately."

"Well, that's wonderful!"

I pull my hand back out of his. "What's so wonderful about it? He's an asshole loser who abandoned his family twenty years ago without so much as a postcard and now he's writing my mom love letters or something. He probably just wants money, which she doesn't have, no small thanks to him."

"Maybe he's changed."

"Changed into what? Some saint? And if he's all saintly now, why is he not writing to me, his daughter? Mom was a grown-up; she had a chance to get over it herself. I was just a kid. Think of *your* daughter. How she would feel."

That was perhaps a low blow. He grimaces. "I'm sorry, you're right. I just . . . Aren't you curious? Don't you want to see him?"

"What for? So he can complicate my life again? He can say, 'Hey, sorry about all those years and stuff I missed, and oops! Gotta run!' I've spent twenty years making sure he has no effect on me whatsoever and I'm not about to muck that up now by having a conversation with him. Anyway, he doesn't want to talk to me; he wants Mom."

"Now what's going to happen?"

Before I can answer, Beck's phone bleeps at him. He looks at the screen and cringes. "I'm sorry, Annie, just a sec." He starts typing, holding the phone at an angle to shield the screen from glare.

I was only ten, but I remember that day. I remember my mom screaming at Bill, that no-account loser who came to bring the car back but not Dad. I remember her screaming at him, "You're help-ing a man abandon his family!" and she was holding her stomach with both arms, doubled half over like she'd been stabbed. She was right there out on the sidewalk. She'd made me go inside, but I was peeking between the newspaper rack and the beer posters to see what was going on.

I knew what *abandon* meant, so when she told me that night that Dad was just taking a trip and he'd be back eventually, I also knew she was lying to me.

Beck finally puts his phone down. His face is long and his frown is heavy.

"Everything okay?"

"Sure, it's fine. Sorry about that. It was Sam."

He puts his hand on my knee. I move my leg away from him. "Don't."

He clasps his hands in his lap. "I just hate to see you hurt."

"Who's hurt? I'm not hurting. I said I'm worried. I made Mom promise not to write him again, but what if she doesn't really stop? The return address was Tennessee, but he could call or just show up one day at the store. Then what?"

Beck doesn't reply. He's staring at me, but it seems that he didn't hear a word I just said.

I brush the sand off my feet so I can slip my sandals back on. "I'd better let you get back. Seems like you have an emergency brewing anyway."

I help him fold the blanket and then we walk in silence back to his car. At the car, he reaches for a hug, but I take one step back, waving at him instead. He gets in his black BMW and drives off, and I wish I wasn't still thinking about the warmth of his hand on my knee.

CHAPTER 12

Maeve

IT'S HARD TO BELIEVE MY DAUGHTER WILL BE GONE AGAIN ON Sunday. Is it possible to miss her and want Sunday to get here, all at the same time?

I can see Anna chafing in this shabby little store. She's still walking around in the few skirts and trousers she brought with her, and more and more she's on her phone to the office, lining up appointments. She's gone swimming in the lake and taken walks with Cami once or twice, but I can tell from all her fidgeting and restless working she's about to the last thread on the end of her rope.

Can I blame her, really? Yet her restlessness feels like a rebuke to me. Even now, all the shelves dusted and gleaming and all the canned products lined up fastidiously, it looks accusatory. *Look how you let this place go!*

Well, it wasn't my idea to spend my life selling people their vices. So I don't do it perfectly, big deal.

When the phone rings and I answer "Nee Nance Store," a young lady says, "Anna? Hi, it's Amy. I was wondering—"

"It's her mother, Amy. Anna isn't here. I can leave her a message."

Amy wants Anna to come see her wedding dress. I break it to Amy that my daughter is leaving on Sunday and probably won't be back all summer. Anna keeps going on about how much work she has to do to make up for being gone these measly two weeks.

No sooner do I put the phone back in the cradle than two men walk in, one wearing overalls and the other a dark business suit.

"Mrs. Geneva," says Paul Becker. "You'll excuse the interruption, but Jack and I need to discuss some plans for the property."

I grip the edge of the counter hard. "You can't do that when the store is closed? I open late on Sundays. And how about a little notice?"

Paul was looking at his cell phone while I was talking to him. He affects a laugh that must seem very deep and manly to him. It sounds theatrical. "Oh, Mrs. Geneva, no need to drag Jack away from his family just to bring his tape measure inside, really now."

This Jack person pulls out a digital camera.

"What are you doing now?" I ask, though I can tell what they're doing. They're deciding what to demolish. *Flash!* And he snaps a picture of the wall I share with the gift shop next door.

"That'll have to go," Paul says, frowning at a clipboard.

Carla comes in and gives me a look, wrinkling her face up at the invaders. I hand her the scratch-off Lotto and Virginia Slims without her having to ask and shake my head at her questioning eyes.

I might as well rent a billboard, though, because Carla will stop in to Doreen's or down to the Tip-A-Few and tell people that Paul Becker was in here with a guy in overalls, and they'll all figure out right quick that this place is getting gutted and Maeve is being evicted.

I'm thinking I'd better tell Anna before the gossip winds its way to her when she walks in the door. Guess she'll hear it right now.

Anna drops a shopping bag on top of the newspaper rack, whips off her sunglasses, and demands of the men, "Who are you? What are you doing here?"

Paul Becker turns around and Anna jumps back as if splashed with cold water. "Paul? What are you doing?"

Paul comes charging toward Anna with his hand out, all glad-handing business. "Hey, thanks for coming to my party the other day. Nice to see you there, just like old times. Well, not *just* like, I guess," he says, laughing at his own wit. Anna's mouth is slightly open and she's got a little crease between her brows.

"What's going on here?"

Jack, the contractor, has continued his measuring and snapping of pictures.

Paul holds up one finger with a smile on his face, like he's going to show us something delightful, like a cuddly puppy or a birthday present. He grabs a big case off the floor and withdraws a rolled-up tube of paper. This he spreads out triumphantly on my front counter.

It's an architect's drawing of what will no longer be my store.

"It's going to be beautiful. We're going to have high-end lofts up here, and downstairs, right where we're standing, is going to be a grocery. But not just any grocery! It will be upscale: imported cheese and wine, olive oils, ciabatta bread. It'll serve the residents of the lofts upstairs and down the block, but of course in time we hope to attract the tourists from Chicago. And, of course, the business crowd who will stop in here on their way to their lakeshore homes."

Anna stares at me now, as Paul babbles on. I draw myself up tall, folding my arms. She asks, "So, you're overhauling the store, Mom? This is the first I've heard of it."

Paul breaks off in mid-sentence, looking between Anna and me.

"You know, we can finish this up another time. We'll call you, Mrs. Geneva. Sorry for the intrusion. Jack? Let's get out of their way now, okay?"

Anna says again, "Mom?"

I say nothing at all as Paul rolls up his dream and slips it back in the case. Jack nods to me on the way out.

I clear my throat. "My lease is up," I tell her. "End of August. They're not letting me renew."

"What are you going to do?"

"Well, that's still up in the air a bit."

"Up in the air? Mom, that's only a few weeks from now! What the hell?"

"Watch your language."

"You've got no plan B at all? Where are you going to stay? Can you afford to move? How are you going to earn money without the store? Why can't you stay and run this stupid yuppie grocery?"

My head is starting to ache again, so many questions. "I can't afford the rent. You wouldn't believe what he wants to charge. I've got a little money to tide me over."

"Only a little?"

"Quite a lot of it went out the window taking care of a child by myself for all those years, and don't forget college!"

"I paid most of that myself, and I am still paying off those loans and will be doing so until I die." She shakes her head and touches her temple, now speaking more calmly. "I've always appreciated that, but it's beside the point, Mom. I can help you financially and I will, but—"

"Who says I need your help?"

"You just said you have no place to live, no other job lined up, and only 'a little' money. Of course you need my help." She waves her hand in the air at this and props it on her hip.

"I can stay with Sally."

"In that shitbox trailer out in the sticks?"

"It's a roof! It's just temporary!"

"Isn't that what Dad said about the Nee Nance?"

I flop into the office chair, turning away from her hard gaze. She comes around the counter and crouches in front of me.

"Mom. I'm just saying that your livelihood and place to live are going to be gone in a few weeks. You have to be thinking more than shacking up in Sally's trailer. We need a long-term plan. We need to start applying for jobs, looking for places to live that you can afford. Worse comes to worst, you could come stay with me in Chicago, but you don't want to do that, do you?"

"Don't talk to me like I'm a child. And what's this 'we' business? 'We' don't need to do anything. It's my problem and I will solve it myself, which is why I never told you to begin with. I knew you'd get like this."

Anna stands up away from me now and folds her arms. "Get like what?"

"Bossy. Patronizing."

"I'm just trying to take care of you. Someone's got to."

I stand up roughly from the chair and it bangs back into the back shelf. "I can take care of myself."

"Then why are you in this mess? Do you know all the years you paid rent in this dump you could have bought actual property? Something you owned and couldn't just be cast out of? What were you waiting for?"

My headache is shrieking now. I can hardly keep my eyes open. I stand up and fumble past her like I've gone blind, stumbling up the stairs to my room, where I choke down two Excedrin dry and lay on top of my quilt, curled up like a wounded animal protecting my soft insides.

When I awake, my mouth feels cottony and I'm dizzy, disoriented. It takes me several moments to remember what just happened. I creep down the hall to peek down the stairs. From this view I can see the store in operation, and I can hear Anna's voice as she rings up purchases. She also seems to be on her cell phone with her office.

I slink back to my room, avoiding squeaky spots on the hallway floor. I close the door gently and press the lock down. It snaps into place and I relax a bit.

From under my mattress I withdraw Robert's last letter and a pad of paper. My pen remains on my nightstand from when I last used it.

Dear Robert, I begin.

You asked me when you first wrote if I believe in second chances and at the time I said I didn't know. I needed time. And actually, just recently I tried to stop writing you. It suddenly seemed so foolish to even entertain the notion of seeing you again, after everything.

But I re-read your letter every night and I couldn't bear to think this could be the last I hear from you, if I didn't write back at all. It was like you were disappearing again, only this time it's up to me, it's in my hands.

I can't promise it will be like it was. But you're sorry and you love me and you're coming back after all, and since I can't stop thinking of you . . . I guess this means I still love you, too.

All this means that yes, I'll meet you. Just tell me when and where.

I don't know what the future holds for us, if anything. But I'm willing to see.

Maeve

The envelopes are downstairs. I'll have to wait until Anna is asleep, or out, or, if not before, I can mail it Monday, when she's gone back home with her fancy education and expensive suits and her utter confidence that she's so much smarter than I am.

CHAPTER 13

Amy

MY MOM LOOKS AROUND FOR A CHAIR TO SIT ON.

We're in Agatha's Boutique, and for most people a chair is nothing, almost nonexistent, like the spoon in your hand or the mirror on the wall, serving only as a means to an end.

Only when you're fat, none of this is nothing.

"Here, Mom," and I take her elbow and point her toward a low bench, upholstered in crushed velvet. It's wide enough for two, or wide enough for her. I remember sitting there myself when looking for a prom dress. I gave up in disgust and stayed home.

She nods her relief at finding a place to land. She crosses her legs at her ankles because she can't cross them at her knees.

I still remember the joy the first time I realized I could cross one knee over another.

She's still breathing a little hard. We had to park far away.

"Well," she says with a little puff of air, fanning herself with a tissue. "Let's see this vision of a dress."

It's still the store model. Mine isn't in yet, but Mom wanted to see it, insisted on it, in fact. Aunt Agatha appears with the dress over her arm.

Mom gasps. "Oooooh, look at that. Will you just look at that."

I accept the dress from Aunt Agatha and step into the large bridal fitting room, alone, by prior arrangement with my mother. She fussed at me over it, complained, "Why are you so modest? I wiped your butt; I can see you change into a dress."

I told her I just wanted her to see it all at once, and get the full effect when it was already on.

I don't let Agatha in here, either. She offered before, because climbing into a wedding dress alone is hard. Too big to step into, too heavy to pull comfortably over the top of you. So I hang it on a hook and wriggle into it from underneath, reach up, dislodge the hanger, and then let it fall down on me. I perfected this after trying on a dozen or more dresses, with Kristi, Sarah, and Nikki tittering outside the doors.

I poke my head out and let Agatha in so she can do up the buttons at the back. The model dress is too big—such bliss! For something to be too big!—and she pulls on it and bunches it up in her hands behind me so it hugs my body.

Only then do I look in the mirror.

We head out into the store like that, me holding up the hem so I don't step on it in my bare feet and Agatha like a caboose hanging onto the back.

Mom puts her hands over her face. She looks horrified, only I know she's not. Her tears are running over her fingertips and sliding down her cheeks, but she makes no sound.

"Well?"

It's an off-the-shoulder white gown, with seed pearls and lace, and lace swooping down the skirt, and a crinoline.

"I know it's a bit lacy and princessy for a woman my age," I say.

"Nonsense," breaks in Agatha. "Every bride can be as princessy as she likes, I don't care if you're eighty."

"So beautiful," my mom says. "Just . . . I always said you were such a beauty."

"Well, now, Maryann," Agatha says to my mother, who also happens to be her niece. "What do you say we look at some gowns for you?"

At this she flushes deep. "I don't know, Aunt Agatha, I'm not sure I'm up to that today. I'd like to drop a little weight first, you know . . ."

"Mom," I say as gently as I can. "The wedding is in August."

"I know, sweetheart, I just . . ." She looks up at Agatha.

Agatha blows a piece of her gray hair off her forehead. "Maryann, I can always take it in for you when you lose those pounds. It wouldn't hurt to start looking. I'd hate for you to be stressed and rushing, last minute. How about I just find you a few candidates, for starters?"

Without waiting for a response, Agatha disappears toward the mother-of-the-bride dresses.

The gown is loose now that Agatha has let go of the back. I feel like I'm lording over my mother, so I crouch down next to her, sitting cross-legged under the billow of my dress. "What's wrong?" I ask her, though I already know.

Her voices comes out raspy. "I'm a disgrace to you."

"No, you're not at all! You're beautiful." I almost choke on it because I heard her say that to me hundreds of times when I was fat and I knew it was a lie every time.

She sniffs hard. "Don't kid a kidder."

"Do you want me to help you lose some weight?"

"Oh, I can't do it like you did it, honey. I'm too old to go running around town in some Nikes or something."

"You don't have to run. What about swimming? You could join the Y, and . . ."

"I can't swim and you know it."

"They do those water aerobics, right in the shallow end."

My mom shakes her head, loose pieces of red hair flopping over her eyes. I would love to talk her out of that dye job. It's fire-engine red and tacky to the extreme, but her appearance is a touchy subject.

I can't stop thinking about how it will look in the wedding pictures. How she will look.

The hair, though, isn't the real problem.

"Mom, you've got to do something."

"Something like what? Like you said, the wedding is in August. This"—she sweeps her hand through the air over her lap—"is a lost cause."

"I wasn't talking about the wedding," I rush to say, but I can feel a flush creep up my neck as soon as I get the words out. "I'm worried about your health."

"Don't start on me with the health thing. It's not like I don't know it. I have lousy metabolism. So do you. You had to run your-self to death and eat like a rabbit while your girlfriends ate what-ever they wanted."

"But you can't—"

Agatha has returned with an armful of gowns, which she hangs on the outside of fitting room doors, to display them. They're all tents, really. Huge sacks with some neck detail, in pastel colors. Gargantuan parodies of Easter eggs.

I squeeze my mom's hand as she flinches away from them.

Stepping out of the air conditioning at Agatha's, we get the full smack of afternoon sun right in our faces. Mom grimaces. "Oh, Lordy, it's hot," she says, and I know what she means. Heat is so much worse when you're already wrapped in layers of excess skin and fat. It's like being cocooned.

"Let's get you a bottle of water before I take you home and head back to work." The Nee Nance is between Agatha's and our car.

Mom lumbers to a bench outside the store, next to the ice cooler. The Nee Nance isn't air conditioned, anyway.

Anna's at the register. "Hi!" I wave to her.

She looks through me for a second, before she blinks and says, "Oh. Hi, there. You'll never guess who was just here," she says, scrubbing with vigor at the surface of the front counter while I grab two cold waters from the cooler.

"Who?"

"Your fiancé."

Her voice sounds odd. I feel like I'm missing a punch line or something. "Oh," is the only thing I can think of to say. "Well, his work is just down the road."

"Right. His work at Becker Development, my mother's new landlord."

"Really?" I put the bottles on the counter, but she doesn't look at them. She has stopped scrubbing the counter and she's staring at me now. "Isn't that interesting."

"The new landlord who's evicting her."

Evicting? "What? No, he wouldn't . . . Are you sure?"

Anna narrows her eyes. "How would I be unclear on something like that?"

I know he must have a reason; there's more to this story, something important I'm missing, that Anna's missing. But I don't know what it is; I learned early on Paul hates to be pressed for details. He shares on his own agenda.

"I don't know what to say. I don't get involved in the business, really." I drum my fingers on the counter and check on my mom, in silhouette out the front window. She's fanning herself with her hand. She's baking alive out there. "My mom is waiting for me, and I'm late for work."

Anna punches the register buttons hard, and it seems like she has had to start over, because it takes her longer than it should.

"Look, I didn't know anything about it. Anyway, it's not up to me."

"I suppose that's true. Do you want a bag for this?"

I shake my head, and I take my change from her. "I'm sure Paul has his reasons for what he's doing. He has the best interests of Haven at heart."

"Because this store, my family store, is a blight on the neighborhood?" Anna gestures around the store.

"No, but . . . I mean . . . He's not a bad guy."

"I'm sure he's swell. I bet he rescues kitty cats from trees."

I snatch the water off the counter and stomp outside.

I help my mom stand up and we begin our slow progress down the block to the car. I look over my shoulder at the outside of the store with its pukey green siding and the one *e* hanging sideways and the beer posters, and come to think of it, actually, it does look like crap.

CHAPTER 14

Cami

LUCKY FOR ME, IT'S NOT HARD TO BEAT MY DAD TO THE MAILBOX.

Lucky is not a word I use often, or if I do, I have to laugh as soon as it occurs to me. Lucky that my dad is usually so drunk he's still passed out when the mail gets here on Saturday?

I take what I can get. The mail truck pulls away with its distinctive rumble, and I dash out into the hard summer rain.

It was sticky-hot all morning until the clouds crashed the party around lunchtime, and now all the wet is pouring out of the air. I love it, actually. If it weren't for the rain streaming so hard into my eyes I can't see, I'd just stand out here and let it soak me cool.

But anyway, the letter. By my calculations, Trent has had enough time to get the letter by air mail, look at the photo, and tell me who those people are. I only hope he hasn't forgotten it and tossed the envelope in some big stack of bills. It's not like he spares much thought for anything back here in the States.

I see it right off; the foreign stamp gives it away. I slip the envelope into the back of my pants and put my shirt over it, in case Dad or that skank Sherry happened to wake up just now.

The house still seems quiet, so I duck into my room and latch the door.

Cami,

Sorry to say I can't figure out who these people are. They don't look at all familiar to me. I guess I can't help you.

I'm a little worried about you. Do you need anything from me? I could loan you some cash if you're strapped. Just let me know.

Trent

I study the photo again. The people look wealthy, though it takes me a minute of squinting to figure out exactly why it seems that way. It's the setting. There's a low stone wall, and a large porch behind them. A huge old tree, and in the distance, yes, there's water. A huge lake. Maybe the sea.

I look at the back of the photo again, and it does not specify a date or place.

I slip the photo carefully back into the Bible and ball Trent's letter up in the palm of my hand. I'm about to go throw it in the kitchen trash when I think better of it. No, better keep this one hidden. I shove the crinkled ball in the back of my old dresser, behind my socks, and slam the drawer shut.

I unhook the door and go in search of some lunch.

In the kitchen I find none other than Sherry, hunched over a coffee and wearing one of Dad's old T-shirts and seemingly nothing else. I look away from her quickly, not in the mood for her to gloat over the fact she has the run of the house, or needle me about our last encounter.

There are some fruit flies buzzing over the dishes. I suppose I'd better cave in and wash them.

"Good morning," croaks Sherry.

I start to pick the dishes gingerly out of the filthy water.

"I said, 'Good morning,'" she repeats.

"I heard you. It isn't morning anymore."

"La-di-freakin'-da."

I drain out the filthy water and fill the sink again with the hottest water my hands can stand.

Sherry startles me by appearing at my side. "Here, lemme help you."

I look her full in the face. She doesn't seem sarcastic and it doesn't seem to be a prank.

I shrug and hand her a towel. "You can dry, I guess."

We slosh around in silence. My dad must have really tied one on to be asleep still. Or maybe they were screwing until late. That thought makes me queasy.

"Hey," she says. "I'm sorry about the fruit thing."

"What?"

"What I said about your brother. I got the impression from Tim that it's kind of a sore subject around here, his boyfriend and all."

"He doesn't speak for me."

"No, I guess he doesn't."

Sherry lowers her voice and glances back over her shoulder at the empty hall. "Did you, uh . . . Did you get in trouble or anything? Over what happened?"

"What kind of trouble do you mean?"

"I mean . . . I hope he wasn't too mad at you over it."

The puzzle piece drops into place. "Oh, you mean you're wondering if he beat me up, yeah? Boy, you sure did pick a prize one in my dad."

She clanks a plate down on the counter. "He treats me all right."

We make small talk about pleasant June weather and exchange polite inquiries about family. His parents are fine; his sister is fine at Harvard. I tell him my mother is fine. There's no reason for him to ask about my father.

"Nice that your brother is getting married," I say, carrying on the family thread and stirring my iced tea. "Is he in the family business, too?"

"Yeah, so far Dad has kept us all on the reservation, except Tabitha, but she'll probably stay out east, she says. New York or somewhere. Boston, Philly. Somewhere like that."

"What's it like working for your dad?"

Beck's smile is thin. "It's swell, you know. He's so experienced and everyone knows him. It's gratifying to see buildings go up that you first saw on blueprints."

He doesn't meet my eye for the "gratifying" part.

I already know from e-mails that he works for his dad as an environmental consultant, adding green spaces and proper drainage to the Becker Development projects.

"Hug any trees lately?" I ask him as our food arrives: salad for me, a Reuben for him.

"As many as possible. Though I don't have much time for petitions and such these days. I do recycle and compost at home. Couldn't talk Sam into cloth diapers, but we'll try that next time, I guess." His smile fails completely and he looks down into his lap.

"You okay?" I ask him. He's ignoring his sandwich.

"Yeah, I'm okay. I'm just a little frustrated at home. Sam has been so mad at me all the time lately, like I can't do a single thing right. Like just today, I left a dish out on the counter this morning and she called me at work to yell at me over it just before I had a big meeting with the city planners. She said it showed I didn't care about how much work she had to do all day."

I clear my throat and glance around. In all our friendly e-mail

"Goody for you."

After a couple more dishes she says, "I'm going out back for a smoke," and leaves me to finish up the rest. I finish the dishes as quickly as I can and decide to head for the Nee Nance, rain be damned.

I had to use an old phone book as an umbrella, so when I round the corner off Shoreline Drive, everything below my shoulders is soaked.

"Cami!" Maeve says. "Oh, honey, look how wet you are! You weren't scheduled to work, were you?"

"Nope, this here is a social call." I drop the phone book and try to wring out my T-shirt.

"We're pleased to see you, but what got you out here in this monsoon? You should have asked Anna for a ride. She would have come to get you."

"Nah, I don't want to put anyone out, yeah? Besides, I like the exercise. I just really felt like getting out."

Maeve nods, understanding without me having to say. People don't know exactly what Tim Drayton is like, but they know enough.

"Anna is upstairs packing. Why don't you go ask her to find you some of my clothes. You're taller than me, but there should be something you can borrow. And then for heaven's sake get Anna to take you home when you're ready to go."

"Thanks. I'd hug you, but I think I'll wait until I'm dry, yeah?"

"Yeah," Maeve says, chuckling. Then she stops and rubs the bridge of her nose.

"You okay?" My hand is on the stair rail.

"Fine, just a little headache, is all."

I climb the steps, and though I don't pray, not really, I glance up to the ceiling and smile as a thanks to the universe that there are a few decent people in my life.

"Hey!" I call up the stairs so I don't startle Anna. I poke my head in to tell her I'm ducking down the hall to borrow dry clothes.

In a few moments I come back to her room wearing a white shirt and some shorts, my wet clothes hung up over the shower door in the bathroom.

"Need any help?" I plop down on her bed. "I came over for an impromptu visit, to see you off and say hi to your mom."

"Nah, I'm just about done."

Anna looks younger than I've seen her look since she's been back. It's because she's dressed down, I think. Her hair is its naturally wild, curly self, and she's wearing cut-off jean shorts and a U-M T-shirt.

"So, will you miss the bustling metropolis of Haven?"

"Oh, absolutely. I don't know how I'll fill my social calendar."

"Will you miss Will Becker?"

She looks at me sharply, then resumes folding. "We'll e-mail, like we always did. It was nice to have lunch with him, that's all."

We both turn at some ruckus downstairs. Anna drops her folding and we skip down the steps in time to see Maeve shouting out the door, "And you're banned for life, you rotten brats!"

"Mom, what the hell?"

Maeve holds onto the newspaper rack with one hand, a broom in the other, bristle side up. She's leaning on them both for support. Anna and I rush to her. I take the broom and lay it aside, and we both walk her to the office chair behind the counter. Her skin feels damp and clammy.

Maeve puts her elbows on her knees and her head in her hands. "Stupid kids were stealing from me. First I didn't care, because we're getting kicked out anyway, but then I thought . . ." She pauses to pant, and Anna reminds her to breathe deep. I think, kicked out?

Maeve begins again. "I thought if I let them get away with stealing, they'd come back all the time, knowing I wouldn't stop them. They wouldn't leave, so I whacked one with a broom."

Anna shoots me a look over Maeve's head. "Did they assault you? Did any of them threaten you in any way?"

Maeve glares at Anna. "Stop lawyering me!"

"I'm just wondering, Mom. Are you okay? What's wrong?"

"I'm just feeling a little shaky, is all. They made me so mad. I need to go upstairs."

We help her out of her chair, but she shakes us off. "I'm not some frail old woman!"

She uses the counter for support as she walks toward the stairs, Anna and I trailing close as we can get without touching her.

When she gets to the potato chip rack, she pauses, frowns as if she forgot where she was going, and touches her hand to her head.

She folds like a puppet cut from its strings.

"Mom!" screams Anna, and I vault the counter, reaching for the phone.

CHAPTER 15

Amy

AS I'M SHAKING MY SNOW PEAS INTO THE WOK, I KEEP REPLAYING MY talk with Anna and arguing in my head for why my fiancé isn't evil for evicting her mother.

Only, I feel bad about it, and since I didn't even know, I can't come up with the logical arguments I'm sure Paul must have. The microwave clock says it's 5:35, and I decided not to wait for Paul anymore, and I just have to start dinner.

Frodo whines at the patio door.

"Not now, Frodo, it's pouring outside. You already went pee."

I add the sauce and skip the tofu, because I know Paul hates it.

A key turns in the lock and my shoulders relax. I didn't even know I was tense until just then. I move the wok off the heat to come give Paul a kiss.

"Hey, babe," he says, dropping his suitcase on the couch and throwing himself into the nearest chair. My kiss has missed his cheek, and for a second I'm puckered into the air like some kind of fish. Paul says, "Can you get me a beer? God, what a day."

I go fetch him the beer but don't take the cap off for him. Then I throw some tofu into the wok. And then a little more.

"I'm sorry it was a bad day," I say. "Want to talk about it?"

He's tipped his head back on the chair, squinting his eyes shut. He shakes his head slowly.

I check the brown rice and it's done, so I start scooping it onto plates.

"I saw Mrs. Geneva today at the store," I say.

He grunts and massages his temple in response.

"Sounds like you have an interesting project there," I say brightly, setting the plates down. I go turn on some Norah Jones. "Do you want some wine?"

"I'll stick with my beer."

I pour myself a sparkling water. "Okay, dinner's on."

He hefts himself out of the chair and drags over to the kitchen table. He's walking like he's eighty.

"So, what have you got cooking for that corner? At Washington and Shoreline?"

"Oh, a high-end grocery and some loft apartments. It'll look great." He's picking at his stir fry, frowning at the tofu and scooting it to the side.

"Oh, good, how exciting."

Paul frowns into his food. "Can we shut the music off?"

I scuttle over to the stereo and punch it off. "So the Nee Nance Store is gone, then?" I ask as if it's nothing, just a question of logistics, and that's really all it is, I'm just curious.

He grunts and says through a mouthful of food, "We're really trying to class up that corner. It's a gateway to the community." A piece of broccoli falls out of his mouth.

"Oh, well. I guess so. She can't be part of it, though?"

Paul groans and pushes back his plate. "Aww, c'mon, don't you start, too. Change is hard, like Dad always says. Improvement to a neighborhood sometimes pushes out the previous residents, but what's the option? Never make anything nice?"

I shift in my chair and ask him, "But isn't there a way to give her a part of the project? Let her run the store?"

Paul folds his arms on the table and gives me a look, the same one I've seen him use at planning commission meetings and on investors. "I don't mean to be rude, but what does she know about high-end wine? Imported cheeses? I don't need someone just to punch a register, I need someone who can advise customers what's the best thing to eat with pinot noir. And anyway, she can't afford the rent. Haven is evolving. We're getting more and more tourists from Chicago, Grand Rapids, Detroit, businesspeople with money who want a lakeside retreat. Not some Miller Lite and a package of hot dogs."

"I just feel bad, is all."

He pushes his food around with his fork, frowning down at his plate. "So do I, believe it or not. I hated to send that letter." He looks up. "But she's got Anna; she's doing well for herself. It's not like she'll be sleeping under an overpass, right?"

I want to say, *Who are you trying to convince?*

He takes his plate to the kitchen and I can see he's barely eaten. "Also, you've gotta look at it this way: The housing market is getting softer, and there's only so much money to be made in that right now. We had to cancel phase three of Poplar Bluff already. Urban redevelopment might be just the thing to save our bacon, because we can get grants and stuff to offset the cost, which investors really like."

"Our bacon needs saving?"

"I exaggerate," Paul answers, but it comes out too quickly. "I just mean this is kind of a tough time to be in property, so we need to move when we have the opportunity."

He comes by and kisses the top of my head. "Because if I'm

going to have the prettiest house in Poplar Bluff for you and all our pretty babies, I've gotta pull my weight at Becker Dev. Just because I'm the son doesn't mean I'm guaranteed anything. Especially since I'm not the *namesake*."

Paul seizes his beer bottle and resumes his position in his chair, flicking on the TV and flipping channels, settling on a ball game.

When we were first dating, he had too many beers one night and got all misty and emotional. He laid his head down in my lap as we sat on his leather couch, and he stared past me at the ceiling and told me about every teacher in school always saying at the start of the year, "Oh! You're Will Becker's brother," and they'd get these delighted little grins. But Paul's grades were never quite up to par. He had more friends than Will, more fun, played more sports, but that all-important grade point average never caught up.

I toyed with the fringe of Paul's hair while he insisted to me that the teachers graded his papers tougher than the those of the other kids, holding him to an imaginary Becker standard set by his brother.

And then Tabitha blew them both out of the water and took off for Harvard.

Paul is still playing catch-up, obviously, but he's got something his brother doesn't. When I first fell in love with him, he was telling a story at the bar about a playoff football game that came down to one final play, and as he geared up for the exciting conclusion, no one even breathed in that clustered audience, and my heart was pounding. I don't even like football. It was his dad's charisma at work.

But charisma doesn't measure like letter grades. A successful project, though . . . That kind of thing can't be denied.

I look down at my own dinner. The stir-fry sauce has gone cold. I push my plate away and watch the rain hammer the glass of my patio door.

* * *

I wake up with the sunshine pouring through my bedroom window. I look up at the glass and I have to smile because the pane is still wet and the sun shooting through the drops makes my window look spangled.

I sit up in bed and take a deep breath from my abdomen, in, out, and whew! Just like that I expel yesterday, expel the whole rotten week, including my hangover and last night's awkwardness, when it took until nearly ten o'clock for me to get a laugh out of Paul and at least a kiss or two before he went home. Early meeting, he said.

But wait, I just expelled all that.

I take my temperature and record it, though it's just a formality because I already ovulated this month. I'm just staying consistent. Though I miss snuggling with Paul in the mornings when he's not here, it's so much easier to take my temperature without having to be all sneaky and hide under the covers and try to muffle the thermometer's beeping.

He'd never understand and probably get all freaked out, which is why I haven't shared my plan with him. See, I figure since we're getting married in August, that would make for a May baby, which is perfect, because with that jogging stroller I've been eyeing at Babies "R" Us, I'd be able to get my figure back in no time.

By charting my temperature for a few months, I'm figuring out my most fertile time, so as soon as we're married I can throw away my Today sponges and we can get down to business.

See, I'm already thirty-five. They call that advanced maternal age and I haven't even conceived.

I let Frodo out of his crate and pull my hair into a ponytail. EVERY THIN DAY IS A GOOD DAY, the sign on my mirror says, and yes, by God, it is. I throw on my jogging shorts and running shoes, and we're off.

Everything sparkles this morning. The leaves are still beaded with the storm rain and it's like the sun is trying extra hard to shine, making up for its absence yesterday. I might run a little longer this morning, speaking of making up for lost ground. It wasn't my best week last week.

But I'm not thinking of that anymore.

Frodo starts hauling me off stride and suddenly it all comes back to me, though, my hangover on Sunday when I almost lost my dog and that guy, what was his name? And that little scruffy dog. Because there they are.

We're going to meet where two sidewalks join together into a single path, and if he hadn't already seen me, I'd turn around to avoid it. He'll want to chat and I can't slow down, and he for sure can't keep up. He's not even wearing jogging shoes, but floppy man-sandals. He obviously doesn't have a girl in his life because she'd never let him out looking like that.

"Hi," I say breathlessly as we meet up, preparing to trot on by. Frodo has other ideas, though, and pulls me back to the scruffy dog. "Dammit, Frodo, come on!"

If this guy had any manners, he'd get his dog out of here and let me run. I mean, at least he can pick up his dog if he has to. The thing is no bigger than a medium-sized cat.

"Feeling better?" he says.

"I've really gotta go," I tell him, pulling on Frodo.

"Oh," says the guy. Ed! That's it. Ed looks down and then he does scoop up his dog. "Sure. I don't want to slow you down. That's enough, Lucky."

Lucky whines and Frodo goes into his "play with me" crouch, and darned if Ed doesn't look a little crushed.

I remember when I first started jogging and all I ever saw was the backs of fit people zooming by.

"Oh, I suppose I can walk for a bit," I tell him. "Give our dogs a chance to be friendly."

"Yep, we've got to socialize them, don't we?" Ed says, squinting into the sun as we move on down the sidewalk. The dogs fall into step, Lucky's legs going about twice as fast as Frodo's.

For a few moments we just listen to the dogs pant, and then Ed says, "I really admire you."

"Huh?"

He glances briefly at my body—not leering at all, just a look—before he looks back at his dog. "You've worked so hard."

"Oh, geez, it wasn't anything special—"

"The hell it wasn't. Believe me, I know."

"Well, I just . . . I always get embarrassed when people talk about it."

"What's to be embarrassed about? You could just say thank you."

"Okay, then. Thank you."

"But I guess you probably are sick of hearing about it, too."

At this I shrug, and look down as if I have to concentrate on my footing, like I'm climbing a mountain and not strolling along a level sidewalk. I find myself noting with surprise that Ed is actually keeping up a pretty good pace. It's walking, but his stride is long and we're really moving.

"Well, how about this," Ed says again. "I'll never mention it again. You can just remember that I believe it."

"Oh! What time is it?"

Ed tells me it's 8:45.

"Shit, I've gotta go; I'm late for work." The dogs entangle each other for a while until Ed picks up Lucky and Frodo finally relents, and I run off back to the apartment complex. Ed calls out, "See you tomorrow maybe?" and I say, "Sure!" and I actually mean that.

CHAPTER 16

Anna

MY MOM'S FACE IS SO WHITE IT SEEMS TO GLOW AGAINST HER coppery hair.

"I'm so sorry, this is all a lot of fuss for nothing." She kneads the edge of her hospital sheet in her hands. I put my hand on top of hers to still them.

"I know you didn't mean for this to happen."

I'm startled by how much our hands look alike. Our veins and tendons stand out so clearly. My nail polish is chipped completely off, and one nail tore down to the quick the other day when I was trying to scrape some gum off the Nee Nance floor.

"I called the office," I tell her. "I'm not going back on Monday."

She gasps and sits up. "No! Anna, you can't do that. I won't have you put your career in jeopardy over me. You've worked so hard . . ."

I try to ease her back down to the pillow, but she resists me. "It's fine; they understand about family crisis. Things on hold will hold a little longer. I'm not trying to get anyone off death row or anything. Dorian can fill in on things that can't wait."

"That can't be good for you. You're always going on about how competitive it is. The doctor says I'll be fine—"

"So far it seems that way, but we still have to get your pressure down with pills, not the IV meds, before they'll let you out of here." The doctors had performed all kinds of tests—blood tests, chest films, even an MRI—to make sure she hadn't had a stroke or suffered organ damage. "Your pressure was 200 over 110, for God's sake. I picked up three months of your prescription. I can't believe you weren't taking it."

She looks down and away from me, and I'm chewing the inside of my cheek to stop myself from continuing the scold.

"You're a good daughter," she tells me. "I wish they'd get me out of this stupid bed."

"Cami will be fine at the store until we get back, and by the way, you're not working at all this week, and I don't want to hear any argument."

My phone trills.

"I'll be right back, Mom." I hand her the television remote and take the phone out of the room.

I walk down the hall to a distant corner. "Hi, Beck," I say when I answer.

"What's wrong? You sounded awful in your message."

"It's my mom. She fainted at the store. Her blood pressure was through the roof."

"Is she okay?"

"For now, yes. But I'm worried. My father's writing her and now I find out she's being evicted. And frankly I'm surprised you didn't give me a heads-up."

"Why would . . . How would I do that?"

"It's your company doing it. Paul is doing it."

"Shit."

"Yeah, shit, Beck, why didn't you tell me?"

"I didn't know."

"Bullshit."

"No, I'm serious. Paul never tells me anything. He thinks my job is to sink every project he wants to do. He's still pissed off about Golden Valley. He won't believe me that the project would have failed anyway, the way he drew it up, without any runoff or drainage and—"

"I don't want to talk about drainage."

"Sorry."

"You really didn't know?"

"I swear, Annie. On my daughter, I swear."

I exhale and I feel my strength slicking off like melting springtime ice. "Beck, she collapsed right in front of me. I thought I was orphaned."

"Where are you?"

"The hospital."

"I'll be there in ten."

"Maybe you shouldn't . . ." I picture his wife's stony face.

"Don't go anywhere. I'm coming."

"Okay," I whisper into the phone. "I won't."

When I see Beck trotting down the hall toward me, he opens his arms and I let him fold me in, pressing my face against his shirt. He puts one hand on the back of my head. I pull away and he puts one arm around my shoulder, and together we walk into my mother's room.

"Are you all right, Mrs. Geneva?" he asks, and if my mother is surprised to see him here she doesn't show it.

"Oh, Will, I'm going to be fine. Nice of you to come."

He asks if we need anything, and I realize just then I'm ravenous. So he goes off to find me a sandwich.

"He was always such a nice kid," my mom says, settling back

on the pillow and flipping the television to mute. "It's too bad he couldn't have gone to Michigan, too."

I settle into the chair next to the bed and try to roll some knots out of my neck. "Going to the same school wouldn't have guaranteed anything, Mom. We were just kids. Who marries the man they date in high school?"

My mother smirks and says, "I did."

"Yeah, exactly."

"Will is nothing like your father."

"That's true."

It's the first time my dad has come up since I found the letter. I sneak a look at my mom and find she's staring directly at me. "What?" I say.

"Nothing. Can't I just look at you?"

"Mom, I need to ask you something." She nods and I think back to seeing her fall to the floor, that moment when my first feeling was nothing more than a panicked scream in my head followed by a storm of possible actions to take, anything to keep her safe. In the midst of that I noticed something that swims back to the forefront of my mind only now that my mother is physically stable.

"Mom, why do you still wear your wedding ring?"

Her hand goes to her chest, then her eyes widen as she pats the space under her gown where the ring was hanging from a chain. "I have it," I tell her. "The nurses gave it to me. It was getting in the way."

She relaxes, then seems to shrink on the pillow. "If you're just going to scold me for it, save your breath."

"I was just asking."

"You wouldn't understand."

Try me! is the retort that comes to mind, but I bite my lip. She's so vulnerable in that flimsy cotton gown speckled with polka dots and her hair a tangled mass. "Why don't you think I'd understand?"

She looks at me a long moment before answering, her eyes narrowed slightly as if trying to see something clearly. "You've never loved like I loved your father."

"You think I'm so cold-hearted?"

"I don't want to fight."

I reach out for her hand, but she pulls it away, slowly, as if trying to sneak it out of my reach. I put my hands back in my lap. "I don't want to fight, either; I just don't understand what you can still feel for him. What he did was unforgivable."

"It's a memory," she says, her voice raspy now. "Just a memento. Of better times."

"So you're not writing him anymore, then?"

She turns fully to face me and her cheeks are bright pink. "I knew this would get around to that. Do you have to cross-examine me?"

I flinch.

Mom is breathing hard and I shake my head, wishing I could roll back time, because she doesn't need this now. There's more I want to say, more I want to ask, but I can't. Not now.

"I'm sorry—" I begin, but Beck comes through the door.

"Okay, I've got a tuna salad on rye and coffee, which I know you take black, but I grabbed creamer . . ."

He prattles on, organizing my lunch on the bedside table. I'm trying to catch my mother's eye, but she's turned away from me, toying with her hospital gown where her ring had been hanging.

"Maeve Geneva! What the hell is wrong with you!"

We look toward the door as Aunt Sally comes in, wearing her black Cher wig again. "Wasn't anyone going to call me? Mailman Al drove all the way out to my trailer to tell me. He heard from Doreen, who . . ."

My mother waves her hand at Sally and shifts on the bed. "Yes, yes, I get it."

I tell her, "We tried to call you but couldn't get through. It just kept ringing."

"Oh, right. I got a prank call and unplugged it from the wall so they wouldn't call back. Guess I should fix that." Sally stared into space for a moment. "Come to think of it, that call was a week ago. Anyway, sister dear, haven't I told you that rock 'n' roll lifestyle of yours would catch up with you?"

At this my mother grins, and I stand up to offer Sally my chair. I tell them I'm going to take my sandwich into the lounge to eat it, and Beck follows me out. We settle on opposite sides of a round fake wood-grain table.

Do you have to cross-examine me? Mom said, sounding so much like Marc. I'd blown up at him for throwing out terms he'd learned watching *Boston Legal* just to undermine me.

Marc followed that up with this gem: "Can't you drop the lawyer thing for one second so we can have a real conversation?" and I'd said, "What lawyer thing? This is me, take it or leave it."

"No way, there's a real person in there, a real girl who can feel something."

"Feel what," I asked him, "What am I supposed to be feeling, and how is my job somehow an impediment to that?"

"Who uses words like *impediment* in everyday conversation?"

"Stop changing the subject," I said.

"I want to talk to you about having a family and all you can do is respond with arguments and logic, and your career . . ."

"And now we get to the point," I told him. "My career that you seem to find so threatening."

"Can't you just have some feelings, for God's sake?"

And so I gave him feelings. I screamed at him for all I was worth about my feelings. And the next day I came home to find his set of keys on my front table and the closet half empty.

Beck says, "Are you in there?"

"I guess."

"What's wrong?"

I shrug. "What isn't wrong? Mom's getting evicted, she could have had a stroke, my dad . . . Forget it. I better eat something or they'll have to pull up a bed for me next to Mom."

The sandwich tastes like dust, but I force myself to chew every bite, appreciating Beck for his respectful silence.

CHAPTER 17

Maeve

SINCE I'M BANNED FROM WORKING, I MIGHT AS WELL TAKE ADVANtage of the privacy.

I slip my hands into the handles of my sewing shears. Sitting on top of my bed is not the most reasonable place for a sewing project, but it's the only space I have that's big enough. Back in the old days, when I used to sew clothes for Anna, I'd set up a card table in the office space and duck back there during slow moments.

That's not an option for this particular project.

Back in the old days I also would have whipped up this dress without a pattern, but it's been a long time since I've done much serious sewing. The rhythmic, metallic *snip, snip* is calming, which is good for me, all in all.

The doctor had discharged me with an armload of pamphlets, including one about stress reduction. I almost laughed in his face, but he was just trying to help.

I suppose, in her way, Anna is also just trying to help, but she must have realized the last thing I need is harassment, because since the hospital she's backed off.

My wedding ring taps my chest as I sit back for a moment and stretch. I didn't even hesitate when I put it back on, though I made sure Anna wasn't looking. It's my ring and I can wear it how I like. As I sit forward to snip again, it swings briefly into my view, a glint of white gold.

Small white flowers swirl over a field of blue in the shade of a cool spring sky. It will be a shift dress, sleeveless, to the knee. It's always been flattering on me and I can't find them anymore. It was the style of dress I was wearing when I met Robert, in fact.

Dean Martin croons on my CD player about pillows and dreaming. I used to take so much flak for my taste in music, because all the other kids were shimmying to the waning days of disco or getting stoned listening to The Who. I didn't like the teasing, but I didn't change my ways, either. I wasn't like all those other girls, and maybe that's why Robert liked me back.

It was 1973 when we met. I used to tag along with Sean, my older cousin and the closest thing I had to a brother. Sally was hanging out in the group, too. She was quirky, and her quirky was still cute. She was eight years older than Sean and shaving years off her age even then. Her wild, kinky black hair and heavily kohled eyes were exotic and exciting to me. Sally called me "doll" and I loved being included that way in their circle of sophisticated people. I was only eighteen, still in high school.

One night in early fall I went to the drive-in. I was supposed to meet Nick, a pock-marked boy with big teeth who I'd thought was nice. I'd grabbed a ride with Sean and then wandered around the concessions and through the rows of cars trying to find Nick, getting colder and colder because I hadn't brought a sweater.

When I finally gave up, embarrassed but not all that crushed that Nick hadn't shown up, I wandered back to Sean's car. No one was paying any attention to *American Graffiti*, and in fact no one was in the car at all. Sally was passing around a flask.

Robert saw me approach first and said, "Well, look here, a fair Irish lass."

His voice was rich in a way that set him apart from the other boys. Not deep, exactly, but warm and resonant. He had a shock of dark, dark hair, and in the faint light from the movie screen and the moon, his smile made my stomach shiver.

I looked at my shoes and rubbed my bare arms with my hands.

"Hey, you're cold," he said, draping his jacket around my shoulders like a cape.

"Won't you be cold?" I asked him. I could see goose bumps on his arms where his short-sleeved shirt ended.

"Nah." He winked at me. "Not a bit."

He drove me home himself that night and walked me to the door, so I wouldn't have to spend one cold moment without his jacket. He stood on the porch while I let myself in, smiling at me but doing no more than that. I was just a kid, after all.

I had to lean on the door to catch my breath.

Of course, Robert understood the effect he had on me. He was a savvy twenty-two years old by then. I was just a teenager and experience-wise barely out of puberty. And I thought I was playing it cool! I was a puddle every time I saw him.

We saw each other at the drive-in, the bowling alley, the pizza place. Always in a group, always with Sally or Sean or both. But then, he never brought around other girls, and at the end of the night, I always seemed to end up with his jacket.

Now that I've finished cutting out the front of the dress, I scoot my sewing to the side and rest back on my pillow. I close my eyes and conjure up the jacket. It smelled like him, and the crackled leather rustled slightly when I moved. I could cry now to think that I gave it away to a thrift store in a fit of pique right after he left.

After I graduated, Robert asked me out properly. I was already a goner by then, and our first real kiss nearly made me swoon, just like in my favorite romance novels.

I didn't mean to insult Anna by telling her she's never known love like that. I just don't see how she possibly could. She was always so very serious, even when she was with Will Becker in high school, insisting they break up because they couldn't possibly maintain a long distance relationship, with him at Michigan Tech way up in the frozen north and Anna at University of Michigan. I tried to talk her out of it then, to give Will a chance, because he looked so utterly wrecked when he left here that day. Anna, on the other hand, glided down the steps after he'd gone, with her hand lightly on the railing. She simply started mopping the floor.

She probably had boyfriends in Chicago, but none that she ever told me about. I've never seen her giddy, not since . . .

Well, not since she was ten years old.

Another memory of Robert comes to me, of him pushing her on the swings at the park and Anna shrieking, "Higher!" Her freckles sparkled in the sun and her limbs were all akimbo, and Robert was hooting and laughing and running underneath her swing.

I shake my head, stretch, and pick up my scissors again. I'd better get busy if I want this dress done by August.

CHAPTER 18

Cami

WHEN I SEE THE COP COME THROUGH THE NEE NANCE FRONT DOOR, the first thing I think is, *he's dead.*

He asks me, "Is Mrs. Geneva present?"

So my dad's not dead. I should be happy. Or something. "She's resting right now, Officer. Can I help you with something?"

When I say "officer," Anna pops out of the back office, where she's been rummaging in papers. Her hair springs out of her head, and without her makeup in her casual clothes she looks like an overgrown twelve-year-old. She says to the cop, "I'm Anna Geneva, her daughter. What's wrong?"

"We need to talk to your mother about an incident here a couple of days ago, with a boy and a broom."

"You've got to be kidding me," I say, remembering the scrawny kid and the shoplifting.

Anna shoots me a warning look, so I sit back in the office chair and let the attorney-at-law handle this one.

"She was defending her property. She believed the boys to be stealing and she ordered them to leave and they refused to go."

The cop folds his arms. On closer inspection he looks younger than I would expect. Then again, I'm getting older, so these people are going to start turning up younger than me. Cops, doctors, and so on. He's got a shaving nick on his jaw and I can see a tiny piece of toilet paper stuck there. He tells Anna, "She can't go around hitting kids with brooms. She should have called us."

"And what, made a citizens arrest? What if they'd turned on her? They were already showing a blatant disregard for her rights as proprietor of this store. Are you going to charge her with a crime?"

"Felonious assault with a cleaning implement. Very serious," I intone. "We're just lucky it wasn't a Swiffer."

"Cami!"

I unfold from my chair. "Seeing as this officer needs to talk to your mom, why don't I go see if she's awake."

As I pass between them, I stop just in front of his face. He looks overly tense, like it's a hostage situation. So I think better of actually reaching for his face to flick off the toilet tissue. "You've got something stuck to your jaw," I tell him, and proceed up the stairs.

I knock on Maeve's door and she says she's awake. There's a great deal of rustling before she opens the door.

When I tell her what's going on downstairs, her jaw falls open.

"Yeah, I know," I tell her. "What a world. Let's get it over with before your daughter decides to file suit against the Haven Police Department."

"Billy Patterson!" says Maeve as she comes down the stairwell. The cop swallows hard and stares at his shiny black shoes.

Turns out Maeve has known him since he was a kindergartner and used to stop in with his mom to buy a Snickers bar when they ran errands downtown. Billy, rather, Officer Patterson, is visibly relieved when Maeve shows him the offending broom. He'd thought it was a heavy shop-floor-type broom, something that could have done some damage.

He has to write up a report, he says, since the kid's mom complained, but he felt pretty sure the prosecutor wouldn't be bothered.

Anna shoos her mother back upstairs, and with Officer Billy safely down the street, Anna picks up a pencil and begins to twirl it in her hand.

"I cannot believe she hit that kid. She could still get sued. I read his notebook upside down; the kid was only twelve."

"Take it easy, yeah? The little hoodlums were stealing from her."

"I know, I know. I just . . ." Anna squints at me, then glances over her shoulder, checking for customers. We're alone at the moment. She leans in closer, dropping her voice low. "Her decision making lately hasn't been stellar. She's not thinking clearly and I'm worried."

"She didn't decide to get high blood pressure, and she was worried about the cost of the drugs . . ."

"That's not what I mean." Anna looks down, working her jaw, and I think she's working up to tell me something.

The bells on the front door clang and a couple of customers straggle in, one after the other. Anna holds my gaze for a moment, then sighs and returns to her papers in the office.

In a half hour, she taps me on the shoulder and we switch places. Her turn to work, just like back in school.

"I can close up for a few minutes to drive you home," Anna says, wrapping her wild hair up in a ponytail off her face. "Wouldn't take so long and you wouldn't have to sit around here."

"I've got nothing there to do, yeah?"

"You still painting your room?"

"Yeah, and I'm tearing up the carpet, but . . . Well, my dad usually has a *houseguest* this time of day and I'm not in the mood to run into her."

"Ah. Charming."

When the door opens, Anna stiffens, her hand frozen in the act of restocking cigarettes.

"Hi," says Amy Rickart quietly, looking like she just ran over Anna's dog with her car.

Anna doesn't acknowledge her and goes back to her stocking. Amy nods at me briefly, then addresses herself to Anna's back.

"Is your mom okay?"

"She'll be fine," Anna says, not turning around.

"I was sorry to hear she was ill."

Anna slams the cigarette packs in place, denting some of them in the process.

"I'm really sorry about what's happening to the store," Amy says, cringing as if those words cost her much effort.

Anna pauses at this and turns to Amy, her face a still mask.

Amy continues, "Paul does have his reasons. He's really not a monster, honest, but it is really awful, and I just wanted to say I'm sorry for being so defensive before."

Anna relaxes one degree from her ramrod posture. "I shouldn't have yelled at you. It's not your fault."

"You've had a rough few weeks, I guess."

Anna nods slightly but doesn't elaborate or allow her mask-face to betray her thoughts.

"I do have a question, Amy," she says. "Has this project been approved by the city council yet?"

"Um," Amy looks up toward the ceiling. "I don't really know, because the other day was the first I'd heard of it. He doesn't really tell me much about his work, not specifics."

"Well, I can find that out easily enough." Anna resumes her stocking, with less force.

"Why do you ask?" Amy says, and she's clutching her purse, I notice, as if someone's trying to rip it out of her hand.

"I might want to attend the meeting, is all."

"Oh. Well, I'm glad your mom is okay."

As Amy leaves, I notice a tiny wrinkle puckering her pert little forehead.

"Anna, how long are you planning to stay in town?" I ask her. "The meeting couldn't be any sooner than next week at the earliest. How much time off did they give you?"

She shrugs. "I was not specific about how much time I needed to help my mother."

"Aren't you . . . Your bosses might be a little mad, yeah?"

"They'll get over it. I can't abandon her right now. She's been abandoned quite enough, I'd say." Anna dusts off her hands. "Hand me that phone book. I'm going to call city hall."

I walk home after a time, not wanting to interrupt the running of the store or disturb Maeve to get a ride. It's not all that far. Nothing is far away, here. I have to thread through the tourists and the kids on summer break slopping ice cream around, and seeing the messy, sticky kids reminds me of my job waiting for me in the fall and how much I've grown to loathe kids. Okay, not all kids, I guess. Just about nine out of every ten kids I've tutored.

At least it's a job, and even though I'm not making much money now, I'm also not spending it on rent and not gambling it away, so it's something I can offer to Steve, some money and a mea culpa and a *Look at me, I was so good all summer.*

I glance back at the Nee Nance when I turn the corner. It looks older than its neighbor stores, like the weary grown-up standing watch over the shiny young kids. So Anna is fixing to save the store somehow, bringing her law degree to bear at the city council meeting, which she discovered on the phone is in two weeks, just before the Fourth of July. I then heard her lie to her bosses on the phone about her mother's delicate state of health, and from what I could hear of her end of the conversation, things were a little testy.

I see no signs of my dad's truck, but that's no indication of whether Sherry will be there. She stumbles home from here on foot, I think, though I don't know exactly where she lives.

I hear breathing inside, a deep, rattling snore. As I creep down the hall in my bare feet, I see his door ajar. He's in his bed, alone. Sherry must have driven the truck somewhere.

I never go in his room. As kids, Trent and I knew there was "hell to pay" if we crossed that threshold, and he reminded me of that when I first got back. So that's why I've never noticed this particular pile of stuff in the closet, which is diagonal from his door. The closet door is one of those folding shutter-style doors and is dented, off the track, and open. Looks like photo albums in there.

Dad's no shutterbug, so these must be family pictures, from when we were still a family, before Mom's cancer ate her up.

I'm still outside his door, just a few feet from his head, but not inside. I have broken no rule. I strain to see how many albums there are . . .three? . . . and try to guess their age based on how yellowed they look.

He's sleeping really hard. Passed out from a good lunchtime drunk is my guess.

The door squeaks when I swing it open, but his snoring doesn't even change pitch.

I pick my way across his floor, over landmines of smelly laundry and glass bottles. I slip the top album off the pile, resisting my desire to open it right then. I slip it under my shirt.

The snoring stops.

I snatch some crumpled clothing off the bottom of the closet and hold it over the rectangular bulge in my shirt. I freeze there, waiting.

"You little bitch," he slurs.

I turn, still in my crouch. "Just doing some laundry, thought I'd grab some of yours."

I straighten up slowly, balancing the album in my shirt, making sure to keep the clothes in front of it.

"I told you . . ." he says. His tone is menacing, but he's not gotten off the bed. He's only up on one elbow; his finger pointing at me is weaving in the air. ". . . to stay outta here."

"I'm going."

I skirt the bed as far as I can without looking like I'm doing so, because *What, are you afraid of me?* is another thing I really don't want to hear.

I almost drop the bundle when he hollers at me, just as I make it to the hallway, "And close the fucking door!"

I do close the door and force myself to carry out the ruse by walking down to the basement laundry, though I want nothing more than to shut myself in my room and study this piece of my past.

CHAPTER 19

Amy

EVERY TIME I WALK INTO THE BECKER HOUSE, I HAVE TO REMIND myself to stop gawking at it like some kind of hick.

But honestly, I can't help but look up in the two-story foyer at the winding staircase and the "light fixture," as Mrs. Becker dismissively called it the first time I gasped about the chandelier.

Mrs. Becker escorts me to the kitchen while the men prepare for the city council in Mr. Becker's upstairs office.

"Want some wine, Amy?"

"No, thanks, but I'd love a sparkling water, if you have some."

She gives me her hostess smile and takes a glass from the cupboard. She's wearing only flannel pants and a T-shirt, but she still looks regal to me. "Big night for Paul, isn't it?" she says. "You'll get used to the nerves. I used to chew my fingernails to bits wondering how the projects were going. You get so tied up in it sometimes, their work, and the business. When it's a family business, it's not just punching a clock. Everything can seem like it has such high stakes."

I take her water and glance away. I am nervous, but not for the reason she thinks.

"Paul doesn't really tell me that many details, actually."

Mrs. Becker waves her hand through the air, looking briefly like she's conducting an orchestra. "Oh, well, it's not very interesting anyway. Easements and zoning variances and drainage. Don't get your brother-in-law started on drainage! In the old days he was always going at us about green spaces and the danger of run-off and using up farmland."

I sip my water and remember Paul one night telling me how his big brother sank one of his family's projects when Will was still a high school kid by hanging out with this group called Youth for Earth. The newspapers loved it, Paul said, his face thunderous with old anger. The developer's kid fighting his own family's project. At the time I pictured Paul at the dining room table, just a kid, watching his brother and his dad fight, and I wanted to hug him. So I did. He'd kissed me on the forehead and said, "Thank God you understand me."

Paul comes down the stairs behind his father and I feel a rising pride. He's so handsome in his suit, so professional and accomplished with his briefcase in hand and those rolled-up plans under his arm.

"Ready?" he asks. "You sure you want to sit through this?"

"Of course!" I hop down from the kitchen barstool. "I can't wait to see my man in action."

The meeting room is surprisingly full, and for a moment I start to panic that everyone will start waving signs and protesting, but the room nearly empties out after a proclamation for the Boy Scouts. They were just a crowd of proud parents.

That's when I spot Anna, dressed in a suit with these really tall heels on. Her hair is up in a bun. As the room empties out, she looks around and notices me sitting next to Paul. I give her a wan smile and she looks away. It doesn't seem rude; rather, like she didn't really register me. Her face looks very still and calm, like it did that day in the store when I apologized.

I squeeze Paul's hand. He glances at her, then looks at me and rolls his eyes. That's unbecoming to him, the professional man, pulling a face like a surly teen.

The city council goes through a bunch of boring stuff, and finally they invite Paul up front to discuss the site plan for the redevelopment project.

I'm probably beaming like a First Lady gazing at her president. He sounds polished; the project looks wonderful; the councilmen are nodding, sitting forward and engaged. When he wraps up his presentation, he gives me a little wink.

The council asks for public comment, and there's a rustling as Anna rises.

"Gentlemen," she begins. "I have some concerns about this project I'd like to raise."

I swallow hard and steal a look at Paul, who's got that same dark, angry face that he wore that day he told me about Will fighting his family.

Anna is impressive, too, I must admit.

"I notice that Becker Development has requested and received from the zoning board a variance for the height of the building, and I maintain that . . ."

The councilmen at first seem bored, then they sit forward with deepening frowns as she continues. Paul scribbles notes on his legal pad, pressing so hard the pen comes through the paper in spots.

"And so, I submit to you that the building codes and ordinances must not be applied capriciously, and that the applicant can surely alter his project to suit the law instead of asking for special exception. And further, we should consider whether displacing a longtime business that has a loyal customer base for an unproven business model whose prices are likely out of reach for this community is truly a wise decision for maintaining the character of our downtown business district."

The councilmen are tapping their pens and staring hard at Paul, who is rising and returning to the podium.

Paul rests his notebook on the podium and frowns down at it for a moment.

"In that impassioned speech, what the speaker failed to inform you is that her name is Anna Geneva, and her mother is the operator of that store, so her motive here tonight is hardly altruistic; rather, it's a self-interested desperation move in the eleventh hour."

I keep my eyes trained on the back of Paul's head, the only view of him I can see from my seat. He grips the sides of the lectern hard.

He goes on, "I don't dispute the longevity of the Nee Nance Store, but I submit that its 'character' no longer suits the neighborhood. Other businesses up and down Washington Avenue have maintained and improved their facades, while this liquor store has let its sign fall into disrepair in recent months, and Mrs. Geneva has been cited by the building department for having beer signs in her window that are too large. Haven is changing, gentlemen, and if we want to keep moving forward and increasing our tax base, so we can continue to provide the services on which our citizens depend, we need to be on the leading edge, not playing catch-up, and to do that we need to make tough decisions."

Paul stands up straight and sweeps his gaze over the councilmen as he sums up: "Don't let one woman's attempt to sabotage this project for the sake of a family member hold up the forward progress of our community."

When Paul turns around, I try to smile at him. He seems a little breathless, and he fumbles his notebook when he picks it up off the lectern.

I risk a look at Anna. She rises to her feet again as the mayor says, "I'll now entertain a motion."

"Mr. Mayor," interrupts Anna, walking to the front. "I have a response."

"Miss Geneva," the mayor says wearily. "You've had your say. It's time to start deliberating."

"Sir, with all due respect, he made several accusations in that speech of his and I believe I should be allowed to respond."

"You get one turn at the podium," the mayor says, holding up his finger like a parent talking to a stubborn child. "And you had yours."

From my vantage point, I can see Anna's right hand ball up into a fist. She says, "Mr. Becker was given two chances to speak."

"He first presented the information on his project and then he gave public comment, two different things. Now please sit down or we will ask you to leave."

Anna pivots on her heel and walks out slowly, her head erect, the picture of grace.

She does, however, push the swinging door hard enough that it slams into the wall behind it. The door hisses itself back closed slowly, and everyone in the room stares at it, waiting for it, and through the door I can see Anna's retreating form growing smaller down the hall.

I look at Paul and he's smirking. He meets my eye and shakes his head. It seems like it's all he can do not to laugh out loud.

The councilmen begin deliberating. There is no discussion about any of the points Anna raised. The only concern is about off-street parking.

As carefully as I can, I rise from my seat. I shake off Paul's hand on my arm and take the long way to the back door and slip out into the hall.

City hall is small, and for all I know she's outside and driven home already. But maybe she walked, in which case . . .

I almost trip over her. The foyer of city hall is only dimly lit with some faint security lights—everyone came in the back door for the meeting. Anna sits against the wall, her legs out in front of her, ankles crossed. Her handbag and heels rest next to her. Her hands are folded loosely in her lap.

I stop in front of her, and she looks up at me and says nothing for what seems like a very long time.

Finally, she says, "Don't apologize for him again. Because he himself is not sorry, so it's meaningless, and you can't do anything about it, so, no offense, your sympathy doesn't exactly help matters."

I sit cross-legged in front of her, and for a moment I savor a flash of gratitude I can do this at all.

"I just wanted to see if you're okay."

"I'm swell."

"Anna . . ." I falter, not knowing exactly what to say. "What's wrong?"

She inclines her head in my direction. I can't read her face exactly in the poor light, but her demeanor seems to indicate, *What are you, an imbecile?*

"No, obviously. I mean, you seem so different from back when I knew you."

"Aren't we all?" she says dryly.

I chuckle at this. "Okay, point taken. But you used to be optimistic. Well, maybe not optimistic in a cheerful sense, but you had such . . . confidence that everything would turn out right."

"Hmmmm. Yeah, I guess I did. Life happened is what." At this, she rises to her feet, slips back into her shoes, and picks up her purse. We both turn at the sound of the council chamber's door opening, far down the hall.

"When are you going back?" I say. "I want to say good-bye before you leave. Don't sneak out of town."

"I don't know when I'm going back, exactly," she says. "I just don't know."

She steps out the front door and I stand there for a moment. I hear footsteps behind me, and without turning I know it's Paul. He slips his arm around my waist and nuzzles my neck. "Where have you been? We got it. It's all systems go. Demolition can start in September and we should be open before the end of next summer."

I step away from his embrace and start walking briskly back down the hall, toward his car. "I've got to get home and let Frodo out," I tell him, walking a little faster when he tries to catch up.

CHAPTER 20

Anna

THE NEE NANCE IS DARK WHEN I PULL MY CAR INTO THE ALLEY. IT takes me three tries to get my key in the door, and then the door sticks so I have to slam it open with my hip. It hurts, but I find that distracting and not entirely unpleasant.

I hit the door again, just because, with the flat of my hand.

I restrain myself from doing it once more, though, as my mother must be sleeping.

I step out of my heels and go on tip-toe up the steps, flashing back momentarily to the few times I snuck in late after a date with Beck, once a little drunk on punch that we'd snuck out of the "grown-up" punch bowl at a Becker family party. I decide to get a drink of water from the kitchen before heading off to my room.

What I see when I flip the kitchen light switch makes me gasp and flatten myself against the back wall.

A half second later I realize it's just Sally.

"Aunt Sally!" I try to keep my voice to a whisper. "What are you doing here?"

"I let myself in with that key your dad gave me, you know, when y'all went camping? Remember that, doll?"

I put my hand to my head, thinking. That had to have been . . . a quarter century ago. Of course my mother has never changed the locks; we've never had a reason.

"I guess I remember, but . . . Aunt Sally, why are you here? Mom's asleep, isn't she? And I was out, so . . ."

She's sitting in front of a cup of coffee, and I do notice then the smell of Folger's. But surely she has a coffeemaker in her trailer.

"I'm waitin' for your daddy. He said he'd pay me back and I need to fix my truck. Thought he'd be coming back anytime now."

I wait for her to laugh. I search her face for that twinkle in her eye, the slight crinkling of her nose that always lets us know she's putting one over on us.

She stares back at me and finally says, "What?"

I try to remember any article I might have read about people with dementia. Are you supposed to tell them the truth? Or do you play along, like guiding a sleepwalker back to bed without waking them?

"Sal? Um, Dad's not here. You know he . . . left. A long time ago. Right?"

She bursts out laughing. "Oh, honey! You should see your face!" She slaps the table and I shush her. "You thought I was off my rocker, didntcha? Ha! I had you going for sure. Well, missy, I better be off. Just wanted to say hello, but it's late, doll. I'll let myself out the back."

She pats my shoulder as she cruises on by, gliding down the stairs and humming.

"Not funny," I say out loud, though she's gone. "Not funny at all."

I get myself the water, shut off the coffeemaker, and dump Sally's cup out, then go back to my room.

I pause for a moment as I close the door. My room. Not my *old* room, as I'd been calling it since I first got back.

I start to pull off my suit and my eye catches that old magazine clipping. *Go confidently in the direction of your dreams . . .*

I rip it off the mirror and wad it into a ball before throwing it into a dusty corner.

The morning dawns cool and the sky is masked by cottony clouds in a dingy gray. Now and then there's a spitting rain, and it's enough to keep out the tourists running in for snacks. We only get the regulars on days like this: Carla for her Lotto tickets and Virginia Slims; later Randy will come by and pick up a forty-ounce, or maybe just a Coke, depending whether he's punched out for the day.

I've just said good-bye to Carla when my cell phone rings, the caller ID indicating Shelby.

"Shells!" I answer. "What's up?"

"Hey, Annie G," she says. "How's Smallville?" Her tone has a forced cheeriness.

"What's wrong?"

"I was going to ask you that."

"What do you mean?"

"Well . . . I don't know how to bring this up exactly, but . . ." She turns her voice to a stage whisper. I can picture her cupping her hand around the phone to try to be sneaky. She must be at the office. "Are you crazy?"

"Crazy for what?"

"Dorian is going around hinting that you're mad with grief and too shattered to come back to work, and going on about how she has to pick up all your slack, and she is picking up your slack, too. She's running to Jenison all the time and 'offering' to do your work and complaining about having to do it. Meanwhile she's basically stealing all your clients and, like I said, trying to make everyone think you're shopping for a rubber room."

I recognize that I should be shouting into the phone, throwing my clothes into a suitcase, and driving as fast as I can down I–94. Instead, I say, "That does sound like Dorian."

"The worst part is that she's making it seem like an act of charity on her part, like she'd do anything to 'help' you. She's going to help you right out of making partner and, if you don't get your butt back here, out of a job, too."

I find that I have a hard time remembering what I was even working on when I left.

Shelby drops the whisper, her voice strained. "What's going on with you?"

"My mother collapsed and could have had a stroke, and it might happen again, especially because she's under a lot of stress right now. And that's not the only thing going on . . ." I pause for a moment and weigh how much to tell her.

In the background I can hear the sounds of Shelby's office. Her radio is tuned to NPR, volume almost to nothing. Her e-mail dings to alert her to a new message. That's when I hear typing.

"This is important, Shelby."

The typing cuts off. "I was listening; I heard every word. It sounds rough, but Anna, how will you be able to help her if you lose your job, too?"

"They have lawyers in Michigan, too, you know."

"Hold on," she says, and for a few beats there's silence until I hear her slam her office door. "You've got to be kidding me. After all the hours you've put in at Miller Paulson, as hard as you've worked to make partner, when you're almost there, you're going to give it all up? Maybe Dorian's right, maybe you are going a little crazy."

"All I did was take a little time off, and I might point out Jenison insisted I do it, and now that I took him up on it . . ."

"A couple of weeks, and it's going on a month, now."

"Did you call just to harass me?"

"I called because you're brilliant and you're my friend and I hate to see you screw yourself because August died. Anna, did you . . . Did you have a thing with him?"

"What are you talking about?"

"Were you having a relationship with him?"

"No!" I stand up from the office chair. "Is that what's going on? People think I'm pining over my dead lover? Who's thirty years older than me?"

"Okay, okay, I didn't really believe it, either, but since you've been acting so strange, I didn't know what else to think. And yeah, Dorian's dropping hints about that, too."

"People are so sick. Two people of opposite gender treat each other nicely and everyone assumes they're fucking. Nice."

"If you don't come back and perform like your old self again, Dorian's version of the story will get more traction, and pretty soon it might as well be true. And if the partnership committee thinks you were sleeping with him and are now too addle-brained and emotional from his death to work, you're done for."

"I just told you, it's my mother's health. Her business is closing. And my . . . there's a lot going on."

"I believe you. But right now I'm the only one who does."

"I just can't leave right now."

"Just get back here as soon as you can, and come out swinging, okay? Also, I want to buy you a drink or six and tell you all about Simon."

"You're not still seeing him, are you?"

"I think it might work this time. See, last time we were together . . ."

I can't follow the thread of her conversation. Randy comes into the store, and I smile at him as he wanders the aisles, killing time on his break. My mom comes down the stairs, looking a little pale but otherwise about normal. Maybe if I can just buy her some time in the store, time for a proper back-up plan, then I can get back to work.

Randy approaches the counter.

"Shells, I gotta go. I'll call you later." I pocket my phone and ring up his purchase. "You feeling okay, Mom?"

"Fine," she says, wandering over to the newspaper stand. "A little tired. Who was that on the phone?"

"Shelby."

Mom picks up a *Courier* and then gasps, slapping it down on the counter like it just bit her. "I can't believe you did that!" she shouts.

I pick up the newspaper to see the headline: SITE PLAN AP-PROVED FOR WASHINGTON AVE. REDEVELOPMENT. The smaller headline beneath it reads: DAUGHTER MAKES STAND FOR MOTHER'S STORE.

She jabs the newspaper with her finger. "We look pathetic!"

"I was just trying to help, and for what it's worth I had some legitimate questions to raise about his project; there's no precedent for the exceptions they granted him, and according to the town's planning—"

"I don't care! I didn't ask you to do that, and you knew I wouldn't want it so you snuck behind my back."

"This affects me, too! I can't take off for Chicago and leave you here not knowing where you'll live or how you'll survive come September."

"I'll be fine. Don't worry about me."

"Considering I'm one stroke away from being an orphan, you'll forgive me if I'm a mite concerned."

She flinches but then sets her jaw. "You have another parent."

"Like hell, I do."

She snatches the paper off the counter and drops it back in the newsstand. "I didn't ask for you to humiliate me in front of the whole town."

"There's nothing humiliating about taking a stand to save your business."

"Easy for you to say. You'll go back to your law firm and your fancy suits and I'll be the one sitting here every day while people cluck their tongues down at Doreen's."

"Do you see me taking off for Chicago? Do you see me ditching you to run back there? You're mad because I tried to help, and now you'll be mad if I leave?"

"Why don't you go somewhere," Mom says. "Go get some lunch."

"You're supposed to be resting."

"I don't feel like resting, and Cami will be here soon. I checked my blood pressure and it's fine, or it was, until now, until I came down here to that." She jabs at the paper.

"Why don't you go out, and I'll—"

"Just *go*, please? I don't care where, just . . . go."

I grab my purse from behind the counter and head out into the wet afternoon, jogging between awnings until I'm three blocks away in front of a low brick office building. I walk in and say to the receptionist, "Is Will Becker in?"

CHAPTER 21

Maeve

AS ANNA TAKES OFF INTO THE RAIN, I CRINGE AT HOW I MUST HAVE sounded to her. But all these years since she moved out I've been in control of my own agenda, my own business. No one nitpicks what I read, or whether I should be working or not, trying to solve my problems for me, when I've got a plan already.

Not that I can share this plan with her, yet. She's clearly not receptive.

Mailman Al comes in, and I have to grip the counter to keep myself from pouncing on him and ripping the mail out of his hands. Al peruses the shelves for his midday snack, and I flip through the mail, as casually as I can manage. Junk, junk, junk, charity solicitation, bill, bill . . .

There it is. I slip the letter into my pocket, as much of it as I can manage to fit. I make a pretense of sorting through the rest. Al doesn't seem to have noticed my sleight of hand.

He finally leaves after making some small talk and buying a bag of chips.

With one more glance out onto the sidewalk for impending customers, I tear into the letter.

Maeve!

I knew you could find it in your heart to forgive me. You were always so good, too good for me.

I'm coming up there in August, only I don't know yet the exact date. Charley is still firming up his plans.

Can I call you at the store? I've been afraid you'd hang up on me but to hear your musical voice again!

Write me back, as soon as you can. I can't wait to see you.

Love from your prodigal husband,
Robert

I glance at my watch. I've got a little time before Cami is due. I slide a legal pad out of a stack of papers under the front counter. I settle into the low office chair, prop the pad up on my knee, and begin my response.

Dear Robert,

I haven't forgiven you, yet. I said we could talk and meet. It's not going to be so easy to make me forget what you did. Because you didn't just walk out on me, you walked out on your little girl, and I'm the one who had to explain to her something that made no sense, something no little girl should have to hear, that her father is not coming back.

It's a dream come true to find out that you're not only still alive but that you're sorry and want to come back, but it's not like we can erase twenty years of loss and absence like scrubbing out a grass stain.

Speaking of your daughter, she's back at the Nee Nance for a little while, and I don't know how long. So when you write again, use a typewriter, or get someone else to address the envelope. And for heaven's sake, don't call! She doesn't know I'm still writing you.

If she had her way, we would never see each other again. Now is not the time to let her know we're staying in touch. I want us to be a family again, and if we go about this the wrong way, it could be ruined forever. First, I need to see you for myself, and you need to explain to me everything that happened, and all your plans for the future. Then I can show her you're serious, and that we have a future together, and then you can apologize to her directly, in person, and with sincerity.

She always loved you, and despite what you've done, I don't think she could just shut that off like flipping a switch.

It won't be easy, but that's what I want for us.

So please, don't call. And remember, when you write, make sure it's not obvious that it's you, from the outside envelope. We have to proceed carefully.

I'll be counting the days until August.

Maeve

All the times I wished for this over the years! At Anna's graduation, I looked for him in the crowd. On her birthdays, I watched for cards in the mail. Our anniversary every year I stared out the front door of the Nee Nance. He's missed a great deal, but yet, not so much. We're both only in our fifties, and Anna hasn't yet married or had children. He could still attend her wedding someday, maybe even give her away! Dance with her! All my old dreams seem possible again.

I address the envelope—the return address is different again, this time in Kentucky—and as I seal the envelope, I feel a wash of regret for that argument with Anna. She puts on such a hard shell; sometimes I forget what it must be like for her, that inside she's still my little girl, no matter how capable she seems in her high-heel shoes and sharp black suit.

I affix the stamp and whisper a prayer of gratitude that this letter didn't arrive while I was in the hospital, because that would have ruined everything. I slip the letter inside my purse so that next time I walk by an outside mailbox, I can drop it in.

This was definitely meant to be.

I said that to my mother, during that fraught, anxious year Robert and I were openly dating.

"It was meant to be! He loves me and you can't stop me from loving him!" I bellowed, one of the only times I dared raise my voice to her, and nothing horrible happened when I did, either. I didn't turn into a pillar of salt and the earth didn't spin off its axis.

"You're throwing away your life on that piece of trash! He's probably seeing another floozy or two behind your back, and you're too naive and starry-eyed to see it! I know his reputation, I hear the talk about that family, with that crazy sister of his, too, and what's wrong with them, anyway, hanging around a bunch of teenage kids?"

"If I'm naive, it's because you hardly let me out of the house! You're just mad because for the first time in my life I'm doing something you can't control!"

She slapped me then, but I was wild for our forbidden love and I barely felt it and, in fact, had to stop myself from slapping her back.

My wedding photo is still hanging upstairs. I've seen it so often I can close my eyes now and picture all its detail. Robert's wearing a suit with huge lapels and a loud tie, and I'm wearing a plain white sundress and a flower in my hair. We're standing on the courthouse steps. I'm clinging to his arm in the picture, and I remember being giddy with the freedom and romance of marrying in secret with only Sally and the court clerk as witnesses.

No, it was never easy for us. Why should it be any different now?

CHAPTER 22

Amy

I POUND ALONG THE PAVEMENT, LETTING THE SKY SPIT ON ME AS Frodo pants along, keeping pace.

I surprise myself at my disappointment, not seeing Ed out here with Lucky, but then it is raining and that keeps lots of runners and walkers indoors. Calories know no weather, though, and I don't have a treadmill.

Also, I've been slacking off the past few days, walking with Ed instead of running. Unless I add another run to my schedule, I need to keep moving forward. My mom is always at me to relax and ease up on myself, but she should know better than anyone why I can't do that.

I adjust my cap, and as I do, I see a flash out of the corner of my eye, someone red-headed. I turn for a second, thinking *Anna?* But it's not her. She has no reason to be here, and anyway, what would I say to her?

She's right. I can't keep apologizing for Paul and it's not my fault.

But watching him tear into her in front of the council, watching her fist clench up . . .

Back in school once, Maeve sewed me a dress for a National Honor Society thing. It was a pretty pattern in a lovely fabric, and at the time I thought it brought out the blue in my eyes.

"Nice dress," a girl sneered at me when I wore it that evening, and it was just that same tone of voice that Paul used last night for "liquor store" and "beer signs."

He's not like that, I think, defending him even to myself.

He's never been snobby around my mom, though she's no cover girl, and he's been nice to my kid brother even though he's a plumber; in fact, he's thrown some subcontracting work Kevin's way.

Now that I think of it, though . . . He once told me how proud he is that I "rose above" my circumstances. At the time I just lapped up the attention—he was gazing at me with such worship and adoration—but now, I hear *nice dress* and *liquor store* and *your circumstances* and it all sounds the same to me.

My knees start to throb. All those years of carrying a whole extra person around on my frame already did some damage, and I should really know better than to push myself so hard. Frodo, for that matter, is trying to lap up puddles, he's so thirsty.

I force myself to cool down and walk back slowly, reminding myself with every step that I love Paul, I'm going to marry him, and the wrecking ball hasn't yet crashed into the Nee Nance.

I flick on the lights in the reception area of Lakeshore Realty, and as my computer chimes to life, I take a moment to straighten my desk. There's a film of dust on a snapshot of Paul and me taken last summer, soon after we started dating. I blow the dust off and wince as some of it flies into my eyes.

When Tiffany grabbed the camera to snap a picture, out of

reflex I hid behind Paul, throwing my arms around his neck and cuddling my face against his. It came off as a larky, fun-loving gesture, at least.

The girls are always carrying on over my figure these days, but pictures are still a trial for me.

"Good morning, Amy," says Kelly, my boss and the agency's broker. She's an acquaintance of Paul's dad, and that was how I got this job, when it turned out I might have to relocate to find work and I was so sad about leaving Haven. Mr. Becker heard about it and hooked me up with Lakeshore because they needed a receptionist.

The Beckers have taken such good care of me.

"Amy," she says, stopping suddenly in the hall and turning around. "I'd like to have a word with you this morning, if I might, before it gets too busy. Do you mind?"

"Not at all."

I follow Kelly down the hall. She's tall and wears spike heels every day, even so. Her hair is shiny black and cut short in a way that flatters her sharp features. She also happens to be one of the few black businesswomen in Haven, make that Ottawa County, something that's a source of pride to her, and I think also a burden. Sometimes the light goes out of her eyes when people praise her excessively.

She selects one of the two chairs in front of her desk and indicates the other one where I am to sit. I do sit, and pivot to face her. Our knees are almost touching.

"I just wanted to let you know that although we're keeping you on, times have been very tough here lately and we'll be cutting your hours, effective Monday. You'll be working ten to three instead of nine to five."

I must have done something wrong. I remember the time my English teacher found me reading a novel behind my notebook and snatched it away from me in the middle of class, giving me a withering stare in front of everyone. I had to beg for the book back. I've got that same sinking, sickening feeling in my middle.

"Kelly . . . I know I've been taking a little time here and there to go out to do wedding stuff, invitations and fittings and whatnot, but I always work through lunch to make it up and sometimes stay late . . ."

She raises her hand. "That's not it. It's just numbers. People aren't buying houses, and when that happens, no one here makes money. I'm sorry to do this to you when you're probably saving for the wedding, but I have no choice."

"I understand," I tell her, slowly standing up from the chair.

All morning I catch myself staring at people, the other agents and brokers in the office, and I think about how long it's been since they've each made a sale, and I realize my phone isn't ringing so much, and when it is, it tends to be a client desperate to know if there have been any offers.

I'm disappointed my hours are cut, but to be honest, the Beckers will pick up any wedding slack. They won't want their boy married off in anything but high style.

And I'm not Fred, who has three kids to support now. His wife just had twins.

"Lakeshore Realty" I say, with a little less cheer, perhaps, when my phone next rings. It's one of our Spanish-speaking clients. *"Hola, Señora Martinez, cómo estás? . . . Sí,"* I say.

Señora Martinez is very worried about not being able to sell her home, which is a cute bungalow. Unfortunately, it's in an iffy part of town and her adjustable mortgage rate is spiking. I tell her that her agent, Mary, is doing the best she can, and ask, would she like to talk to her? She tells me no in a voice that sags with the weight of those payments.

I call Paul next. "Can we meet for lunch today?"

"Geez, babe, I don't know . . ."

"Paul, please. I'd like to see you."

I hold my breath. I never do this: make demands. He's got enough going on.

"Okay, fine. Sure. Come by when you have lunch and I'll take a break."

"Thanks, honey. See you soon."

He only mumbles into the phone and I would have liked a cheerier send-off, but I'll take it. Anyway, a lunch will go a long way toward erasing last night's post-council-meeting unpleasantness.

"What do you want from me?" he'd shouted, actually raising his voice at me. I was curled up on the couch. His face was so red he looked burned. "You want to live like a Mrs. Becker and have this storybook wedding? Then we need to make money. I try to make money and you whine about how I do it! You're worse than my brother. Damn bleeding hearts. You sure don't mind the fancy car and the nice house, though, any more than he does."

"But . . ." was the only word I managed.

"If we only did projects that never bent a blade of grass or displaced a single soul, no one would have any place to live and I'd be a . . . a . . . plumber."

"Hey, my brother's a plumber!"

"What's the . . ." He clapped his hand over his forehead. "Amy, that's not the point. I could have said gas station attendant—"

"But you didn't. You said plumber, which now you say is the same thing as a gas station attendant."

"I just . . . Jesus, stop taking this so personally. You were the one who jumped on me, which, by the way, this was supposed to be my big night, thanks for the support, *darling*."

And with that, he'd slammed his way out the door.

I sent him a text later to apologize, and he sent one back that said "I love you," but it's hard to know how sincere that was.

Yes, lunch is just the thing. I'll praise him for his accomplishment and we can get back on track.

* * *

When I step through the front door of Becker Development and shake out my umbrella, I see Anna standing before the reception desk.

She's wearing shorts and a T-shirt, both spotted with rain. Her hair is back in a barrette, but what isn't pulled tight has frizzed out in the muggy air. She turns to face me, then looks quickly away, her jaw set.

The receptionist, Barbara, waves at me, nods, and buzzes for Paul.

First, Will comes out to greet Anna. His face is grave, and he steps close enough to Anna that I can't hear them talking. He puts his hand on Anna's elbow and leads her a couple steps away from Barbara.

Barbara shoots me a look and I shrug back at her.

Paul comes out, his hair mussed from where he must have been messing with it. I reach up to smooth it down and he flinches away, then smooths the hair himself. He then gives me a weak smile and kisses my cheek. "Hi, hon. I've only got just an hour. I really shouldn't even break away, but . . ."

Paul notices Will and Anna in the corner. Will is putting on his trench coat and grabbing an umbrella. Anna hitches her purse up on her shoulder. I see the brothers' eyes meet, but they don't say a word.

Paul leads me out into the rain. We have separate umbrellas so it's hard to get close. I'm glad to get into the warm, breakfasty smell of Doreen's.

The door opens behind us, and Paul and I both turn to see Anna and Will coming in from huddling under one umbrella.

We all stare at each other for a moment's surprise, then there are uncomfortable chuckles all around. "Fancy meeting you here," Will says.

"Four, then?" the hostess asks, and no one disagrees in a moment's hesitation, so we all follow the hostess to a booth.

Anna and Paul are diagonal across the table, each avoiding the other's gaze.

Paul clears his throat after we order finally and says, "No hard feelings, eh?"

Anna narrows her eyes and doesn't respond. Then she exhales deeply and says to me, "So, tell us all about the wedding. You must be very excited."

Now this is safe ground. So I tell them about my bridal party and the colors and my stunning dress and the reception out at the country club. This gets us halfway through our meal.

While I'm prattling on, I can't help but think how natural and relaxed Anna and Will are together. They're not doing anything wrong, really, here. They're old friends and clearly not sneaking around because they're having lunch right out in the open with us.

But if I were Samantha, I'd be pissed. And knowing Samantha the little I do, she will be, when she hears of it.

Under the table, Paul strokes my knee with his thumb and I relax. Even though we couldn't talk privately, now I know: All is forgiven.

I squeeze his hand back. *I forgive you, too.*

The check comes and we ask the waitress to split it by pairs. I also ask her to box up the remains of my fresh fruit for my snack later today. I see Anna make a grab for the check, but Will gets to it first, and there's some whispered debate before he wins, slapping down his Visa.

I start to get up as they do, but Paul gently takes my arm. "Wait a minute, babe?" he asks.

"Sure . . ." I glance at my watch. I'll have just enough time to get back. Barely.

Anna and Will nod to us, and I notice as they leave that his hand hovers behind her lower back, not quite touching, as if she might fall at any time and he needs to be at the ready. I also notice they make a wrong turn outside the door, walking the opposite direction from their respective workplaces. As they pass the large front window, Anna's head is down, arms folded, and Will is speaking to her, his posture bent so he can be close to her face.

I turn to Paul in the booth, and my breath catches in my chest because he looks positively gray.

"What? What is it?"

"Amy . . ." He takes my hand in his and it's like when he proposed, only he's not on one knee, this place stinks of bacon fat, and he looks like he might throw up. "We may need to postpone the wedding."

CHAPTER 23

Cami

I THINK THIS IS WHY JESUS WAS A CARPENTER: IT'S EASY TO BE serene and turn the other cheek when you can pound nails and saw wood and sand until your biceps turn rubbery.

The mattress set I bought at Salvation Army is propped up on my sunny yellow wall, and the finished floor is smooth under my toes. And now I'm building myself a bed because, why not, yeah?

It's that or take a bus to an Indian casino and fall right off that cliff again. So, bed it is.

Also, I know Sherry is still asleep in here somewhere, and I'm pounding as loudly as I can so she'll leave. I haven't touched her again and don't plan to. But I never promised her a monastery.

My thumb explodes in fire, only it doesn't really, that's just what it feels like when I smash it with a hammer.

I can hardly see through my watery eyes as I fumble out to the kitchen and fill a baggy with ice. This is as good a time as any for a break, I'd say.

I drop the lock-hook into place back in my room and sit cross-legged, cradling my iced thumb, with a photo album on the floor in front of me.

It's not as old as I'd hoped, this album. It's from my own youth, not my mom's, so there aren't any clues in here as to the identity of the mysterious rich family who called my mother Pammie.

I'm tempted to call my Aunt Clara and ask, but just picturing her pious pout makes me want to spit in her face.

I'm grateful there are no pictures in here of my mom sick. I don't need to see that. Because she was always the family photographer, when she fell ill, the pictures stopped.

Not that it's easy to look at pictures of Trent and me gallivanting in a park somewhere, knowing my smiling mother was behind the camera, clicking.

My thumb's throbbing eases up and I sneak a look under the ice bag. The thumbnail is turning purple.

I pull my phone out of my pocket and dial.

"Hi, Steve."

"Oh, Cami."

"I know you said not to call, but . . . well, since when have I done what I'm told, yeah?"

"Yeah."

There was a smile in his voice, I just know it. "So listen, I've been really good so far. Not so much as a poker chip anywhere near me. I'm even staying away from potato chips just to be safe."

"Well, good. So you're okay, then."

"Sort of." In the pause, my gaze falls on the photo album, on a rare picture of my mom and dad together. Trent must have grabbed the camera. My dad is smiling at my mom, apparently unaware of my brother the paparazzo. "So, keeping my side of the bed warm for me?"

I cringe at myself. I'm not good at needy.

He clears his throat and I clench my eyes shut, wishing I could pull those words back. I should hang up. My good thumb hovers over the "end call" button. I wait for his answer anyway.

"Actually, I'm seeing someone else."

"You are, yeah? Good for you." I suck in a breath and move the phone slightly away so he can't hear the effort this takes to hold it all in.

"I'm sorry, but I did tell you not to call."

"I know."

"Cami? Are you there?"

"Mmm-hmmm."

"Say something."

"Something."

He laughs at this, like he always laughs at my jokes. Always used to, I should say. "C'mon, I want to know you're okay."

I put the phone on the floor long enough to let my breath out and pick the phone back up. "I'm fine, yeah? Aren't I always?"

"That's my girl. Look, take care, huh?"

"Yeah."

I hang up and drop the phone on my bed. My door rattles against the hook-lock and I hurriedly shove the photo album into my closet.

I open the door to see Sherry in all her wrinkly, smeared, hung-over glory. "What?"

"What happened to you?" she asks, squinting at my face.

"I hit my thumb with a hammer. If you'll excuse me, I have to get to work."

"Are you okay?" Maeve asks me as I come in. She's at the register.

"Allergies," I answer. "Also, I hit myself with a hammer. See my amazing Technicolor thumb? And where's Anna?"

Maeve's jaw clenches briefly before she says, "I sent her out for a break. It was getting a little crowded in here."

Sally is in the store, restlessly wandering from shelf to shelf, picking things up and putting them down. "You sure you don't need help, sister dear?" she calls. "I could straighten up some . . . Whoops!" There's a loud crashing, and in the rear of the store I can see a display of cereal come tumbling down.

"She's making me crazy," Maeve hisses. "I'll pay you a million dollars to take her out of here for the day."

"Wouldn't you rather get out somewhere? Let me hold down the fort?"

"I don't feel like going anywhere. Honestly, I just want her out of my hair."

"In that case, I'll do it pro bono. What does she like to do?"

"She likes the Indian casino," Maeve says. "She'll sit there at the nickel slots for hours."

I walk to the back of the store and start setting up the boxes again. "Hey, Sal. You feeling lucky today?"

It's not quite as grand as the Detroit casinos, but none of them are much different. They're all loud, for one thing, both in decor and volume. Sally zooms right over to the cheapest slots as fast as her skinny legs can go, a plastic cup of coins in her hand.

I'll wander around a little, I tell her. Just to poke around.

I didn't bring much cash, on purpose. But I did bring my ATM card. For emergencies.

My wandering brings me past the blackjack table, and all I do is watch, at a distance back. One of the players sees me and gestures to an empty seat. I raise my hand and shake my head: no, thanks.

I can't believe he just took another card. Imbecile. He groans and I groan inside my head because anyone with brains saw that coming. I shift my weight, tapping my foot. I adjust my glasses and finally rip myself away.

It was Steve who first brought me to the casino. Little did he know.

I was still living with Elizabeth then, before she moved out to live with her boyfriend, sticking me with half the lease left and no roommate. My tutoring paychecks were flimsy, and I was just seeing Steve. We were bored of movies and the weather was too rotten to take a walk, so he suggested ducking into the MGM Grand. We were laughing about it, poking fun, having drinks, all the while acting like we were above this kind of thing.

I sat down at a table of five-card draw and won Elizabeth's share of the rent for the next three months. Then I tore down the poster in my grocery store advertising for a new roommate and moved my things into her side of the closet.

By the time I moved in with Steve, when my lease was up, I'd discovered online gambling, and sure, I had my ups and downs, but I was mostly up.

Until I wasn't. And every attempt I made to get back on top, I only lost more. I just knew I was about to get back on track. He was never supposed to know.

I walk up to the bar to fetch myself a 7-Up.

"Having a lucky day?" asks a round-faced blond guy next to me. His hair is sticking up funny and he looks like Dennis the Menace in a midlife crisis. He's actually wearing a Members Only jacket.

"Not really, no."

He smiles at me, too huge for the occasion, and looks me up and down. "I'd say my day is lucky, now."

"Spare me, Casanova."

"Bitch," he spits, and stumbles off his barstool.

The bartender hands me my pop and smiles. "Good for you. He's used that same line on the last three girls that came up here. Everyone else just ran away."

I turn my back to the bartender and put my elbow on the bar. He's flirting, too. Everyone's always out for something.

A blackjack table is in my line of sight, and as a matter of fact, so is an ATM machine. Maybe I'll just check my balance, and only take out a little bit. Only what I can afford to lose; isn't that what the public service announcements say?

My hands are quivering just a bit as I punch in my PIN number. It's not nerves or fear. This is the beginning of the buzz, and I want to weep with how happy it makes me to feel it again. I'd almost succeeded in burying it in the recesses of my animal brain, pretending I never enjoyed the cards, the winning, the battle.

I snatch the cash out of the mouth of the machine and stuff it down into my pocket, striding over to the little window where a young man supposedly named Felix fetches my chips.

"Good luck," Felix says, and winks.

The dealer greets me extravagantly, like an old friend he hasn't seen in years. The feeling is mutual.

CHAPTER 24

Anna

WHEN I RETURN TO THE NEE NANCE, MY CLOTHES STILL HAVEN'T completely dried from this morning's sprint in the rain. The sensation is sticky and I can't wait to get these clothes off, especially since I felt like a rube sitting there in my shorts and cotton shirt next to three people dressed for business.

My mother is at the counter, leafing through a tabloid.

"Mom, I thought you were resting. Where's Cami?"

"The store isn't busy. I was going batty upstairs anyway, and Sally was making me batty down here. I sent Cami and Sally to the casino."

"Want me to run down to the store and pick up a book for you? Or the library?"

My mom glances down at the magazine, closes it, and then slips it to the side. "No, thanks." She comes around the counter and glances around. We're alone in the store. She reaches for my hand and I let her take it, though physical affection now that I'm an adult feels strange to me. "I'm sorry I yelled at you. You were trying to help. And this was your home, too."

I glance around at the store, which I hated as soon as my dad left. It quit being a fun place when he wasn't there to hand me candy off the rack, ignoring Mom's *tsk* about screwing up the inventory and the enamel on my teeth. Plus, I was just starting middle school and kids started to notice who was wearing second-hand clothes and who couldn't have sleepovers because there was no room in her tiny cubby above a liquor store.

But all that was before someone was trying to take it away from my mother, from me.

"I don't want to give up on this, Mom."

She squeezes my hand again. "Honey, what's the point? You hated this place, and this isn't exactly what I wanted for myself."

"But you don't have any time! You won't get unemployment as a sole proprietor, and you don't own any property. You need some kind of income, and . . . jobs aren't so easy to come by these days." I'd started to say *unskilled jobs* but knew how that would sound.

A customer approaches the counter with an armload, and a few more come in the door. I join my mother at her side, bagging up the stuff to speed things along.

I'm immediately distracted by the mental play-by-play of the lunch I just endured. I'd hoped to catch Beck for a quick bite, one measly hour with an old friend outside the confines of this lousy store. We just had to bump into that brat brother and Amy Rickart in the same restaurant and get stuck with them. So when the meal ended and the rain had finally faded away, I walked with Beck even as he turned in the opposite direction of Becker Development and the Nee Nance.

First he invited me to his family's Fourth of July party, insisting it was no problem with his wife and saying I could easily avoid Paul in the crowd. I laughed at that, because I couldn't even avoid

Paul at lunch. After extracting from me a promise I'd think about attending, he asked about my job, when I was going back.

And I told him, much to my own surprise, I don't want to. So don't, he said, and I told him it's not that simple, and he replied, in effect, I was the only one making it complicated.

He stopped walking in front of a store selling Petoskey stone renderings of the lower peninsula and other whimsical magnets, and I stopped in front of him. He put his hand on my elbow and said, "I'm just saying life is too short to do something you don't want to."

"Oh, like you always wanted to work for your dad's business."

"Low blow, Annie. I'm not saying I'm perfect in that, either. But I've been thinking along these lines for a few months now, and sometimes forcing yourself to go through the motions of what seems sensible is the biggest waste of time possible. What if twenty years from now we both look back and say, 'Why did I put up with that?' Think of the pain of all that time just lost, forever."

"Are you thinking of quitting your job, then?"

"Not exactly. I'm just saying, you're not locked into anything. You don't have to keep doing something just because you always have, especially if it's hollow."

Hollow. Beck always could do that: put just the right word to my emotions.

The flow of customers finally dries up and I turn back to Mom, trying to find the thread of our conversation again. I'd forgotten that about being back here, how every discussion is halting and disrupted.

"So, Mom, here's what I'm thinking about the store. Let's work up a plan and go to Paul. I've got savings, if you want to call it a loan, call it a loan then, and I'll pay your rent in the new building for a while. We can spruce up the exterior, change the name, and, fine, work on a long-term plan for you. But in the meantime you won't have to live with Sally in that stinky trailer."

She sighs. "But I can't do all that myself. I wouldn't know where to begin."

"I can help you."

"You've got to go back to work!"

"I don't know about that. I'm thinking of making a change myself."

She gapes up at me, searching my face as if she's not sure who I am.

I know the feeling.

CHAPTER 25

Maeve

MY FIRST THOUGHT, WHEN I SEE ANNA WITH HER HAIR FRIZZY IN her grubby clothes, telling me she's thinking of giving up her job at Miller Paulson, is to scream, *No! I will not allow it!*

My second thought: *This is all my fault.*

Customers interrupt us, and Anna takes charge of them like she was born to it, and this thought stings me because in a way she was born to it, you could argue, learning to pull up and toddle along the shelves with the canned cat food and toilet paper and Slim Jims.

She would bring home those gold stars on her homework, and I'd sit there in the crowd as she collected accolades for National Honor Society, and I'd know down to my toes that she would have a better, bigger life than I ever dreamed of.

And she did it, by God. She did it.

If only I could tell her that she doesn't need to hover over me, that her father is going to build me a house. I can just see her sneer, though. She was too young to remember him at his best. A person shouldn't be boiled down to one mistake, especially if that person is sorry and was a decent sort to begin with.

Now that Anna is at the register, I wander back upstairs to have my own lunch and think about her suggestion, fixing up the store to serve some snobby summer people. A waste of time and energy when I'm going to leave anyway. And all the while beholden to that Paul kid! Beholden to the whole Becker bunch.

I take my egg salad out of the fridge and start scraping it on the bread, after a tentative sniff to make sure it hasn't gone over.

Mr. Becker was always nice enough to Anna, but it always seemed to me he treated her like a pleasant pet: a little too amazed at her success, as with a dog who can open a refrigerator door. If I end up crawling to them and begging for a chance to clean up my store, it would confirm his view of us. Of me.

I can't let her throw away a career she slaved for just so she can save a store I don't even want and, in fact, don't need.

But if I don't do something visible that she can see and understand to provide for myself, she won't go back.

And to think I exhaled at her college graduation, thinking I'd leaped some towering hurdle: She'd made it through childhood and four years of college unscathed and poised for success.

Parenting never ends, my old friend Veronica told me once.

I dump the remaining half sandwich in the trash because it tastes like cardboard anyway. I'll grab something else to eat on my way to see Veronica.

At first glance, Veronica's house looks modest and unassuming. That's only because it's built on a hill, so the front view is of a simple, low, ranch-style home with a nice picture window.

Out back, the house sprawls down the hill with another two floors. The kids used to have such fun stumble-running down that hill, back when Alex was just a boy who was maybe a little more active than the others.

I hear Veronica call "I'm out back, Maeve!" when I come in the front. I cross her entryway (she calls it a "foy-yay") and down a winding path. She and Grant have an in-ground pool now, though I've never seen her use it for actual swimming. She seems to have installed it only for its reflection of shimmering sun.

She's under a monstrous umbrella, lounging in a terry-cloth wrap of some kind. After this morning's rain, the sun has been heroically pushing through the thinning clouds and it's nearly bright.

We dispense with the small talk about the weather, and she pours me an iced tea from her pitcher.

"How's Alex?" I ask, by way of steering the conversation toward our children.

She has been sitting facing me, but at this she stretches out again on her chair, staring through her sunglasses at the underside of the umbrella. Or maybe she closes her eyes; I can't tell from here.

"I wish I knew. He never tells me anything anymore because he doesn't want me to harangue him for it. I send him money when he asks because I'm afraid what will happen if I don't."

I swallow hard. This makes my worry about Anna seem so petty. "I'm sorry."

"I don't know what else I can do. Grant says I 'enable' him, but at least he's alive. At least I know if he's getting some money from me he's not doing something out of desperation. The last time I tried to be tough? He was beaten within an inch of his life by some man, and I can't even imagine the details of how that transpired. It was horrifying to get that call. Grant watches too many documentaries. They don't do documentaries about the kids who end up dead when their parents cut them off. That wouldn't be very inspiring, now, would it?"

"I know you're doing the best you can."

"I'm sorry, I know this isn't what you wanted to hear today."

"No, don't apologize. I want you to talk about it."

"How's Anna? Still a superstar?"

This could have been said with bitterness, but it comes out weary. Kids make you tired at every age, every stage.

"I'm worried about her, honestly."

Veronica sits up again, pushing her huge glasses to the top of her head, where they perch on her blond-frosted, feathery hair. "What's wrong?"

"I think she's going to quit her job."

"Okay." She waits for me to continue.

"She's worked so hard for it, her whole life."

"Well, she'll land on her feet, I'm sure. Why does she want to quit? Is she burned out?"

"I think . . . I think she wants to quit to save me . . ."

"Save you from what?"

My next words catch in my throat. She'll think I'm asking for charity from her if I explain it. And I've never done that, not ever, not even when I had to borrow money from the bank at a ridiculous rate just to buy Anna a Christmas present, not even when I had to spend my retirement savings to help make her tuition payments when things were slow at the store.

And Veronica always knew better than to offer.

"I've been ill a bit," I offer. "My blood pressure. She thinks I'm too sick for her to leave," I say, because it's part of the truth.

"Well, you'll just have to be the picture of rosy health and have fabulous blood pressure, because you're right, she shouldn't throw away her job for that. Would it help if I told her I'd keep an eye on you?"

I nod, knowing it wouldn't help a bit.

"You know," Veronica says, sliding her glasses back down. "That might be just a cover story."

"A what?"

"What if she wants to quit, but she needs a convenient excuse? I mean, look at Anna. She's outdone herself at every turn, and she's come so far. What if she just doesn't want it anymore? But she can't just *quit*. Girls like Anna don't do that. She might be looking for a reason."

I chew this over for a moment while Veronica continues. "You remember, Alex was always such a bright kid. Remember how he learned his multiplication tables before his class even started on them? How he could spell any word he ever read—he'd just look at it once and know it forever? We praised him so much, so extravagantly for that, but then he'd get to school and something else was always more interesting, like putting gum in a girl's hair. I think he felt it."

"Felt what?"

"Felt the responsibility of his brain. He cracked early. Maybe Anna is cracking late."

"She's not cracking!" I stand up, sloshing some tea out of my glass, which I haven't even touched. "She just wants to take care of me. Anna is a responsible, well-adjusted child."

"You mean, unlike Alex."

"Don't take it personally."

"You're the one taking it awfully personally." Veronica stands up with me. She's taller than me, and as I look up at her this way, she seems haughty. On a pedestal, like a statue in a museum. "Maybe you're a little more wrapped up in her success than you'd like to admit."

The ice rattles in my glass as I set it down slowly. "I'm sorry about the trouble with Alex. I feel for you. I shouldn't have troubled you with my problems."

"I'm not saying that's definitely what's going on. But it's worth considering. Anna has gone so fast and so hard her entire life, maybe for the first time she's really wondering what she wants."

"And I think maybe you've watched too much Dr. Phil. Have a nice afternoon."

I have to wrestle the slider open, and I don't bother closing it behind me as I scuttle across her slick tile floor and back out to my beat-up old Buick.

In the car I have to take three tries to get my key into the ignition. In my mind's eye I can see teenage Anna's creased forehead as she handed me a paper with a "B-" scrawled on it, her face red and shiny wet. *It's a B*, I told her, and she choked out, *It's nearly a C*, and as it happened, she begged the teacher to let her rewrite it and he caved in. She was nearly shaking with relief when she later showed me the big letter A on the top with the note *Much improved*.

CHAPTER 26

Amy

"HONEY?" I CALL OUT TO PAUL, WHO HAS *SPORTSCENTER* ON IN MY living room. "Want to go to the parade?"

He grunts his answer, which means it's probably no.

I adjust my jewelry in the mirror and stare at my engagement ring a moment. It's just what I wanted, princess cut, classic, the band platinum, which I think is so much more elegant than gold. Mrs. Becker's wedding ring is platinum, too.

I convinced Paul not to tell anyone about his reconsideration, and told him I was still going to wear my ring. In return, I promised not to do anything else to plan the wedding until we make a decision.

But "we" really means Paul, because I've never wavered.

It's a good thing I'm such a planner. We've already got the country club reserved, the church lined up, and in fact we attended three of the four premarital counseling classes as required at First Presbyterian. My dress, thank goodness, is already on order, on its way.

True, we don't have invitations yet, or flowers, but those won't take so long. Soon enough Paul will have gotten over his problem, and we'll have lost nothing, really.

I exhale and look into the mirror again to steady myself. I'm the same blond Amy that Paul fell in love with and proposed to. Nothing's changed. Nothing important, anyway.

"Can I get you anything?"

"No, thanks."

I curl up on the couch next to him. Frodo hops up next to me.

"You know, you can't be letting that dog up on the furniture all the time. He's too big."

He's thinking of when we live together! A good sign. "Down, Frodo," I say, nudging him by his collar off the sofa. He flops at my feet.

I trace a figure-eight on Paul's shoulder lightly with my fingernail. "The party tonight should be fun, don't you think?"

"As much fun as a root canal."

"What do you mean?" The annual Becker Fourth of July party is a major part of the Haven social calendar. A huge barbecue, summery drinks, and a private fireworks show over their private beach.

"Everyone will want to talk wedding."

"Well, we'll just tell them we're tired of talking about it, change the subject."

Paul rolls his eyes at me.

"Come on, it won't be that bad."

"I don't know why we can't just be honest with people about it."

My palms film over with sweat, and I sit back from Paul so I can wipe them on my dress. "Because nothing's definite, that's why. Right? Isn't that what we said the other night?"

"The other night" after that awful lunch when Paul dropped that bomb on me—I will never get over his doing that in a public place and when I had half a workday to endure—we had it out for sure. He claimed that financially it was too iffy to get married now, that the company was "a little strapped," and it seemed like a bad idea to drop so much money on a wedding in that situation.

I'd already told my boss I was sick and gone home to hug my pillow and worry, since I couldn't bear to discuss it right there at Doreen's. I'd spent the whole afternoon spinning theories about why he'd gone cold on me. I panicked about another woman. I weighed myself at least ten times to remind myself I hadn't gotten any bigger. I re-read our old love notes on the computer and even counted them: just as frequent as before.

So when he was pacing and started going on about finances, I was left stammering. It was the one thing I hadn't imagined.

"It doesn't have to be so fancy." I made a grab for his elbow so he'd stop that awful pacing, and in my head I thought, *just don't make me give up my dress.* "We can scale back the guest list and serve cheaper food. I'd even change the venue; I don't care. I want to marry you."

He shook his head. "I wouldn't do that to you; you want me to get married in a dream wedding. You've told me that a hundred times, haven't you?" He finally stopped pacing and put his hands on my shoulders. "I know what it cost you to change your whole life. You deserve to have the best of everything. We can still move in together, you know. It would just be putting off all the pomp and rice-throwing till maybe next summer when things pick up again. By then the Washington Avenue rehab should be done, and we should have some tenants and be getting more cash flow, maybe phase three of Poplar Bluff will be a go again . . ."

"What if it doesn't work next summer, either? What if you don't get to do the Washington rehab?" *Rehab*, my foot. He meant the Nee Nance demolition. I knew he did.

"Well, that would make it tougher. Is it so hard to put it off a little while?"

I swallowed hard and wiped under my eyes. "Paul, I'll be thirty-six by then."

He embraced me then and said into my hair, "Baby, it's just a number. You're stunning at every age."

Tell that to my ovaries, I thought.

My period came early this month, and my temperatures have been erratic. No clear answer on the ovulation predictor sticks, either. Early menopause could strike, for all I know.

"Paul?" I try to get his attention again now, because he seems to be sucked into the commercials. I know he gets distracted by the television, especially sports, but it's salt in the wound when he's ignoring me for the sake of advertising. "Nothing's definite, you said."

"Yes, that's what I said. Okay, we'll go to the party and steer the topic off the wedding."

He still hasn't taken his eyes from the TV screen, and now I notice what he's looking at. It's a beer commercial, and a buxom girl in a bikini frolics with her lime-flavored beer. I stare at her unmarred, taut skin, then scrabble for the remote, punching the button. I toss the remote aside, startling Frodo.

Paul says "Hey—" but then he stops because I'm straddling him, pulling his hips toward me. He groans into my kiss and starts to fumble with the zipper on the back of my dress. He tugs it down.

I jump off his lap and head for the bedroom, supporting my dress with my arms. He pulls at my arm. "No, here," he says, voice husky. "I like it out here."

"The bed," I reply, but he won't let go of my arm.

"Nah, c'mere, it'll be fun."

Now I pull like I'm at the end of a leash. "It's cold in here. I need the covers. Come on, Paul, let go . . ."

He relents, and I run into the bedroom, dropping my dress only moments before I slide safely into the sheets.

"You know," he murmurs as he moves against me. "I'll want to see my wife naked in the daylight someday."

"Then you better hurry up and marry me." I kiss him harder so he'll shut the hell up.

CHAPTER 27

Cami

I SMACK THE TIN CANS INTO THEIR BOXES WITH A SATISFYING THUD. I can almost imagine this is my stuff and I'm packing to leave. Where am I going? New York City, of course; isn't that where restless Midwestern kids always go? Or Los Angeles, if they want to be in pictures.

"What the hell is this?" growls my dad from behind me.

But this isn't my stuff, and I'm no kid anymore.

"I'm cleaning up." I don't turn around, only pause briefly in the removing of cans from the pantry. Without the cans to obscure it, a brown sheen is now visible over the shelves. I've got Soft Scrub at the ready on the counter and, if necessary, new shelf liner.

He grunts in response. He's closed the shop for the Fourth, but I'd been hoping he'd go whoop it up at the campground or the Tip-A-Few. "Where's Sherry?" I ask him, modulating my voice to keep out the sarcasm.

"She's pissed off at me."

I turn around slowly and steal a look at him. He's not wavering where he stands, and he doesn't stink too badly, yet. His eyes are relatively clear and his hair might even have been combed. His skin is even freshly shaved, though reddened. I should buy new razor blades next time I go to the store.

I can't think of a safe answer to this, so I don't reply.

"Kitchen's not that dirty." He moves a little closer, watching me.

I shrug. "It's something to do." After a moment's pause, I add: "I might also paint the cabinets."

He frowns at me. "Why the hell would you do that for?"

"It's something to do, like I said."

"This ain't your house, little girl."

"Never said it was."

"That room is one thing, 'cuz you sleep there. But this is my kitchen, and what if I don't want my cupboards painted?"

I shrug again, leaning against the counter. He sits on a kitchen chair sideways, one elbow hooked over the back, and the sight startles me: Trent always used to do that. I have a brief flash of my brother in London, sitting on a chair like that, reading a paper. With my father clean shaven, I can even see a ghost of Trent in him.

"Thought you'd appreciate the help. You work so hard down at the shop, yeah?" I toss my hair and cringe inside because I know this is a tell of mine, flagging a bluff, a lie. But he doesn't know me well enough anymore to see my giveaways. And I've gotten better at not tipping my hand.

"Hmmph." He aims a finger at me, staring down the length of it like sighting a rifle. "You stay out of my room. I don't care if you want to play decorator everywhere else in my house, but don't you set one foot in my room."

I nod and try not to toss my hair, or exhale too hard, or even move.

"So what are your plans today?" I turn back to my can stacking.

An odor has begun to creep out of the pantry. I discover a bag of something that according to the label had once been potatoes. I retrieve a trash bag from under the sink and dispose of them, trying not to look disgusted.

"I dunno. I was supposed to spend the day with that bitch Sherry."

"What's her problem?" I risk stirring his ire out of curiosity.

"You know women. She thought I was looking funny at this other girl, and then I didn't call her right the damn minute I said I would. Shit, she ain't worth it. If I wanted to be nagged to death, I'd get married again. How come you never got married?"

"I'm not an old maid, yeah?"

"Old enough. You ain't queer, too, are you?"

"No."

"So what the hell is your problem?"

"Maybe I don't want to be nagged to death, either."

Done with the potatoes, I retrieve my plastic gloves and begin scrubbing the shelves. But having my head inside the pantry—my hearing and sight dulled from the box-like effect of the shelving— kicks up my adrenaline.

"Men don't nag," my dad says, raising his voice, either because he knows I can't hear or because he's getting worked up.

"Maybe I'm just a stupid bitch, then," I shout back. I can tell from the location of his voice that he has stood up. I will not give him the satisfaction of pulling my head out of here and turning around.

I will not.

I breathe deep to slow myself down, but the fumes from the Soft Scrub make me dizzy in this tiny space.

"You ain't stupid. No kid of mine is stupid."

My face safely hidden in the pantry, I can smirk openly at this.

"You had a fight with your boyfriend, I figure." He's very close now, within arm's reach, I'd say. "No other reason you'd be crawl-ing back here."

This makes me pause in my scrubbing. But I'm not even close to done yet, so I renew my effort with vigor, not answering.

"I'm gonna go work out downstairs," he tells me, and his voice retreats across the kitchen toward the basement steps. "Make me some lunch at noon. There's money on the table if we need gro-ceries."

When I can hear him clanking around the free weights, I with-draw my head from the pantry, glaring furiously at my stubbornly shaking hands.

He starts with the beer at lunch. I count during his sandwich: three. This is a speedy pace, even for him.

I can't say a rich folks' party is normally my favorite place, but tonight I much prefer the Becker manse to Chez Drayton. I think Anna made sure I was invited, because despite my distant-cousin relations with Amy Rickart, I don't think I'd be at the top of the guest list.

It takes me all afternoon, but I take everything out of the cup-boards and scrub until my fingers ache and my arms feel weak. By four o'clock, I wash down some Advil with a Diet Coke and admire my handiwork. The whole place smells vaguely of lemon, and the empty cupboards seem inviting, as if no one lives here anymore and they're waiting for a fresh start. Half the food should really be thrown away, as it's out of date, but I know what will happen if I start throwing away his food. Instead, I'll just inspect the labels when I cook and leave the oldest stuff at the back.

I spent my modest casino winnings on fresh white paint and new cupboard hardware almost as soon as I got back from the casino with Sally. It was exhilarating to win, and frightening, too, in the same sense of a near-miss on the highway.

And what if Sally hadn't gotten lost among the slot machines and had me paged while I was still ahead? I remember cursing when I heard the page and pounding the table with my fist, drawing startled glances from the other guys sitting at the table. The dealer eyed me curiously, drawing back slightly.

I was like a hungry dog, and someone was trying to take away my food.

A wave of disgust hits me, just as familiar as that buzzing high I got when I bellied up to the table. That's how it was, the whole time I was trying to get on top again when I was still with Steve: the lightheaded thrill followed by the crash when I realized I'd only dug in deeper.

All these years since my mom died I've hated my dad for his drinking, and then what do I go and do? Steal money from my boyfriend so I can keep gambling. And then just yesterday, I threw money on the table I didn't have to spare, because if I had even two months' rent for the smallest hovel in town I'd be gone, not to mention that I'm gonna pay Steve back no matter what he thinks of me.

Even with the intercom system calling my name at that casino, I almost anted up again anyway, but then Sally must have seized the intercom phone because her voice crackled over the speaker: "Hey, Cami! You didn't leave me, didja?" I wasn't sure, but she sounded slightly panicked. She was pacing like a zoo animal when I got to her at the courtesy desk.

That's why I spent that cash on the paint, so I wouldn't have it to gamble again. Then I cut up my ATM card. If I need cash, I'll go to the bank and get it out in the daylight, when I have to stand in line and think about it, and sign a paper to get it, just like they used to do in the old days, before punching buttons and swiping plastic.

Because if I can't stop myself from doing it again, even knowing what it costs me, I'm more like my father than I ever wanted to admit.

The front door slams open. Sherry charges in. "Where's your asshole father!"

I jerk a thumb toward the hall. "In his room."

My adrenaline revs up again. I had the feel for the afternoon, but Sherry changes things and I don't know exactly how.

Raised voices come from down the hall. I glance around the disheveled kitchen, but I think I'd better retreat to my room while the going's good.

Too late.

The two of them burst out of the room, looking for a moment like those old cartoons of the cats and dogs fighting so hard all you see is a cloud of flailing limbs.

I backpedal down the hall ahead of the maelstrom. They've got each other by the arms. If they weren't trying to kill each other, they could be square dancing.

Grab your partner by the throat . . .

We all scramble into the relative openness of the living room. This is when I notice something about Sherry: She's about half the size of my father.

I throw an arm in between, pulling on whatever I can grab of the pair of them until I find myself directly in the middle, like some kind of demented version of the children's game London Bridge. *My fair lady!* The kids shriek, and you're caught.

"Bitch, get outta my way!"

I tumble to the side, over a chair, onto something really hard and metal.

CHAPTER 28

Anna

I'D FORGOTTEN HOW SMALL THIS PLACE IS. NOT THE BECKER HOUSE, which lords over its front lawn. No, I mean Haven.

I park my car where everyone else did, along the huge circle drive, and begin trudging alone to the backyard. Haven isn't just physically small, but claustrophobic. Why else would I be attending the party of the family who wants to evict my mother and destroy the store she spent her life building? Because another son in the family happens to be my old friend and he's the only person I feel like seeing now. Not my mother, who is angry at me instead of at the man who left her. Not Sally, who grows more irritating by the day. And certainly not Paul Becker.

Shelby, back in Chicago, has started to feel like a mirage to me. So has Dorian, though once the mere mention of her name would make me work harder, longer, just to make sure to stay out ahead.

August is a dream. Nothing left of him at all.

Mr. Jenison was disgusted with me, I know, when I called to extend my leave. They weren't paying me anymore, he said, as if that would make me hasten back to my desk. He expected me to answer all e-mails from anyone at Miller Paulson promptly, because it wasn't easy picking up someone else's work.

He, too, mentioned the partner selection committee.

Before hanging up, he wished my mother a speedy recovery in a tone that revealed his doubt that my mother had so much as a hangnail.

I wonder if I can stretch the Family Medical Leave Act to my purposes. That would give me up to twelve weeks, though they'd deduct the weeks I've already been gone. Still, it would get me through the summer.

The first thing I notice when I walk through the garden archway is Beck's daughter, Madeline. She's whirling away on the grass with that abandon only children have, that innocent lack of self-consciousness. Or, if she's conscious of people watching her, she probably already knows how wonderful she looks. She has that kind of beauty. I glance around for her mother. Samantha is never far behind, to hear Beck tell it, always in Maddie's orbit. No sign of her, though. The party has a general watchfulness about it, with various adult heads turning at intervals to gaze at her and meet the eyes of the others: *She's just spinning; no danger right now.* No mother nearby, though. No Beck, either.

Something charging at me from my left gets my attention.

It's a chocolate brown dog galloping away, its tongue hanging out.

"Frodo!" shouts Amy, running up behind him. She seizes the dog's collar just as he leaps to either slobber me or eviscerate me. Probably slobber, given how his tail is wagging, and he's got one of those dopey-looking dog grins. Amy was knocked off stride by grabbing the dog, and she's bent over awkwardly now. She looks like she might saddle him up.

I put my hand down to let him snuffle me.

"I'm sorry," she pants. "I brought him because I hated to think of him locked up in the apartment all night with the fireworks, thinking he might be spooked—he's not crazy about thunder—only I'm having to grab him off people all the time. He already knocked over Maddie once."

I give Frodo's ears a scratch. "Oh, it's okay. As long as he's not going for the jugular, I don't mind. Go ahead and let go of him."

"You sure?"

"Sure. I like dogs, but a pet was out of the question for me with no yard or anything."

Our eyes meet briefly, and her expression is soft with understanding that hovers just above the point of pity.

Frodo jumps a couple times, but after sniffing me and being rewarded with the scratches, he bounds off in search of new friends to make. Amy watches him go.

"I'm sorry to horn in on your lunch the other day," Amy says, looking at me sideways, still watching her dog romp. Someone has produced a tennis ball and is throwing it. "They'll be throwing that ball all night now."

"You didn't horn in. It was just a lunch. We shouldn't have interrupted you, the lovebirds getting married."

"Yeah, well, it just seemed so rude to say, 'No, we don't want to sit by you.' "

"And yet that's what everybody wanted. Isn't that funny, how people can't say just what they want so they end up doing the exact opposite?"

"I don't know about that. I do what I want."

"Aside from awkward lunches."

"Well, maybe occasionally I endure something out of politeness, but in general I do live my life just the way I want."

I look carefully at her. She's wearing a candy-colored sundress, a fine gold chain, and her hair gleams in the angled late afternoon sun. "I'm glad for you, then."

I spot her trio of friends who were nasty to me at the engagement party, the ones with the snotty remarks about my SAT score. "What about them? Do you endure them out of politeness?"

Amy's mouth hardens into a thin line. "They're my friends. Don't talk crap about them."

"Do you have amnesia? They were awful to you in high school."

"We were all just kids then. Everyone's changed, don't you think? God, I hope so. I'd hate to be the same as I was at fifteen. And I'm not just talking about being fat."

"I do know what you mean. Where can a girl get a drink around here?"

She points me toward the bar on the patio and spies Frodo doing something naughty across the grass and goes scampering after him.

I wish Cami had come. She called my cell just as I was leaving, saying she had a terrible headache and couldn't get away. I offered to drive over with some intravenous morphine if I had to, but she chuckled and said she really needed to stay in.

I almost gave up on the party, but my mother about shoved me out the door, saying I needed to do something that resembled fun.

Now I just feel conspicuous. No date, no friend to stick by my side. Just the memory of Marc last year, when we were still together and he'd been watching kids tumble around on the grass at Grant Park.

"We'll make even cuter ones, don't you think?" he said, nudging me playfully.

For days afterward, whenever this conversation came up, he'd swear he didn't mean anything by that, and I'm the one who overreacted. He said I "hit the panic button at the mention of commitment to anything but the job."

I told him he was being such a girl about it and offered him a tampon. That didn't go over well.

Marc was not a direct guy by nature. He'd hint at something, sidle up to it, and try it out like tossing a baseball in his hand on the pitcher's mound. That's why I didn't believe that he was just kidding around.

Oh, here comes Beck. By now I've got my mojito, and my shoulders sag with relief that I won't have to stand so alone anymore. It's not the aloneness that bothers me—rather, the spotlight effect it creates in a party setting. Also, people will start whispering, if they haven't already: *Why is she still in town? Has she moved back for good? Did she lose her job?*

His face brightens as he approaches, and he greets me with a hug. It catches me by surprise, so I don't have time to move my glass out of the way; it gets squished between us. We share a chuckle over that.

"Maddie looks cute today," I tell him, gesturing toward her. She's now got a dandelion and she's plopped down in the grass, blowing fluff. Paul Becker is standing nearby, one eye on her and another on some city councilman. I look away from the pair of them.

"Yeah, Sam bought her that dress."

It's brown, pink, and white and makes Maddie look like Neapolitan ice cream.

"Where is Sam today? I haven't seen her."

"Ah. Well, she wanted to go visit her parents in Indiana for the Fourth. Maddie pitched a fit about going for that long drive and wanted to stay here, so . . ."

"Oh, well. I'm sure Sam will appreciate the break."

"You'd think that, wouldn't you?"

Maddie runs over to Beck, and he scoops her up in one arm. She nuzzles his shoulder and steals a shy look at me. That's when I notice her eyes are the same sea-glass green as her father's. I wave at her and she buries her face, then wiggles down and goes skipping off across the grass screaming, "Aunt Tabi! Aunt Tabi!"

"They change your life, don't they?" I say.

"Do they ever."

"Remember when we used to say we'd have five kids?"

"Three boys and two girls. You said you hated being an only child."

I stare out over the bluff at the sun sinking toward the water. We used to have those silly conversations on this lawn all the time, sprawled over each other on the grass, Beck toying with one of my curls. We used to talk longingly over how we could walk around naked if we wanted in our own house. Such glorious privacy, the holy grail of teenage lovers.

Beck clears his throat just as I'm wondering if he's having the same memories. "Is your . . . You hear anymore from your dad?"

I shake my head. "I'm not the one who heard from him in the first place, but no, I don't think so. I haven't seen any more letters, and Mom did promise. I'm so furious with him for toying with her like that." I grip my drink harder and take a long, cool sip. "If I could get my hands on him . . ."

"You probably could. Get your hands on him, I mean. Your mom knows where he is, right?"

"Where he was at the time, anyway. Who knows where he might be now?"

"At least you know he's still alive."

I turn fully away from Beck and walk a couple of steps toward the lake and away from this conversation. I never really figured he was dead, anyway, though I used to say so all the time. I can see now I was only trying to make myself feel better about his absence, as if he were on his way back to us and he got run over by a truck, only he didn't have his wallet so no one knew how to track down his survivors . . .

Beck says from behind me, "I'm sorry to bring it up."

"Don't be. I know you care, which is more than I can say for a lot of people."

"When are you going back, do you think?" Beck steps to my side but doesn't face me, joining me in staring out across the water.

"I haven't decided. I'm still worried about Mom and I extended my leave a bit."

"Good of them to do that for you."

"Mmm. They're not all that thrilled about it, but I've never asked them for any favors before. I think they're hoping I'll turn back into my old self." I smirk at this. "Back into a scullery maid when the spell wears off."

Beck drapes an arm across my shoulder. "So you're Cinderella, now?"

I step sideways out from under his arm. "Hardly. I, um, I'd better go, and . . . I have to talk to Amy. I'll see you later."

I walk backward for a few steps before I turn around and head toward the crowd, feeling uncomfortably hot, though the breeze has taken the heat out of the air.

After an hour of drifting around the edges of things, shaking hands and enduring small talk with three or four people and not-at-all-subtle inquiries as to whether I'd lost my Chicago job, I'm ready to get home, screw the fireworks. Beck seems to always be in my peripheral vision and I keep meeting his eyes, and I'm all too aware of all the other eyes at this party.

I'm heading to my car when I bump into those three girls again, the supposed new friends of Amy Rickart.

They fill my ear with bridesmaid chatter, and I don't try to hide how bored I am. The last wedding I celebrated was my coworker David's. He flew to Vegas with his girlfriend, got married, came back, and got his closest friends drunk over tapas and sangria at their new apartment.

"Saw you talking to Will Becker," Nikki says.

"Yep."

"Must be nice, catching up with an old flame."

"It was a pleasant conversation."

The other two girls watch with naked greed in their eyes, so I change the subject, interrupting Sarah, whose mouth is open to say something else.

"Amy looks wonderful," I say, nodding to where she's standing next to her mother.

"She does," chirps Kristi. "It's amazing that she ran all that weight off. Too bad her mother can't do it."

"Oh, yeah, running is great. You should try it, Anna. It's really amazing."

"Try what?"

"Running. It takes the weight right off."

I pivot on my heel and turn back away from them, those idiot magpies standing between me and my car. One of them calls something after me and I fold my arms, pinning my hands to my side with my elbows, to keep from flipping them the bird.

I take the wooden steps down to the Beckers' private beach, enjoying the sound of my shoes smacking against the hard wood. At the bottom, I don't get the privacy I was hoping for.

The partygoers have begun to filter down here, spreading out blankets preparing for the small private fireworks show that will start just after dusk. But I don't see Beck, or his brother, or anyone else annoying, so I stand apart from them at the water's edge. I slide my feet out of my shoes, drop my handbag, and curl my toes in the warm sand. The dune hugs this stretch of shore close, keeping the wind at bay, pulsing with the warmth of the day's sun.

The lake's motion is soothing and steady, though strong. I step into the lake, just far enough that the waves won't soak my knee-length skirt. The undertow sucks the sand from around my feet and I sink farther in, feeling rooted. It's an illusion, though. I can pull away anytime.

Something gold catches my eye. Gold in the lake?

I stride into the water and then push off from the bottom in a surface dive. I pull the water toward me until I reach the swirling gold and pull Madeline up by her tiny torso. I flip onto my back to kick us back to shore, arm tucked around her chest. There is screaming from the beach, but silence from the little girl.

CHAPTER 29

Maeve

IT'S HARD, SOMETIMES, NOT TO HATE THE CUSTOMERS.

They don't see you, for one thing. Most of them. Their eyes are on their purchases, their wallets, their money, their kids, and even more these days, their cell phones. I used to fold my arms and wait for a customer to finish talking before I would ring up their items, instead of being made to feel like an intruder on this critically important phone call they can't stop having for five seconds, long enough to meet my eye and hear me say, "Have a good day."

But after I spent too many transactions standing there like a servant waiting for orders and endured too many disgusted sneers when they finally caught on to what I was waiting for, I gave up my one-woman crusade and just took my revenge out in little ways, like stacking their tin cans on top of their bread.

Holidays are the worst. Lots of people work holidays, people with important jobs, like doctors and police officers, saving our lives no matter how much fun everyone else is having. But for me and all the other service-industry types, we live to serve someone else's fun.

I can't count how many years it's been since I've seen fireworks. For that matter, even been to the beach, though I can see it from my front door.

"That'll be $12.32," I tell the woman who has come in for sunscreen. She snorts at the price tag, then at me. I argue in my head, *I've got overhead, you know, and bills to pay.*

Today would be a great day for the beach, nice and warm, a breeze to keep you from sweating too hard. The water has warmed up at last, enough to make a swim merely bracing instead of heart-attack cold.

My hands fly over the keys on auto pilot, the customers blurring together.

I remember Robert on a hot day like this, just twenty-three years old, hair coffee black, with that crooked smile.

We'd stolen away to Crescent Beach, an isolated sliver of sand that only the locals could find because it was hidden down a winding path of streets with no signs to indicate its presence.

My mother knew I was going to see Robert and ordered me to put something on my shoulders. It was 1975, but the sexual revolution mattered not at all to Mrs. Callahan, and I was not going out with bare shoulders to meet the likes of him.

I still had the sweater draped over me, cape-fashion, staring up at Robert in the sun, as we paused during a walk on the beach. I was dizzy with the heat and with his nearness.

"Baby, look at you. It's too hot for that sweater." Robert looked down at me, eclipsing the sun, which shone so bright around him I could barely see his face. With one thumb, he nudged the sweater off my shoulder. I made to pick it up, but with the slightest pressure, he stopped me.

"It's only sand," he said. "It'll wash."

I felt no cooler. I'd barely eaten after fighting with my mother about going out at all. The emptiness in my stomach spread to my limbs, to my head, and I felt like all my air was gone and I really needed to sit down . . .

Next thing I knew, I was stretched out on cool sand under a stand of trees at the far edge of the beach, something cold and wet on my forehead. Robert was lying next to me, shirtless, one arm supporting my head like a pillow. He must have used his shirt to stroke my head with cool water. I snuck a look around to see if anyone was nearby enough to see us.

"You scared me half to death," Robert said, but he was smiling and not looking very scared. "You okay?"

I sipped the shady air and tried to play it cool, like the sophisticated woman a man like him should have, not some swoony kid. I tried to sit up, but Robert pressed me gently back down, to rest, he said.

"I just got too hot, too hungry," I said. "No big deal . . ."

"I didn't know that, though." He gave me that sideways grin of his. "For all I knew, you were afflicted with a rare teenage heart attack."

"Oh, shut up."

"No, I'm serious. I thought, *This girl could die right here and I never made love to her.*"

I put my hand to my chest, my heart stopping, then barreling off like a sprinter at the starting gun. He slowly withdrew his supporting arm from under my head until I was lying properly flat. I might have fainted again, if I'd been standing.

He kissed me. We'd kissed before, even engaged in some light petting, but we'd never been horizontal, in broad daylight, with an item of clothing already removed. I pushed against his chest, just gently, thinking we were going too far, but he just kissed harder, and I kissed back myself, turning that push into my own caress.

Then I felt his hand on my breast, and I gasped, scrambling backward away from him like a crab.

Robert gulped hard but made no move to come after me or coax me back. "I'm sorry. You're just . . . You're a good girl, aren't you, Maeve Callahan?" His voice was raspy.

He was going to break up with me and return to his worldly girls who would make love to him anywhere, anytime. I hated my virtue suddenly, so out of place and even freakish, and what good did it do me after all?

He looked down at the sand, and then back up to me, his face solemn. "Well then, I have no choice in the matter."

He scooted forward on the sand in a seated position and took my hand. I was losing him. The love would never go away, though; I believed that. It was far too powerful to simply wink out like a candle flame.

"Maeve, my good girl, marry me."

"What?"

His eyes twinkled. "You heard what. Marry me. I love you, I want you, I don't want anybody else, and we're old enough. I believe that means I should marry you."

My breath caught in my throat, so I could only nod, and when he folded me close, I soaked his bare chest with my tears.

I made him promise to buy me an engagement ring and told him we'd keep our engagement secret until he did—that way maybe it would look better to my parents. And it might have stayed secret, but one of the times I fought with my mother over him, when she insisted he was a Don Juan and had other girls on the side and would dump me any minute, I screamed, "He's going to marry me!"

My mother's face contorted into an exaggerated wounded expression and stayed that way until she died and the mortician rearranged her face.

Robert's father eventually paid for the ring, which Robert swore to pay him back for. I don't believe he ever did. I loved him too much to care about any old ring, or who paid for it, though I admit the town gossip was hard to hear.

It was gossip that made me start wearing it inside my shirt, come to think of it. I overheard someone in Clawson's Drugs talking about how they saw me in the store still wearing my ring, "pining after her runaway husband, so sad."

I wasn't pining. I'm not pining, now. But is it so wrong to have a little hope?

Carla jostles me out of my daydream by asking for a Lotto ticket. "Easy Pick," she says, dropping her huge satchel on the counter.

At dusk, the customers stop coming in. By now they're all arrayed on blankets on the beach or maybe on condominium balconies. Anna is at the Becker house. Is she talking to Will? I wonder. Or hanging out with Amy? Likely not Amy; she'd be too close to Paul. I hope she's having a little fun. At least she's outside the store. She's been getting too comfortable here.

I prop open the Nee Nance front door and face the lake, standing in the doorway. The dusk is cool and there's a light breeze, like a sigh of relief that the heat of July has burned away. From here I can just about see the rows of heads facing the water.

Robert and I used to alternate taking Anna to the beach on the Fourth of July, to stake out a good spot. Then, as soon as customers stopped streaming in, the other one of us would sprint to the lake and search the towels for redheaded Anna. Our little girl would hold her ears closed against the bangs, but her face would be bright with joy at the burning sparks lighting up the sky.

Then, when Robert left, I had to stay and run things. Sally would sometimes help, but even back then, the register drawer was a mess when she was done with it. I just couldn't close the store during those pre-dusk hours, though. I made too much money. Sometimes Anna would go with a friend; sometimes she'd stay with me and, like I'm doing right now, we'd stand in the doorway and watch from here, though the downtown buildings obscure some of the display. Then we'd step back through the door and talk about how everyone else had to fight traffic; weren't we lucky to already be home?

Lucky us.

Then she got to be a teenager and fell in love with Will, and his parents, too, for that matter, and she spent nearly every holiday with them.

I tried not to mind, because she was enjoying herself, at least.

The crowd cheers as the first lights spark to life. Somewhere, a sound system is playing Sousa marches. Next year Robert could be with me again, and we'll be rid of this lousy store, watching the fireworks in some quaint northern town before retreating to our own actual house.

Inside, between bangs, I hear the Nee Nance phone ring. I ignore it and it stops. Minutes later it starts up again, and this time I run to it.

CHAPTER 30

Anna

I'M ON MY HANDS AND KNEES WHISPERING *HAIL MARY, FULL OF grace* . . .

I started CPR, but a doctor from the crowd rushed to her, elbowing me aside. Now I crouch, shivering, whispering the only prayer I can think of as he grunts over Maddie, still and white on the sand. The party crowd stands in a gaping horseshoe around us, their faces forming a wall of shock: all mouths open, hands over their faces.

Over the doctor's noises and the relentless splashing of the lake, I try to silence my own ragged breathing to listen for sounds from that little girl.

Hail Mary, full of grace . . .

And then sounds come. A cough, then more coughing, and a vomiting sound, and a wail that's heartbreaking and beautiful because it's human and alive. I drop my head on the sand and breathe: *Thank you.*

Now I hear pounding on the wooden stairs, fast and uneven; they're skipping several steps. I look up to see Beck, wild in his running, his parents behind with blankets, all their faces pulled tight with fear.

I pull up to my feet, my body aching with cold and effort and tension.

The wailing continues from Madeline as the adults bundle her and Beck cradles her, soothing, yet crying himself. I can see him shaking, even at a distance, and watching him I feel just a taste of his fear, and I feel faint with it.

Beck and his family move up the steps still urgently, but now smoothly and with care. A siren grows louder as it nears the top of the hill.

Beck and his parents have gone to the hospital, where they must have called Samantha, and here in a guest bed in the Becker house, I clench my eyes tight against imagining what it would be like to get that call.

Beck's sister, Tabitha, finally noticed me, shivering on the sand. She thanked me in such a formal and serious way it was hard to imagine she was once the dorky kid in spectacles we all called Tabby Cat. She attended to my practical needs by leading me to the guest room with an adjacent shower, sink, and bathrobes. As always, it was stocked with soap and shampoo, in both manly, spicy scents and girly, fruity stuff. This is a family who attends to details. How do they miss a little girl walking into a lake?

Of course, I missed it, too. Some lifeguard I turned out to be.

I pull the bathrobe closer on my body, hugging a pillow and staring at the dark window, trying not to think about all the times Beck and I had sex in this room when his parents were out of the house. It felt risky doing it at home, but it wasn't, really, not with

the door locked, and the house was so big that by the time someone walked throug the huge, creaky front door and came upstairs,
there was ample time to scramble our clothes back on and dash out
into public spaces again.

Tabitha tossed my clothes in the dryer and promised to bring
them back, but that was ages ago. Also, I don't know where my
purse is, which has my car keys in it. I've been forgotten in all the
commotion. I can go traipsing through the house in a bathrobe and
a smile or hope someone remembers me.

I'm too tired to go home anyway right now.

I can't stop picturing Madeline's face. She didn't look asleep
or romantically unconscious the way people do on TV. She just
looked dead.

How long had I been staring at the water before I saw her? Had
she been on the beach when I first came down?

I see her limp whiteness in my memory again and sit up, gulp-
ing water from the glass on the nightstand. Then I stagger to the
bathroom and retch the water into the white marble sink.

The party was cancelled, but the city-operated fireworks carried on, and now, partyers out there are setting off firecrackers and
sparklers, and the pops and bangs filter in here. Don't they understand a near tragedy has taken place? Of course not. But there are
always tragedies, somewhere.

I flip off the lamplight. Surely the Beckers won't mind if I rest
a little while longer.

"Anna?"

I fumble until I find a nightstand, a lamp. The room comes into
view and it all hits me: Madeline, the water . . .

Beck.

He's standing just inside the door, looking like he hasn't slept
in a week.

"Is she okay?"

He closes the door and comes fully into the room. I sit up and swing my legs out of the bed.

"Yes, thank God. The doctors think she's going to be fine, but they're keeping her overnight. Sam is with her now; she must have been doing a hundred miles an hour all the way from Indiana."

I glance at a digital clock on the nightstand, which reads 1:37 a.m. "Oh, Jesus. I'm so sorry to still be here. I was just resting . . ."

"Don't be sorry. My God, if there's anything . . . I mean, a place to rest for a few hours is the least of what we could offer you, considering."

Beck sits on the other side of the double bed. His hair stands up, probably from being raked through with his fingers. Stubble is growing in, and his eyes are watery and shot through with cracks of red.

"I don't know how it happened," he says, looking down into his lap. "I could have sworn I saw her just a minute before, and the whole family was there, and I thought we were, I mean, I thought someone was watching . . ."

He chokes on the words and pushes his palms into his eyes, curling himself over.

I cinch my robe tighter and arrange the neck for maximum coverage and join him on the other side of the bed. I put one arm around him, feeling him tremble. I squeeze tight, trying to stop the shaking.

He gulps out, "What if you hadn't . . ."

"But I did. She's okay. Don't do this to yourself. No one can watch a child every minute."

"Samantha does. She would have. She . . ." He gasps and lets the air out in a shuddery exhale. "She said it's all my fault."

With this, he turns to me, staring into my eyes for a moment.

Then he leans forward, resting his forehead on mine. He closes his eyes.

For a moment or two, we stay like that, just silent. Then he moves his hands to my shoulders. He pulls me forward, so gently it seems that I imagined it, until his lips press down on mine.

We push aside each other's clothing with the practiced ease. I allow myself to tip back on the bed with him, almost weeping that his touch is tender as it ever was.

The shame creeps up on me, like lengthening late-day shadows.

My limbs entwine with his, in that old familiar way they have, like there are Beck-shaped grooves on my calves, arms. We haven't yet spoken.

I'm suddenly uncomfortable, despite the pleasing warmth of Beck's body and its familiar contours.

I jerk myself straight up.

"This was a terrible mistake." My quiet words seem to blare across the silence. I yank on the robe and my hands shake like an old drunk's as I fumble with the tie. "Get dressed," I hiss at Beck. "Get up."

Beck pulls himself upright but makes no move toward his clothes.

"Beck, please! What if your sister remembers I'm in here? She was supposed to bring back my clothes."

"She's not here. No one's home but Mom and Dad, and they're asleep."

"Where did she go?"

"She was going to stop at the hospital, then go to her boyfriend's house."

"Beck, for the love of God, put your clothes on; smooth the bed. I'm going to have a panic attack. I'm going to jump out this window unless we look presentable in the next forty-five seconds."

Beck sighs and gathers his clothes, stepping past me into the adjoining bathroom. I make the bed again, smooth it taut, then remember I'd been sleeping in it. I climb back in, wrinkle up one side, and get back out again.

Now Beck emerges, still looking like hell but dressed, his face unnaturally flushed. Now, his presence can be explained. He could be just saying thank you.

I drop onto a bench at the end of the bed, my head in my hands. "This is by far the worst thing I've ever done."

"It wasn't just you." Beck's voice is effortful and gravelly.

"I'm sure that will make your wife feel a whole lot better."

"She's not going to find out. I'm certainly not going to tell her."

"I should have known better."

"So should I."

"Well, yes, now that you mention it." I glare at him through a tangled curl. He joins me on the bench. "What the hell was that for?"

"It's not working out with Sam, I told you that. The fight before she left for Indiana was a little more serious than I let on. We are— well, we were, at least—going to be separating."

"That doesn't make this okay." He puts his hand on my knee, and I walk away from him to the window. All I can see outside is blackness. The lake is indistinguishable from the sky. "And you can't separate now. Not like this."

"We'll wait a decent interval. Make sure Maddie really is okay."

"How okay is she going to be? First, she almost . . . Then her parents split up. I can't be responsible for that. I went through that. I won't do that to somebody else."

"I'm not like your father! I wouldn't leave her forever. This is different. I'm telling you, we were on the rocks anyway."

"So, if I hadn't come back, you would have left your wife and come to Chicago to be with me."

Silence.

"Beck, go find my clothes. They're in the dryer."

"Anna, I—"

"Just find my clothes. I'm calling a cab. And where the hell is my purse?"

I cut off anything else he might say by grabbing the bedside phone and barking orders at the Information operator. I turn my back to him as he slips out of the room.

CHAPTER 31

Maeve

MY HANDS SHAKE ON THE STEERING WHEEL, PARTLY OUT OF RELIEF that the call wasn't about Anna, partly with anger at my dimwit, irresponsible, chain-smoking sister-in-law, who nearly torched herself.

As it was, it was only her trailer that went up like a Roman candle.

That wrinkled old ninny fell asleep with her cigarette dangling out of her hand, most likely over the side of the bed, so it dropped on some garbage on the floor, as opposed to right on her bed sheets.

Then, Anna still hasn't come home and isn't answering her cell phone. I've heard her curt, cool voice mail message—"This is Anna Geneva. Leave a message"—ten times now, so I've stopped bothering. She'll call when she can.

If she can.

No, stop. The universe would not do that to me, not on the same night. She's just late, out having fun, not hearing the phone ring.

The hospital looks disgustingly cheerful, all lit up and bright.

A weary woman at the information desk tells me where to find Sally, and as I shuffle off in that direction, another memory overtakes me, of that time Robert piled the car into a utility pole.

I'd had to roust Anna out of bed. She was only four years old. The poor babe was rubbing her eyes against the harsh light and drowsing on my shoulder as I talked to the doctor, wanting to brain Robert with an IV pole. He wasn't seriously hurt and had the nerve to smile. Anna reached out for her daddy once she woke up enough to see something was wrong. After being reassured his "owies" would go away, she cuddled up next to him in the hospital bed. Robert sang her a silly song of his own invention. I can still hear him, in his whispery tenor.

> Anna my banana, how I love my girl,
> Anna my banana, every freckle and curl,
> Anna my banana, won't you always stay with me?
> Anna my banana, I love you, can't you see?

How could the same man who sang nonsense love songs to his little girl then disappear on us just six years later?

If he would only write back like he promised, maybe I'd at last find out the reason, and if there's a reason—there has to be—there can be forgiveness, eventually.

I turn the corner to see Sally in her room. Her wig is off and her short gray hair is smashed flat like a worn shag carpet. Her face still looks a little sooty, though someone has wiped it partway clean. She plucks off an oxygen mask to greet me. Her usual cockeyed smile is gone as she says, "I know you always told me not to smoke in bed, but honest, I didn't fall asleep, I promise."

I don't bother arguing with her. What difference does it make now?

Now that it seems clear she will survive, another reality smacks into me like a wrecking ball. Sally has no place to live. The Nee Nance just got more crowded.

I confer with the doctor and promise to retrieve her tomorrow and help deal with the paperwork. With that, I am dismissed to go home.

Robert has never asked about his sister in the letters. Maybe he figures that Sally moved on with her life. Will he be delighted or dismayed to find out she's still hanging around? I'll wait until I see him to broach that one.

But she is not moving in with Robert and me. I don't care if we have to build her another trailer with our own bare hands.

After I drag myself to bed and fall into an uneven, unsatisfying sleep, I jolt awake at the ringing buzzer for the front door. I pull on my old robe and fly down the stairs barefoot. I peer through a small window in the door.

Anna stands in the circle of weak yellow light cast by the bulb under the awning. In the seconds while I fumble to open the door, I scan her for signs of trauma. She seems intact, but her posture is hunched and she's hugging herself, like she's afraid she might fly apart otherwise.

"What's wrong?" I say. "Where's your car? Your purse? Oh, God, were you mugged?"

Anna lets out a heavy sigh. "You've got to be kidding."

"What is it?"

"I'm sorry to have to wake you up. I lost my purse and had to take a cab home. I'm sure they'll find it in the morning, and I'll get my car later."

I wonder why she didn't just stay there, in one of their gajillion rooms, rather than take a taxicab without her purse and wake me up in the middle of the night. Who paid for the cab? And for that matter, why is she home so late? Why couldn't one of the Beckers have brought her home hours ago? Not that I mind being awakened; now I know she's safe.

If she lost her purse with her phone in it, that explains why she didn't get my calls.

"Honey, I should tell you that Sally is in the hospital. Her trailer burned down. No serious injury, just smoke inhalation. Actually, the way she packs away the cigarettes, her lungs are probably better tonight than they are most nights, since she's not allowed to smoke there."

Anna leans against the newspaper rack and steps out of her shoes. "I assume the trailer is a loss."

"I assume so, too."

"Shit."

"You said it."

Anna curves over slowly to pick up her shoes, as if every muscle aches. "Where is she going to go?"

"Where else? The Nee Nance, home of the Wayward Genevas."

Anna gazes around the darkened store. "Where the hell are we going to put her?"

"I know. Where the hell, indeed."

CHAPTER 32

Cami

I'M NOT MUCH FOR MAKEUP, BUT THEN, I DON'T NORMALLY HAVE a shiner, and I just know what everyone's going to think the minute they look at me—that is, everyone who knows my dad.

I squint into a mirror on the back of my closet door and slather another layer on. It looks cakey and orange, but from a distance you probably can't tell.

My plan A of staying inside until it healed has derailed. Anna called to say she needs me, so does Maeve, at the store, and besides all that, the sounds of Sherry and my dad making love like wildcats is worse than the fighting. At least, I assume that's what they're doing in there.

I already know Anna won't believe what really happened, but she's a lawyer and has spent a career trying to pin down weaselly liars. I suppose that will predispose a person to be cynical about the honesty level of the general public.

But he didn't hit me, beat me, or do anything that dramatic. I just had to play Supergirl and defend the scrawny, drunk skank who was about to be throttled by my dad. I got in the way, is all, and those dumb tin cans were still all over the kitchen, and that part was *my* fault.

I blacked out for a second or a minute, I'm not sure, and when I opened my eyes, Sherry was screeching that I was dead and my dad was screaming at Sherry, blaming her for my fall. I laughed; they were so concerned about who was going to get blamed for murdering me. Manslaughtering me, I guess, would be more likely.

I don't know why that was funny. Probably because I'm a sick individual.

My dad startled when he heard me laugh and yelled at me, "You think this is funny?" as if I'd arranged to knock myself unconscious as some kind of practical joke.

Sherry interrupted him by saying I'd gotten "knocked silly" and we should be glad I'm not dead. Real sweet of her, though she didn't offer to help me up. I was wobbling all over the place, trying to pull myself upright again while they carried on arguing. I got my own bag of ice and a roll of paper towels for stanching my head wound.

Well. That's as good as my face is going to look. If only I had time to buy a hat before I meet Anna. I'd love to buy some huge Jackie O sunglasses, too, only I need to wear my eyeglasses, which are fashionably taped together, since my fall cracked one stem.

I make a pucker face in the mirror. Yeah. Sexy.

Anna called my cell this morning with her voice barely under control, and that right there got my attention. She said her aunt's trailer burned down and she wanted some company while she went to go check the wreckage for anything she could salvage.

I think something else is up, though. Clinical, collected Anna wouldn't be that shaky over her aunt's knickknacks.

She's going to pick me up at the corner in her mom's Buick. She said something else about her car I didn't quite catch.

I heave open my bedroom window. I lift out the screen and slide it between my headboard and the wall. I sit on the sill, swing my legs out, and drop myself to the muddy strip of dirt that used to be a garden.

I prefer the escape route to the front door and the risk of being interrogated by my father and Sherry, who seem to be extending their Fourth of July to the fifth as well, never mind opening up the shop. With luck, when I come back, they'll be sleeping or my dad will finally have gone to work.

My head throbs. I forgot to bring my Motrin.

The first thing I notice in Anna's car is that my black eye is on the opposite side of the car from her, so this delays any interrogating from the attorney-at-law. Stealing a glance at her as she pulls away from the curb, I see she's so pale the veins in her cheek appear ghostly and blue.

"Thanks for coming," she says.

"What are friends for, yeah?"

She doesn't respond, steering the car out of Haven to the two-lane state highway.

"How was the party?"

She shifts in her seat, checking over her shoulder, though she's not changing lanes or anything. "It was . . . Well, I've had better nights."

Her face tenses up as she clenches her jaw. I turn away and watch road signs click by until we turn onto a gravel road.

We both take the Lord's name in vain as we pull up to what used to be Sally's home.

To call it rubble would be charitable. The acrid stench of melted plastic hangs in the air. There's nothing here but a scattered pile of charcoal. Sally was lucky to get out of there alive. Considering she lives out in the sticks on a patch of someone else's property, the volunteer firefighters probably took some time to get here.

Not even Sally's car survived. The fire ate that up, too, via the attached carport. I can't even tell what kind of car it used to be.

The Buick chimes *ding, ding, ding*, reminding us we're standing there with the doors open. I slam mine, and Anna pushes hers shut listlessly.

I wonder if Sally has keepsakes. Sure, she probably does; everyone does.

"Was she insured?"

Anna shakes her head, eyes riveted to the wreckage.

"Where is she going to live?"

Anna leans one hip against the side of the car. "We'll lay her out on top of the beer cooler or something, I guess." She looks down, and her curls hang between us.

I come around to join her at the driver's side, putting myself between her and the fire scene. "What's wrong?"

She raises her face to me, then puts her hand to her mouth. "Oh, my God, he hit you!"

Shit. For a second there I forgot about my prizefighter face.

"I knew you were going to think that, but no. I fell."

"Sure, you fell."

"Don't start, yeah? I fell. He and Sherry were fighting and I got caught in the middle. I mean, I stupidly put myself in the middle."

"You really just fell."

"Don't cross-examine me."

"I hate it when people say that to me, you don't know how much."

I look her straight in her eyes, which I see now are red-rimmed and tired. "I swear to you. I only fell."

"This is still not good. If your father and . . . who? Sherry? whoever, are fighting violently, you should get out of there."

"We're not talking about me, now. Something's wrong. Now, what?"

"Cami—"

I hold up a hand. "No. Subject closed."

She walks a few steps away, staring into the green woods around the trailer. "It's petty, now. Forget it."

I walk to her side, keeping far enough away she doesn't feel under siege. "Don't do that. Don't play the 'your problems are worse than mine' thing, because people did that after my mom died, and you know what it meant? No one ever talked to me again. Girls didn't complain to me about their own moms being mean, or about their divorced parents, or their bad hair days. And because they couldn't do that they never invited me anywhere, and you know what? Having a dead mom and no friends was worse than listening to other people's problems."

"You might hate me."

"Try me."

Her answer comes out as a whisper.

"Come again?"

"I slept with Beck."

This startles me so much I take a step back. Miss Superstar Honor Roll sleeping with a married man. But even Anna Geneva has her days, it seems.

"Well, you seem pretty sorry about it."

She laughs with no mirth. "You could say that."

"How did . . . How did that come about, even?"

She folds her arms tight as she tells me about rescuing his daughter, Beck's admission that he and his wife were splitting, how he turned to her for comfort and kissed her, and from then it was one escalation after another with neither of them thinking at all.

"We just picked it up again like an old habit. It's probably what alcoholics feel like when they fall off the wagon. I can't say what he felt, I guess, but I know I didn't think a bit because if I had . . . But I suppose I had to willfully shut it off, didn't

I? Somehow I shut off the part of my brain that knew it was wrong."

"Look, nobody's perfect. It was a mistake, and it wasn't just your mistake. He's the one who should have been thinking of his wife, yeah? He didn't have to come to the guest room that night; he could have waited to talk to you in the morning. And you said you did a terrible thing, but you saved a girl's life. That's not nothing."

"No."

She's not at all mollified by that. She's got a mental report card and has given herself an F in sexual morality.

"What are you going to do?"

She shrugs. "I'm not going to see him. I'm going to stay as far away as I can."

"Chicago is pretty far."

She tips her chin up and gazes up at the treetops. "Yes, it is."

After a moment, it seems our talk is over and I start back to the car.

Anna stops me by saying, "I don't know if I'm going back."

"Ah."

"I can't give you, myself, anyone, a good answer for it. Beck told me the other day that if something feels hollow I shouldn't keep doing it, just because I always have."

"He's right about that. Life's too short, yeah? Like that quote Amy gave us."

"But I did imagine life as an attorney. I've gotten everything I ever wanted."

"And you don't want it now?"

She scowls at the ground. "Stupid. I'm sure it's just a phase. I mean, God, my student loans, all that work, those hours I put in at Miller Paulson? I'm just having a childish midlife crisis."

"Yeah. But . . ."

"But every time I think of going back, I get this crushing weight on my chest."

"So what's the other plan?"

"I've gotta help my mom figure out something. I can do that best from here. I think I've got a plan that will work, at least for a while, until we can find her another job. I just can't bear to think of her tossed out on the street with nothing and no job, having to stand there with her hat in her hand in line at some grim government office."

"What about after you get her settled?"

"I don't know." She shakes her head. "It's the most curious thing. All my life I've known every single step I would take, and I've always done it. For the first time in my life I think of my future and it's a blank."

"Hmmm." I know the blank feeling. But then, I've never known any different. "So, are you quitting for sure?"

"I can't imagine that phone call, either, to my boss." She laughs, but her face is clouded, her eyes narrow. "Maybe I'll just stand here until I rot."

"By the way, what happened to your car?"

"Oh, that. Shit. It's at the Becker house. I lost my purse doing my lifeguard thing, and I took a cab rather than let Beck drive me home. I suppose I'd better find it."

Anna starts back toward the Buick, barely picking up her feet, kicking up clods of dirt in the process. "Hey, if you need a place to stay, we'll figure something out. A cot in my room or something, anything. You've gotta be safe, you know." She cocks an eyebrow at me over the top of the car. "You've gotta watch your own back because no one else will do it for you."

CHAPTER 33

Anna

IT TAKES SOME TIME TO DRIVE BACK TO TOWN. VACATIONERS ARE out in abundance now, and traffic meanders along as if everyone's got all the time in the world.

Cami insists I drop her off at the same corner where I picked her up, saying, "I'll be fine, yeah?" She strolls down the street toward that house—can't really call it a home, considering—with one hand in her pocket.

I don't believe Cami for a second about her black eye. But I also know that you can't make someone help herself. There was this attorney, back when I first started at Miller Paulson, who was really bright and quick on his feet.

He was also a drunk. He'd come in reeking of booze, probably still from the night before. Sometimes, we'd see him sober, and he'd be dazzling and brilliant and charming. He'd go out at lunch for a refresher. We sent him notes, letting him know we noticed. A few of us confronted him late one night in the office and he got so angry he threw a stapler.

Three weeks later he was gone, his cube empty and his desk cleaned out. No one had to ask what happened.

Shelby had been so angry with him, furious that her attempts to help him had been rebuffed. I shrugged and reminded myself that each person is responsible for his or her own actions.

You just can't save people. You can spread out the safety net, but they have to jump into it.

I come through the Nee Nance's propped-open front door, and I stop short.

Beck is at the counter, talking to my mother. My purse is between them.

Immediately, in my mind, we're naked in the guest bed, and I can't stop the hot flush sweeping over my face. He glances away from me, looking pink at the tops of his ears, and then meets my eyes, leaning on the counter with one hip. He's trying so hard to look casual.

I don't look at my mother. I don't want to know what she makes of this.

"I've brought your purse," Beck says. "And I drove your car. I'll get a ride back from my dad later."

"I can't believe you're thinking of my car now. I'd think you'd want to be with Madeline."

My mother interjects, "For heaven's sake, come in out of the doorway."

I walk in all the way, careful not to stand too close.

Beck clears his throat. "Samantha is at the hospital now, getting ready to bring Maddie home. She, uh, she doesn't want me around right now."

Mom pats Beck's arm. "She's probably a mess. She'll calm down later, I'm sure." Mom turns to me. "Beck told me about last night."

For a crazy half second I think she means the sex.

"Why didn't you tell me you saved her life?"

"I didn't want to talk about it. And I still don't, actually."

"I won't press you, honey. I'm very proud, though." At this, my mother comes around and hugs me hard. I fight not to push her off me.

"What's to be proud of? I mean, who would do any different? And I was a lifeguard. Actually, I'm kicking myself for not noticing earlier."

Beck croaks out, "You're not the one who was supposed to notice."

My mother releases me and gives him a kind smile. She should have had more children; she's brimming over with kindness.

She says, "Why don't you drive Beck home?"

I shoot him a look and try not to seem alarmed. He says, "No, really, it's fine, my dad can take me home . . ."

"Well, you said he'd drive you later, but Anna can take you now. You should be at home as soon as possible to see your daughter. Even if your wife is upset now, your little girl will want to see you."

Neither of us can dispute the simple logic in this. In fact, the way my mother has framed it, I'd be a cretin to refuse.

"Well, then," I scoop up my purse. "Let's get you home."

I can drive this route in my sleep. Everything here in Haven has clicked back into place. The cash register keys, where Mom keeps the register tape, all my old driving routes . . .

Sex with Beck.

I shake off the thought, trying not to look at him in my passenger seat.

I hope to God Samantha isn't home when I drop him off. I am absolutely not coming in.

The drive is uncomfortably long. The Beckers live on the outskirts, where the properties are bigger, separated by acres of velvety lawn.

"So now what?" Beck says.

I keep my eyes on the road. "There is no 'now what.' Now you go back to living your life."

"And you go back to Chicago?"

"Yes."

This is a lie, or, at least, I don't know if it's true.

"I wish . . ." He pauses. "I wish you wouldn't."

I miss the turnoff. "Damn." I check over my shoulder for traffic and turn into a driveway. "Beck, you know last night didn't mean a thing. Nothing. We were together a hundred years ago when we were kids and fell into an old habit in a moment of stress." I finally cut my eyes over to him before backing out onto the blacktop and shifting into drive. "Don't get any romantic notions. I don't love you." I punch the accelerator a little too hard. "Not even close."

He braces himself on the dash. "Bullshit. You didn't change that much, Annie."

"You don't know me anymore."

"I think I'm the only one who does know you, actually."

"Oh, really?"

"I know you're lying about going to back to Chicago."

I squeeze the steering wheel and drive a little faster.

"Anna?" he says. He reaches out to touch me and I slap his hand away. I refuse to speak to him for the rest of the drive.

When I walk into the store, I see four guys wrestling a cot up the narrow stairs. Randy is among them, I see, and Mailman Al in his postal shorts.

My mom points at the men with her Diet Coke bottle. "We'll put Sally in with me. I can squeeze the cot at the foot of my bed, T-shaped."

"She should be in with me. We're both the ones crashing your party." As soon as I say it, I want to cringe.

"No. I want you to have your privacy. That's your room, for however long we've got left in this place. It's fine."

"Where is she?"

"I'm about to go get her. I guess she's really whooping it up there, annoying the hell out of the doctors. So, about the trailer. Can she save anything?"

I shake my head. "Not a thing."

My mother sighs. "I don't know how she's going to take this. Normally she'd just laugh it off, you know how she is. But lately . . . Hasn't she seemed a little . . . off to you?"

She has, but I don't want to worry my mother. "Nah, not really. Want me to go get her?"

Muffled cursing comes from the stairwell, and the cot slides and rattles halfway down the steps.

"No, I'll go. I'll just run upstairs a minute and straighten up there first. Anyway, you've got some interesting reading material here."

She points to the newspaper as she picks up her keys and comes around the counter, squeezing my arm as she goes.

The headline on the *Courier*'s front page reads: CHILD NEARLY DROWNS, and another headline underneath in smaller type reads: DEVELOPER'S GRANDDAUGHTER SAVED BY FAMILY FRIEND.

CHAPTER 34

Amy

THE SUNSHINE STREAMS ONTO PAUL'S BACK, CREATING SHADOWS in the valleys of his muscles.

It makes me want to lick him.

But instead I turn away, hiding the thermometer with my hand and hoping the soft *beep beep* as it works doesn't disturb him. I yank the thermometer out when it begins its rapid "I'm done" beeping and muffle it under the covers until it stops. I look at the temp and frown. It doesn't make any sense at this point in my cycle. I didn't drink hardly anything yesterday, and I wasn't up so late . . .

Though I'm told stress can throw off a reading.

He turns over next to me, and I slam the thermometer in a drawer.

"Babe? What was that?"

"Nothing."

"What nothing?" he says sleepily, tossing his arm across his face to block out the light. "Can't you draw the shades in here?"

I like the light; it helps me bounce out of bed in the morning, early enough for a run. I stretch up and pull the blinds down, though. He grunts and rolls back over.

The party turned out okay after all, at least until poor Maddie . . . Tears prick at my eyelids again. God, I love that kid; always have since I first saw her and played My Little Ponies for an hour straight. I've always liked kids, but when I met Maddie, the penny dropped and my body said, *Yep, let's have us some babies.*

I had to wait a year until Paul proposed. And now, he might not marry me at all.

I snuggle close to his back and now I do lick him, a playful teasing on the back of his shoulder blade, his earlobe.

"Hmmm." He sighs but doesn't respond. So I run my tongue across the back of his neck, which I know drives him crazy.

"Babe, I'm really tired," he says.

He'd watched a West Coast baseball game, drinking beer in front of the TV, while I paced by the phone and waited for word on Madeline.

I swallow down my irritated sigh. "I'm going for a run. Call my cell if you hear anything about Maddie."

They told us she's fine, but until I can see her, I won't believe it for sure.

When I see Ed this morning, I do a double-take. Once for seeing him out here the day after a holiday, and twice because he's running. With actual running shoes.

His running is more of a walk with some bounce in it, really. His little dog, Lucky, has no trouble keeping up. When I overtake him, I could shoot right by in a split second.

I slow my pace a bit. Frodo looks up at me as if he's baffled.

"Hi!"

Ed turns to me and he smiles wide. "Hi," he pants. His face has gone florid, and little rivers of sweat are tracing their way down from his damp hair. "You . . . inspired . . . me . . ."

"I'm glad. Nice shoes."

He just nods, watching his footing now as if he doesn't trust himself.

"Did you stretch first?" I ask. He looks at me briefly with a small grin. "Well, at least stretch after, and cool down with some walking, too. I'll show you some stretches when we stop."

He flaps his hand at the sidewalk ahead, then pantomimes pushing me forward.

"I don't mind," I tell him. "Actually, maybe you want to slow down just a bit. You should be able to speak, really."

He settles into a walk and, after a few paces, pants out, "Thanks for the advice."

"I'm happy to help."

"How are things with you?"

"Oh, fine."

"No, they're not."

"What do you mean?" Frodo stops me to pee. I'll have to run after work to make up for this slow-down. That annoys Paul sometimes; when we have dinner together, it means we eat late.

"The light just went out of your lovely eyes when you said that." He smiles at me, and he actually winks.

Oh, so it's like that, then.

"Well, there was a problem last night, with my niece. She . . . I don't want to talk about it. But I'm just fine. Look, I'd better turn around."

"What about those stretches?"

"Maybe another time. I really should go."

"Amy, I'm sorry." He's got his hands on his knees, still breathing hard.

"You better walk a little longer. It's not good to stop suddenly."

"Amy, I didn't mean anything by it, I was just trying to—"

"I know what you were trying to do," I tell him, shouting so he can hear me as the distance between us increases. I'm walking backward away from him, gradually beginning to jog. "I thought you were just a nice, friendly guy I could talk to, and then here you go with my *lovely* eyes and trying to hint I'm not happy with my fiancé."

"I never said you weren't happy with your fiancé; you said that, just now."

I turn around and run a little harder yet, leaving Ed panting on the sidewalk behind me.

I walk away from the apartments and down a winding trail that leads to a rugged patch of gritty sand between a couple of small hills. It's our apartment's version of a beach. I unhook Frodo's leash and throw a stick into the water. He's going to stink like hell, but he's having fun.

I was really starting to enjoy Ed, and then he had to remind me of Kyle—someone I've worked very hard at forgetting.

When I first started dropping weight, Nikki had come into the office to see about buying a house. We got to chatting and she invited me to a club. I was still leery of going out, but the club was nice and dark and I thought it would be my treat for the 30 pounds I'd lost. That's three bowling balls' worth, I figured.

My face burns to remember Kyle. He played water polo in our high school and had the kind of chiseled chest that most high school boys would sell their own mothers for. All of us girls swooned over him; it was impossible not to.

He was at the club with the same crew of guys that had flocked around him in high school. I dared to give him a flirty look once, and shortly after that, he started dancing behind me, very close to me, his dick pressed right to my ass, actually.

I want to slap my twenty-nine-year-old self upside the head for the way I acted that night, grinding back against him, responding not only to his erection but the hoots of approval from Nikki and the girls, and his crew of baboons. I'd never—*ever!*—had that effect on a guy. Feeling that power made me as drunk as the whiskey sours.

By the time the last song played, we were plastered to each other in the back corner of the place, and we fumbled to his truck, and he drove me home. Of course I invited him in, desperate fat-ass that I was, and of course I let him fuck me, and I let him do it again even though the sex was terrible.

When I woke up, he was gone. I remember for sure that I gave him my number, but—yet another "of course"—he never called.

Nikki told me later that all the girls were "so mad" at him, because he'd been overheard laughing about screwing "the heifer."

"He's, like, such a dick," she'd said, and I muttered, "Why did I have to know that?" I don't think she heard me.

Frodo takes a break from stick-throwing to dig a pit in the sand, so I flop down and put my head in my hands.

Paul has got to marry me. I just can't put myself out there again.

I'd rather buy a vibrator and have a test-tube baby.

CHAPTER 35

Maeve

I'VE TOLD ANNA I NEED A MINUTE TO STRAIGHTEN UP MY ROOM before I go get Sally.

I really just want to drink in my last few moments of anything like privacy.

With the cot at a T at the end of my bed, it's a squeeze to walk between its corners and the doorway. I'll have to roll the sewing machine back in my closet to have any room to move at all. How will I finish my reunion dress now?

I haven't been exactly hiding my sewing project from Anna, but I haven't been advertising it, either. I can make myself a dress if I want; I don't need a special reason. But she's cunning, my daughter. She'd know.

I shove the machine hard into the closet, and with the *thud* I feel a memory slam into place.

It was my birthday, a frosty day in October. I had the space heater going, but the autumn chill still crept in every time someone opened the door. We could never keep the outside out at the Nee Nance.

Robert strutted in the front door of the store with a goofy smile plastered on his face. He still had a piece of toilet paper stuck to his chin where he'd nicked himself that morning. I reached up to flick it off and gave him a quick kiss. Anna was still at school.

"C'mere," he said. "I've got something for you."

He'd remembered! A rare treat. Normally Anna would prompt him when she got home from school, and then he'd dash down to the bookstore to grab a card and a romance novel, which I'd probably already read.

I pulled my sweater tightly around me and followed him out to the sidewalk.

A shiny red foil bow twinkled from the top of a large cardboard box, which read BERNINA on top. Only the week before, I'd been sighing over the machine in a catalog. My old Singer was constantly jamming, and I'd given up sewing, not having the patience to wrestle with that old beast. But with this top-of-the-line Bernina, I could whip up enough dresses to clothe Anna for the rest of her educational career.

"Damn you!" I shouted through fresh tears. "We can't afford this! Where did you get the money?"

Robert's face crumpled. "Honey, I know how much you wanted . . ."

"Wanting is different from having! Where did you get the money?"

"Babe, we have some in savings, and the store is doing well, so we'll make it back . . ."

"Our savings? Robert, that's for emergencies! What if Anna breaks her leg tomorrow!"

"She's careful. Look, honey, you said you wanted it, and think of it this way, with all the money we'll save on store-bought clothes, it will be worth it."

"But it's money we don't have to spare, we can't . . . You have to take it back." I knew I was making a spectacle for them all to chew over at Doreen's, but I couldn't stop myself. The blessed wrongness of the gift, the hugeness of his tactical error, pained me. And yet I loved him for trying.

Robert dug his toe into the ground. "Um, that's the other thing, sweetness. I didn't exactly buy it brand new. I mean, it's in perfect shape, don't get me wrong, but . . . It's not like I can take it back with a receipt."

I wiped my face with the sleeves of my scratchy sweater. "So, the money is gone."

"Look, I didn't know it would upset you so much. I thought you really wanted it, and I was just trying to make you happy. You deserve to be happy, you know, and one day I'll do that for you."

He looked grave, all his merry light gone. He continued, "One day I'll be the man you deserve. I promise you that."

And without another word, he hefted the box around to the alley entrance, leaving me shivering in the autumn wind.

With one more shove, I squeeze the machine deeper into the closet. After all that, he'd been right. The Bernina—wherever and however he'd obtained it—had lasted for decades and saved us untold money on store-bought items. I'd never have been able to do that with the broken-down old jalopy of a machine I'd had before.

Maybe I'll tell him that. He was right after all. I know he was tired of being wrong all the time. Almost as tired as I was of being right. It's no fun being right about everything going to hell.

I sure wish he'd hurry up and write me back.

Sally is quiet through the check-out at the hospital, and for most of the car ride home, for which I am thankful but also disturbed. A quiet Sally is something out of a parallel universe.

"Can I smoke, sister dear?"

"Just don't set the car on fire."

"Well, aren't you funny, Miss Robin Williams."

Sally's wig is back on, but it's tangled and ratty-looking. I should offer to wash it for her. It reeks of the fire, which is a different kind of stench than her cigarettes'. Sitting next to her is like standing downwind from a burning trash barrel.

"So, you okay?"

She nods, tipping her head back on the seat. "As long as I've got my health," she says, hacking suddenly and so hard I worry she's going to ram her head into the dashboard and we'll have to turn back around to the hospital. When she settles, she laughs again, her voice sounding like it was scraped by sandpaper. "My health, right."

"You know, didn't I always say those things would kill you? You didn't have to try and prove me right."

She's turned away from me. "Sorry," she mumbles.

With the back of her head facing me like this, ageless, I can almost imagine we're on our way to the drive-in with Sean and Robert and the gang.

I bring my eyes back to the road. We're almost back to the store, and traffic is heavy, the streets clogged with people who can afford to take a week off from work around the Fourth.

Sally's voice is jarring when she speaks again, louder than necessary in the confines of the car. "Why are you still wearing that ring?"

I drop my hand away from my chest. I'd been touching my wedding ring through my shirt without noticing it. "Since when do you pay attention to what I do?"

"Oh, I've known for ages you have it, doll. I just never thought to ask until now."

"Why do you ask now?"

"Why don't you answer?"

"Because I don't feel like it."

Sally taps her fingers on her knee to some beat in her head. "My brother was such a jackass, leavin' you like he did."

"I don't want to talk about it."

"No, you never did like this subject."

"Why would I like it?" We're at the store now, and I pull into our alley parking space.

Back when Robert first left, Sally tried to be consoling and I'd always push her away, make her drop it. I didn't want it in my face all the time, is all. I didn't want her in my face, either, with those dark brown Geneva eyes. So she quit talking about it, and eventually I let her come around again.

I always wondered why she wasn't more upset herself, her only brother taking off like that. But I never wanted to raise the subject, once she'd finally dropped it.

"Do you need help out of the car?" She had remained still while I took the keys out of the ignition and zipped them back in my purse.

"Nah. I just can't believe this is all that's left of me," she says, looking down at her own purse, which slouches in her lap, half open and ready to spill its contents at the slightest nudge.

CHAPTER 36

Cami

I DIAL THE SHOP AND A YOUNG KID ANSWERS, MAYBE NINETEEN years old, whose voice still has that scrapy echo of adolescence. I don't know who he is, but I pity him because having Tim Drayton for a boss is no trip to the candy store, I'm sure.

"Can I talk to Tim?" I ask, pitching my voice unnaturally high.

"Um, he can't come to the phone right now."

"Is he working or what?"

"He's rebuilding an engine. He's gonna be a while. Can I take a message?"

"No, that's okay."

I hang up and smile. Good. He'll be out of the house all morning, at least. And for once Sherry isn't here.

I walk out of our now-clean kitchen with its fresh white cupboards onto the dirty hall carpet, past my sunny yellow room, and turn into the cave where my father lives. If you can call this life.

Piles of clothing dot the room. I don't know which ones are

supposed to be clean and which are dirty. I'm not sure he knows, either. I did his laundry when I first came back, along with mine, but then he thundered at me about not being able to find his shirts, which were hung up on a clothesline in the laundry room. So I quit doing it.

Even if there were clean clothes in here, they wouldn't smell that way long. The room's odor is something like a zoo crossed with the Nee Nance's bottle-return bin. I spy an ashtray and some crushed cigarettes. My hand clenches as I stare at the ashtray.

He never used to smoke in here. Mom wouldn't allow it. So he'd suck on his cigarettes on the back porch, glaring across the yard. Sometimes, if he were really upset, Trent and I could see his face flash up bright and yellow in the light of another match struck for another cigarette. The night Mom told us about her cancer, I think he smoked half a pack, one after the other. His beer, then, was still a relatively moderate habit.

Now he's smoking in here. He could torch the place in a pickled stupor, just like Sally and her trailer. My mother's house, where she raised us.

She used to spend Saturday mornings cleaning, all the windows open in the spring and summer. Trent and I would wake up to the sound of disco on the stereo and the scent of lemon in the air, and Mom would be bopping along, humming and scrubbing and dusting, a kerchief tied over her hair.

And look what he's done to it, the smelly, drunk old bastard.

I pick up the ashtray and walk out the back door, across our squeaky porch, and stand in our yard, feeling the weight of the ashtray in my hand. We've got a wooden fence around our scrubby patch of grass; Mom insisted on it for us kids, worried because this isn't the greatest neighborhood. It used to be painted a rich brown. Now it's faded to a color like weak tea.

I fling the ashtray, discus-style, into the back fence. It only cracks once, alas. I'd been hoping for a satisfying shatter.

He'll not likely notice it. Or if he does, he'll think he misplaced it himself.

I go back into his room and crouch down by the stack of photo albums in his closet. With one ear cocked toward the front door, I leaf through them.

This is harder than I thought, watching myself and my family regress in age as I work my way from top to bottom in the stack.

A picture of Trent and me at the beach, arms around each other, stops me short. I gaze at it for a minute or so. I look at my watch: It's four o'clock in London. I wonder if he's having tea.

Then I slam the book. No time now.

Here's one. It's smaller than the rest, visibly older, too. I whip through the pages and notice that in this one, someone has written dates and names under the photos.

Part of me cries out to stop and linger on these pictures of my mom as a girl, but that's not my goal now, to wallow in what I can't have anymore. I need to—

There. That couple again.

Alice and Richard Gray, 1968

Though I'm sure I'd never forget this, I jot it down anyway on a slip of paper I'd brought in with me just for this purpose.

Also, though I know rebuilding an engine takes all morning, my adrenaline cranks up and I begin stacking the albums again, not taking particular care to get them in order; Tim Drayton is not a detail man, as a rule.

When I put the last one on the stack, something curious draws my eye.

In the very back of the closet is a perfect square that had been cut out of the wall, replaced, and sealed over. But never sanded or painted. I tap around the square and onto it: hollow.

The sound of an engine outside the house causes me to jump upright, jam the off-track closet doors back closed as best I can, and sprint over the laundry out into the hall. I dash into the living room and then concentrate on breathing evenly.

When I look out the front window, I see only the mail truck, rumbling away.

I sit for a long time, cross-legged on my bed, trying to remember a Richard or Alice Gray in our lives. I call Trent again but only get his voice mail, so I leave him a message to call my cell phone and I give my next working hours, translated to UK time. The last thing I need is to get a call from Trent in front of my dad.

I resign myself to calling Aunt Clara.

"Hello?" she answers, suspicion already tingeing her voice. She has caller ID, I'll bet, and it probably says C. DRAYTON on her little screen.

"Hi. It's Cami." Silence. "Your niece."

"Oh, Camille! Heavens. I wasn't expecting you."

I'm sure she wasn't. "Could I just ask you something?"

"Yes." She draws the word out slightly.

"I mean a question, not a favor."

"Of course," she answers, sounding a little offended. As if I had no reason to doubt she would help me, the hypocritical old wench.

"Do you know Alice and Richard Gray?"

"Them? Why on earth . . .? No, I don't know them."

I can hear her tapping her long nails. She'd make a lousy gambler. "If you don't know them, why did you answer, *Them?* Don't lie to me, *Clara.*"

She always preferred for me to call her Aunt Clara, and she wanted me to pronounce *aunt* to rhyme with *want.*

"Well, I don't *know* them. We weren't friends."

I choke down an exasperated scream. "You've heard of them, though."

"Why do you ask?"

"I found a photo of them among your sister's things." I throw the *sister* in her face deliberately.

"That's all?"

"Yes, that's all." What else could there be? I don't press her. She might hang up if I don't play this right.

"Mrs. Gray was Pamela's violin teacher."

"My mother played the violin?"

"Oh, yes; she was very good." Clara doesn't say this with pride—rather, as if she's got something sour in her mouth.

"So why does she have a photo of her violin teacher and her husband?" And why was it inscribed with such affection? I hesitate to give Clara this information, sensing I've crossed into sensitive territory.

"They both took a liking to her. Mr. Gray played piano and he would accompany her on her solo pieces. The Grays used to include her in their family events, having had no children of their own."

"What happened to them?"

"Same thing that happens to everyone. They died."

I flinch at this, not realizing until that moment I'd been hoping to find them, to quiz them about my mother's youth, her musical skill, which I'd known nothing about. I never even saw her hold an instrument.

"Is that all?" Clara asks, her voice weighted with a display of boredom.

I grip the phone a little tighter in my hand. "I'll just say thank you for the only useful thing you've ever done for me, answering this simple question, however grudgingly you did so."

"You're still so angry."

"Why shouldn't I be? I lost my mother, and my one female relative acted like I was dead, too."

"We were never close. It was a bit late to start acting like best friends, I thought."

I snap my phone shut and place it gently on my bed to keep from slamming it into the wall. Then I stand up and punch my mattress, again and again, until my fury sputters out amid daydreams of my mother playing a song on her violin, something sweet, just for me.

CHAPTER 37

Anna

I RING THE BELL AT THE BECKER HOUSE AND WIPE MY PALMS ON MY skirt. It will take some time for the housekeeper to answer, so I suck in a breath and puff it out.

I made a mistake. I don't intend to make that mistake again. I'm only human.

I say this so I can forgive myself before the door opens and I'm confronted with Beck's wife.

Magda answers and greets me with glee. "Oh, Anna! Mr. B and Miss Sam are so excited to see you, and wait until you see Maddie! She's as good as new!" She pulls me by my hand into the foyer.

I force a smile as she leads the way to the family room, where Mr. Becker, the elder, is standing. Samantha sits on a chair with Madeline in her lap, looking at a picture book. She looks up as I enter but flicks her eyes back to the book.

Mr. Becker steps forward and wraps me in a hug. "Our hero!"

I didn't want to be here, but Mr. Becker invited me to this

little thank-you lunch, and what was I supposed to say? *Sorry, I can't face your daughter-in-law because right after I rescued her daughter, I screwed her husband.*

My attempt to let myself off the hook on the porch failed utterly. I'm torn between a desire to run out the door and never come back to this incestuous hick town, and an unsettling urge to scream out the truth: I'm no hero, that's for damn sure.

"Sit, sit," he tells me, and I do because one does what Mr. Becker says. It's the way of Haven. "I'm sorry Will can't be here. He got caught up with something at work and he really couldn't get away. He's such a hard worker; I'm so proud of him. I remember that of you, too, Anna. You two were always working. Or, at least I think it was working!" At this he winks and booms laughter. I don't dare look at Sam.

"I want a snack!" shouts Maddie, jumping off her mother's lap.

"It's almost lunch," Sam says mildly. I look at her fully for the first time and stifle a gasp. Her hair hangs in matted strings like that of a neglected doll. Her face is waxy and pale.

"I want a snack!" bellows Maddie, her body going rigid.

"I'll get you a string cheese." Samantha sighs as she starts to rise.

"I want Grandpa to do it!" Maddie shrieks.

Grandpa leaps to his feet and happily leads the way to the kitchen, leaving Samantha and me alone in the spotless family room.

"How are you holding up?" I ask, to fill the silence.

Samantha shrugs. "She's going through an 'anyone-but-Mommy' phase right now. I suppose when we're together all day, every day, that's to be expected. But it isn't easy to be rejected by her. Especially now."

I can't add anything to this, so I say nothing. I glance out the picture window at the lake beyond.

"I have to thank you," she tells me, which forces me to face her again. "I almost lost my life that night. It's scary to love one fragile thing so much you feel you'd die if . . . I've been trying to get Will to have more babies, but he doesn't want to. Which is funny, because he used to say he'd have ten of them, as many as I could squeeze out."

The sound of my swallowing seems loud in the room. Samantha's staring at me, expecting me to respond. "Well, maybe he'll come around."

"I doubt it. He moved out."

I gasp before I can stop it. Samantha raises an eyebrow at me.

"I'm sorry to hear that," I say.

"Are you?" She turns toward the kitchen. "Where are they? Honestly, he's probably making pancakes, if she asked him to. I swear it's like I just donated the uterus sometimes, and none of them would notice if I wandered off."

"The Beckers can be intimidating, as a group. I used to feel that way myself."

She turns back to me, two bright pink spots flaring on her cheeks. "Are you comparing your little high school thing to my marriage?"

"No! I was just commiserating, I mean—"

My fumbling is interrupted by growling sounds and shrieks, as Maddie runs back into the room, her face purple with jelly, and William Becker behind her, making like some kind of animal, hunched over and chasing her. Mr. Becker pauses in front of me as Maddie does a loop around the room and takes off again. He rests his hands on his knees and pants out, "See? In perfect health. Aren't you glad you came over to see that everything's okay?"

He can't see Samantha behind him, glaring at me, her mouth forming one hard line.

"Where's Mom?" I ask Cami as I come back in the front door of the Nee Nance, toting my fast-food lunch in a paper bag because I couldn't eat a thing at the Becker house.

"Upstairs watching TV with Sally. Paul Becker called. He said your meeting date is fine."

I nod. "I should have brought you lunch. Do you want me to run out and get some?"

"Nah," Cami says. "I ate already. What's up with Paul?"

I fill Cami in on my plan to get my mother a reprieve, at least temporarily. "I think he'll go for it. I hope so, anyway. I know it's not what she wants forever, but she has to do something while we figure out the rest of her life."

"What does she want to do?"

I pop a fry in my mouth. It's too salty; I have no appetite, anyway. *Beck left his wife,* I keep thinking. "She's oddly detached from the fact that this store as she knows it will be gone. Maybe she's distracted by Sally and her blood pressure and everything. Maybe she can't accept it. It's been part of her for so long, she just can't believe it's going to be really gone."

My phone rings and the screen says W. BECKER. I just left there; what does he want?

"Excuse me, Cami, I'll take this in the office."

"Hello," I answer, dusting fry salt off my hands as I step behind the metal desk piled with invoices and balance sheets.

"Hi."

"Beck! What's going on?"

I glance out into the store, and then I close the office door, slowly. I catch Cami's eye as I do this and she raises an eyebrow.

As he speaks, a crack runs through his voice. "Sam and I split up. I moved out."

"What happened?"

"It was ugly. I don't want to talk about it."

"She doesn't . . . You didn't tell her, did you?"

"No, of course not."

"But she suspects, doesn't she?"

"Can we meet up? I hate talking like this over the phone. I want to see your face."

"We'd better not." I can't imagine a single place in Haven that would be safe. Even if the news isn't public yet—his dad didn't even seem to know—before long everyone will know that he left his wife.

"Let's meet in Muskegon."

I calculate the distance, the drive time, how long Cami is scheduled to work. "I guess I could get away, but I don't know . . ."

"Please. It would mean a lot to me. You're my friend. You never stopped being my friend."

He listened to me about my dad's letter when I dared tell no one else.

"Okay. Yes." We decide to meet at the mall, in the parking lot in front of one of the stores.

When I hang up and tell Cami of my plan, she says, "You sure you want to do this?"

"He's a friend. He's having trouble, and I think I caused it."

She only nods. If she's judging me, she's not showing it.

As I drive north on the highway, my phone rings again. This time it's a Miller Paulson number. From my quick glance I can see it's Mr. Jenison. I let it go to voice mail.

CHAPTER 38

Maeve

TWO THINGS JOLT ME AS I WRITE MY RENT CHECK FOR AUGUST.

The last month in my home, in this store.

The month Robert said we would meet, only he still hasn't picked a date or sent me a proper letter. A couple of weeks ago he sent a postcard. A postcard! With his name and his own writing, after I'd told him to be careful! He signed it *love*, which would have sent Anna through the roof. I'm just lucky she wasn't in the store.

The postcard was for the Rock and Roll Hall of Fame in Cleveland. At least he's made it to the Midwest.

I'm in the office, with Cami manning the store. Sally is upstairs, sleeping, her wig draped across the top of my dresser like some sort of exotic carcass. At least she let me wash the smoke out, as best I could.

I'll still have a job if I want it, it seems, thanks to Anna. The pay she negotiated isn't much, but it's income. Paul won't let me lease the space, even with Anna's help, to run the new business myself. I'm not good enough for that, I guess. I'll go from proprietor of my own store to some retail clerk with a boss telling me whether I can have a day off or not. Even that is temporary. He let it be known he would be hiring a new manager, eventually, who would handpick his own staff.

I'm glad I wasn't there to witness Anna try to wring money out of him, arguing about how much I'm worth to punch register keys.

Dean Martin croons on my tape player about being king of the road. Robert always loved that one, crooning along with his voice a bit too sharp, drowning out Dean.

The Nee Nance will be gone, though, even if I stay. It will be shut down for a while, gutted, rebuilt. I won't recognize the place. Meantime, I'll have to find an apartment. Anna will help me pay my rent. That's how she put it, "help me," when in fact she'll have to pay it all, at least for now, until the renovation is complete. Without the income of the store, or wages as Paul's lackey, I've got nothing.

Any savings I managed to scrape up always went out the window for medicine, or a new-old car, or repairing the broken boiler.

I look up at my citation on the wall from the Rotary club, for organizing that food drive for years, rallying the chamber of commerce to collect cans for the needy.

And now here I am, hand out to my daughter, pockets turned inside out. At the ripe old age of fifty-two.

As Grandma Geneva used to say, "How do you like them apples?"

I hear Sally stomping down the stairs. She pokes her head into the office. "Hey, sis, can I come apartment hunting with you?"

I suppose, since she'll be living there, too, it's only fair. "Yeah. I'll be with you in a minute."

I rest my head on my folded arms.

*   *   *

The balcony overlooks a vast sea of hot blacktop, with fresh yellow parking-lot stripes.

The rental agent behind me is showing Sally all the "features" of the kitchen. I hear the sink sprayer fire off and Sally apologizes. Honestly, I can't take her anywhere. And now I'll have to take her everywhere.

Below and to the right I can see the gray sign which reads EM-ERALD COVE: A BECKER DEVELOPMENT PROPERTY. I didn't even know. It was just one of those I circled in the paper yesterday. Anna had told me not to worry about the expense of the rent.

"Even if you picked some place fancy," she said, "it will be so much cheaper to live here than in Chicago."

And that's when I knew. No fanfare, no big announcement. Just like that, with her use of definite future tense, Chicago and Miller Paulson became a piece of her past.

All because of me.

Well, not just me. I turn away from the stunning blacktop vista—the air so hot it shimmers above the pavement—and see Sally trying out all the cupboard doors as if one of them will somehow work differently from another.

I suppose if it were me alone, I could have sponged off Ve-ronica, distasteful as that would have been, or at least Anna could have headed back to work and just sent me a check for a while until I got on my feet.

But with Sally homeless, too, and somewhat battier of late, it must have seemed impossible for her to go back to her old life and leave us to our devices. Poor Anna, saddled with a tiresome sense of responsibility.

I find myself wishing she had just a little of Robert's devil-may-care attitude, just enough so she'd go back to the big city and not worry about me. I'd get along without her if I had to. Especially if her father would finally write me. "Got held up a bit," his postcard had read. "Sit tight."

"Well, ladies," chirps the rental agent, brushing at speckled dots of water across her dress. "How do you like it?"

"I like it fine," I answer, as Sally crows from the bathroom, "Hey, sis! Check it out, two sinks!"

The agent smiles at me confidentially, like she's going to let me in on a delicious secret. "His-and-hers sinks. All those annoying little beard hairs? They all go in one sink only."

"Hers and hers, I guess," I say. "It will be just me and my sister-in-law here."

"Ah," she says, suddenly busily rummaging in her purse. "So, can I get an application started for you?"

I lick my lips and take in a breath. How to broach this?

"Well, this place is fine, but my situation is a little, well, it's unusual, because my daughter is going to be paying my rent, at least at first. I run my own business, but my lease is up, and as of the fall, I . . . I don't have any income, so I don't have any W-2 statements or anything to show you."

The air conditioning hasn't been on and it's already stuffy in here. Having spelled out my life like that, I can scarcely breathe.

"Hmmm," she says, tapping a pen against her pursed lips and squinting at me like I'm a confusing modern art piece. "I'll talk to the folks down in the business office. I'm sure we can figure something out. You can't be the first person to have this situation. College students and whatever . . ." She starts to walk out, and then turns and says, "Your daughter has verifiable income, I presume?"

"Well, she . . . She's got a lot in savings. She just moved back to town, but she's a lawyer, so she'll have income in no time."

"I see. I'll let you ladies continue looking around. I'll be down in the office if you have any further questions."

The door swings itself shut, too hard, and it echoes so loud in the beige emptiness that I jump.

I should have let Anna come do this, like she offered, but I had to say "No, no, I'll find a place myself." Maybe she has to be the one to rent it and we sublet or something . . . ?

My head is now throbbing. I wonder if this is a blood pressure thing . . . No, I'm sure it's the heat. My pressure has been up a little, but nothing like it was that one day. I notice just then how quiet it is in here.

"Sal?" I head down the short hallway. I thought this place seemed more spacious from the outside, but it's not much bigger than the upstairs of the Nee Nance. "Sally!" She's prone on the carpet in a patch of sun.

At my exclamation, though, she props herself up. "What? Just having a rest."

"On the floor? What are you, a housecat? Get up, for Pete's sake."

"So is this the place?" she asks as I help her to her feet.

"I don't know. Maybe."

"'Cuz I like the double sinks. Classy. We can both put on our faces in the morning. Or our hair!" She guffaws and whacks at my arm, staggering a little with the glee of her own joke.

In the hall I take a deep inhale of the common-area air conditioning. It would be nice to have AC for once in my life, though I'm not sure it's worth the price of living with Sally.

"Anyhoo, I love it," Sally says. "It smells better than my trailer."

"No smoking in this place!" I shout suddenly, whirling on her so quickly she draws herself back against the stairwell wall. "I will not have you turning my home into a pit like that stupid trailer."

"Well, aren't we fancy. I'll smoke on the balcony."

"And you'll empty the ashtray every day."

"Yes, ma'am, your ladyship." She salutes me.

"Oh, shut up."

We clamber into my old Buick and back out of the parking space, and I glare at the Becker Development sign. "You know, Sal, they're not going to rent to us, anyway."

"Why not?"

"Because neither of us has a job or income."

"I got Social Security. And my pension from the school system."

"Oh, I'm sure it's a massive amount for being a janitor!"

In my peripheral vision she draws herself up straighter. "Custodian."

"Sally, I'm quite sure we can't afford this place, and come to think of it today, Anna doesn't have any income right now, either, and she's the one who's supposed to be paying for us."

"Ah, we'll figure something out. It'll be fun! We can stay up late, paint each other's toenails, and hey, with two bedrooms we can bring over gentlemen friends—"

I punch the brakes at a stoplight hard enough that we bounce off our seatbelts. "No, it is not going to be 'fun'! We'll be destitute and living off other people, and with no jobs we'll be staring at those damn beige walls until we want to kill each other. Does that sound like fun to you? And then I get a job, only what kind of job will that be? With twenty credits at a community college three decades ago? I'll come home and hang up my hairnet and have no one but you for company, you batty old broad!"

A horn blares behind us. The light is green. I punch the gas and the car makes one massive charge forward and dies with a clank and a gasp. I try the key with a shaking hand as the cars behind us lean on the horn again. From the side, I see Sally open the door. I look and she's glaring at me through some stray strands of her black wig. She flips me the bird, and then slams the car door so hard the keys jingle in the ignition.

"Fine," I mumble to myself as she recedes into the neighborhood beyond. I put on the hazard lights. "Just go, already."

I sit back and wait for the traffic streaming past me to clear enough for me to get to a phone and call Anna.

* * *

"Where's Sally?" is the first thing Anna asks me when she picks me up off the side of the road, moments before the tow truck arrives.

"She took a walk."

"Funny time for a walk."

"She's a funny gal; what can I say?" I rest my head against the side window and close my eyes. Anna is quiet as she drives me back, reopens the store, and sends me up to my room to rest.

"Oh," she says, as I have one foot on the bottom step. "This came for you. Doesn't look like business mail so I didn't open it."

I come back across the store, trying not to look too eager, only mildly curious, as I accept the envelope.

The address and return address are typed, badly, on a manual typewriter. It appears to be from a "P. C. Harming." I scurry up the stairs, biting my lip to keep from laughing and crying at once. Prince Charming, indeed.

CHAPTER 39

Amy

I SHOULD HAVE PICKED SOMEWHERE ELSE FOR THIS, BECAUSE THE beach should be romantic and beautiful, and I fear that now I've ruined it for myself forever.

Paul scowls at his feet. His khaki pants are rolled up to his knees and his feet have sunk into the sand. I've been pacing next to him, leaving footprints on the cool, firm sand continuously soaked by the waves. We're on the private strip of beach behind my apartment, and I just demanded he marry me.

"We talked about this. I told you it doesn't feel like the right time."

"I don't have all the time in the world."

"I don't like being pressured."

"It's not my fault I'm thirty-five."

"What does age have to do with it?"

I grab chunks of my hair and groan. Men. They must be this blind on purpose; there's no other explanation. "I want a baby, dammit!"

He startles and finally stops looking at his feet.

"Don't look so shocked. We've been talking about starting a family, both of us have."

"Yes, but . . ."

"When did you think that was going to happen? When I'm forty? Do you even know what the statistics are for birth defects after my age, if I can even get pregnant at all?"

He puts his hands up like I've pulled a gun on him, and he takes a step back. "Holy shit, Amy, I'm not prepared for this, either."

"You said you'd marry me and I don't understand what changed. You can't even use the economy as an excuse; the council approved your project and Anna isn't trying to stop it now. You promised."

"I know."

"So, are you a liar?"

He flinches. "I'm not. Things change!"

"What changed? I didn't change!"

"I'm just feeling a lot of pressure right now and I can't take wedding pressure. I don't want to talk about invitations, I don't want to pick a first dance song, I don't want to be a big spectacle."

"So fine! We elope!" As I say this, though, my heart drops. I did so want a wedding.

"My parents would never forgive me. Neither would you," he says.

"You think I'm going to forgive you for jilting me?"

"Oh, God, I'm not jilting you; I'm just postponing."

"No! We are not postponing. We have to send our invitations. I have the pattern picked out and the wording. If you want to marry me, do it now. Otherwise," I suck in a deep breath and ball up my fists, "forget it."

"Amy?"

"You heard me. I will not be jerked around like this. I am not going to be hanging on the line like some fish and you're debating whether to throw me back."

"That's not what I mean—"

"You loved me in June enough to commit to me forever. If you don't feel that way now, then we're done."

He shakes his head and picks up his shoes from the sand, walking slowly away from me. He pauses to look back at me, and I can't tell from this distance, but his face might be wet. If he's crying, why won't he come back? I watch him walk all the way to the wooden staircase and disappear over the top of the dune.

It isn't until my feet touch the sidewalk at the top of the steps that I realize I left my sandals on the beach. I look across the parking lot, half expecting to see his car still there, that he's upstairs in the apartment, waiting for me with an apology.

No car.

It takes effort to get up my apartment steps. I have to pull with my arms along the railing because I doubt my legs will get me up the stairs alone. I cross into the apartment and Frodo begins his happy, bouncing "You're home" dance. Almost right away, though, he sits down in front of me. I crouch down and wrap my arms around him, burying my face in his furry neck, which he tolerates. My engagement ring glints in the early evening sun.

It's really too late for invitations anyway. I'd sent out the "Save the Date" card, and by now everyone who got one is already wondering why the invitation hasn't arrived. Half of Haven probably already realizes the wedding is off.

Pitiful of me, really, to keep walking around talking about the wedding. Then, I always did have a healthy denial muscle, the same one that let me think I was just big-boned, it was hereditary, and I was in fairly good health for all those years. That being a nice person would get me far in life, and I'd find a mature guy who didn't care about looks.

Dunce cap for Amy Rickart.

I release Frodo at last and notice that my phone is blinking for a voice mail. Maybe he called when I was coming up the steps?

"Amy? It's Aunt Agatha. Your dress is in. I know you'll want to come in for the fitting soon so I can get it altered, and your bridesmaids should have their final fittings soon, too. The big day is coming up quick. Just call the shop when you're ready and we'll set a time."

I delete the message and realize I'm hungry. I hadn't eaten dinner when I got home from work and decided I couldn't go one more moment without knowing whether I was getting married or not.

I pull myself up off the floor and rummage in the fridge. Lentils, bean sprouts, hummus. A pasty piece of baked chicken from yesterday. I try the freezer. Some Lean Cuisines with their pieces of rubbery meat the size of a playing card and bland, limp vegetables.

I'm ravenous. I need something with some substance.

In the back of the freezer is some ice cream, which I bought for Paul and forgot to mention to him. Cookies and cream, his favorite.

I grab it out of the freezer, and speaking of Paul, he left a beer or three here.

The carton is cold in my lap so I put a pillow underneath it. I throw a bride magazine on the floor, startling Frodo, and open up an issue of *Glamour*. A greeting card falls out, the front showing a soaking-wet Chihuahua glaring at the camera with the thought bubble reading, "I've had better moments."

In spite of myself, I chuckle and reread Ed's card, which I found slipped under my door the day after he flirted with me.

Amy,

I'm really sorry to come off like a typical scuzzy guy just trying to get in your pants. I won't lie, you're a very pretty girl but more importantly, you're very nice and you set off my "flirt" mode. I should have known better, though. Hey, isn't that an '80s song?

Anyway, you do inspire me, at the risk of sounding like a cheesy ballad. I never mentioned this before, but I wasn't always fat. I used to be in pretty good shape, actually. Then I quit smoking and got a desk job and one thing after another happened. I figured this was just what happened to people when they got older, you know? I only walk at all because of Lucky.

Then I saw you and remembered you from high school and thought, damn, what's my excuse?

So anyway, I have lost a couple pounds. I'll change my jogging schedule, though, so I don't bump into you anymore. I don't want to make you uncomfortable and frankly I can't help but flirt with you a little. Forgive me my male weakness!

I hope this note doesn't cause you trouble. I saw you into your apartment that one day, remember? I'm not stalking you or anything, promise.

Anyway, my high-powered binoculars are broken. (Kidding! Really!)

Your friend,
Ed

I spoon in the ice cream and roll my eyes back with pleasure at its creamy sweetness. After so long without it, it's like a dream of perfection in sweet, frozen form.

It would be simpler if I had a crush on Ed like he does on me. Then I could call him up and we'd get together and talk about how we met, and it would be just like a movie starring Reese Witherspoon. People tell me I look like her, now that I'm thin.

But, sweet as this note is, it just reminds me of Paul, and how he lit up when I first met him, and how happy he was when I came into the room, and how he used to hold my hand every chance he got, and just how much he admired me. And that wasn't all; I admire him, too, so smart and determined even though he doesn't have the support from his family that his brother does. He can be really funny when he's relaxed, and he rolls with everything. Long walk on the beach? Sure, babe. A chick flick? Whatever you want, babe. Try some sushi? Yeah, why not, babe?

Until recently.

I look down in the carton and a wave of disgust at how much I've eaten threatens to ruin the experience. I set the sweating, damp carton on top of another bride magazine—are they multiplying in here? How many did I buy?—and take a long swig out of the beer bottle, channel-flipping to find something to watch, anything that has nothing to do with love.

CHAPTER 40

Cami

I LOCK THE FRONT DOOR AND DEADBOLT IT, TOO. THEN I WEDGE A chair under the doorknob, just like they do in the movies. I lock the back door and make sure the windows are shut, though that means it will soon be the temperature of a kiln in here.

My dad is off camping with Sherry, but I'm taking no chances, considering.

Two things bother me about his room.

Now that I've cleaned up and painted most of the house, his room sticks out like a festering boil. The door won't even stay closed; it keeps swinging open, exposing itself to the rest of the house.

Also, he forbade me from going in there, and since I discovered that hollow spot in the wall, I now know there's a reason. For once it's not just a random demand for the sake of being a bully.

So I've now got my spackle and my saw and trowel. I figure now I've got plenty of time to open this wall up, check it out, and seal it back shut before he's the wiser.

The piece of the wall caves in easily with one punch of my trowel's handle end. The anemic light from the closet bulb at first reveals nothing, and I curse myself for thinking like some kind of Cold War–era spy. But then, just below the hole I've made, I can see the edge of a rolled up document, held together by a rubber band. I snake my fingers into the hole and fish out some yellowed papers. They smell of mildew and have black flecks along their edges. This has been in here a long time, whatever it is.

"Camille Ann Drayton!" booms a voice from the porch, and I scream before I can check myself.

The key rattles in the front door, but the chair and deadbolt are holding him back. I shove the papers down the back of my pants and fluff my large shirt over them, checking with my hands to feel if they might be visible.

There's a cracking sound from out front. The deadbolt has torn from the doorframe.

"Cami! What the fuck is going on here?"

The chair's legs scrape against the front hall linoleum.

I rearrange his hanging clothing in front of the hole I've made, and kick at my supplies, trying to get them under the bed. There's stuff already under there, though, and they won't fit. I would try shoving them into the closet, but I don't want to turn my back.

I kick a filthy pile of laundry over them.

The chair gives way and crashes to the floor, the door banging into it once, twice, as he shoves his way through.

Even if I try to leave the room, he'll see where I've been.

I stand, clasping my hands loosely at my waist, like a kid about to sing for the choir. My blood pounds in my ears.

He appears in the doorway, face contorted and florid. This is the worst of him, I know. I haven't seen this in a very long time.

"You're back early—"

"Surprised you, didn't I?" He grins wide. The alcohol stench rolls off of him. He starts to walk around his bed. I consider leaping over it and making for the door. But the room is small; his reach is long. And running might set him off. Activate his predator instinct. "That asshole campground ranger said we were making too much noise, and I told him what for and he threw my ass out, if you can believe that bullshit. And I'm a taxpayer and everything."

"Where's Sherry?"

His eyes narrow and his face clouds over.

"She was embarrassed to be seen with me. Can you imagine? A whore who dances for money, embarrassed to be seen with an upstanding businessman? A regular pillar of the community."

He has a hard time saying "community." Too many repetitive syllables. Now he's angry with both of us, maybe all women.

He steps toward me again, and then stops, looks down. I follow his gaze. He's kicked the pile of laundry under which I'd stuffed my supplies. He glares up at me through the hair that's fallen across his forehead. "What did I tell you," he begins slowly, in a low voice, *about coming in here?*" The last is said at almost a scream.

He lunges for my face. I duck, but he catches a handful of my hair. He twists his hand into it and pulls me out of the room. I reach up to try and dislodge his hand, but the hair is woven into his fingers. He pulls me across the junk on the floor, and I can't keep my footing. He bangs me into the hallway wall as he yanks me out toward the living room. As we reach the end of the hall, he pulls me up to my full height and slams me into the wall, his face so close to mine I can trace the red cracks in the whites of his eyes. With his other hand, he seizes my chin, holding my face right in front of his.

"I had one rule. One lousy fucking rule and you couldn't respect it."

He takes his hand off my chin and slaps me so hard my eyes lose focus and the stem of my glasses cracks.

"Dad!"

"Don't you 'dad' me. You stupid little bitch."

He yanks me off the wall again, dragging me through the living room. With his free hand, he throws the chair out of his way and uses his foot to prop open the door. He yanks his hand out of my hair and seizes me by the front of my shirt. With this, he throws me across the porch and I tumble down the concrete steps.

"And don't come back unless you learn some respect!"

He slams the front door, but it doesn't stay closed. I can see him stumbling back toward his room. My glasses have fallen off my face, so I pick them up along with the broken stem, forcing myself to stand on quivering legs. He might yet investigate his closet and realize that I did more than just cross his threshold.

I taste blood. I think I've bitten my tongue, or maybe it's my lip from where he hit me.

But still I smile. Because under my shirt, down the back of my pants, I still have those papers he sought to hide.

CHAPTER 41

Anna

IN THE DANK CONFINES OF THE TIP-A-FEW, IT TAKES ME SEVERAL moments to search out Cami. When I do see her, she's curled over a glass of beer, a pitcher at her elbow. Her hair falls like a curtain down to the table. As I approach, I can see she's concentrating on something, a stack of papers.

"Sorry I'm late, I had to wait for my mom to get up from . . ."

My words fade away as she looks up at me. One side of her face is puffy and discolored, and a shadow has begun to spread from the bridge of her nose under her eye. Her lip is split and swollen. On the injured side of her face, there is no stem on her glasses; they balance on her nose and other ear.

I watch her notice that I've seen it and hold my breath waiting for her to explain it.

"Okay, this time he hit me. But I didn't lie before; that really was a fall."

I nod slowly. "Are you . . . are you in pain?" I was going to say, "Are you okay," but that seems ridiculous to ask.

"Not much, but that's not why I asked you here."

She pushes the papers across the table at me.

"Cami, we should call the police."

She rolls her eyes and slaps the papers. "Don't bother. Read this, I'm telling you."

"But, he's—"

"Forget the cops. He'd get out in no time, yeah? Just read this, I'm beggin' you, read it."

My phone chimes, letting me know I have a message. I ignore it and read, TRUST OF PAMELA SUE DRAYTON.

I glance at her with a questioning look, but she just points down to the paper, wanting me to read. The paper smells musty, and it's brittle in spots with long-dried dampness.

I can't believe what I'm seeing.

"Cami. You won't believe this. You have a trust fund worth a hundred thousand dollars. You should have gotten it when you turned eighteen." I try to reconcile this with the state of their shabby house in a dodgy neighborhood.

She nods, takes a swig of beer. "You want some of this?"

I shrug, not really caring. She waves at the waitress and points to me, raising her glass in the air.

Cami continues, having to push her glasses up on her nose continually. "I thought that's what this said. And I think I know where she got the money, too. I found out that she used to play violin—I know, I had no idea—and that her violin teacher and his wife sort of became like godparents to her, and they were wealthy and had no kids of their own."

"Oh. So you think they left her money."

"Sure, I don't know how else she would have gotten it. And she didn't spend it. She saved every bit. For us."

Cami frowns at the table, then rips off her glasses and tosses them down, where they rattle across the waxy surface. She covers her face in her hands, gripping the hair over her forehead with the tips of her fingers.

"Excuse me," she says, stumbling out of the booth and to the ladies' room.

I'm not going to follow her, because she doesn't want anyone to see her fall apart. Sometimes the greatest kindness is space, and preservation of dignity.

Once, in my earlier days at Miller Paulson, I thoughtlessly answered a call from a client on my speaker phone. My hands were full, and this was before the days of the earpiece I eventually wore so often it was like jewelry.

He'd gotten drunk and was upset about a setback in his case. He started shrieking at me, blaming me for everything wrong in his life.

My office door was open. People started to collect in the doorway; others stared as they went by, rubbernecking. I snatched up the handset to switch him off speaker. I kept trying to interrupt him, to bring the conversation back to a something professional, to appease him without simpering, but he ridiculed my attempts to speak.

August came in then. I don't know if he heard what was happening or just happened by, but he strode right in my office.

Tears were quivering at the edges of my eyelids.

August took the phone, listened a moment, then shouted over the client's drunken venom, "You can call us back when you've composed yourself," and hung up.

I looked at his face and thought, *Don't pity me. Don't you dare.*

He said, "Make sure you bill him for that," and winked. The crowd of gawkers laughed, I laughed, and we moved on with our day.

The reality of August's death hits me in the chest. It's been easy to put that aside here in Haven.

The waitress plunks down an empty glass for me and fills it from the pitcher. I check my message on the phone. It's Beck.

Tough day today. Visit from Maddie and she asked me to come home with her and Mommy. She doesn't understand why I can't. Miss you.

Text messages and e-mail only, we agreed. Phone calls only in dire circumstances. Otherwise, we would avoid each other without doing so conspicuously. In the few weeks that have passed, we've bumped into each other twice in town, said hello, and carried on.

He broke the rule once already, though: when he left me a copy of Thoreau's *Walden* on the doorstep of the Nee Nance, ringing the bell as I was closing up for the night, and then disappearing down the street without a backward glance.

On the title page was this inscription: *I imagine life with you. Beck.*

There was a bookmark toward the end, and he'd underlined one passage.

I learned this, at least, by my experiment: that if one advances confidently in the direction of his dreams, and endeavors to live the life which he has imagined, he will meet with a success unexpected in common hours.

And I was happy to see it. Despite that he's still married, despite that I never wanted to come back here, despite his brother and the demolition . . . I was happy.

It makes no sense, but frankly I'm a little tired of making sense all the time.

Cami returns with the familiar gait that I recognize from across the bar before I even see her face. She moves so smoothly it's like she pours herself from one step to the next.

She pauses after she sits down and gives me a smile which seems to say: *Thanks for not following.*

And I nod in return. We will never discuss this moment, I know.

"So," I say, patting the trust papers. "Will you let me sue his ass?"

"Go for it," she says. "But what if he spent it?"

"He certainly hasn't been living a lavish lifestyle."

"But maybe he's just living off it. I've been wondering for years how a drunk like him runs an auto shop. Who would take their cars to him? Maybe no one does, yeah? But how could he do that? Wouldn't he have to forge my signature and stuff, fool a court?"

"You'd be surprised," I tell her, dryly. "There's no end to ways people can get screwed over. Don't worry, we'll get you something. He hid this from you, and he's not going to get away with that."

"So, what's your going rate?" Cami says.

"Oh, God, no. This one's on me. This'll be fun, in fact."

I sip my beer and ponder that Cami could never have afforded me in my Miller Paulson days. I also start writing the complaint in my head, to be filed in circuit court the minute I can get to my laptop and to the library to print it out.

"One more thing," Cami says. "He threw me out, and by that I mean literally . . ."

"Oh, you can stay with us, definitely."

"I'm sorry about it. I know how cramped it is there. I won't stay long, just until I figure something out—"

"Shut up already. It's fine."

"Well, okay then. But I don't even have so much as a toothbrush, or any clothes at all. Can you help me go get my stuff tomorrow? After he goes to work?"

"Of course."

We sit in silence for a few moments, listening to the clack of balls at the pool table and the low rumble of a baseball game on one of the small televisions.

"So, I guess you're back for a while, yeah?" asks Cami.

"Yeah."

"You okay with it?"

"It was my call."

"The siren song of Haven too much for you?" Cami casts an eye around the shadowy interior of the Tip-A-Few.

"There are worse places to be."

"I'll take your word for it," Cami says.

My phone rings and I glance at it. It's the store, and for that number, I answer: "Mom?"

"Oh, good, I caught you. Sally isn't back yet and I'm really starting to worry."

"She's not back *yet*? That's not a walk—that's an epic journey."

Cami cocks an eyebrow at me. I whisper to her: *Sally.*

"I didn't tell you this before, but . . . we had a fight. An argument. And she stormed off."

"She's probably off having a tantrum or something, then."

"She never stays mad. She doesn't have the attention span." I can hear my mother's voice start to shake.

"Don't panic. We'll start looking. Okay, Mom? Don't panic."

Cami is already draining her glass. She dusts off her hands as in *that's that* and says, "Well, I've always wanted to be in a search party, yeah?"

CHAPTER 42

Maeve

THE NEE NANCE IS CLOSED.

Now and then someone comes by and rattles the front door. Sometimes they knock. I imagine they cup their hands over their eyes and peer inside. Maybe they think I'm dead on the floor.

I just can't deal with customers now.

Anna searched for hours last night and came back with Cami—beaten up by that hideous louse of a father, poor thing— and they fell asleep upstairs in Anna's room. Slumber party style, both of them on the floor in some musty old sleeping bags I dug out of the back room. I looked in on them when I gave up on sleeping before dawn this morning. It pinched my heart to see them sprawled like that, their hair wild, their faces relaxed in repose. I could almost imagine the room scattered with *Tiger Beat* and *Seventeen* magazines, and a stale bowl of popcorn in there, too.

I called the police this morning, and they said although she's not officially missing yet, they would keep their eyes open for her. *Should I let the local media know?* the young man asked.

I held my breath. Once again the Genevas were falling apart in public. But if everyone saw her face on the news . . .

So this is what brings me into the kitchen with my too-strong coffee, paging through old photo albums to find a usable picture to put on the news.

Only she's wearing the wrong wig, or pulling such a face that no one would recognize her, or her back is to the camera.

And I keep stopping where I know I shouldn't linger: pictures of Robert making a muscle for the camera, giving Anna a horsey ride, and then pictures of a teenage Anna with no parent in sight—because Robert had left and I had the camera, always.

I should set these aside and bring them with me. I glance at the wall calendar—a gift from Lakeshore Realty—and see that it's just ten days until our appointed meeting date. His letter, from "P. C. Harming," finally came through with a definite date and place, even a hand-drawn map on the back of an IHOP placemat. He'd drawn hearts and flowers all around our destination, the piece of land he's promised to build a cabin on, for the two of us.

Only, what if I haven't found Sally by then? And what on earth would I say to him? *Hey, remember your sister? The one you never talked to again, either? Well, she's missing, by the way. No, she never did marry anybody; no, I was all she had, actually . . . until I lost my temper and drove her away . . .*

Or, worse. She goes for a swim and they find her in the channel or smashed on the rocks . . .

I slam the album shut. Maybe the school system where she used to work has a picture on file.

It's been years since I prayed, since before Robert left. The church ladies never came by with casseroles for me, like they did for the widows. No visit from the priest to see how I was getting on. In church, they seemed to steer their husbands away from me, as if I might reach out and snatch myself a replacement. That might have been paranoia on my part, but the chill was there, for whatever reason. It was palpable, like the pain in your lungs on a January morning.

None of that was God's fault, though, was it? I fold my hands and rest my forehead. I can't think of any words, so I trust that God will know what I'm trying to say and simply whisper, "Amen."

I turn in my chair at the sound of footsteps. It's Anna, in a huge old T-shirt that says UNIVERSITY OF MICHIGAN on it, still looking so much like a kid.

"I called the police," I tell her. "They say they'll keep an eye out, and they'd like a picture. They can put it out to the media, too . . ."

"We'll find her," Anna says, clearing her throat and coughing. "I need some of that coffee, then I'll get dressed and head out again. Did she have friends she would stay with?"

"She used to have casino buddies, but she hasn't been on one of those trips all summer. I don't even know who she used to go with."

"Maybe they—"

The phone rings, and Anna seizes the kitchen extension. "Hello?" Then her eyes get big and she stares at me, saying, "Sal, where are you? . . . What? . . . Well, tell me what you can see from there. Any signs, anything. Are there people around? Why don't you stop and tell someone you're lost? . . . Listen, honey, it's okay, we'll come to get you; we just have to know where. . . . Uh-huh . . . Who's Pete? . . . Oh. . . . You need to ask someone where you are. They won't think you're silly; just say you need to get a ride . . . Uh-huh. Oh, good." She starts snapping her fingers at me, making scribbling gestures. I scramble in drawers until I come up with a geriatric ink pen and rip the cover off the phone book. Anna turns the phone book cover over to the blank side and starts writing, balanced awkwardly, using her knee as a table. "Yes . . . okay, I know where that is. Thank you, Ma'am. Listen, can I ask you something? I hope this isn't awkward for you. Just give me a yes or no: Does she seem okay to you? Physically? . . . Okay, thank you."

I sink down into the kitchen chair, holding on like I might tumble off at any moment. I hate to imagine what my blood pressure is right now.

Anna seems to have Sally back on the line. "Sally? Hi, doll, it's Anna. Look, I'm going to be there as soon as I can, but it's about a thirty-minute drive. I need you to promise me that you won't move. You've gotta stay put. Can you do that for me? Okay . . . I'm sure you're hungry. We'll get you some breakfast the minute I get there. Okay, I'll be there soon. Sit tight."

Anna hangs up, and I follow her as she rushes down the hall to her room, where she steps over a sleeping Cami and slides on a pair of shorts. She wraps her hair into a ponytail and hisses to me in a whisper: "She's in Saugatuck."

"How did she get there?"

She shrugs and steps across Cami again, grabbing her purse off the floor. I follow her down the steps.

"I want to come with you."

Anna shakes her head. "You'd better not. If she moves again, she might call back here, and you'll need to call me and tell me where she is."

"But you told her to stay."

Anna stops in the doorway, her keys in her hand. "Mom. I hate to say this, but I don't think she knows what's going on right now. She might forget she said that and just wander off. She might get a ride from somebody; I think that's how she got where she is now. She said she was riding with . . . an old boyfriend."

Our eyes lock. Anna clearly understands just as I do that she didn't get a ride from any boyfriend.

"I'll call you the minute I get her. Keep an eye on Cami. Tell her to put some ice on that eye."

My daughter dashes out the front door, and I raise my eyes to the ceiling. It might have been luck but maybe not. *Thank you.* And, *Please, let her be intact.*

CHAPTER 43

Amy

"LAKESHORE REALTY," I ANSWER, RUBBING MY TEMPLE WITH MY free hand. "Yes, one moment." I hit the disconnect button instead of transfer.

"Shit."

"Amy? Is everything all right?" Kelly has stopped by my desk, her arms full of paper.

"Sorry, just a little—"

The phone interrupts me, and I answer and this time manage to transfer the call.

I hope she doesn't fire me, because then all I'll have is Frodo and my apartment, which has wedding stuff scattered all over it like lacy land mines.

Kelly glances down at my desk, which is somewhat more bare of late, considering I've taken down all personal pictures. "Come with me," she says, gesturing with her head because her arms are full.

Here it comes. I should have known.

"Cover the phones," she says to Bill as she passes, and I follow her, with my eyes on the carpet.

"Please sit," she says, dropping the files on her desk and straightening her lapels. "I've been concerned about you. Is everything all right?"

"I'm fine. I know I've been a little distracted . . ."

"It's not that. A couple of disconnected phone calls are of no concern to me. But you took down all your pictures, and I saw you actually eat a Snickers the other day. I thought aliens abducted the real Amy." She smiles at me, a little bigger than her cool, professional smile, but I can't see the humor.

I look down at my lap, at my ring, which I still can't bring myself to remove.

"I don't want to talk about it."

"I just wanted you to know you can discuss it with me, if you'd like."

A piece of hair has fallen out of my sloppy ponytail. I push it back and squint at her for a moment. "I have friends."

"I didn't mean to imply that you didn't."

I haven't talked to them, though; in fact, I haven't been returning their prying calls and e-mails. They're asking me about dress fittings, why haven't they gotten their invitations, when should they schedule the bachelorette party . . . I know what they'll say. They'll insist I take him back. Or maybe they'll try to get me drunk, which seems to be how they solve most everything.

"Would you like some time off?" Kelly asks, tapping a pencil, eraser-side down on her desk.

I shake my head, hard. "No, please, I'm okay. I'm sorry about the dropped calls. I'll do better."

"That wasn't a threat, you know."

"I know. I'm sorry, Kelly . . ."

"Well, back to your desk, then. But one thing, Amy. Keeping a problem secret doesn't make it disappear. In fact, sometimes putting it out in the daylight is the only way to solve it." She holds my gaze as she says this, and I nod to her before backing out and returning to my station.

Kelly is famous—or infamous, depending on whom you ask— around here for suing her boss at her old job because he continually passed her over for promotions, although she was better educated and worked harder than her white coworkers. According to the article in the paper, it had been going on for years before she spoke up finally. The guy settled out of court, and Kelly used the money to start this business.

She caught a lot of flak for it. People said she should have handled it quietly, without all the fanfare of a public lawsuit. But something she said at the time stuck in my head. She was quoted in the paper as saying, "A whisper doesn't always cut it. Sometimes you need to shout."

Back at my desk, I send Paul a text.

I need to see you. Meet me at my apartment after work. 5:30?

I've only just set my phone down when it trills again.

I'll be there.

One good thing about getting out of work at three o'clock is, now I have a jump on Paul getting here, assuming he's on time. He often gets distracted at work.

I'm still in my work clothes and Frodo cocks his head at me when I put him on the leash. He wants to go for a run. "Not now, Frodo. You're going on a playdate."

Ed had put his address on the card he left for me, and he's only a few buildings away. I lead Frodo along, pausing to let him pee, and

I knock on Ed's door, hoping he's home because honestly I don't know his schedule or even what he does for a living.

Ed draws back slightly when he opens the door.

"Amy! I don't suppose you're going for a run right now."

"I need a favor, actually."

"Name it."

"Could you keep Frodo for a bit? I just . . . It's a long story, but . . ."

"You got it, no problem. How long?"

"Um, I'm honestly not sure. Give me your phone number, though, and I'll call you."

So we exchange numbers, and before I leave—with Frodo romping all over poor little Lucky, who's getting clobbered but enjoying it nevertheless—I shake Ed's hand. "Thanks for being so genuinely nice. I bet you would have been nice even when I was fat."

"Well, I'm in no position to judge. Pot and kettle, you know."

As I head down the steps, Ed calls after me, "Good luck!"

Back in my apartment, I take a long, hot shower, and this time I don't grab the robe and avert my eyes.

Still swathed in steam, I make myself look at my naked self, complete with stretch marks and the saggy skin around my thighs and middle.

I dry my hair in the mirror, looking at my breasts, which seem thin and tired. My mirror quotes remind me: EVERY THIN DAY IS A GOOD DAY!

Not true, I know. I tear it down.

Reflexively I reach for my mascara, my concealer and blush, and then I stop, put it down.

I brush my hair straight. No curlers this time, no hairspray.

I start to close my window blinds, and then stop. I yank the cord, letting the light flood in. No one can see in here, anyway; the apartment is high enough.

Still time before Paul arrives. I slip on my silk robe I always wear when Paul is around. I fish my journal out of a drawer in my nightstand and sit down to wait.

At 5:15 my doorbell rings, and I think it must be Ed or someone else. Paul never rings the bell; he has a key.

It's him, though. Through the peephole I can see him looking down, hands in his pockets.

"Hi," he says inside the door, leaving his hands where they are. He seems to flinch away from me. "You're not dressed."

"I was wrong," I say.

"About what?" He looks like someone hollowed him out. He's standing there all bent over, concave like an old man.

"To break up with you. I was also wrong to hide from you."

"Hide what from me?"

My hands fumble with the robe tie. It's not a complicated knot, but my fingers feel fat and clumsy, like when it was easier to use a pencil to dial a phone than use my fingers. I drop the robe off my shoulders and suck in a sharp breath, like I'm bracing for a slap. I squeeze my eyes shut.

I know what he's seeing, since I made myself look again this afternoon. From the shoulders up and knees down I'm pretty, and with clothes on I can pass.

It's all out there now.

"Can I . . ." He stops, clears his throat. "Does this mean we're not breaking up?"

I crunch my eyes closed harder for a moment, then force them to open and look right at him. He's waiting, looking like a kid on the first day of school, both hopeful and scared to death. I shake my head. "Not if you don't want to."

At this, he rushes to me, embraces me. "Why would I want to?" he whispers into my hair.

He kisses me so long I'm breathless. I push back a little and say, "Even with all this?" I glance down at my body.

"Can I show you how much I don't care?"

He scoops me up and carries me off to the bedroom, where the sun frames my bed like a spotlight and we stay on top of the covers.

I say to Paul, "Tell me not to crawl under the sheets."

"Don't crawl under the sheets." He takes my hand and kisses it. The only thing I'm wearing is my engagement ring. "I was beginning to think you only cared about everything looking perfect."

"I only got close to perfect recently. I can't just let go of it."

"You thought I wouldn't love you if I saw your whole body?"

"Not exactly. I didn't want to chance it, I guess. We never met when I was fat. But look, be honest, Paul. Would you have dated me when I was fat?"

He props up on his elbow, his dark hair flopped over one eye. His face is somber. "It would have been my loss."

I close my eyes and let that sink in. It would have felt better if he'd said, "I would have loved you at any weight." But I know that the weight is a wall that keeps so many people out, and not only shallow, vain, nasty people. Even when I was huge, I didn't date fat guys, either. And even if not for Paul, I still wouldn't have dated egg-shaped Ed, either. Nice as he is.

"Will you still love me if I get fat again?"

"Well, now I know what I'd be missing."

"So why won't you marry me?" I cringe after I say it. I wasn't going to pressure him.

"I'm sorry I did that to you," he says, his voice soft. He rests back on my pillow, turning his eyes to the ceiling. "It wasn't fair to let my work stress mess up your dream wedding. I suppose it's too late, at this point."

"Probably." My voice cracks, despite my earlier resolve that it shouldn't matter if we get married on our original wedding date in a big ceremony. It does, dammit. It just does.

"Well, does it have to be too late, though? Maybe some things won't be so elaborate or whatever, but it's not like we cancelled the country club. Did you?"

"I couldn't bring myself to make that call. Or even tell anyone."

"Ha, me neither. I could just imagine my dad's reaction. I've been putting it off."

We turn to each other, both of us with that same half smile. "So, maybe we can still do it?" I say.

He embraces me on the bed, kissing my cheek and saying, "Hell, yeah."

So this is the new us, all honest and open and, literally, naked. It feels so good, I'll even tell him about my fertility charts and the temperatures.

Later.

CHAPTER 44

Anna

MOM QUIZZES ME ABOUT SALLY AS I TRY TO ADJUST THE STOCK ON the shelves to make everything look less ravaged. We haven't been reordering, except the most popular items, so things are looking even more sloppy and haphazard than usual. I've deposited Sally upstairs on Mom's bed, and when I left her, she was snoring away.

"She was just sitting on a park bench, kicking her feet like a little kid waiting for a ride, and she chattered the whole way home."

"About what?"

"Nothing. Old stories about people she used to work with, stories about you as a teenager, working at the bowling alley. Drive-in movies."

"Did she say anything about what she'd been doing all that time?"

I stand up and stretch. Mom is leaning on the counter, and that's when I notice something inside her shirt, pressing against the cotton. She's still wearing that ring.

"Anna, did she talk about it?"

"No. Every time I tried to gently inquire, she either shut right down or changed the subject, told me a joke. She wasn't wearing shoes, which you noticed when she came in, and it sounds like she got a ride, at least one ride, from a man. But I don't know anything else. Her shirt did seem like it was a little dirtier on the back than I remembered it, like she'd been lying down in the dirt at some point."

"Should we . . . have her checked out?"

I shrug, thinking of her sleeping upstairs, looking so frail now. "I don't know if I'd take her to the hospital, but maybe just have Dr. Simon give her a once-over."

Mom glances at the door to make sure there are no customers coming in. She drops her voice lower. "I hope she didn't . . . You don't suppose, if she forgot what year it was and thought some guy was her boyfriend . . ."

"I hope not, but I don't really know. Like I said, she wouldn't talk about it."

I don't say it out loud to my mother, but along with the chance that Aunt Sally had sex with a stranger because she was out of her head, she could have been raped. Actually, one is the same as the other, because the guy in question would probably have known she was acting strange, not in her right head. I suppose we could drag her to the sexual assault crisis center, have a rape kit administered, and try to get to the bottom of it.

Or, we could leave her alone.

"It's not your fault," I tell her.

Mom averts her eyes. "In any case, we'd better watch her close."

My cell phone bleeps. I read Beck's message.

Moving into a house in Poplar Bluff. Buyers pulled out of sale. Dad needed a tenant. Big enough for two.

He includes the address in the message.

I snap the phone shut and resume straightening the cans.

"Who was that?" Mom asks, leafing through a magazine.

"Shelby."

I've got duplexes and apartments circled in the newspaper, mostly two-bedroom. Mom is assuming all three of us will be staying together, at least for now, and it's the only option that makes sense. I have savings, but not so much that I can pay rent on two apartments without a second thought, especially given how grim the job market's been looking lately.

The thought of sharing four beige walls in a rental unit with my mother and batty maiden aunt is almost enough to send me crawling back to Chicago and begging Miller Paulson for my job back. Almost.

And now here's Beck with his "big enough for two."

Too fast, and yet, wasn't it years in the making? His text from last night said his wife had found an attorney.

So it seems she's prepared to divorce.

They are, however, keeping everything as quiet as possible until after Paul's wedding, in which Maddie is going to be a flower girl and Beck is a groomsman. That will be their last public appearance as husband and wife, he'd said.

My invitation to the wedding had arrived just yesterday, along with one for Mom. Mom threw hers in the garbage. I've got my RSVP marked with "regrets" and ready to go out with the day's mail.

"I think I'm just going to close the place down," Mom says abruptly, slapping her magazine closed. "Who cares now?"

"Right now?"

"Not this minute. Maybe next week—Friday should be our last day. Then I'll take a drive up north."

"A drive?"

"Sure, why not? I never get weekends off. I'll just drive up north and get some air."

"Want me to come with you?"

"Would you be offended if I said I just need some alone time?"

"Not at all." I understand all too well.

I glance at the calendar behind the counter. That's the Friday before the Becker wedding. "Well, it's as good a time as any. I'll make a 'going out of business' sign."

"Don't bother. I don't want any fuss."

Indeed. That's all we've had lately. A whole lot of fuss.

Cami comes down the stairs, her face looking much better already. She's pulled her hair back.

"Hey, you fixed your glasses," I say, noticing they're back on her face as normal.

"I glued them. I can't fold them up anymore, but at least they stay on. And no tape on them, yeah?"

"So, are you feeling okay?" Mom asks, giving Cami that slit-eyed once-over she always used on me after a bad test at school or a tumble on the playground.

"Right as rain." She puts her hands on her hips. "Need a break, Maeve? I'm bored."

"You're on."

"We have to look at some apartments, anyway," I tell Cami after I line up the SpaghettiOs. "And I have a complaint to file in circuit court, and then we'll go get your stuff from your dad's."

It felt funny, last night. I couldn't sleep after failing to find Sally, so instead, I got back to lawyering. This time I wasn't sitting at my huge desk in my office with my high heels kicked off under the desk; I was cross-legged on my narrow childhood bed with my laptop, Cami asleep on the floor. It didn't take me long to write; climbing back in the saddle was easy. I saved it to a thumb drive so I could go print it out.

It was fun, even, gearing up to kick some ass. Not that I didn't kick ass at Miller Paulson; I kicked plenty, and though I believed every word I wrote, everything I said at the time, looking at my

work there with some distance, all the battles were usually between huge entities or wealthy people scrapping over money.

This ass-kicking is personal and deserved. I'm not a mercenary
now, hired to carry out the battle plan; oh, no.

Cami reclined in the office chair. "How long could this take?"

"It will take some time. It depends how hard he fights, whether
he hires his own lawyer. He might settle, which would be faster
but might get you less than what you're owed."

"Hmmm. Less, huh?"

"Sometimes speed is preferable. Depends what your goal is.
What you really want."

"Mmm." Cami tips her head back in the chair and spins herself
in half circles, idly stroking her fading bruise with the tips of her
fingers.

CHAPTER 45

Cami

ANNA SLOWS HER CAR IN FRONT OF MY HOUSE—SCRATCH THAT, Dad's house—and if we see his truck or any sign of movement in the windows from Sherry, we are outta here. Seems safe, though, so we exchange a look and pull up front.

I go quickly across the grass, pulling out my keys as I do. I'd like to just mosey, as an act of defiance. I'm not afraid of him. He already knocked me cold and slapped me around. *Do your worst!* I would like to say, and spit on him, just for that extra hit of drama, because why not? But I've got Anna here, and I wouldn't like her to get beat up on my account.

The key doesn't even go in.

"Piece of shit changed the locks on me."

We look for open windows, but they're all shut.

"C'mon, let's head out back."

Our feet crunch on the gravel and as we walk down the drive.

That's when my dad's neighbor slams her window shut. Anna jumps. "Hey, cool it, there, 007," I say, elbowing her.

On the back porch, I find a window open halfway. "Stand back," I tell Anna, and grab an old beer bottle. I smash the end off, then use the jagged edge to rip the screen out.

I turn to Anna and wink. She looks like she might throw up. "You'll defend me against a breaking and entering charge, yeah?"

"You bet." She doesn't smile, though.

I wriggle in through the half-open window and open the back door for Anna. I gesture for her to follow me into my room, where I stop so quick she bumps into me from behind.

My dresser drawers are standing open; my folding closet door is off the track and hanging akimbo from the hinges. Everything's empty. Even the sheets are ripped off the bed, which has been moved away from the wall.

There are shoeprints all over my sunny yellow paint.

I lead Anna down the hall and there, in the living room, is my stuff in a pile, like it's ready for a bonfire. On the top of the mess is the framed photograph of Mom, Trent, and me, the one that fell off my wall the first day back. Its glass is cracked with a spider-web pattern, as if punched.

I slide the photo out of its frame and fold it inside an old math book.

"Let's go," I tell Anna.

"Don't you want me to find some boxes or something? For all this?"

I shrug. "It's just stuff. None of it means a damn thing."

A pounding on the door make us both jump this time. It's not my dad because this person is too short; anyway, he must have his own key.

I open the door to find Sherry, looking around her frantically, like she's being chased by a lion.

"You guys have gotta get outta here. Now."

"What's going on?"

"Your dad got a call at the shop. I was on my way out when I overheard. The neighbor called to say you were breaking in, and he started cursing and talking about a citizen's arrest. He's really lit, too."

I don't have to be told twice. But halfway across the weedy yard, I stop and turn back to Sherry, still on the porch. "Hey, um, thanks for that. He'll be pissed if he catches you here, yeah?"

"Probably," she says, pronouncing it "prolly."

"So, go already."

"Yeah, I guess I'd better."

She looks lost. She might not have any class and she's definitely no intellectual giant, but she just risked her ass for me and I can't just let her stand there. "Hey!" I snap my fingers at her. I can see Anna has already started the car. "You gotta go."

"Well, I kinda got tossed outta my place, so . . ."

"Uh-uh. I'll tell you right now that a cardboard box is better than this. You know that yourself; tell me you don't."

"Cami!"

We lingered too long. His truck skids around the corner, and I flinch because he's headed right for Anna's car.

"Dad!" I scream as his truck slides, fishtailing, until it's nose to nose with Anna's bumper.

He stumbles out the door, looking from me to Sherry. "You!" he bellows, jabbing a finger at her. "You helped her bust into my house. My own house!"

"I didn't, Tim, I swear!" She holds her hands up like he's going to shoot her.

I sure hope he doesn't have a gun.

He whirls on me, but I don't shrink away. For one thing, he's still several feet from me, and it's broad daylight. In the corner of my eye, I can see Anna muttering into her cell phone.

"And you! You're always leaving me!"

"What the . . . ? You threw me out! After beating the crap out of me!" I point to my eye.

"How could you leave me all alone like this?" he bellows like a wounded bear.

I gasp and clutch my chest. He said that to my mom, just before she went into the hospital that very last time. As if she got sick on purpose, just to hurt him.

Movement to my left catches my eye. Anna strides across the grass, looking very lawyer-like, despite her capri pants and pony-tail. She walks right up to my father and smacks him in the chest with some papers.

I suck in a sharp breath, but he seems to be so stunned all he does is take the papers and frown at them.

"You're being sued, asshole. For the money you stole from your daughter."

"C'mon, Cami," she says, and walks backward to her car, one eye on my father, who is reading and becoming more scarlet by the moment.

"Sherry! You coming?" I say, doing my own backward walk. She just shakes her head.

Please? I mouth the word to her, across the lawn, pointing at the car. *C'mon!*

She shakes her head slowly, waving her hands at us. *You go on.*

Anna does a Y-turn and drives off in the opposite direction of the sirens.

"She'll be okay. The police just got a tip about a drunk and disorderly. If we're lucky, he'll get in his truck and start driving so they can get him for that, too."

"Lucky, yeah." I say, sinking back in the seat and taking out my family picture to look at myself in my pig-tailed youth. "We could use some of that."

CHAPTER 46

Maeve

I'M IN FRONT OF MY BATHROOM MIRROR, PRIMPING. WHEN WAS THE last time I bothered? My freckles stand out bright against my skin, like someone scattered dust across my chest. Robert won't mind, though. He used to kiss them, pretending to kiss each one individually, until . . .

I haven't felt this way in so very long.

I stayed up most of the night finishing the dress. Sally did ask me what I was working on, and I just told her I wanted a new summer outfit.

I wish I could get a full-length view, but we don't have a full-length mirror in the place. I'll have to content myself with admiring the neckline in the bathroom cabinet mirror, and trust that the hem is even.

The last day of the Nee Nance. The day I see Robert again. There's a certain poetry to that.

My wedding ring is in a zippered pocket in the lining of my

purse. It would be exposed if I wore it with this dress and its scoop neck, and I don't want Robert to leap to any conclusions if he sees it there.

I hope I can put it back on my finger, though. And soon.

I have makeup in my purse, too, which I haven't worn since the last wedding I went to, which was probably two years ago now. I dare not put it on yet; Anna would ask too many questions. Anyway, it would fade off in the long drive to Cadillac.

It was good of Veronica to lend me her car, since the Buick died, and agree to keep an eye on Sally for me. I'd brought her a cake from the bakery in the next block by way of apology for blowing up at her earlier suggestion Anna was "cracking." I told her I was hoping to get away for some personal time, and she readily agreed to help, telling me I should ask for assistance more often.

Anna will watch the register today. I told her I didn't want to be there for the end of it all, and she could close up whenever she felt like. There's no point in commemorating the last sale or the last customer. I'll be punching a register again anyway.

I walk back to my bedroom and put a pair of medium-high heels into my large bag and slip some flat sandals on for the drive.

I may buy some perfume on my way out of town. I sniffed some from my old collection, but they all whiffed vaguely of vinegar.

I come down the steps, catching sight of my own legs in the dress, and the effect is dizzying, because I mostly wore dresses around Robert. If I don't look too close, my legs could be those of a twenty-year-old.

At the bottom of the stairs, I do a double-take at the store's bones sticking out. The shelves emptying, the advertising posters taken down, the sign with our hours gone.

"Hi," says Anna, then she stops sweeping, leans on the broom. "Well. Don't you look pretty."

"Feels like an occasion, somehow."

"Sure you don't want me to put a sign up? People around here might be sad to know they missed out on the Nee Nance's last day."

"They can come gawk at the wrecking ball." That came out as more venomous than I meant it. I take a deep, deliberate breath. "You know I don't like a spectacle."

"Right. No fanfare." Anna resumes sweeping. "So, Cami's bringing Sally to Veronica's house. She sure is being a sport about this, and lending you a car, too."

"That she is. I just don't want you two to have to worry about Sally while I make this little escape." I laugh to cover what I just said, though there's no way Anna could know what I'm really doing.

I will tell her, and soon. And by then I hope to make her understand. She has been less guarded lately, since she rescued that girl. Maybe all is not lost for father and daughter.

I step forward to hug her, and I don't feel her stiffen under my arms like she has so often. She rests her chin briefly on my shoulder, curving down to do so. It's still time-warping, feeling my daughter loom over me, when I used to hold that chubby little hand, reaching up to grasp my pinky finger.

"I better go. I need to get going . . ."

I turn away hastily before Anna can ask me what's wrong, quickly wiping under my eyes as I walk out the front door and the Nee Nance jingle bells clang against my knee.

There's too much time to think on this drive. I should have brought along some tapes. I can't abide talk radio, all those people yelling at each other. I have no use for current music. I hear enough of that thumping out the car windows of wannabe gangsters cruising Shoreline Drive.

I flip on the oldies station, having long ago reconciled myself to being out of date, when I was still young enough to try being hip. I always felt older than my peers, partly due to my mother's strict rules for my clothing and comportment, and partly because of my own mysterious preference for the movies and songs of a previous era. I've always been nostalgic for a time I can't even remember.

The Eagles start wailing in harmony about giving me the best of their love.

Two memories assail me at once. Robert crooning that to me over the phone, badly on purpose, trying to make me laugh after a fight with my mother.

And that day at the bowling alley.

I was working for my uncle Mike, waiting tables from the snack bar. Certain memories are so fierce they crystallize, complete with smells, sounds, full color, slow motion, and instant replay. Fresh smoke and sweat, the thunderous crashing of ball into pins, and echoing hoots of victory, and yes, even the Eagles singing over the tinny speakers about the best of their love, *sweet darling, every night and day* . . .

There was this guy. That's all he was, I tried to tell myself, just a guy, of a certain type who liked to be lewd. I certainly never invited this with my conservative attire, but for a certain malicious subset of his kind, it was like blood in the water to wear a high-necked, shapeless blouse.

I had learned to step away from grabby hands and to lean away when setting down drinks. But waitressing—even at a bowling alley—forces physical proximity. No protective counter or cash register.

There was nothing special in how his hand grazed my breast when he reached for a napkin and I set down his friend's drink. Nothing revolutionary about the smack on the bottom he gave me when I walked away or the jeering I got for refusing to cooperate with a sexy wink or a knowing smile.

This is what I told myself when holding my hand over my heart behind the bar, trying to breathe.

Uncle Mike was so busy that night—a Saturday—that he barely

glanced my way, and anyway, I was a big girl, right? I was eighteen, after all. A grown-up. I was afraid he'd fire me if I couldn't handle the customers, and then my mother would accuse me of asking for the attention.

Then Robert and Sean and the gang came in. My heart leaped; I was saved! But they chose a seat so far away from that man, they'd never see a thing.

I served them some sodas, and when Robert asked me what was wrong, I smiled at him and said nothing's wrong, everything's fine.

Moments later, I steeled myself to approach the Wolf Man's table. As I was trying to hear his buddy's snack order, I found myself in the wolf's lap, encircled in his meaty arms. I pushed against him and he squeezed tighter. I kicked my feet and he laughed, his oniony breath in my ear, my hair. I could feel his erection under my thigh and I hollered, "Let me go!" and wanted to cry with how pathetic and fearful I sounded.

The next moments happened all at once. The chair was knocked down, and in a moment I was back on my feet and Robert was on top of the man, pummeling him in the face. His buddies were closing in and pushing up sleeves.

"Robert!" I screamed, because he was not a big man, and the other men were, in fact, all rather large.

At last Uncle Mike and my cousin Sean and a couple other friends of ours finally swooped in. The wolf and his whole pack were ousted into the parking lot, banned for life, and threatened with jail and worse if they ever came near the place, especially that night.

Uncle Mike pleaded with me not to tell my mother. No doubt he feared her wrath, too, that this should happen under his watch.

He insisted I take the night off. I tried to refuse, playing it cool, though my hands trembled in my lap like I'd been taken with some kind of palsy. He sent Robert and Sean to guard my walk to my car.

Sean beat it back to his bowling game the minute he established that there were no villains lurking about.

Robert put his arm around me for the rest of the trip across the parking lot, and I still tried to play the woman of the world.

"It was nothing," I said. "Some horse's ass." The curse word felt strange in my mouth and sounded too quiet for the circumstances.

"It wasn't nothing. He was scaring you, and doing it on purpose, which makes him one sick prick. You don't ever let anyone do that to you, Maeve. You come get me, or if you can't, get somebody. Don't ever let anyone hurt you like that."

He squeezed my shoulder and helped me into the car, even slamming my door for me. He stood in the circle of light under the parking lot lamppost until he disappeared from view in my rear mirror.

Rumble strips startle me back to the present with a loud, grinding growl.

I aim the car straight again and roll down the window, tuning the radio to a talk station. No more daydreaming allowed. The real thing will be in front of me soon enough.

CHAPTER 47

Amy

WHEN I SEE MYSELF IN THE MIRROR, I TURN TO LOOK OVER MY shoulder. My mother thinks I'm looking at her, and she smiles and gives me a thumbs up, tears carving furrows through her makeup.

In truth, I thought for just a moment that this reflection belonged to someone else, and I was turning to see the other bride in Agatha's, wearing my dress.

Now that the dress has been ordered to size and altered to fit me just so, the effect is astonishing. My waist has never looked so tiny, and the special strapless bra I ordered makes it look like I even have a chest.

I vow I will not let one sweet, one carb, one glass of wine, pass my lips until after the big day.

My bridesmaids were horrified that I cancelled my bachelorette party. I told them to go get drunk without me, and I think they're going to do exactly that. Considering how close I came to not having this wedding at all, "celebrating" my single life hardly seems worth the effort.

No one has been speaking. They're waiting for me, I realize, Agatha and my mother.

"It's beautiful." My voice breaks.

"You're beautiful," Agatha says, fluffing out my gown here and there, pulling on bits of the dress to make sure it fits. Of course it does; she's a genius, and every bride in town knows that.

My mother starts to speak and has to clear her throat and start again. "I wish . . ."

She doesn't have to finish her sentence. She sits behind us on a cushioned bench, wearing a column-shaped lavender dress with a jacket. It falls nearly to the floor. The embroidery on the jacket echoes the lace on my dress. It's perfect; rather, the best Agatha could possibly do.

"You look lovely," I tell her.

"Not hardly," she answers, but waves away further protest and starts digging in her purse. I know enough to give up at this point. Persistent argument will only escalate, and she'll just get more and more vicious with herself in an effort to convince us she truly is hideous.

I notice Aunt Agatha has paused in her dress-fluffing to rub her hands. They look knotty, like branches on a dying tree.

"Are you all right?"

She seems to only just realize what she'd been doing. "Oh, this. My arthritis is kicking up. I don't know how many more weddings I can do. I'm just glad I held out for yours."

"Will you be hiring someone, then?" Agatha has had shop assistants before, girls who work the register, if she can find someone reliable enough and the business is brisk. But she's never had anyone else do the tailoring.

Agatha steps forward with my veil. It's old-fashioned, an actual veil that comes over my face, attached to a headpiece that will be combed into my hair in its updo. I didn't want one of those cascading bits of tulle stuck in my bun. I wanted a real veil. I wanted for so long to see the candlelight muted through the tulle, to have it pulled back for complete clarity just as I reach my husband.

"No," she says, stretching to reach over my head. I bow at the neck, feeling like royalty. "No, I'll probably just close up."

"Oh, no, you can't!"

Agatha shrugs, but her eyes are sad. "Well, it couldn't be forever."

My mother interjects. "Why don't you hire someone?"

She shakes her head firmly. "You don't keep your own business going for forty years and then just hand it over. It would be like handing your kid to a stranger and telling him 'You be careful now.' No way."

This speech sounds rehearsed, giving me the impression she's had this talk before. "You don't have to give up everything," I tell her, thinking of all the brides in Haven who won't have her personal attention, all the fat girls crying in fitting rooms who won't have Agatha to make their clothes fit. "Just hire an assistant. For the sewing."

Agatha looks up at me, honest surprise on her face. "My dear. The sewing is everything."

My cell phone rings, and I flap my hand toward my purse. My mother reaches over and she can't get up fast enough, she knows that, so she passes it to Agatha, who hands it to me, fire brigade style. It's Paul, and I'm a little breathless when I answer.

"Hi, babe," he says.

"Hi, honey!" I chirp.

"Listen, um, do we have anything going on tonight? Anything that can't be rescheduled?"

"Nope, not at all!" We were supposed to be finally deciding on a first song, the one we'll dance to as husband and wife. It was one of the many chores that got dropped in the last weeks. We only just got the invitations done, telling everyone who asked that there had been a typo in the first batch and we were *so* sorry for the delay.

He sighs, a huge whoosh right into the phone. "Oh, good. I've just got to stay late tonight, I . . . I'm sorry, honey. I'll make it up to you. Let's go out for a late dinner? Or maybe tomorrow?"

I think of the calories in a restaurant meal, even in the so-called salads. "No, it's okay, really. Do what you need to do."

"You sure?"

"Yep!"

"Bye. I love you."

"I love you, too."

I click the phone closed, and Agatha takes my purse from me, fluffing my veil again. "So nice to hear," she said. "That's the nice thing about a bride who's not a twenty-year-old. You know how to take things in stride."

My mother laughs, and it startles me because I don't know what's funny. "Lord, yes!" she cries. "When Marlin was working so late in the garage all the time, I used to get so angry I think I smashed a dish on my own kitchen floor. And of course he was only doing it because he thought he had to be the hardest worker in town, and . . ."

My mother and Agatha start their patter, reminiscing about their own days as newlyweds, and their words trail to nothing in my ears. I can think only of Paul, hunched over his desk, his sleeves pushed up and his tie tossed over his shoulder so it won't hang down on his papers.

My phone rings again and I sigh and extend my hand for it, knowing now that Paul has gotten my blessing for late work, it won't be him calling again. Next I hear his voice will be tomorrow at the earliest.

"Hello?"

"Amy? This is Nikki's mom. Listen, I'm afraid there's some bad news. Nikki was trying to water-ski last week on her vacation and she broke her leg, quite seriously. She'll have to have surgery and she's in a lot of pain. She's not going to be in the wedding. I'm so sorry."

I stumble through some polite words of sympathy for her injury and add to my mental list of chores a get-well card for her, but all I can think about, truly, is the problem this creates.

It's asymmetry. An orphaned groomsman.

My heart starts to flutter in my chest like a frantic bird, and a wave of heat breaks over my skin. I start to zip myself out of the dress, because if I faint I might rip it.

My mother and Agatha ask me what's wrong, and I can hear myself telling them Nikki broke her leg, but I'm not really in the room; my brain is whirring away at how to fix this.

The Beckers can't demote any groomsmen at this late date; all their people are important. Snubs in a large, rich family can carry on for generations, so I'm told. Not that the guys would care, no. It would be their mothers, their wives.

But what do we do with a groomsman alone? Walking down the aisle with no woman on his arm? "It would look awful," I murmur.

"What? What's awful?" asks my mother as I step out of the crinoline. I seize my sundress and throw it over my head as fast as possible; in my distraction I hadn't realized I was undressing in front of them. I'd intended to ask them to step out of the dressing room first.

"It's all wrong," I say. "It won't look right."

"Your dress? But you just said it's gorgeous." Agatha frowns, clearly worried about where she's gone wrong. She starts inspecting the dress, which is once again on its hanger.

"Oh," says my mother. "Oh. I see."

She slips out of the dressing room door, with Agatha right behind.

I need a substitute. I need a fill-in bridesmaid who can wear a size ten dress, because my dresses were special ordered, and because of Paul and his "gee, maybe we shouldn't get married" stunt, we're so far behind . . .

"Amy!" calls Agatha, and I seize my purse and run out of the room at the urgency in her tone.

The look on her face freezes me in mid-step. She beckons me with one finger.

As I get close, she folds her arms. "Young lady. Your mother is in her own dressing room now, and I'll have you know she's bawling her eyes out because you're so upset her weight will make everything look all wrong."

"What? No! I didn't mean her! I meant we lost Nikki as a bridesmaid and so . . ."

She doesn't change her expression one bit.

"Agatha, I'm telling the truth. I'm upset because now we've got a groomsman without a partner!"

"I'm not the one you have to convince."

I tap the dressing room door where my mother's feet are showing. She nearly crashes the door into me when she slams it open. I try to stop myself from grimacing at the way she waddles when she's in a hurry, swaying her bulk from side to side on her way past Agatha, to the car.

"Something tells me I'm going to suddenly take ill on your wedding day," she says as she hits the sidewalk.

"No, Mom, please, I wasn't talking about you!"

I load her into my car—parked mercifully close this time—and climb in my side, explaining to her all the way about Nikki and how stupid it will look to have one groomsman alone.

My mother shakes her head, but her frown has softened into a look of weary exhaustion. "Fat mother, lone groomsman—what does it matter, Amy? You should have seen the look on your face. You looked like someone just died. I thought I raised you to believe that looks weren't important."

"Ha!" I smack the steering wheel. "Remember high school?

Me, and the girl with cerebral palsy, and John with the huge nose and horrible acne, all in the Loser Club. Then I lost the weight, and huh, guess what? Miraculously people look my way. Men ask me out. I get a job sitting at a reception desk instead of working the stock room at T. J. Maxx. Looks don't matter? My size six ass."

"So then explain to me why your fat-ass mother should be in your wedding?"

I drop my head back to the car's headrest. "Mother. Of course I want you there. I love you more than . . ." *a perfect wedding*, I finish in my head. "More than anything."

"I'll be there. But I won't be in the pictures."

"Mom, please . . ."

She holds up a hand to me and turns to look out the side window. "I'm not going to be looking at those pictures the rest of my life thinking about this moment. Take me home."

I can't help but try one more time. "But what if this is the day you decide to change things?"

She snorts and doesn't turn around. I drive her back home and walk her up the porch steps in silence, her wheezing filling the space between us.

CHAPTER 48

Anna

WHEN THE TENTH PERSON SAYS, "I HEARD THIS IS YOUR LAST DAY!" I turn to Cami and say, "That's it. Close up."

I don't know how they figured it out. Maybe it was the absence of my mother that tipped them off, or maybe somebody just made a guess down at Doreen's, and the rumor gained traction, and for once it turned out to be true.

Whatever, I'm sick of the funeral this has become, everyone parading in here to tell me some sappy memory of me in pigtails selling them a Snickers bar.

It was especially cloying to see the chamber of commerce crowd in here, that bunch who used to praise Mom so extravagantly until Haven started gentrifying and they gussied up their businesses, and all of a sudden the Nee Nance became a "liquor store" instead of a "family-run shop."

Cami turns the key and slams the door with her hip to make sure it's locked. She salutes, starts to hum "Taps."

I wad up a piece of register tape and throw it at her. She flinches harder than I would have thought, and I regret it at once. She must be skittish about things flying at her face. Considering.

On an old invoice, I take a Sharpie and scrawl CLOSED FOREVER and hand it to Cami.

"Got any tape?"

I look around at the desk, momentarily at a loss.

She shrugs and sticks it to the door with her chewing gum.

"Let's box up this stuff for the food pantry, especially the baby formula and stuff. They could use it. I'll get some boxes from the back."

We start stacking and I try not to look at the gaping shelves. I shake my hair out of my face and try to think of something else. "You sure you want to come with me to meet with your father?"

As soon as I'd heard from Mr. Drayton, I offered to let Cami come to the meeting and instantly regretted it, watching her face get hard and her eyes turn to slits.

"He's not going to hit me in front of the lawyers, yeah?"

"I didn't figure the chances for actual violence were all that high, but—"

"I just want the house."

"What?"

Cami has straightened up from her packing, hands on her hips. "I know he owes me more, but all I want is that house that he's been fucking up all these years."

"Oh, come on, that house can't be worth more than . . ." I stop to think, and she carries on talking.

"I don't care what the valuation is. I know it's a crappy neigh-borhood and it's falling apart." She angles her head so that she's glaring at me over the tops of her glasses. A piece of long hair slides in front of her face. "That house and a few old photos are all that I have of my mother."

"All? Not a piece of jewelry or anything?"

She grabs a box of cereal and whips it into the box at her feet, overhand. "He sold it. Said we needed the money. Donated her clothes. Threw away boxes of her stuff." She heaves the box up onto her shoulder and walks toward the back, calling out, "That house is all there is."

"You're the boss," I tell her, but I still want to grab the rat bastard by his ankles and shake him upside down until every last cent falls out.

For all those years in the store, it only takes a couple of hours for us to box up the stock. Cami and I looked at the beer and wine cocktails in the cooler and shrugged. Let Paul have it. He can throw it away himself, or just let the wrecking ball smash it all to bits.

A frantic pounding at the door startles us out of inspecting the naked shelves of what was once my family's livelihood.

Amy peers between her cupped hands, calling through the glass. "Anna? You in there?"

I let her in and rush her into the store like I'm running a speak-easy. I just don't want any more looky-loos in here reminiscing.

"What's the problem, Amy?"

She looks gaunt to me, instead of attractively thin. The skin under her eyes is shiny and bruised. Her rouge stands out bright against her skin.

"I have a huge, huge favor to ask, and please say yes."

I fold my arms, stiffening right away. "Tell me what it is, at least."

"Nikki broke her leg, and I need someone to fill in as a brides-maid. Please, will you do it? It's just a few hours, and you were invited to the wedding anyway."

"What difference does it make?"

She rolls her eyes and sighs. "I've been dreaming of this wed-ding since the time I had a Barbie doll, only I thought it would never come true. I figured if I ever found some poor bastard to marry a walrus like me that we'd end up on the courthouse steps somewhere instead of dragging my enormous ass down an aisle. Then I lost the weight. I know it's stupid; you're a sophisticated big-city type and you think I'm being childish, but sue me for wanting symmetry in my wedding, okay?"

Her words came out in a waterfall, and she pants slightly now that she's done. She wrinkles her pert nose up at me, and damned if she doesn't clasp her hands like a kid wanting a new bike.

"Geez, Amy, isn't there anyone else?"

I'd forgotten to RSVP because I wasn't going to go. I didn't want to be anywhere near Beck and his wife, much less in the wedding party with him.

She shifts in place and glances down at her feet. "Well, you'd fit the dress, I figured. But it's not just that," she hastens to add. "You were always so nice to me in school, even when other people called me fat-ass. We would have stayed friends, I think. If you'd stayed."

It's only a few hours, only a dress. She bites her lip at me.

"Fine. Okay, fine."

She sags as if she just put down a two-ton weight. "Oh, thank you!" She hugs me with reedy arms, and then out of her purse she pulls a slip of paper with her loopy cursive on it. "Here's the information. The rehearsal is tonight, and the dress is at Agatha's; she can do a quick fix if it's super-long or loose or whatever, and here's what time we're all getting to the church tomorrow."

I already regret this.

She hugs me again, and I catch Cami smirking at me over her head. I stick my tongue out at her.

Amy says, "Thank you, seriously, so much. I mean, considering everything with Paul, and . . . I know it's stupid, but it really does matter and . . ."

"All right, sheesh, go plan your wedding . . ." I steer her out the door and lock it again, this time shutting off the lights.

"Well, aren't you Mother Teresa?" says Cami, still smirking.

"Shut up. Let's go hide upstairs before someone asks me to cure a leper."

"I'm just kidding you. It's nice, yeah?"

"Sucks to be nice."

"You said it. That's why I hardly ever am." Cami takes the stairs two at a time with her long, loping gait.

As she disappears up the steps, I sit in the dark with my phone and send an e-mail to Beck.

Amy just begged me to be in the wedding as a last minute sub. Just thought I'd alert you.
A.

The reply comes in before I've even pocketed the phone.

Damn! That's going to make things really awkward, with you being there in front of Sam and the whole town, in the bridal party. Jesus.

I have to keep fixing typos as I reply, cursing my slow thumbs and the tiny keyboard.

Don't give me shit, please, I can't take this right now. I was just trying to be nice. She's a wreck about it. It will be fine. Right?

This time I stare at the phone, crouched in the office chair, ignoring the rattles as would-be customers try yanking the front door open.

Finally, his answer comes.

Sorry. Of course, you were just being nice. We'll get through it.

The Nee Nance phone makes me jump in the chair, the ringing

echoing shrilly against the empty shelves.

"Nee Nance," I answer automatically, opening my mouth to say, "we're closed."

"Babe! Don't react, I know you said Anna is there. Just tell me that you got my note."

I grasp the side of the counter and swallow hard. Coming through the phone line, I hear traffic noises, honking, conversation. The flick of a lighter.

"Yes," I whisper.

"Great! Good. I'll be there. The address is 506 Huron, right? Not 605. Couldn't remember what I'd written. And it's just outside Cadillac. Use the first exit, not the one for the downtown. Got that?"

"Yes." I scribble on a paper beer sack with the Sharpie.

"Can't wait to see you, Maeve. Love you."

And he's gone.

I find myself staring at the paper sack with my scrawled notes until my eyes lose focus. I look at my watch, think about how long Mom has been gone, and also about how slowly she drives whenever she has to venture onto the highway.

I take the stairs two at a time myself, racing to find my car keys.

CHAPTER 49

Maeve

MY FEET CRUNCH ON THE GRAVEL AS I WALK UP THIS LONG, CURVING driveway.

I parked out of sight on purpose, so I could slip into my dressy shoes and fix my makeup in the mirror. I gave up on eyeliner. My hands are too unsteady; I could have impaled an eyeball.

I also needed a moment to gather my thoughts. I didn't want Robert rushing out to ambush me before I'd even gotten out of the car.

I'm surrounded by piney woods, the carpet of needles muffling every sound except my own footsteps. I can hear squirrels chase each other in the branches and birds tweet and call from the treetops. There are no phones here. No cash registers, Lotto tickets, rumbling beer trucks with their exhaust seeping into my atmosphere.

I pause a moment before coming around a bend in the driveway to suck in a breath and close my eyes, feeling my smile unfurl across my face.

My step slows as soon as I make the crescent-shaped turn.

Before me is a trailer with rust stains down the side and a graying wood porch.

I look past the trailer for signs of a cabin or perhaps imminent construction. Stacks of wood or some excavation. The silence remains total, especially now that I've stopped walking, and then I think with both fear and hope that I have the wrong address. Robert never was good with details.

The door of the trailer slams itself open, the sharp sound echoing around the trees.

I put a hand to my lips.

He runs hitchingly down the three steps of the porch and over the gravel. Something is wrong with his leg; he limps. His hair is the gray of steel wool; he's wearing a baggy sweater over a plaid shirt, both of which look two sizes too big.

Yet. The twinkle in his eye is unmistakable.

"Oh, baby, I knew you'd come." He folds me into a hug and I relax into his arms. His smell is just the same: Old Spice aftershave mixed with the stale tang of beer breath and old smoke.

"Robert," is all I can muster.

He takes my hand and leads me to the trailer. The porch steps moan under our feet.

Just inside, cloths and sheets and doilies cover misshapen piles of unseen junk. A cloying strawberry candle burns on the table in the kitchen area to my right. Underneath the aggressive strawberry, I detect an aroma much like the interior of the store.

Dean Martin is on the stereo, asking me to send him the pillow that I dream on.

He's gawking at me, up and down, and I tear my gaze away from the inside of the trailer to look down at my feet and blush.

"You look wonderful," he says, his voice coming out so quiet it's like a breath more than words.

I want to say the same to him, but I'm still assimilating this present-day Robert with the dark-haired husband of my memory.

When I'd imagined this reunion, it was usually at home because I always pictured him coming home to us, while Anna was still a child. In my fantasies, I'd sometimes thunder at him, other times swoon, and now twenty years of competing emotions all jam themselves together like typewriter keys that went so fast they collided.

"So, where's this property?" I ask him. "Are we going to see it later?"

"This is it, baby. Isn't it beautiful?"

I nod, and he leads me down to the couch, which underneath the large throw blanket is rather droopy and tips me nearly backward. I perch on the end and cross my legs primly. He's staring, hard, at all of me. I can't remember the last time I'd been studied with such intensity.

"But wasn't there a cabin?"

"Well, babe, it's going to take a while to get the money for that, but this Charley that I'm working with? He's going to fix me right up. I'm buying this land from him."

"Buying? You don't own it?"

"Not yet, but I will. It's a . . .whaddya call it . . .land contract."

"What does Charley do, anyway?"

Robert stands up suddenly, jarring me on the couch. "Want a drink? I bought some rosé. Didn't you used to like rosé?" He pops open a can of beer. The soundtrack of our married life.

"No. Well, I did like it, I guess, but . . . I don't want anything now. You didn't answer me about Charley."

"You know, this and that. He's an investor. An entrepreneur."

I close my eyes. Bill was an entrepreneur, too. "Robert, shut that music off, please."

He limps his way over to the stereo and hits the button. The limping makes him look frail. Dean Martin cuts off in mid-croon.

He puts the beer down on a scuffed faux-wood coffee table and joins me on the couch again, taking my hands in his.

"You haven't asked me about Anna," I say.

"You said she's back."

"Yes. She's a lawyer, you know."

Robert sits back, folding his arms, and a beaming smile comes over his face. "Is that so. Is that a fact."

A burning sensation rises in my chest. What right does he have to that pride? Did he hunch with her over book reports? Did he drive her to predawn swim practice and sit on hard plastic bleachers surrounded by muggy chlorinated air? Did he fill out college applications and stay up late when she couldn't sleep with worry?

"I put her through school myself; plus, she took on so much debt she'll be paying it off when she's a grandmother."

"Honey, I . . ."

"Why didn't you come back?" I stand up, backing a few steps away from him. My voice sounds shrill and loud in the trailer, and it feels so familiar, all those shouted conversations in the Nee Nance back room, trying to hide from customers, from Anna.

"I got arrested, okay?"

"You . . . you what?" All the scenarios I ever imagined, none of them included jail.

"Bill had this great idea to sell cigarettes, you know, buy them where there aren't so many taxes and bring 'em back to Michigan and sell 'em cheap, but still at a profit. I didn't know it was smuggling. I thought he was enterprising."

I close my eyes against the trailer, his weak explanation.

"You didn't even call."

"What could I have said? Bill got a lawyer and got himself sprung but left me high and dry. I knew we didn't have the money ourselves to get me out, so I did my time. I was ashamed of myself, sweetheart. I couldn't write you from jail. It would be just like your mother always said."

I flinch because I can hear him coming toward me now.

He continues, his Old Spice cologne filling my nose. "I didn't want to come back until I straightened myself out as a real man."

"Do you think your little girl cared about that?" Now I open my eyes to stare right at him. "Do you know what it was like for me to try to pretend you were just on a business trip? To hear her crying at night and know it was because of you? To see her look down the street for you night after night?"

"She did that?" Robert cocks his head like a confused dog.

"Of course she did! What did you think she would do?"

He digs his toe into the thin carpet. "I . . . I tried not to think about it. Her. And you. It was too painful."

"For *you*? Painful for you?"

I wrench myself away from him and step toward the door.

"Maeve, baby, don't leave. I said I was sorry; I'll make it up to you, I swear I will, but you've gotta give me a chance. I didn't mean for it to happen. One thing just kinda came on top of another . . . There was never anyone else like you."

Anyone else. I stop at the bottom of the porch steps.

Robert isn't the only one who was fooling himself all those years. In my daydreams of our reunion, I also hadn't considered other women in those empty decades.

"Don't follow me," I tell him over my shoulder, because I can't bring myself to turn around and watch him recede in my view. "This was a terrible mistake," I say, but he probably can't hear it, as my voice comes out in a choked, weak mumble behind the loud, fast crunching of my stupid high-heel shoes in the gravel.

CHAPTER 50

Anna

CAMI'S DRIVING BECAUSE I CAN'T HARDLY SEE. EVERY TIME I LOOK at something, I see my father's face instead, trying to imagine what he looks like now, and in my mind's eye, he seizes my mother in his clutches like a predatory bird grabs a mouse.

I told her to step on it, and I'd pay the ticket for her if she got one.

According to my car's GPS, my mother arranged to meet my father in some desolate, forested area. She has no idea what the years have done to him. He might not even be alone.

Even the best possible outcome—a happy reunion—is a disaster, because he will do this to her again, I'm sure of it. One thing I've learned in my years at Miller Paulson: People don't change for the better; they don't learn their lessons. If anything, they only learn how not to get caught.

"Cadillac," Cami says, pointing to the exit sign. "That's it, right?"

"Yes," I say, consulting my paper-bag notes.

My heart only beats faster as the car slows down. My anger at my father has for now eclipsed the betrayal of my mother, who promised—promised!—she wouldn't write, but then not only wrote, she made plans to meet, and hid all of this from me.

But then, she once promised he'd be coming home, back when I had pigtails and still believed what grown-ups told me.

"Who's that?" Cami asks, slowing the car down on the shoulder of a narrow two-lane road slicing through woods.

Ahead of us is a bright yellow Hummer, backing out of a driveway. A green reflective address sign at the edge of the driveway matches the address we have for the rendezvous.

In the passenger window, I see a vague male silhouette.

No evidence of my mother or the car she borrowed from Veronica.

"Follow it," I tell Cami. "But hang back."

She nods and lets the Hummer get ahead of us for several yards before she pulls gradually back to the road. I turn in my seat to peer through the pine trees at the land, trying to catch a glimpse of my mother's car. All I see is a rusted trailer.

We're parked outside a bar on the main road of Cadillac's downtown. I have my hand on the door to open it, when Cami puts her hand on my shoulder. "Wait. Maybe I should go in alone first."

"Why?"

"We can see who's in there, what he's up to. Who he's with."

I nod, numb. I wish my mother had a cell phone. Her absence alarms me. I'd had visions of charging in to find them clinched together and then demanding to know what the hell they were doing. But now that I'm here, and she's nowhere to be seen, I'm not sure what I want.

"Be back soon. Sit tight."

Cami lopes into the bar slowly like she does reconnaissance every day.

I wonder why my parents chose to meet in Cadillac. We tried camping around here, I know, but there was no significance to that address that I can remember.

Our couple of camping trips were dismal failures, largely due to my dad's lack of preparation. He'd forget something important like pillows, so we'd end up sleeping on rolled up towels.

The stars were magic, though, I remember that much. Haven is no metropolis, but the light from the streetlamps and the businesses is enough to ruin the night sky, at least in town, where buildings also help break up the view. The stars were nice out on the beach, but I never had that much time to admire them between working at the store, band practice, and homework.

Out camping, up north, I could stare up through the dark trees until my neck ached, my eyes so wide that I'd forget to blink until they itched with dryness.

One of those neck-aching nights I heard my parents fighting in the tent.

Supposedly they were just going in there to look for something, but soon their murmurs turned into normal talking, like they'd forgotten those thin nylon walls weren't real and I could hear every word.

My dad was saying, "With just a little investment it could pay for itself in a few years or so . . ."

And Mom interrupted: "*Could* pay, a few years *or so* . . . When will you learn to listen to yourself? You can't keep gambling with our future like this. The store was supposed to be temporary."

"It is, it is, babe . . . but . . ."

I tried to tune my ears into the singing of the nighttime frogs out on Goose Lake, the way you can focus your eyes on something far instead of something near, but it didn't work. I heard it clear as a bell when my mother said, "I should have listened to my mother years ago."

"You mean . . . you should have left me?"

I couldn't take it anymore and cried out in fear of an imaginary animal, and they came rushing out of the tent. My dad took a big stick and charged into the dark outside the circle of firelight, chasing away the big bad monsters.

In the flickering light, my mother's jaw was set and her face looked grim. But in the cool morning, as we sipped our hot chocolate warmed by the camp stove, my parents were jovial and relaxed again.

At the time I was relieved. As an adult, I don't understand why she didn't follow her gut.

Cami startles me by hopping into the driver's seat, leaving the door open with her foot still on the pavement.

"Okay, this is the deal. They've got a card game going at this address." She shoves a bar napkin at me. "I think your dad and this guy, his name is Charley, are running a card sharp scam and I got myself invited."

"What? Why?"

"We won't know for sure it's a scam until I sit in."

"What difference does it make?"

"Listen, your dad is a charmer, yeah? Isn't that what you said? You need to know what he's up to so you can tell your mom exactly what's going on."

"So what do you want to do?"

"I just said I'd come out here and get my money, then I'm going to ride over to the house. In an hour I'll excuse myself and we'll know exactly what's going on."

I grab her arm and square myself to her in the seat. "Cami! You are not getting in this strange man's car, especially if he's up to something illegal and you want to bust him. I think we've seen enough. I want to get home and find my mother."

She yanks her arm back. "And I'm pissed on your behalf and I want to know what's going on. Come get me in an hour."

She pulls away from me and disappears inside the bar.

I can't believe she's so reckless. Maybe that's what happens to a person who lives with someone who might beat the crap out of her at any given moment. Maybe she feels strange without a sense of danger.

The door opens and a husky guy with a shaved, stubbly head and goatee walks out first, and I dive down as if I'm picking something up off the floor of the car. After a few moments I sit up slowly, taking a peek and watching the trio walk down the block toward the yellow Hummer a few spaces down. Cami is in the middle and bringing up the rear . . . That can only be my father, wearing a huge sweater and limping, his hair gray like a stormy summer sky.

They drive off, and when they're out of view, I look down at the scribbled address and reach for my phone to look up the directions. For good or ill, Cami has gone with them and I need to stick close by.

I'll admit to curiosity myself, now that I've caught a glimpse. And for all I know, my mother is waiting at this house. She wouldn't approve of an illegal card game, but who knows what lies he's telling?

First, I type a message to Amy.

Amy, I'm sorry but I can't make the rehearsal dinner. It's a long story, but a family emergency has come up. I'll be there tomorrow and do my best to follow along.
Anna

Next, a note for Beck.

Beck, I can't come to the rehearsal dinner after all, but I'll still be there tomorrow. I'm sorry it's awkward for you, but I'll be glad to see you, even so.
Something's going on and I don't have time to explain. I really miss you, especially now.

I pause for a moment. I want him here, to squeeze my hand and look at me with those sea-glass eyes until my breathing slows down and I feel okay again.

So I add:

XOXO
Anna

I'm halfway to this mysterious card game house when my phone bleeps. I pull over on a side street to check the message.

Anna,
Can't talk right now, at home with Sam and Maddie.
Will

Of course he'd be home the day before the wedding. They'll go together after all, since Maddie is the flower girl. But . . . since when is he "Will"?

I shake my head and pull back out onto the road. I don't have time to think of it now.

The house is on Lake Cadillac, a huge brick ranch with a hooked driveway that curves down toward what must be a walkout basement. It took fifteen minutes to drive, counting the phone distraction, and I've now been sitting here playing mindless games on my phone for an hour. She's overdue and I can't stand it anymore.

I leave the car on the street and walk slowly up the drive, taking care not to smack my shoes too hard on the pavement. As I approach, I can hear noise coming from downstairs; someone must have left a door open.

I come up on a patio slider from the side. There's only a screen door closed. I can hear sounds of a baseball game on television, shuffling cards, deep male voices. I can't hear Cami.

I yank the slider open and look past the stunned faces of the men for a sign of Cami or my mother and think, *What has she done? I should have stopped her.* I turn back to the men at the card table. The large bald man is half standing, his hand moving toward the waistband of his pants, but someone's hand is on his arm, halting him.

And that man is my father.

"What the fuck is this?" demands the bald man, but no one answers him.

My dad's mouth is open slightly, and his lips are moving soundlessly, like he's trying to talk underwater. His hair is thick as ever, despite being gray. His face is more furrowed than I remember, but he's still got that stubble he always had by this time of day, his eyes still that deep shade of coffee brown.

Cami exits from a door to my right, drying her hands on a towel.

"Oh, hi," she says. "Sorry for the delay. The boys here were anxious for a chance to win some of their money back, so they convinced me to stay."

Despite her casual tone, she fixes me with a hard, significant look, and darts her eyes over toward the big man, who must be Charley.

My father turns toward Cami, understanding dawning on him. "You! You're together? What are you, cops or something?"

"No," I say quickly, for fear of alarming Charley, who seems fidgety and hasn't moved his hand away from what is probably a gun in his pants. "We were simply . . . curious."

Charley begins again, reddening: "What. The Fuck. Is going *on*?"

My dad stands up and walks over to me, taking my elbow. "I'll deal with this." I let him lead me to a side room, some kind of study. Cami follows me, and I'm grateful for the back-up; also, I don't like the idea of leaving her out there with those men.

He closes the door and flips on a radio to mask our conversation, I suppose.

"It's really you," he says, peering at me through narrowed eyes.

"Yes."

"You look so much like your mother."

"Where is my mother?"

"She left. She's a little upset with me."

I laugh, but the sound, even to my own ears, comes out harsh and sickly, like a tune in a minor key.

"Gee, she's really upset?" I ask him. "Now why on earth would she be upset with you?"

"No call to get snippy, young lady."

I draw myself up straight, noticing up close that I'm taller than he is. "Don't you 'young lady' me. I don't know what you were thinking trying to win her back after abandoning her for twenty years in that shithole store. Did you think that gorgeous trailer would do the trick?"

"It's just temporary; that's a beautiful piece of land."

I should feel triumphant now, having been proven right. But there's no joy; in fact, I now realize part of me, somehow, had been pulling for him since I got that call.

Cami clears her throat. "We should probably go, yeah?" She jerks her head toward the door.

Oh, right. The armed man.

"Wait," my dad says, reaching out to grab my hand. His touch startles me, not having felt it in twenty years. A hard stone settles in my throat and I suck in a breath, blinking rapidly. "Let me make my case. Look, I'm earning money now. That's why I wrote your mother; I'm finally getting ahead a little, working with Charley here. I really am gonna buy that land and make her proud of me, and make you proud of me, too . . ."

"So proud you snuck around with Mom but didn't dare acknowledge my existence."

"Your mom said you'd be upset, so I wanted to do it right, you know, gradually and all."

"Do *what* right, exactly?" Cami interjects. "Card scams? What do you do when your rich sap out there finds out you're cheating?" She pulls a card from her pocket, shows it to us, and then flicks a barely perceptible notch with her fingernail.

"Hey, now," he addresses himself to Cami, still grasping my hand, and I look down at it, noticing how much older he looks based on his hand alone. "Where do you get off—"

I say, "What's your wife's name?"

"What?"

He turns back to me and then looks down at his hand himself and winces.

He's wearing a wedding band. It's yellow gold. My mom's ring is white gold.

"I said, what's your wife's name?" I yank my hand away and fold my arms.

"Technically she's not my wife, seeing as how I'm not divorced. I just got this to shut her up about it."

"She throw you out, then? Or did you abandon her, too?"

He steps toward me, his arms outstretched. "Anna Banana . . ."

"No!" I jerk my finger at him. "No. Just . . . Don't. Don't you dare."

I pull open the door and figure if we walk fast enough, heading straight out without looking around, maybe the men won't care that we were here at all.

"Let 'em go," I hear my dad say, and I can see Cami in my peripheral vision, looking determined and moving more quickly than I've ever seen.

Out on the driveway I start to breathe again. My dad's voice stops me.

"Wait . . . Anna, do I have grandbabies?"

I scrunch my eyes shut at this, at the unexpected stab I feel in my gut at his question. "No. Do I have siblings?"

He actually smiles a little. "Twins. Boys, fifteen years old."

"I hope their mother has her own source of income."

We scurry up the drive, Cami and I, as the angry Charley shouts from inside for Robert to get his ass back in the house. It's clear who's the boss in that room.

Cami takes the driver's seat without having to ask, but as she sits down, she fishes around in her shorts pocket, slapping a wad of bills into my lap.

"What's this?"

"Winnings," she says, buckling up. "Now let's get the hell home, yeah?"

CHAPTER 51

Maeve

THE SIGN SAYS "CLOSED FOREVER," AND I HUSTLE MYSELF INSIDE before any busybody types can intercept me to grill me about the closing, or the new store, or whether I'll be staying with Anna.

I pull myself along the counter and tumble into the office chair, face in my hands.

"What did you expect?" I say out loud to myself.

I'm glad Anna isn't here, because I couldn't look her in the face now. I'd never be able to keep my composure, and somehow she would know, she just would.

Also, I need to tell her. Let her know that her father is back in the state and where she can find him if she chooses to. She won't choose to, of course. She's smarter than stupid, foolish me. Anna will probably snort and roll her eyes and say, *What would I want with him?*

Someone knocks hard on the front door, and it feels like someone kicking me in the head. I fumble under the counter for my bottle of Excedrin, and when the knocking has stopped and the intruder has moved on, I force myself up the stairs.

I flop on my bed with my feet aimed at the headboard, the better to stare at my wedding picture. I was so utterly certain, that day. Not a bit of doubt. My jitters were all related to getting caught by my mother and having a dramatic scene on the courthouse steps. When we finally got married, I was so lightheaded with relief I think I giggled the whole way to that cabin in Ludington where we finally made love and I walked around completely naked, giggling again at how womanly I was at last.

I choke down the Excedrin dry.

He still looks like himself. A little damaged by time, but who isn't? I've got varicose veins popping up, and my hands are looking wrinkled and scarred. I have a healthy start on an excellent pair of crow's feet, too.

I close my eyes and remember his tight embrace, and suddenly I'm angry, not at him but at myself for my haste. So he hasn't started the cabin yet. The land truly was pretty, and it was so quiet out there. Maybe this time he'll listen to my advice, knowing how wrong it all went before, knowing I was right. In fact, he'll have to listen to me, because I won't put up with anything less. This time, I'll leave *him* if he doesn't toe the line!

I'm in a position of strength, in fact, leaving him angrily like I did. I'll send him a letter at that address, explaining exactly the conditions under which I'll see him again. Yes, that will work. It could all work out yet.

My eyelids are heavy, and my limbs feel shaky. I hadn't realized how tense I was until just now when I'm finally relaxing. I could turn around and crawl under the covers properly, but I prefer to drift off to sleep looking at this wedding picture and the new start we could yet have.

* * *

"Mom?"

I pop awake on the comforter, squinting in the afternoon sun falling directly over my eyes.

I hear rumbling feet up the steps, and when I pull myself upright, Anna is framed in the doorway, hanging on as if in an earthquake.

"Oh, thank goodness. Are you all right?" she says.

I clear my throat. My headache has receded to a dull echo of pain. "Yes. I decided to come back early—I got bored all by myself." Weak excuse, but she surprised me; forgot to think of a better one.

"Mom. You don't have to lie to me. I know."

I pull myself to stand next to the bed. "Know? What do you mean?"

"I followed you."

I put my hand to my chest. "How dare you!"

"Well, not right behind you. But my father called here, thinking I was you. He gave the address, so I went. I was worried about you."

"Oh, I'm sure you were *worried*. You wanted to ruin it!"

Anna puts her hand to her head. "Mom, can't you admit now this was a bad idea? You saw that trailer, no better than the one Sally torched. And you must have figured out he's got no legitimate employment."

"He just moved back to the state. Times are tough."

"When are you going to stop defending him? He said himself you were upset when you left; think of the reasons you were upset; think of why you took off instead of staying for the romantic reunion. Whatever made you do that, it's all still true. It didn't cure itself in the hundred-mile drive back here."

"Don't take that superior tone."

"Don't change the subject!"

"It's very much on point! Your whole life you've thought yourself better than me, with your education and your job and your smarts, and you're right, you are better than me and I'm glad. That's what I wanted for you. But I didn't expect you to throw it in my face all the time. Just because he doesn't meet your standards of what's acceptable doesn't mean I can't have him back if I want him."

"My standards? Like my standards are so high! How about a man who didn't jilt you twenty years ago with nothing? A man who is gainfully employed and not a liar and a criminal?"

"Get out of my way." I push past her, breathing easier now that she's not blocking my exit. "Criminal!" I shout over my shoulder. "Now you're exaggerating." I storm to the kitchen to get myself a glass of water, just for something to do so I don't slap her impudent face.

She follows me to the kitchen. "Oh, is that what you think? Cami and I caught him running an illegal card game, cheating, no less. The guy who was running the game? Had a gun and was about ready to pull it on us."

I clutch my glass with two hands, force myself to take slow sips so I don't make myself sick. "I don't believe it."

"I'm not the liar here."

I glare at Anna. She stands with her feet apart, arms folded, her eyes narrowed at me. She's got her attorney face on.

"You take that back."

"You're the one who promised me you wouldn't write him."

"I never should have promised you that. It was none of your business, anyway."

"How is it not my business if I have to pick up the pieces when he leaves you again?"

"I never expected you to pick up anything! I can take care of myself!"

"Oh, is that why I have to pay your rent?"

I whirl toward the kitchen sink and throw the glass into it, hard, jumping as it cracks in half, water splashing up. "You don't have to pay anything for me. Your father and I will be just fine."

"Until his new wife wants him back, that is."

"That's crazy. What wife? He can't be married."

"He's wearing a wedding band, and it's not the one you gave him. Says he has fifteen-year-old twin sons."

My heart pounds so loud in my ears I can't hear what she's saying now, though I can see her posture softening from one of righteous anger. She's tilting her head and her face is painted with sadness. She steps toward me with an arm outstretched. That's when her sympathetic expression tips over into pity and I can no longer stand it.

Through the roaring in my head I can't hear myself scream at her to get out, out, out, leave me alone. I cover my face with my hands and just screech until I feel her vibrating footsteps retreat down the steps.

I curl down to the kitchen tile and wait for my blood to slow down, and picture those cool, piney woods with the birds calling to each other in the hushed forest air.

CHAPTER 52

Amy

MY LIPSTICK IS TOO PINK.

I knew I should have done a practice run with my makeup at the salon, but with the *delay*, there wasn't time. Now I look like a tart with lipstick the shade of a child's crayon, instead of the soft, subtle peachy-pink I was hoping for. I keep blotting it, but then it fades off, so I put it back on, all the while my bridesmaids keep chirping at me like squirrels about this and that, and *don't get any lipstick on the dress.*

Sarah and Kristi have been at my elbow since dawn, practically, rushing to get me glasses of water or tissues or whatever I might need, and I would have thought this attention would be flattering—just what a bride deserves—but I have a powerful urge to smash their faces into the wedding cake.

What is wrong with me today?

We've commandeered a nursery room at First Presbyterian and turned it into a dressing room of sorts, though we were all dressed and primped when we arrived, courtesy of Mrs. Becker's fancy salon and the limousine paid for by Mr. Becker. It's hot in here. I'm afraid I'm starting to smell less like a bride and more like a sweat sock. Each time I look in the mirror, something else is wrong.

Like this lipstick. And that one curl that keeps sticking funny out of my updo, but when I pick at it, it gets worse.

Tabitha floats behind me, looking elegant in her bridesmaid dress, the only one of the bunch who really has the figure to suit such a narrow silhouette, though the other girls insisted that's just what they wanted.

"Tabi!"

She stops and approaches me, regarding me with the pleasant, distant smile of a business associate. We're not close, Tabi and me. But I needed her to round out all the men on the groom's side.

"Tabi, is your brother out there?"

"Yes, he is. Do you want me to get him for you?"

"No, I just . . . Does he seem okay to you? In good spirits?"

"Just fine. He's talking golf with the groomsmen."

I sigh a little and tug on the neckline of my dress to make sure it doesn't sag too much, second-guessing the off-the-shoulder look, when I should have had straps so I . . .

"He's not going to take off," Tabi says, interrupting my fretting, having leaned in close without my noticing. "He wouldn't do that."

I meet her eyes in the mirror. *Did he tell her we almost . . . ? How does she know?*

She smiles and blinks, her eyes crinkling up just in the same way as her mother's, a reassuring wink of sorts. "Besides, Dad would kill him. And then fire him."

She glides away. I then ask one of the girls for the time, wondering where Anna is, and if we might have a stranded single groomsman after all.

* * *

As I'm posing for photos between candelabras decorated with delphinium and white Asiatic lilies and rich green ivy, this feels like tempting fate, like I read somewhere that Jewish mothers don't buy anything for the baby until after the child is safely born.

I did insist Paul not be in these pre-ceremony photos, despite the obvious irritation of the photographer who doesn't believe in "bad luck to see the bride" and is trying to "expedite" things.

But I've been waiting a year, and my whole life besides, to take my groom's breath away as I come down the aisle.

The photographer mumbles to himself as he tests the light and I cast my gaze across my wedding.

There weren't enough pew bows. My bridesmaids, contrary to my request, are wearing too much jewelry. I suggested a nice French twist for Kristi's hair, but she insisted on having it down, and there's a riot of ringlets all over the back of her head, which, sadly, only makes her look bigger.

On top of it all, Anna still has not arrived, though when I called Agatha's this morning she said Anna had been in for some last-minute adjustments.

I peeked in at the reception hall earlier. The centerpieces are too tall and showy. It's going to be hard for guests to converse over the top of them. I was in a rush to pick the flowers that day. Paul had to work through lunch and couldn't help me. Also, the cake looks woefully small, though I'm sure I gave the bakery the correct number of guests.

I exhale when I see Anna walk into the back of the church sanctuary. She stands framed in the far doorway. Nikki's dress looks nice enough on her, but it's not a flattering style for Anna's broad shoulders. I send her a mental apology. She seems to be searching the crowd. I nod in her direction and she nods back, but she starts looking again.

Maddie, in her flower girl dress, zooms past Anna on her way to make circles around the pews, followed closely by Samantha, who preferred not to be in the wedding party and is thus wearing a plain black dress. Behind his wife comes Beck, ambling along, and then he stops short in front of Anna. He looks quickly away and walks back out of the sanctuary.

"I need the bride to look this way!" calls the photographer.

I hope someone settles Maddie down soon before she falls and rips her dress.

"Okay." The photographer claps his hands. "Let's get the mother up here, please."

My mother sits in a front pew, her hands folded in her lap. Her hair is too short to pull back, so the stylist just curled it all into little loops, the color of red rubber bands, thanks to her dye job.

She shakes her head at the photographer.

"C'mon, Mom!" the photographer wheedles. "Daylight's burning! It's now or never!" Then he starts to impersonate a crooner, using his flash as a mic. "*It's now or never . . .*"

My mother shoots him a look that interrupts his croon like someone yanked the needle off his record.

"Very well, then." He blinks and proceeds as if nothing at all unusual happened. "How about some with your maid of honor?"

Sarah approaches, teetering a little on her heels. The girls already opened some champagne this morning. They poured some into my orange juice, but I dumped it out when they weren't looking.

I sneak a look at my mother. She stares hard into the middle distance, chin lifted slightly.

Maddie is still tearing around the pews, and Sam has given up the chase, instead standing in the center, rotating to follow with her eyes as if she's on a turntable. Kristi's son, the ring bearer, is chasing, too, and he's six, so he ought to know better.

I won't let our kids get away with this kind of behavior. Assuming I can have some at my "advanced maternal age."

"Stay with me, bride!"

I turn on my smile again.

After dozens of shots, I think they're about to release me to go round up the groomsmen when the photographer consults his list of required photos. "Oops! Almost forgot. Flower girl!"

"Me! Me-me-me-me-me!" and Maddie comes running.

I notice that she's carrying a cup. A cup of juice. A nearly full cup of purple grape juice.

"Maddie! NO!" I holler, and in doing so, I startle her. She stumbles to a halt from her dead-run, trips on the hem of her dress, and grape splashes down her white satin skirt.

I throw my bouquet down. "For God's sake, who gave her grape juice when she's wearing a white dress? And poured it to the top? Seriously? To the top?"

None of the adults respond. Their faces telegraph revulsion. They turn away from me to the little girl, who gazes up with her eyes round and huge, silent tears soaking her little face. The cup, still in her hand, quivers.

The ring bearer next to her is as white as his shirt. "I - I - I - . . . Miss Amy, I'm sorry, she was thirsty and she said her favorite flavor was grape . . ." He bites his lip, which trembles.

Samantha looks like she might tear my hair out. "I hope you're pleased with yourself." She strokes Maddie's hair and crouches down behind her. "You didn't mean it, baby," she coos. "It was an accident."

I peer down at my own dress with its perfect satin surface, delicate beading, and lace and consider what all this has cost me. Everyone watches me intently; I can feel them wondering what kind of freak-out is coming next.

I take halting steps toward Madeline, and it pierces me to see her shrink away at my approach. I fold myself down and gently take the juice cup from her hands, which yet retain some of their toddler pudginess.

"I'm sorry I yelled at you. Do you ever have those days when you think it's supposed to be a really good day, only you don't feel very good? You feel kinda grumpy and strange?"

She nods, but her body is angled slightly away from me, like she wants to bolt.

"Look. I want to show you something."

I tip the grape juice cup, and a purple stream runs down the skirt from my knee to soak the lace at the hem.

Sarah actually shrieks out loud, as if I've snapped a kitten's neck.

"Now we match," I tell her, smiling my first real smile of the day. I chuck her chin with my thumb. Maddie then points a toe, in the manner of a dancer, and curtsies with her stained skirt. I rise and do the same.

My bridesmaids rush in with handkerchiefs dabbed in ice water and start clucking and admonishing me, but I pay them no mind. I share a wink with Maddie. Sarah hands me my bouquet, and I reach in to snag some baby's breath, which I tuck into Maddie's hair, behind her ear.

Samantha smiles softly at me and kisses the top of Maddie's head.

In the midst of all this fussing, I hear my mother call out, "Mr. Photographer, sir! I'm ready for my close-up!"

CHAPTER 53

Anna

MY HEAD ITCHES WITH ALL THE HAIRSPRAY AND HAIRPINS, THIS dress makes me look like I have the shoulders of a linebacker, and I'm about to stand up in a wedding where the groom has evicted my mother to bulldoze her business and I've screwed the groom's married brother.

And now my mother hates me for giving her bad news about my father's other family, the newer one, the one with twin boys, teenagers, which means he wasted no time replacing us.

"Showtime," whispers some lady in a bouffant, waving her hands in a uselessly frantic gesture, which I think is supposed to mean hurry up and get situated.

Since I missed the rehearsal dinner—what with ambushing my father and the screaming fight with my mother, who banished me from the premises—I don't know where I'm supposed to stand, so I hang back, waiting for an empty spot to form.

The last groomsman looks over his shoulder, searching for his counterpart.

It's Beck.

I bite my lip to keep from gasping out loud. We share a panicked look. He starts to tap the shoulder of the groomsman in front of him, but the bouffant woman grabs my elbow and shoves me into place.

Beck sets his jaw and offers me his elbow, eyes forward.

I have this sudden need to apologize, though I'm not sure what for. The order must have gotten jumbled up somehow; these things happen. Amy would have warned me if I was supposed to walk down the aisle with my old boyfriend.

Though we are supposedly just friends, and what would be the harm in that?

When it's our turn, we begin the halting step-pause walk between the pews.

I can see Samantha's pert, brunette bob near the front, but she doesn't turn to face us. Beck doesn't even look at me when we part to stand on our respective sides.

Doesn't he realize that such obvious coldness makes the whole situation look even worse?

The ceremony is blessedly brief. I don't have the stomach for promises to love and cherish, and when I hear "as long as we both shall live," it's all I can do to keep from laughing out loud.

Is this what my mother expects from my father? That he's going to promise *again* to stay until death do they part?

I couldn't think of anything to say to her after she threw a glass in the sink and screamed at me like her hair was on fire. So I abused my credit card, got a motel room, and drank cheap merlot out of a plastic cup all night, flipping channels and staring at my phone, hoping Beck could sneak away to send me a note.

I almost bailed on this wedding completely, but none of this is Amy's fault.

The recessional music cranks up, and I paste on a smile, steeling myself for taking Beck's arm again, this time facing the crowd. At least they'll be paying attention to Amy, not me.

Beck looks past me at the opposite wall when he offers his arm and holds out his elbow, frozen in place like a mannequin. I give his biceps a light squeeze; surely that's a gesture no one would notice. I glance up at his face. His eyes remain forward with military discipline.

I grin through excruciating pictures, and then the photographer claps his hands at last, announcing we're all set, and I practically sprint toward the restroom to find my purse and keys, my obligation fulfilled.

But Amy, more fleet than I could have imagined in that heavy dress, catches my arm.

"Thank you," she says, squeezing my hand hard. "I know that was strange for you. You're such a good soul."

At this I swallow hard. "Hardly."

"Can I ask you one more thing, please? Could you just stay through the bridal party dance? Just so Dave has someone to dance with?"

"Is that who I'm supposed to be paired up with? Dave?"

"Yeah, I'm sorry about the mix-up. I think Sarah has a crush on Dave, so she messed up the order." Amy rolls her eyes and pantomimes shooting Sarah with her finger. Across the room, Sarah laughs extravagantly, bending herself nearly in half at something this Dave fellow has said.

I watch Amy skip lightly across the room to kiss her husband. Her veil is on crooked, her updo is coming down in spots, and I swear I saw a purple stain on the hem of her dress. But she looks more at peace than I've seen her all summer. She glows like a bride should, and because her joy is contagious—and because I don't want to go home just yet—I decide I can stay for one dance. No harm in that.

*   *   *

For the next hour I sip white wine and skirt all the little knots of conversation, ducking and weaving to escape acquaintances, doing several laps around the room in the process. I wish Cami were here, but she wasn't feeling well and I'd already asked her to do enough. She said she was going to stay at the store to keep Mom and Sally company, in case my mother decided to unburden herself about my dad or take off for Cadillac again. Cami had stayed discreetly away for my first talk with my mother and my banishment. Her advice had been to keep calm and that my mother would eventually come to her senses.

Considering her twenty-year track record on that score, I'm not optimistic.

I stop my reception hall loops long enough to watch Paul and Amy sway to "Unforgettable."

The bridal party then starts to filter to the dance floor, and I search out Dave.

Only Sarah has already hung herself around Dave's neck like a lariat, and he's apparently in no hurry to let go.

This leaves Beck alone again, and I stare at him across the dance floor. His face is motionless, with all the warmth of an upright corpse. I'm suddenly aware that every moment I hesitate only draws out the agony.

The wedding singer begins the opening lines of "Someone to Watch Over Me," as I step into Beck's arms. He holds me at a distance, his hand barely touching my back, his hand not clasping mine so much as supporting it.

"Finally, we can talk for a minute." I pat his shoulder gently "Relax a little. We're not doing anything wrong."

He finally looks directly at me. "She knows."

At this, I stumble. He nudges me back to standing and continues to lead me in the dance. "How?"

"She was looking over my shoulder when I answered your e-mail."

I close my eyes, and then I remember I'm supposed to be dancing with an old friend and open them again. I conjure up my cool, professional calm and stare at Beck's shirt buttons instead of his face. "But the e-mail wasn't that bad," I say, trying to remember precisely what I'd written.

He continues, "I told her. She seemed to know already, and she's been hurt before. I couldn't hold on to the lie."

I feel the stares of everyone at the wedding like dagger points on my back. Their faces are dark to me, outside the whirling colored lights on the dance floor.

"Well, then. Now what?"

He clears his throat and meets my eyes. "Well, you see, we talked, and she thinks maybe . . ."

I don't even hear the rest for a loud buzzing that starts up in my ears. But I don't have to hear it. I should have known from the beginning.

"Keep dancing," Beck urges. "They're watching us."

I back away from him, shaking my head, and recede into the shadowy, candlelit room.

I go home to the Nee Nance because the motel room seems even more dire and pathetic.

The lights are out, though, and I'm hopeful that Mom went to bed early. For all I know, she's driven back to Cadillac.

I step out of my shoes just inside the door and carry them dangling from my hand, feeling my way along the shelves in the dark, knowing this place so well I could walk through it with my eyes closed.

I notice someone has left on the kitchen light, so I stop in there to switch it off, only I jump at the sight of someone at the table.

"Sally!"

"Hey, doll. Don't you look pretty."

She's at the table wearing a T-shirt, cut-off shorts, and no wig.

Her hair is growing in patchy, in the color of fog. She sees me notice this and says, "My head itched. Don't worry, I'm not crazy. Not right now, anyway."

"I never said you were crazy."

Sally waves me into a seat. "Take a load off and talk to your auntie. I've got coffee."

The chances I'll be able to sleep right now are nil, so I pour myself a cup and settle into the chair across from her.

"Sally, have you . . . Have you talked to Mom?"

"Not really. Her friend dropped me off this afternoon and she was watching TV, said she didn't feel much like talking. So I let her be."

So Sally doesn't know. With my father's face fresh in my mind, I can see a resemblance now between them, something in the brown eyes that makes them always seem like they're just about to wink. I feel like I should tell her that her brother is not only alive, but only a hundred miles away. But then, I think that's my mother's job. Something for the older generation to work out themselves.

"So I've been getting forgetful," Sally begins, looking down into her cup.

"Happens to everyone."

"Not like this, it doesn't. I forgot how to play cards, and the other day when I got steamed at your mom . . ." At this she looks up at me, right into my eyes, no trace of mirth or pranks. "I lost whole hours of time. I don't know where I was, and by now I've figured out that my ride wasn't any boyfriend I've ever had."

I put my hand over her free one, the one that's not clutching the coffee mug like it's an anchor to reality.

"So, I want you to know, dearie, that you can go ahead and put me in a home."

"Sally!"

"No, I mean it. I'm feeling okay right now, but I know that a brain going down this kind of slide doesn't crawl back up again.

It's only gonna get worse. And you and your mom shouldn't have to deal with me. You should be off in the big city making your fortune. I know you didn't like that job anymore, but there's nothing for you here."

"I wouldn't say 'nothing.'"

"Honey, in some ways you are just like your father. Now, listen to me, don't go getting all upset. In the good ways. He dreamed big, dreamed of getting the hell out of here. See, you got the dreaming, but you also got the brains and the discipline to do it right. Anyway." She takes her hand out from under mine and pats my arm. "Like I said, you go ahead and sign me up for a home. Soon enough I won't know the difference between that and a sock hop anyhow."

With what money? I'd like to ask her.

"So, how else am I like my dad?"

She sits back in her chair, frowning at me like she would a complicated sudoku puzzle. Silent seconds tick by, and I think maybe she's forgotten what I asked her and maybe that's just as well.

"You've got the Geneva nose, for starters. And when you're upset about something, you bring your jaw forward and tip your chin up, just daring the world to knock you silly." She demonstrates, and the effect is eerie, not only because I can see myself doing that so clearly but because I saw my father do it so recently. "When you were a kid, you were a fidgeter, and that was just like Robert. I think he took up smoking because it was an easy way to fidget, flicking that lighter and tapping his cigarettes. Sometimes he'd pack the tobacco down so hard he couldn't light it." She smiles, for a moment seeming to be lost in the fog of memory. Then she looks up at me again. "But you don't fidget so much anymore. And that's the big difference, like I said before. Discipline. And that you got from Maeve and all them Callahans. Your uncle Mike, rest his soul, running that bowling alley, even your grandma Callahan. And though you may not show it, you love like a Callahan, too. Hard and life-long. Not just when it's convenient, running hot and cold."

I open my mouth to protest, remembering Marc and the keys left on the table.

She stops me by raising her hand and saying, "I know you're not married yet, but maybe this is why. You're gonna wait for just that guy you can love hard and for life. That's not just anybody."

I picture Beck's solemn face during the dance, then his inscription in the book. *I imagine life with you.*

"What's eating you?" She takes a sip of her coffee and stares at me over the rim.

"Nothing."

"Don't lie to me, doll. Anyway, I'll probably forget in the morning."

I chuckle at this. "It's nothing, Sal. It's just . . . I'm a little confused, is all."

Sally leans in. "Ain't we all? Look, honey, I waited half my life for a man that wasn't mine."

"What . . . What makes you think I'm talking about a man?"

"I don't know nothing about nothing. But I do know that waiting around on someone else is no way to live. It wasn't my choice not to have babies, honey. By the time I gave up on him, I was too old." She heaves herself up out of the chair with a dramatic show of stretching and creaky bones, as if to drive home the point. She pats me on the shoulder as she passes and plants a kiss on the top of my updo. "But it was sure a pleasure watching you grow up, Anna. You sure are something special."

She walks down toward the darkened bedroom she shares with my mother, softly whistling "Zip-A-Dee-Doo-Dah."

CHAPTER 54

Cami

IT'S IMPRESSIVE, WATCHING ANNA SUITED UP FOR BATTLE. SHE'S IN her severe, chic black suit and she's wrangled her hair behind her head into a bun. She's perched at the edge of her narrow childhood bed, one leg crossed over the other, her foot tapping slowly in her dangerously sharp heels as she stares down at the settlement document in her hands.

Per my instructions, it says that my father gives me the house in exchange for my not suing him over stealing my trust money. According to my watch, our meeting starts in a half hour.

As Anna pointed out, such a document does not, however, protect him from criminal proceedings.

Down the hall, I can hear Maeve rustling in her room. She's packing things, though none of us know if she's joining Anna in the apartment she picked out or if she's made other plans. I wouldn't have thought it possible for two people to ignore each other in such a cramped space, but they have not exchanged words beyond "Excuse me" since their fight.

Anna tells me that she encountered her mother in the kitchen yesterday, the day after the wedding, and they just stared at each other and walked huge circles through the room to avoid actually crossing paths.

Part of me wants to shake Maeve, but I know I'm the one who stayed half the summer with a man I was afraid of, pretending I was too tough to be worried, too savvy to be at real risk.

So yeah, I'm not one to lecture about delusion. Also, I know she won't believe someone else anyway, no matter how reasonable and right that other person might be. Even her own daughter.

Anna looks up. "You ready? And you're sure this is all you want?"

"I just want his drunk ass out of that house."

"Well, then. Let's go."

My dad insisted on meeting at the house, saying he didn't want our business all over town, and seeing as Anna doesn't have an actual office, this was the best we could do.

"So much for neutral territory," Anna had grumbled, but I told her no territory was neutral in Haven.

Anna manages to walk smoothly up the gravel driveway in her heels, her briefcase swinging at her side. She skips the doorbell and hammers on the door with her knuckles.

When my father opens the door, the first thing I notice is that he's clean shaven and smells like soap. His tie is crooked and his shirt is stained yellow at the armpits, but it's an actual buttoned-up shirt.

Maybe he looked something like this when my mother fell for him. It had to be something.

"Mr. Drayton." Anna sticks out her hand. "Thanks for meeting us." She shakes his hand hard, hard enough to surprise him. I stifle a smile. He wasn't expecting much, I can tell. "Is your attorney on his way, then?"

My father clears his throat roughly. "He, uh. He can't make it."

Anna looks around the front of the house and settles on the kitchen table, which is only marginally cluttered. I can see the house has already begun its slide back to squalor in the short time I've been gone.

"Do you need to reschedule, Mr. Drayton? Or, I could schedule a court date if you prefer, and we'll let a judge hash this out. We don't have a great deal of time."

Actually, we have nothing but time, really, since she doesn't have a job. Technically I could go back to tutoring, but I don't have any money of my own, and Steve won't have me back. My pitiful salary there isn't enough to pay rent by myself, so I'm starting over, too.

My dad just grumbles and indicates a chair. I'm sure he couldn't find an actual lawyer to take his case.

I lean against the kitchen wall, preferring to stand.

Anna launches into her legal speak, explaining that he stole what was mine and never even told me it existed, and how much interest he would owe if she took him to court to pay it back now.

"But this could all be solved, right now, today. You just have to do one thing."

He slumps in his chair like a kid in the back room of math class, ready to throw a spitball. "What?"

"Only one asset of yours comes even close to the amount of this debt to your daughter." Anna waves her hand to indicate her surroundings. "This house."

"My house? She wants this house? Bullshit. It's mine."

I can't take it anymore. "It was my mother's!"

He wheels on me but stays seated. "She was my wife! And what was hers then is mine now. I deserve it after what she put me through."

"She put *you* through?"

"Do you know how much hospitals cost? You think I had any

insurance, running my own shop? That little life insurance policy we had on her was enough to bury her and didn't even cover half the debt she left me with."

"You act like she got sick on purpose, you miserable fuck."

He slams his hand down on the table and uses it to prop himself up to stand. He stares at me with the clearest eyes I've seen in months. "I won't have you disrespecting me."

"I won't have you insulting my mother."

I step closer, my heart going wild in my chest, my hands itching for something heavy and blunt to hold and swing.

"I needed that money. Not you. I needed it because I had debt, and a business, and little kids to feed and a mortgage. So yeah, I got the hospital off my back, and I paid off this house so I wouldn't have to worry about it no more. Pam wouldn't let me touch a dime of those rich assholes' money the whole time she was alive, so yeah, I took it when I needed it, and I needed it because of her."

"It wasn't her fault."

"It wasn't mine, neither! She's the one who died and went off to heaven or whatever, and I'm the one who had to stay here and listen to you kids bawl and tell you she wasn't coming back. You kept asking me! You kept asking, even though you were old enough to know! You killed me every time you asked!"

My dad crumples down in the chair, keening and roaring and pounding his fists.

I never saw this, not once, after Mom died. I heard slammed doors, I heard cans being opened behind those doors, and I watched him chain smoke for hours.

I glance at Anna. She has her phone in her hand, thumb on the buttons.

We both wait, until his wailing loses force like the air hissing out of a tire.

He sits back abruptly. "Gimme the paper."

Anna slides it over. "I think you'll find, Mr. Drayton . . ."

"Shut the fuck up and tell me where to sign."

He signs in all the required places and stands up so roughly his chair knocks over behind him.

I clear my throat. "Dad, I . . ."

"I suppose you're gonna sell it and give half the money to your fruit brother and that fag boyfriend. Or maybe you'll just use it to do your whoring. It's still my house for a week. Get out or I'll call the cops."

He yanks open the fridge, knocking over bottles inside.

Anna has to pull me out by my elbow as my father roots around in the refrigerator, cursing into its cold interior.

The drive back to the Nee Nance is silent and slow.

"Thanks," I tell Anna when she parks in the alley.

"You're welcome. I'm . . . I'm sorry."

"For what? We won, yeah?" I swing my legs out of the car and try to feel triumphant. If I feel anything right now, it's relief. I've just snatched something precious out of danger, like a vase that was teetering on the edge of a mantel.

He's stirred up memories I haven't considered in years and would rather not think of now. The tears and the clinging, the massive hole left by mother.

Anna follows me inside the dim store interior, and I prop myself against the front counter, my eyes unfocused on the brown, waxy floor. We did both keep asking my father about Mom's death. We couldn't believe it after so many relatives had assured us our mother was "a fighter" and we just had to keep hoping. We did hope, Trent and me; we even prayed the way my aunt told us. And she died anyway, and we'd been so believing of those grown-ups, but then they didn't have answers; they all drifted away, in fact, after the funeral and the sorting through of her affairs; they all floated away until it was Dad, Trent, and me, and Dad didn't have any good answers, either.

It was his job as a father to answer those questions, though, as best he could. To take care of us, not to drown himself in booze and scream obscenities and knock me down the stairs when I got in his way and then tell the school I fell.

Maeve appears at the top of the stairs, and we both turn to her. "How did it go?" she asks.

Anna shrugs. "She got the house."

Maeve nods, seeming to read the air in the room and understand that *congratulations* is not the word.

"Cami, I hate to ask you this, but could you excuse us, please?"

Maeve seems pale and a little shrunken. Anna sets down her briefcase and folds her arms.

I say, "Of course. I need some air, anyway."

I leave them to their own trials and walk out on the summer-baked sidewalk, trying to let the sun burn dry my freshly turned grief.

CHAPTER 55

Anna

IT TAKES MY MOTHER SOME TIME TO DRIFT DOWN THE STAIRS. AS she does, she holds her own arms tight, as if she's cold.

"I got a call," she says. "While you were out."

I wait, not daring to guess.

"It was your father. He said . . ." She lowers her gaze to the floor. "He said he wanted to check on me and to find out what you had to say about him. He'd wanted to call earlier but said he was giving me 'space.'" She chuckles darkly and looks around at the bones of the store. "As if I need more of that. Anyway. He said there was a change in plans." My mother laughs, again, slightly hysterically. She steadies herself on an empty shelf. "The land? The trailer? Turns out Charley sold it to someone else with actual money and income, but not to worry! He says, babe, don't worry, I've got another spot all picked out . . ." She winks and assumes a stance very much like my dad would: all big arms and big smiles, trying to take up more space, as if to puff up his sorry little idea.

She walks across to me and holds out a hand. It's an odd gesture, to shake the hand of one's own mother, but out of reflex I offer my hand. She takes it and turns it palm up. From her pocket she takes out something small and places it in my palm, folding my hand over it.

She smiles, but her eyes are crinkled up in grief.

I open my hand and her wedding ring sits there, looking so small in my palm, the diamond little more than a chip of stone.

"I don't want this," I say. "What would I do with it?"

She shrugs. " Do whatever you like with it. Sell it, throw it in the lake. It's over. It took me twenty years to say it, stupid broad that I am, but it's done."

I slide the ring onto my pinky finger for safe-keeping, until I get upstairs to put it somewhere safe, and consider its ultimate fate. I look back at my mom, and she seems withered and wrung out. I've felt this way at work, when I've won a tough battle, but both sides—the people, not the lawyers—look drained and white-faced in the aftermath. Victory is not always a pleasure.

"I'm not happy or anything, Mom. In fact . . ." I swallow hard and approach her, finding the words hard to conjure, even to my mother, who has already seen me as vulnerable and exposed as I've ever been in my life. "In fact . . . deep down I was hoping he was coming back for real."

I embrace her and let a couple of unfamiliar tears fall into her hair. I'm too tall with my shoes on. I step out of them so I can be smaller again, more like the child she raised by herself. "Maybe you were the braver one for daring to hope out loud," I tell her.

She chuckles sadly. "Let's not get crazy here. No, I was just blind. I'm sorry, sweetie."

"I'm sorry, too, Mom."

For once, it's my mother who tries to step back first. But I don't let her. Not just yet.

* * *

I help my mother clean up her room after I change out of my suit and put her ring, wrapped in tissue paper, inside a small box of childhood mementoes: certificates, medals, awards. Evidence of my early potential, which so far has brought me right back here, and a future no more clear than the horizon in a morning fog.

Mom has three piles going: keep, donate, trash.

She puts her hand on her sewing machine. "Will we have room in the apartment?"

I consider it. "Sure. More room than we have here, right? And it fits here."

"Well, you'll have your things from Chicago."

"I'll be getting rid of a lot of that. Pretty stupid to have a cappuccino maker and a wine refrigerator."

"Don't be so sure about that!" calls out Sally as she passes, her wig back on but crooked. She's been digging trash out of the kitchen, in merry spirits. Mom told me she's going to sit Sally down tonight and let her know all about Robert.

The phone rings, and my mother and I exchange a look. "I'll get it," I say.

I trot down the hall, and to my immense relief, it's Agatha from the boutique. "Hello, Maeve."

"This is Anna. But don't worry, everyone makes that mistake. I'll get her for you."

"Great," says Agatha. "Because that great-niece of mine thinks we oughta talk."

Amy? Talk about what? I'd like to ask, but Agatha doesn't appreciate nosy types, so I give Mom the phone with a shrug and go back to my own packing.

Twenty minutes later, Mom finds me in the kitchen, stacking pots and pans in a Seagram's 7 box. Our moving supplies make us look like drunkards.

She wanders in, looking lost and perplexed.

"What is it, Mom? What did Agatha want?"

"She's thinking of giving me a job."

"Really?" I abandon the packing and wipe beads of sweat off my head with my forearm. "You don't look happy."

"It's not final yet; she's thinking about it. She said she was all set to retire because of her arthritis, only Amy's insisting she hire me instead to be her seamstress in the shop. She might even let me manage it."

I remember Mom sewing some things for Amy back in school, when Agatha's didn't have anything suitable, and certainly nothing in the mall would have fit. Good of her to remember that.

"Well, if that works out, it would be nice."

"I'm just so shocked. First, Veronica pitching in to help me watch Sally, when I . . . Anyway. They actually had fun, Veronica said. And the other day Doreen came in to tell me her daughter wouldn't mind spending some time with her, either. Rhonda would take Sally with her for her church food pantry volunteering, said she'd enjoy the company because it gets boring sometimes."

My mother's color comes back a bit, and her face gets more animated. "If Agatha gives me this job, you can go back!"

"Where?"

"The Land of Oz. Where do you think? Go back to Chicago! I'll find someplace to rent, someplace small. Sally and I lived in one bedroom before; we can do it again. She's got Social Security, which is something. I can work for Agatha, and with all this help, we'll be fine!"

She's just overwrought. What would they do for health insurance? Even if Agatha hires her, Mom should know that small businesses can't afford quality benefits. And Haven is getting more touristy by the day. Even rent on a small place is going to be pricey.

And anyway, where else would I go?

Mom clasps her hands up under her chin, like she always used to waiting for me to open my Christmas present.

"I'll think about it, Mom."

This seems to satisfy her, and with a contented little sigh, she dives back into the boxes.

By morning, we're mostly packed. We've left out the few things we'll need over the next couple of weeks while we slowly move in to the new place, a two-bedroom duplex I found in a decent neighborhood, owned by a quiet older couple who live in the other side.

Already wearing my swimsuit, I step over Cami's sleeping form. The new place isn't so far from the lake, either. I could walk to the beach in good weather for a swim, then shower and head to work. I don't have a job yet, but I'll figure something out. I could always hang out my own shingle for a time. Haven probably needs attorneys, or maybe Muskegon, Grand Rapids. I can commute if I have to. And once I sell my fancy Chicago crap and stop paying for that storage, I'll have enough to get by modestly, for a little while.

I pause in my walk through the store to let a moment of grief pass, a cramping sensation in my chest for what's gone forever: August, my once-soaring career, my colleagues back in Chicago. The possibility of Beck in my life again.

The morning air already carries a chill. Summer is so brief.

The water's coldness shocks me into the present moment, so that I think about breathing and my stroke, watching the pier over my shoulder to make sure I don't get too far out. Alone, that would be dangerous.

Even with the edge of the pier, I pause and tread water, looking at the skyline—such as it is—of Haven, looking postcard-quaint from this distance.

It's not so bad, being here.

I look south, toward Chicago. Then I inhale sharply and swim back toward shore.

I walk quickly back, my wet hair dampening the sweatshirt I've thrown on over my wet swimsuit. As I approach, I see someone at the front door of the Nee Nance, peering in between cupped hands.

"Beck."

"I wasn't sure you'd be up."

He steps aside and I use my key to let us in. I listen; no one else seems to be up yet.

"What do you need?"

"I told Sam I had an early meeting. Well, I do, but not this early."

"For the record, I did not ask you to tell that lie. That's on your conscience."

"I came by to apologize. For putting you in such an awkward position."

"Well, I had plenty of chances to avoid this train wreck myself."

With his toes turned slightly in, and the way he keeps raking his hair with his fingers, he looks sixteen again.

"Beck, what do you want?"

"Well, first of all, my dad has a job for you, if you want it. No, listen, hear me out. They've been thinking about adding a lawyer on staff at Becker Dev instead of paying a big firm all kinds of money to keep consulting on things. And he adores you and respects you. It's perfect."

"Not for me, it's not."

"Well, could you at least—"

"No."

The sidewalks begin to fill up outside the windows with morning commuters walking to get breakfast at Doreen's, the early tourists out to get their cappuccinos at the café down the street. Without the beer posters in the window, we're exposed here, and I see people glancing inside. Beck still hasn't spoken but is making no move to leave.

"What is it? What?"

"Can you . . . can you give me a little time? Sam said she wants to work things out, but I think she's going to see eventually that our marriage hasn't been working for a long time, that it has nothing to do with you. Then we can really end it, and you and I can . . . we can give it a chance. We just need to give it time."

"I think we've given each other enough time."

"Anna, please . . ." He steps toward me, arms out.

I stop him with a raised hand. "Time to look forward now, wouldn't you say?"

"We're still friends, though, right?"

"I don't think that's very smart. Also, not very sensitive to your wife."

"I don't want to lose you completely."

"There's a lot of things I didn't want. You get over it."

He opens his mouth as if to speak again but then lets himself out the door. He turns and walks with his rounded shoulders off in the direction of Becker Development.

An hour later, all the residents of the doomed Nee Nance are up and at 'em. My mother starts to make pancakes in the kitchen for Cami and Sally. I'm not hungry, so I step into my room to clean it up.

I could leave it dirty, I know, since Paul is going to bulldoze it. I wince to think of a wrecking ball careening into that tiny octagon window through which I watched Haven parade by, watched for Beck to pull up for dates, watched for my father.

No, when I leave for the last time, I want to see this room as my parents saw it when they first moved in: bright and clean with promise, a quaint nursery for their little redheaded toddler.

"Hey," Cami says, startling me so much I almost drop my broom.

She doesn't question my sweeping. I think she gets it.

"Not hungry?"

I shake my head.

"Suit yourself. Hey, I've got an idea, yeah?"

"What's that?"

"Why don't your Mom and Sally live in my house?"

"Why would they do that?" I dump what seem like a decade's worth of red curls from the dustpan into a plastic trash bag.

"Because I think you and I should go to Chicago."

I stop in my sweeping and finally put the broom down. "What the hell for? I quit my job. And I thought you wanted so badly to live in your mom's house."

"I wanted to own it; I still want to own it. I want it to look pretty again, and I want it to be taken care of. Maybe I'll come back and raise a family there if I ever get to do that. But right now I don't need the space. Your mom does. I wouldn't even charge her rent. See? Then she'd be okay with her new job and I could get a real fresh start. I'm a good roommate, as you know. I don't even snore."

She plops herself down on the bed and tucks her hands behind her head, smiling smugly. "C'mon, it's perfect."

"With what money? Neither of us has a job."

"You've got some savings, yeah? I've got the money I won off your dad's sleazy friends. It's a start."

I shake my head and pick up the broom.

Cami sits up on the bed and pokes me in the side. "You loved the big city. You know you did."

This makes me think of how I felt the day I started at Miller Paulson, tiny among the skyscrapers, feeling the speed and energy of the city pulse under my feet, hearing it in the roar of the El.

My mother calls out that the pancakes are ready.

Cami springs up off the bed. "Think about it, yeah?"

I resume sweeping up the dust and sand, listening to the din from the kitchen, as the summer sun focuses through my small window and heats the room like a greenhouse. I shove the broom under my old brown vanity table, and as I pull it out, a half-crumpled piece of paper comes with it, with these words visible: GO CONFIDENTLY.

Maeve

I'M HUDDLING IN THE BACK ROOM OF AGATHA'S, PICKING LINT OFF my black wool suit, when I hear the chime for the front door, indicating someone's come in.

"Anna, you look like a snowman! Let me take your coat," I hear Agatha say.

I sigh with relief. I was worried, what with all the lake-effect snow they were predicting, and the drive from Chicago is more than four hours in good weather.

The door to the back room swings open, and there's Anna in a black pencil skirt, high-heel boots, and a red sweater. "Mom, there you are. Sorry I'm so late. The weather is awful. Also, I'm sorry about the red. I was in a rush to pack."

"I'm sure Sally would approve. She'd love it if we all wore feather boas."

She checks her watch. "Are you ready? They're waiting."

"I can't go out there."

Anna crouches down to be level with my face. "What is it? Are you not feeling well? How's your blood pressure?"

"That's not it. I'm fine, but . . . I wished this on her, Anna. I got so frustrated with her that in my head, silently, I said I wished she'd just die. And then she did."

"Oh, Mom. Dr. Simon said it was a stroke, and what with all the smoking all that time, it's a wonder it didn't happen years ago."

But it didn't happen years ago. It happened after I spent the night bawling into my pillow in frustration.

Anna puts an arm around me and squeezes. "You were a saint. She was no blood relation to you, but you took care of her anyway. You had no responsibility to her."

"Sure, I did. What would have happened to her if I didn't help?"

"Exactly. Now come on. They're waiting."

I let her lead me out of the back room into Agatha's. Cami steps forward, looking pink cheeked and relaxed. Chicago has been good to her; Anna tells me she is tutoring, and studying to be an interior designer at night. Meanwhile, Anna is working hard as she ever did for Miller Paulson, but in running her own practice, she's given up office politics, and these days her voice is brighter; her laughter comes more easily.

Cami says, "Well, Mrs. Geneva, ready to go put the 'fun' in funeral?"

I can't help but laugh because it's exactly the kind of thing Sally would have said.

First Presbyterian is bursting with mourners, though none of them look mournful, which would please Sally to no end.

I walk toward the casket, and Anna follows close behind. Sally looks unnatural in repose, because she was seldom ever calm. Even when she slept, she was all over the covers.

"Nice wig," Anna says. "I don't remember that one."

"I had to order it online. It's what her natural hair used to look like."

She's wearing a black, curly, shoulder-length wig and a plain blue dress. I should have added a red feather boa.

I finally turn away and scan the crowd for familiar faces. There's Veronica and Grant talking to Doreen. They're looking appropriately understated and polished as ever. She sees me and gives me a sad smile and wave. The skin under her eyes looks shiny, and she has a handkerchief in her hand. In helping me out with Sally, she's gotten to know her, too, these last months.

Anna puts an arm around me and lightly rubs my upper arm. I reach up to pat her hand, thanking God she will allow me these small physical gestures again.

A short, gray-haired man approaches. "Maeve, I'm so sorry."

It takes me a moment to place him without his postal shorts and Diet Coke.

"Oh, hi, Al. Good of you to come."

"If you need anything, you let me know, okay? I'm in the book. I miss seeing your face every day, but Ellen just won't trade routes with me." He winks at me, then flushes slightly pink and walks away with a couple of glances back.

The congregants begin to make their way down front when the organ music strikes up.

The service soon evolves into an open-mic memory session, and Pastor Jim is rolling with it, knowing Sally by reputation as most of the town seemed to. Old coworkers from the school where she'd worked as a janitor had the congregation in stitches with tales of Sally's pranks, like dipping an onion in caramel, a la candy apple, and presenting it to the principal.

I've never laughed so hard at a funeral.

No one talked about her more recent oddities, apparently as unsure as anyone when the quirky Sally ended and the dementia began.

Finally, one of her coworkers suggested for the sake of brevity, they adjourn the memories to the Tip-A-Few after the graveside service. It was roundly agreed.

I can't catch my breath enough to sing "Amazing Grace," so I mouth the words, with Anna's steadying arm around me.

Before I leave the sanctuary, I let my hand brush the closed casket.

"Good-bye, dollface," I whisper.

The wind blows right through the mourners, carrying away the words of Pastor Jim. I suspect most of the people here are just counting the minutes until they can retreat to the Tip-A-Few, to do just that in the dank, warm bar.

The crowd breaks up almost before Pastor Jim gets his Bible closed. They're not going to lower the casket until everyone leaves. That's the arrangement.

Anna trudges in her fashionable, wobbly boots through the snow, picking her footing so carefully she doesn't notice right away why I stop several yards away from the limousine.

There's a man standing between us and the car. He wears a gray parka, with a fur-lined hood, and a beard. Sunglasses obscure his eyes, though the sun can't penetrate the shield of clouds and snow.

"Robert," I say.

Cami hustles past, but she shoots us a look as she goes by, as if to say, *I won't go far.*

"You look good," he says to me. I sneak a glance at Anna. Her face is calm beneath the curls, which have escaped from her hat and are waving in the gale. "So, do you hate me?"

"I don't hate anything," I tell him truthfully, though there were a few late evenings after that day I gave Anna the ring when I raged and cursed and stomped, just because I had to. "I am mad at myself for gathering dust waiting for you and then being all too ready to believe anything you said."

"Some of it was true," Robert ventures.

"Some of it was always true. That made it so easy to believe it all."

The wind batters us, and none of us speak for a few moments.

"Were you at the funeral?" Anna asks.

"Yes. I'm awful sorry."

I wonder what for. Our loss? His loss would, in theory, be greater, as they were siblings. Sorry for leaving me with Sally to care for? Sorry for showing up now?

Robert says, "Can you ever forgive me? What if I get rich? Legally and all? And really build a nice house? I won't even call you until it's done, for real."

"You're the father of my daughter, and we spent years and years together. But you'll understand if I don't keep looking for you to come down the street or for your letters in the mail."

I'm about to walk away when Anna speaks up. "I have to ask you something. Are you running from something? From the law? Or from your *business associates*?"

Robert doesn't answer. He looks down at his feet. He's wearing sneakers, and they're wet with snow. She looks at me, shrugs, and starts to walk away to the car.

Robert says, "Is this it, Annie? Forever?"

She stops and opens her purse, digging around in it. She hands him a business card. "This has my office address. You can write to me."

Robert stares at her card and chews his lip. Then Anna reaches out and seizes him in a hug, and just as abruptly she breaks away and runs on tip-toe back to the limo. I follow as quickly as I can manage over the slick ground.

As the car motors down the cemetery drive, we both turn to look out the rear window. Robert is watching us go, blowing kisses into the wicked wind.

A+

**AUTHOR
INSIGHTS,
EXTRAS, &
MORE...**

FROM

**KRISTINA
RIGGLE**

AND

AVON A

Discussion Questions

1. Why do you think Maeve has failed to move on from the store and her marriage?
2. Have you ever felt stuck in the past like Maeve? Were you able to move on? What did you do to get "out of the rut"?
3. Why do you think there's friction between Maeve and Anna? What kinds of issues complicate relationships between mothers and grown daughters?
4. Anna and Beck feel drawn to each other after years apart, and Maeve still pines for her estranged husband, Robert. Do you think old romances can ever come back to life?
5. In continuation of the previous question, do you think old romances *should* ever be revived? Why or why not?
6. How does the absence of Anna's father during her childhood affect her adult life? Did his absence have any positive effects on Anna? What were they?
7. Does a person's past irrevocably color her future?
8. Why do you think Cami comes back to her dad's house despite their history?
9. Have you ever known anyone to remain in a dangerous, abusive situation though it seems obvious he or she should leave? Why do you think this happens?
10. Amy always strives to control every aspect of her life. Think about this personality trait in terms of her dramatic weight loss: Are the two related in some way? What other ways does she try to exact control? Are these actions to her benefit or detriment?
11. Have you ever made a dramatic yet positive change to your life, such as Amy made? Were there unexpected downsides to this transition? Why did they arise, do you think?

12. Anna decides to remain open to the idea of contacting her estranged father. What would you do if you were in Anna's shoes?

13. How did you imagine your life when you were younger? How much is it similar to what you predicted, and is this good or bad?

14. If your life has not turned out the way you wanted, is it defeatist—or realistic—to accept that?

15. The author chose a quote from Thoreau as an epigraph for the novel: "Go confidently in the direction of your dreams. Live the life you've imagined." Why do you think she chose this particular quote? What does it mean to you, in light of what happens in the novel?

16. Consider the novel's four main female characters. Is there one that you particularly identify with? Which one, and why?

17. When you first read the novel's title, what did you think the story was going to be about? What does the phrase "the life you've imagined" mean to you?

A Conversation with the Author

What inspired this book?

This book has been through many drafts and was once known by another title, and I actually started it before I wrote my debut *Real Life & Liars*. I was sifting through my life to find material weighty enough for a novel, zooming in on times when I was most upset and scattered. A moment of disillusionment stood out to me. It was a time when I realized that doing your best, working your hardest, and being a nice person wouldn't guarantee success. It was a painful newsflash to realize the real world is not always merit-based! This brought me to the character of Anna, the attorney who is poised for the career success she thought she wanted, only to find it doesn't bring her the satisfaction she'd expected. Anna's mother, Maeve, was the next character. At first, she existed mainly to support Anna's story, but she emerged with a powerful tale of her own. Cami was simply "the friend," and Amy was a plot device, but their stories became more important as the novel went through its many drafts. I love the fact that it's an ensemble story now. Also, I loved the idea of using Geneva for a last name, if only for the "Geneva Convention" joke made by Aunt Sally.

You mentioned many drafts of this novel. Why so many?

I am ruthless about abandoning projects that aren't working, and this was especially true before I ever had a book deal and thus a contract to fulfill. So, ordinarily I would have just filed this one away as a learning experience. But I always loved the ending chapter. Indeed, the existing ending is not much different than my earliest drafts. I was determined to write a book that *earned* that ending. I'm happy with the result. It was worth every bit of the work.

What inspired your fictional Haven, Michigan?

I had set *Real Life & Liars* in a real city that is very special to me, but this time I wanted total flexibility in the setting so I just made up a town. Originally I'd called the town North Haven, then I decided to drop the "North" entirely because "Haven" alone is so evocative and, for some of my characters, ironic. Haven is loosely based on Grand Haven, South Haven, and similar small towns on the southern shore of Lake Michigan. I worked for a couple of years at the *Grand Haven Tribune* as a reporter. It was my first real job, with a desk and business cards and everything. I was so proud of my own desk! The Tip-a-Few bar in the book is based on the real thing in Grand Haven. It's such an excellent name for a bar, I couldn't help but use it.

The Nee Nance Store is based on various small convenience stores near places I've lived. I love little family-run places—and their whimsical names—and had always thought a family business would make a great jumping-off point for a novel.

How did you come up with the title?

At first, "the life you've imagined" only came into play as a bit of scenery: the magazine clipping Anna had taped to her mirror as a girl and later tears down in a fit of disgust as a cynical adult. As the novel evolved into an ensemble story, I gave each of the girlhood friends the clipping and imagined how they reacted to it. The quote (which is actually a misquote—the real Thoreau excerpt isn't quite so modern and pithy) seemed evocative of this story about adults grappling with the contrast between their actual lives and what they thought they'd have.

Are you living the life you imagined?

No! And I'm glad. I imagined myself by this point sailing along in my career as a newspaper reporter, well on my way to becoming editor of a large urban daily. Novel writing was a vague aspiration for some undefined "someday" point. I always envisioned myself a hardcore career woman who would "do it all." I'm still a career woman, but the career is different, and my definition of success more fluid and flexible. I no longer try to predict my life many years ahead, and when I do imagine the future, it's more in terms of family and home rather than jobs and money. Also, the older I get the more aware I am that it's all so fragile. I'm happy that my family and I are healthy right now, today. And I'm awfully glad that my "someday novel" came sooner rather than later, because who knows what later will bring?

H. Scott Buttman

KRISTINA RIGGLE lives and writes in Grand Rapids, Michigan, with her husband, two kids, and dog. She's a freelance journalist, published short story writer, and coeditor for fiction at the e-zine *Literary Mama*. Her debut novel, *Real Life & Liars*, was named a Great Lakes, Great Reads selection by the Great Lakes Independent Booksellers Association. Though she doesn't live at the shore, Lake Michigan makes her heart happy whenever she can get there.

Kristina Riggle

ALSO BY KRISTINA RIGGLE

REAL LIFE & LIARS

ISBN 978-0-06-170628-8 (paperback)

"This book has heart.
Each of its four stories is
compelling and makes
you keep turning the page
long after you should
have turned out the
light.... Kristina Riggle
gets it exactly right."
—Becky Motew, author
of *Coupon Girl*

THE LIFE YOU'VE IMAGINED

ISBN 978-0-06-170629-5 (paperback)

"(An) engaging,
companionable
novel about family,
expectations, and
adversities overcome....
I devoured it and
wanted more."
—Therese Fowler,
author of *Reunion*